T0367849

SKULLCAP

SKULLCAP

by

Steven Burgauer

SKULLCAP

iUniverse books may be ordered through booksellers or by contacting:

iUniverse
1663 Liberty Drive
Bloomington, IN 47403
www.iuniverse.com
1-800-Authors (1-800-288-4677)

ISBN: 978-1-4917-6182-3 (sc)
ISBN: 978-1-4917-6183-0 (hc)
ISBN: 978-1-4917-6181-6 (e)

Library of Congress Control Number: 2015903413

Print information available on the last page.

iUniverse rev. date: 04/10/2015

To my father,

who held on to sweet life as long as he could

The future belongs to those who show up.

Book of Lore **(12th Edition)**

PROLOGUE

CHAPTER ONE

He could feel them inside him, the spiders, inside his veins, moving this way and that, fixing all the parts that were broken. Hundreds of them, maybe thousands, all tiny, each smaller in size than a chain of nucleotides, each weaving their way through his body, his blood vessels, his lymph nodes and nerve channels, stopping at each layer of tissue, rearranging what was out of place, setting straight what was lousy and wrong.

Age had done most of the damage, age and liquor and tobacco and forbidden drugs. Tiny mistakes cumulated through time, mistakes the body had no way to fix.

Evolution had a downside.

Selfish genes replicated in casual abandonment.

Within the double-helix chemistry of deoxyribonucleic acid, there was no organized apparatus — no biological subroutine — for repairing each and every broken copy. DNA lacked, as it were, a Darwinian imperative compelling it to do so. Thus, the same mechanism that permitted evolution also made death inevitable.

Epsilon 1512 could feel the spiders repositioning themselves inside him. The sensation of movement near the base of his ribcage was not just his imagination. The spiders' work was nearly complete. They seemed to be gathering in his belly, just as Nurse Hopkins said they would.

Every person alive, every person born into this world, was condemned at birth to eventually die. Every last one of us is born into this world infected with the seeds of cancer — and of heart disease and of dementia and arthritis. Only the manmade spiders, injected into a person's pulsating veins before it was too late, could prevent the inevitable. Only those people treated in that particular way could have their death sentence commuted.

The pain in Epsilon 1512's abdomen intensified now. Tears streamed from his eyes, eyes that at a younger age had once been blue.

Now, in old age, those same eyes had lost their bright sheen, a victim of encroaching cataracts. The ugly growths cast a gray hue across his visual landscape.

Now, in old age, those gray diseased eyes were clenched shut to block out the pain in his belly.

Epsilon 1512 was tired. Before this all began, he had actually welcomed death, had looked forward to it for some time. His body was worn out, his zest for life diminished.

It was a natural progression, this thing called aging. A process of Nature. Something man should not mess with. It begins in the womb. Violent Birth. Vibrant Youth. Thriving Manhood. Lustful Marriage. Rambunctious Offspring. Enriching Career. Stimulating Retirement. Pleasant Decline. Peaceful Death. Solemn Grave.

But to lose his identity? To be reduced to a number, to an alphanumeric? How depressing! How downright revolting! *In what world is that fair?* In what world should a man be forced to surrender his name and his history and accept instead the fifth letter of the Greek alphabet accompanied by a four-digit number? *Was this alphanumeric now the sum-total of his existence?*

Epsilon 1512 had wanted to die. — *But don't we all?* He had prayed for death. One life was long enough. Epsilon had already had two. *Who needed resurrection? Tell me — who?*

But times and circumstances had changed. Out here in the steaming jungles of Venus, death was no longer an option, not if a man had skills. Skills were valuable, more valuable than dignity. Epsilon 1512 had skills. He had to be kept alive. *He had no choice.*

Before being captured and made to work in the mines, Epsilon had been a soldier, a Recon Scout. He knew handguns and targeting. He knew land-nav and tracking. He knew code-cracking and ciphers, money and finance. He had been married, had two kids, been married again, had two more. After countless years on Venus, countless years as an enslave held against his will, he supposed the whole lot of them were dead. *By rights, he ought to be dead too.*

Instead, Epsilon 1512 landed on the wrong side of a brutish war. He ended up as an enslave here in Slave Camp #5, Domtar Province, planet Venus. In the Venusian lithium mines there was a chronic shortage of skilled slave-labor. It was cheaper to rejuvenate a trained enslave off-planet than to transport a new, untrained one from Earth lockup. Thus, the choice was clear. — *Keep them alive. At all costs, keep them alive.*

Epsilon felt the pain, now, in his abdomen. A burning sensation, just below the sternum. The spiders were gathering now in the liver, the last organ to be rebuilt.

That it had gotten this far meant he would survive the procedure. It meant that he would live, that the rejuv had been successful. The process was not one hundred percent you know. When they brought him into the Centre, he was dead, at least as dead as a mortal man could be and still be successfully revived.

Technology had redefined the meaning of Dead. Death was no longer an absolute. Neuroprostheses. Laparoscopic surgery. Organ harvesting. Corrective gene therapy. Bio-algorithms. Each postponed the inevitable.

But every last one of these procedures was carried out at the macro scale, an artery here, an organ there, a bone graft over yonder. — And none of it was permanent.

The spiders were the first to get at the heart of the matter. The first to fix things at a micro level. Tiny little manmade creatures, not much larger than a virus, built to attack disease and aging at the cellular level, down where messenger RNA and her many obedient soldiers held sway.

Certain things could not be fixed, of course. Macro things mainly. That rib you broke as a kid, falling out of a tree. That scar on your knee where you hit the pavement, falling off your bicycle. These were macro injuries. The body had healed them in the customary fashion. Whatever scars were left behind from those incidents would always remain. Not even the spiders could regenerate a lost appendage.

But what *could* be fixed — and not with great difficulty — were the ATP factories harbored deep within each cell, the mitochondria.

What *could* be fixed were the errant cells, the shortened chromosomal telomeres, the tumors, the cancers that might spin out of control, destroying one's body from within.

What *could* be fixed was the lung damage from smoking, the liver damage from alcohol, the brain and kidney damage from Deludes. Suddenly a man was twenty years old again, with yet another prime to live.

But it was no longer a case of youth being wasted on the young.

The second time around a man had the accumulated knowledge and experience of an eighty-year-old — or, in the case of Epsilon 1512 — a one-hundred-and-forty-year-old.

God! How he wished they would have killed him instead!

CHAPTER TWO

"Time to go back to work, Epsilon 1512."

It was Nurse Hopkins. He liked her. She had nice boobs, a sweet ass and spoke Terrish, three things he would not have noticed a week ago. *Come to think of it, maybe there was an upside to an involuntary rejuv after all.* A man's favorite muscle worked again, stretching taut whenever the mood suited, never failing to exercise its indefatigable ability to think and act for itself.

Here on Venus, women were scarce, at least the sort of women a man might want to bed. The really good ones were consigned to the Farm. Which left not nearly enough of them to go around. First Law of Economics. *When a thing is scarce, the price goes up.* This is an indisputable fact, like gravity. No amount of liberal legislation or blind faith can hope to repeal a rule so basic.

Scarcity made those few women available the most valuable thing on the planet, more precious than air or food or water. *Could it be any other way?* What was man without woman? Nothing. Not a thing. Lonely men truly did not care whether they lived or died. Epsilon 1512 knew that. Only too well. He had gone long stretches without a woman.

"Out of bed, Epsilon 1512. Time to go back to work."

Oh, the sweet music of Terrish. Such a wonderful language!

Epsilon's first wife had been that way, the way Nurse Hopkins was being now, giving him ridiculous orders she knew he had no intention of listening to or obeying.

Epsilon looked down at his arm now, newly strong and muscular. There was the barcode on his vibrant flesh, bolder than before, a series of thin black bars on a field of white, bars with an alphanumeric underneath, his alphanumeric, a capital Greek letter followed by a number — Epsilon 1512.

The barcode and number reminded the man what he actually was. A human being devoid of civil rights. A disenfranchised enslave. A lowly man sequestered for all eternity to a labor camp on one of the most unforgiving planets in the solar system.

Nurse Hopkins helped Epsilon 1512 to his feet, now. His legs were shaky. He looked around the rejuvenation recovery room. The remaining beds were filled with other oldsters in various stages of repair. — Frank Robinson. Tara Kingsley. Skip Henderson. Rock Hound. — Not all of them would make it.

Lord, what a perversion! If the gods had meant for us to live forever, surely they would have given us eternal life.

But to be forced to work hour upon hour, day after day, more or less until the end of time? Without any rest? With nothing hopeful to look forward to? No vacation? No retirement? No reward for a job well done? What kind of life was that?

Which reminded him. He — Epsilon 1512 — had not always been a number. There was a time when he, this man, still had a name. Before the *Ticonderoga* was hijacked, before this nightmare began, he was born Lars Cabot. That was long ago, in December 2314. He suffered his first rejuv in 2395, his second one — this one — in 2454.

His grandfather, a man history buffs would likely have heard of, was General Felix "Flix" Weinger. This man, his grandfather, was something of a war hero. Flix had been injured in a battle as a young man. Now he carried a cane. He once showed it to Lars, back when Lars was still a kid. The cane was hollowed out inside making room for the rifled gun barrel that ran down the length of the interior.

Epsilon's grandmother, Flix's wife for a short while, was one Krista Leidurmarm of Iceland. Their lovechild, Eleka Leidurmarm, Lars's mother, would marry Hogan Cabot at a young age. Lars would come along two years later.

But this rejuvenation idea, where the hell did it come from?

It all started a couple thousand generations ago, when some genius Cro-Magnon realized he could use a forked branch as a crutch to help relieve a leg that was temporarily disabled.

Over the next fifty thousand years or so, all sorts of adjuncts to the human body were developed, many by accident, more than a few as weapons. Some other early man discovered that the leg bone of that antelope he was gnawing on could also be profitably employed as a club to put down an enemy. Other weapons followed in short order, weapons that could extend a man's reach, others that might help him live a bit longer or control more resources. Spears. Daggers. Bows and arrows. Protective body armor.

But it was not until the Middle Ages that some truly remarkable aids to better living came into widespread use. Some of these adjuncts had peaceful applications. Eyeglasses, for instance. *Can you imagine a greater boon to mankind?*

Before the advent of the more recent ocular implants, eyeglasses made science possible. These simple devices kept people from many walks of life productive into old age. They cut down on accidents.

If not for the invention of the eyeglass, could there even have been a Renaissance? Think of the impact. Two small pieces of glass. When ground properly, they can extend by years the working life of a talented smith or scholar. Think how the world changed beginning in the fourteenth century when it became possible to correct failing vision.

Or consider the artificial tooth. What had once been an instrument of torture soon became a source of happiness and improved productivity.

The list goes on. Peg legs. Plaster casts. Trumpet-shaped hearing appliances. Splints. Sutures. Anesthetic surgical procedures.

With the advent of more modern materials and technology, the development of every kind of artificial limb became possible. Hearing aids. Contact lenses. Replacement hips. Mechanized wheelchairs.

But the meshing had barely begun. Like two frenzied lovers, man and machine were bonding, becoming one. Locked in a symbiotic embrace of flesh and bio-ready steel, the two raced together across a landscape cluttered with rotors and silicon chips and lines of robotic code. Technology. Metallurgy. Personal need. Ego. Money. Physics. Chemistry.

The next generation of mechanical devices was permanently implanted. Arterial stents. Synthetic pancreases. Cardiac pacemakers. Replacement knees. Artificial skin. *And why not?* If a man could greatly enhance any physical or mental ability by having some artificial device attached to or imbedded in his body, would he not jump at a chance to do so? *Of course, he would.*

The triumph of mind over matter culminated with the marriage of the nano-chip to the latest advances in micro-surgery. Now comes the brain-machine interface, the so-called skullcap. With that unholy union it was now possible, in the first instance, to control the movement of a limb by direct mental input. This was the opening step along the treacherous path that led toward the creation of cyborgs, those man-machine abominations long familiar to readers of science fiction.

Manipulating limbs that had been rendered useless because injury had cut them off from the nervous system was not the only application of skullcap technology. Skullcaps could also be engineered to function as literal extensions of one's mind. They could serve as storage devices for retaining obsolete memories. Or act as electronic processing units to help the brain evaluate information. Or communicate with the outside world by direct cable link or, more likely wirelessly.

As with all technical advances, skullcap technology was controversial. Some skullcaps were more equal than others. A richer man might possess a more sophisticated skullcap, one that ran faster, stored more information, and could make him richer still. A poor man might not possess any skullcap at all, not even an inferior one, not even a slow or defective one. Without such a device interfacing with his brain, he would instantly become an imbecile among a race of superhuman beings. The ethical questions were legend.

New questions arose. A brain-machine interface to communicate with damaged limbs is one thing. *But exactly how much of the body could be replaced by this kind of cybernetic technology?*

As it turns out, nearly all of it.

By accepting such solutions, people began to bypass incurable diseases in a very direct way. They began to substitute entire body parts instead. Some even began to question the need for the body itself. *Why not simply house a brain in an entirely artificial life-support system?*

Thankfully, it never came to that. Substituting body parts and adding skullcaps to the head is about as far as it ever got.

But even swapping body parts was still major surgery, no matter how advanced the technique. It took a lot of old-fashioned cutting to replace a damaged or worn-out organ with artificial tissue, even designer tissue grown in a lab. Major surgery. Messy and traumatic. Cutting into flesh. Excising tissue. Recovering lost blood. Risking infection.

The best replacements were three-dimensional scaffolds built from biodegradable polymers laced with embryonic stem cells. The entire structure of stem cells and scaffolding was implanted into the body, forming new tissue. Better. But still major surgery.

It was not long, however, before science devised a better way — the spiders. Rebuild a person from the inside out. No surgery. No trauma. No risk of infection. Just swallow one giant oversized pill or submit to several somewhat painful injections.

"Let's go, 1512."

It was Nurse Hopkins again. She had her hand on Epsilon's arm and was leading him out of the Centre towards the exit. The Platypus would take him back to the enslave camp. Lars knew the routine. He had lived here in Domtar Province, planet Venus, for something on the order of sixty years. He also knew this might be his last chance for another sixty.

"Nurse?"

"Yes?"

"A kiss?"

She did not answer. He was hardly the first to ask.

"For old time's sake?"

"Was there a time before this one?"

"If not with me, then surely with some man."

She smiled. "Yes, for old time's sake."

Nurse Hopkins pursed her lips and pressed them against his.

He gently sucked her upper lip.

She smelled delicious.

Their tongues touched.

His manhood stiffened inside his pants. She reached down and touched the shaft of it briefly, felt its length.

He stroked her breast through the cotton of her white shirt.

She moaned softly then pulled away.

"Until next time?"

"Yes, until next time."

PART I

CHAPTER THREE

As a boy, Lars was a bit of a bookworm. He read everything he could get his hands on. Mysteries. Detective stories. Biographies. Oh, and science fiction.

Lars liked all the science-fiction writers — Montgomery, Clarke, Nagowa. He liked them all. Except when they veered off into fantasy or the supernatural. That is when he lost interest.

But the chance to speculate about the future, to visit other worlds in other times, to think about other ways of living. To see ordinary men and women combat evil or confront an alien ecosystem or be challenged by an oppressive philosophy — these were themes that excited him.

Lars loved to read about heroes. But not the sort who could lift impossibly heavy objects with mysterious superpowers or read people's minds or magically teleport from place to place.

No, the sort of hero Lars wanted to read about was the sort of hero his grandfather was, the sort who had brains and courage and technical knowhow. Such men, such ingenious creative men, knew more real stuff than the bad guys they came up against. These were the sort of men Lars wanted to learn more about.

Lars loved being out-of-doors. He was an avid Boy Scout. He found great solace in his merit badge achievements, in his energetic patrol competitions, in shooting an arrow from a bow he had built or in learning how to tie a proper knot. He spent countless happy weeks at summer camp, tramping around the northwoods with nothing more in his hand than a pocketknife and canteen of water.

His father, Hogan Cabot, an outdoorsman but certainly no Boy Scout, had a proud pedigree. Fifty percent Amerind, fifty percent Scottish, neither half able to hold its liquor. He loved to hunt. But not with a rifle, with a compound bow and arrow.

His mother, Eleka Leidurmarm, was a striking beauty. Eleka was a wonderful amalgam distilled from an Icelandic mother and sturdy American father, both former military, both engaged in covert operations for a clandestine branch of the central government. Some of those adventure-seeking genes got passed down to Lars.

The Cabot family made its home in the boundary waters of northern Minnesota, nearly "off the grid," as Grandpa Flix would say. Their rustic log-cabin-style home was half a million kloms from nowhere, down a gravel lane, deep in the Minnesota backwoods. The nearest town was Ironwood, population 200. Lars's father worked at dangerous trades, logging, mining, fire-fighting. The man was a rebel, complete with overlong hair, harsh words, and a taste for habit-forming drugs.

Lars had a big brother. But the two boys did not get along. The older boy beat up on Lars every chance he got. Lars did not much care for it. But he found himself powerless to put a stop to it. Lars grew up believing that is what big brothers did, beat up on their little brothers. Years later, when Lars was incarcerated as an enslave, he would tell other prisoners he was an only child.

The Cabots were heir to few creature comforts. They simply did not have the money. Their possessions were few, practically none of them new. An old gcar in the garage. An antediluvian vid screen in the front room. A music pod. A family *Book of Lore* on the shelf.

Do not be fooled by the presence of that *Book of Lore.* No matter how much that particular volume may sound like a Bible, the Cabots were not religious. Not one of them attended High Temple, not one. And only one of them believed in the pantheon of gods, which included the local protector Aphrodite.

On the other hand, that *Book of Lore* was a printbook, one forged from paper and ink; this in a day when printbooks were uncommonly rare. That *Book of Lore* was far and away the Cabots' most valuable and prized possession.

The book held special significance for Eleka, Lars's mother. It was a family heirloom. Eleka inherited the book from her own mother, who first inherited it from her own grandmother.

By virtue of its age, the printbook was valuable. If sold at auction, it could have brought in enough money to change their lives. Hogan had pressed Eleka on more than one occasion to sell the thing. But she had steadfastly refused.

Lars had custody of one as well, a printbook. It had been a birthday gift from his grandfather Flix. But unlike a *Book of Lore* or a Holy Bible, this particular printbook was not sacred in any way. Quite the opposite. The book might as well have been written with dynamite not ink, the way Eleka exploded when she discovered what her father had done. "The work of the Devil," she called it.

Devil's work or not, the book Flix gave his grandson was a classic on the subject. One hundred and fifty years old. Nearly in mint condition. Used since its publication by infantry soldiers attending munitions school. A *Primer on Nitrate Compounds*.

The *Primer*'s subject matter was explosives, a business Lars's grandfather, a soldier, knew a great deal about. An unusual subject for a grandfather to be sharing with his grandson, to be sure. But he knew the boy had no outlets for his curious mind and was likely to get into trouble of his own accord. Why not find something the two of them could learn together, a way for a distant grandfather to bond with grandson?

The *Primer* was difficult material for a boy Lars's age to master. The vocabulary was highly technical, well above his reading level at the time.

But Lars was a fast learner. This is where he first became acquainted with the names and characteristics of compounds such as "2, 4, 6-trinitrotoluene," more commonly known as TNT. Also with the names of explosive blends containing TNT, such as Amatol and Composition B and Torpex and Tritonol.

Lars learned from the book that TNT was at one time the most commonly used explosive in military and industrial applications. In the early days it was valued because of its lack of sensitivity to shock and friction. This reduced the risk of accidental detonation.

TNT melted at a temperature far below its ignition temperature. This was a valuable characteristic. It allowed the stuff to be melted and safely poured into a container or combined with other, more powerful explosives. TNT neither absorbed water nor dissolved in it. Thus, it could be put to effective use in wet environments.

In many instances, powdered aluminum could be added in various measure to the TNT to increase the speed at which the explosive developed its maximum outward pressure. When it happens rapidly enough, a shock wave is formed. Whatever material comes in contact with the supersonic detonation wave, whether flesh or bone or concrete, will be utterly shattered.

But the *Primer* from Lars's grandfather was more than just some "how-to" manual for firebugs. The book also provided the boy with a good history lesson. The word Torpex, for instance, was actually short for "torpedo explosive." Torpex proved to be particularly useful in underwater munitions. The aluminum component had the effect of making the explosive pulse last longer, which enhanced its destructive power.

Then too, the *Primer* contained page after page of complex graphs as well as numerous charts and tables. Taken together with the intervening prose, the compendium described how to cook up explosives of various potency.

But reading how to do something is not the same as actually doing it. *How else to understand what happened next?*

From time to time a box or package would arrive at the Cabot's front door in Ironwood by private courier. The package would be from Grandpa Flix. He would send Lars a box filled with the very ingredients the boy would need to stir up some of the simpler compounds described in the book, along with a vid and detailed instructions on how to safely mix them.

When Lars's mother discovered what her father had done, she was outraged. Any good mother would be.

How dare her father do such a thing! How dare he encourage such comportment in a child, much less introduce her son — his grandson — to such a dangerous pursuit!

But, when the package first arrived, Eleka held tight to her fury. She held tight to her fury for weeks, until the occasion of Lars's tenth birthday. It was on that occasion that Grandpa Flix suddenly and without invitation showed up on their doorstep in Ironwood, another such birthday gift in hand.

Eleka was fit to be tied. Her father had a habit of showing up at the house unannounced. He was always spoiling Lars, and in ways she did not like.

Do not get the wrong idea. Mom loved her son dearly, just as she dearly loved her father. But the two — father and daughter — had horrendous fights, and they were usually about Lars.

Eleka could get rather feisty when she wanted to. Lars knew to stay clear when his mother got like this. On the day in question, Lars remained safely upstairs, in the loft which was his bedroom, listening to his mother and grandfather while they argued.

That day, on the occasion of Lars's tenth birthday, father and daughter squared off almost as soon as he walked through the door, gift box in hand.

He saw that she was angry. His go-to response when she was like this was to become stern.

"Eleka. It is high time the boy grew up. High time he saw something of the world beside this dump."

"And just who the hell decided that? Who took a vote and elected you tour guide for my son?"

"Your son; my grandson."

"Yes, your grandson. But Pops, the boy is only ten."

"Well, then explain this to me." Flix picked up a brightly colored brochure from off the coffee table. It was from the Feldman Neurological Institute. "This is what you have planned for the boy? A skullcap?"

"It gives a young man an edge, a chance to keep up with other young men and women his age. I have been saving up for this procedure for years. A top quality skullcap is expensive. Last year, I applied for a hardship financial grant from the Institute. Now the grant money has come through. Lars will be fitted with a first-rate skullcap practically for free."

"Do not do this, girl. Let the boy be a boy. Let him enjoy a normal youth. Do not tech him up like that."

"I don't want him to grow up like his father. — Or like you."

Flix looked at his daughter. "I did such a fine job raising you, I thought I might have a go with my grandson."

"Father, in case you have forgotten, you have two grandsons, not just the one. Anyway, you need not concern yourself with Lars. Hogan and I are doing just fine raising the boy, thank you very much."

"Are you? Are you really? If you ask me, you two did not do so well with the older one."

"That's not fair."

"Isn't it? The older one is a bully. He beats up on Lars all the time."

"We are working on that. But Hogan is not always here to help."

"Didn't I tell you not to marry that man? Hogan is a lousy role model. Smokes cannabis, hunts with a bow and arrow, works in a lumber mill."

"This is not about my choice in husbands, Father. This is about what is best for my son."

"Honey, you have to know I am not the sort to interfere. But surely you can see it for yourself. The boy needs a change of scene. Lars needs to learn a little something of the outside world, something beyond Ironwood. A skullcap is just about the last thing the boy needs at this age."

"And you think teaching my son how to blow up things will make him a more rounded individual?"

Grandpa laughed. "Well, not just that."

"And was it your idea to show *me* something of the world when you and Mama stuck me in that boarding school? I was just a child. I needed my parents. Hell, I needed my friends."

"It could not be helped. You must know that. You must know I had no choice in the matter. You know full well what happened to your mother."

"I mean before that."

"Before that? My God, girl. Before that your mother and I were still in the service. We could not possibly take time out to care for a small child."

"But you two could find time to have one, is that it?"

"It takes two to tango, little one. Or have you forgotten?"

"Sorry, Pops. But somehow I cannot see you as silly. — Or in love."

"But I was in love, child. Your mother and I were very much in love. But we had our careers. Obligations. I apologize if I wasn't much of a father. But now I would like to have the opportunity to make it up to you, if even a little. At least let me try to be a grandfather to Lars. Who knows? I might even be good at it."

"You promise not to fill the boy's head with crazy ideas?"

"Oh, come now. You absolutely know that I will."

Now Eleka laughed. The earlier tension was broken. "Okay, Pops. Lars is in his bedroom upstairs. I will go get him. The boy is yours for the week. That is, if you can stand the little monster that long. He wrecked my pancake griddle with one of his experiments, you know. That griddle was a present from you, Pops."

"Oh, don't worry yourself too much about me and Lars. The boy and I will get along just fine for a week. The two of us are going to fly up to my lodge in Maine, fill our bellies with lobster tail and peanut butter fudge, then hike up Cadillac Mountain, just like you and I used to do back in the old days."

"I suppose that silly flying machine of yours is parked out in front somewhere?"

"You know that it is."

"Some things never change."

"And why should they?"

CHAPTER FOUR

Lars packed quickly and then was out the door with his grandfather.

The boy's eyes opened wide as could be when he got out onto the long driveway in front of the Cabot's log-cabin house. Lars had seen pictures, but never the real thing.

Now, here it was, a great flying machine parked in the tall grass a hundred meters up the drive.

The machine — a military-style airchop — was so advanced and so silent in flight, Lars had not heard it land. Neither had his mother. Now he clambered up into the cockpit ahead of his grandfather.

"Happy birthday," Flix said, barely able to contain himself.

"It is for me? Really?"

"You cannot keep it. But if you promise not to tell your mother, I will let you handle the stick once we are up and away."

"You mean it?" Lars practically flew out of his seat.

"When have you ever known me to be a kidder? Yes, of course I mean it. Now strap in, boy. — Or birthday party is over."

Lars fell silent, now, the obedient soldier. He studied his grandfather's every move, tried to commit the pre-flight curriculum to memory.

Grandpa Flix made some last-minute checks of fuel and Lars didn't know what else. Then he flipped the cover off the POWER switch with his thumb and snapped it into the ON position. Somewhere behind them, power flowed to the turbines, and the overhead rotors began to turn. Grandpa Flix reached over and checked the boy's straps to be sure they were snug. They were.

Lars looked at the domed cockpit, his eyes everywhere at once. An airchop was a hybrid, a cross between an old-style helicopter and a modern jet aircraft. The rotors were short and stubby, the body sleek, the turbine on the central-axis silent. Lars had read somewhere that such airships employed stealth technology.

As they lifted skyward towards the east, Lars cocked his head back to gaze out upon the night sky through the canopy. Ten-year-old boys come in only two flavors — those that want to jump in a spaceship and explore the heavens, and those that want to hear the roar of an adoring crowd and be a sports star. Lars was one of the former. Now, through that overhead canopy, he could suddenly see the heavens in all their glory — the moon, the constellations, the stars.

As the airchop picked up speed, the nose dipped and Lars was pushed further back into his seat. In front of him, filling the console, were dozens of instruments. Most were backlit by green lumens. His grandfather pointed out the important ones to him in turn — rotor speed, ground speed, oil pressure, biometrics, altitude, heading. They were now at 3000 meters altitude, moving at a speed of nearly one thousand kloms per hour on a heading of ninety degrees, due east. He handed Lars a set of headphones so that Lars could hear the comm chatter. The boy's eyes lit up. *It was, oh, so exciting!*

"Okay, son, now pay attention. An airchop is a specially designed and unique flying machine. This craft is as airworthy flying level and horizontal as it is flying upside down or perpendicular to the ground on its side."

"Cool. You mean I can fly this thing upside down or loop-de-loop and still not crash it?"

"No, Lars. What it means is that an airchop is damn hard to stall and harder still to accidentally run into the ground. Now, son, take hold of the stick and pull back on it ever so gently."

The boy's palms were sweating. But Lars did as he was told and the nose of the airchop rose. They started gaining altitude very rapidly.

"The stick is a directional finder. Pull back, your ship climbs. Push forward, she dives. Pull left, she banks left. Pull right, she banks right. Plus, the stick is sensitive to the tightness of your grip. It interprets a tight grip as being imperative. Thus, it responds quicker. Right now it senses your nervousness, so relax."

Lars nodded his understanding and loosened his grip ever so slightly.

"Good. Now level her out."

Lars slowly pushed the stick forward. The nose began to dip toward the horizontal.

Grandpa seemed to approve. "It is all about avionics, son. That big dial in front of you displays the horizon. Gently move the stick around until the red half-circle on the dial fits snugly against the centerline. Then you know you are flying level."

Lars kept his eyes on the dial, as Grandpa instructed, and gradually leveled them out.

"Okay, good. That same dial will show as a heads-up display if you put on your nightvision goggles. But we will save that particular lesson for another day, when you are a bit older. The entire operation — weapons systems included — can be manual, voice-activated, or computer driven. If, for instance, I am logged in and I issue the vocal command AUTO FLY, the computer will take over and the airchop will fly itself until I say different."

"What is the fun in that?" Lars said, trying to bank left. The computer would not let him.

"RESUME MANUAL," Grandpa ordered, and the stick relented.

Lars yanked the stick left and the red half-circle banked hard off the horizontal as the sudden steepness of the turn increased. He felt the g-forces build in his temple, behind his eyes.

"Easy there, kiddo. Early pilots manual-sticked all the time. Computers did not exist in those days. Pilots flew by instinct. Just like that fellow I once told you about. Chuck Yeager. If you ask me, I would rather fly with a good stickman than a mediocre computer. But no matter who has got his hands on the stick, my lunch tends to stay down a whole lot better if the pilot flies level. So do me a favor, will you kid, and level this baby out again."

"Aye, aye, Captain."

Lars looked at his grandfather with deeply respectful eyes and did what the old man asked. *How many ten-year-olds get to pilot a real-live airchop for even five minutes much less an hour?* No way was he going to blow his big chance by not following orders.

For the next hour they flew in silence — Lars, his grandfather, and an ocean of stars. Somewhere along the way, excitement overwhelmed the boy and he fell asleep. Grandpa quietly took the stick.

They passed over the Great Lakes, up the St. Lawrence Seaway, across the mountains of Vermont and New Hampshire, out over the Atlantic, and up along the New England coastline into Maine. When they rapidly descended from out of the clouds, Lars lurched awake.

The night sky was black as Flix set the bird down on a pad near his home. Even so, the moon threw off sufficient light for Lars to make out the lines of a large house a hundred meters away.

It was a scene Lars would never forget, that nighttime landing along the coast of Maine. Even two centuries later, even after surviving a brutal war, after enduring two rejuvenations, after two lifetimes as an enslave on Venus and a year-long overland trek to freedom, even after all that, Lars could still remember his grandfather's house like it was yesterday.

Compared to his parents' own rather simple abode back in Ironwood, Flix's place was enormous. Plus, the location was grand — along a secluded windswept stretch of beach below Bar Harbor.

Now, as the rotors spun to a stop, Lars fairly leapt out of the cockpit of the airchop to explore his amazing surroundings for the upcoming week.

What excitement!

CHAPTER FIVE

The next morning Grandpa fixed pancakes. This was a special recipe all his own. Blueberry syrup, chocolate chips in the batter, thick slabs of sweet butter to melt on top, fresh-squeezed orange juice on the side. Add a cup of hot cocoa and a side of bacon and you have an energy-packed breakfast.

Then, stomachs full, the two of them hit the trail. Walking one behind the other, they lumbered up the South Ridge Trail on Cadillac Mountain.

Lars loved the great out-of-doors, and he loved to climb. It did not matter whether it was a tree or a ladder or a sheer rock wall. He loved to climb. Nothing else could quite compare with being up high. It was where Lars felt most at ease. Later in life, this fearlessness would help make him the spirited spacejockey he eventually became.

The trail up Cadillac Mountain began just below the entrance to Blackwoods Campground on Mount Desert Island, ten kloms in all. Grandpa walked with a slight limp. He used a hardwood cane to help him get by. His initials — FW — were carved into the handle. Lars asked him about it.

"As a young man, I was a pyrotech specialist in the armed forces. I put some of what I learned about firecrackers in that little book I gave you."

"Firecrackers?"

"Yes. The *Primer on Nitrate Compounds.*"

"It is about a bit more than firecrackers, Grandpa."

"I suppose."

"Mother was angry with you for sending me that book. — And for sending me that wonderful assortment of chemicals."

"Still have all your fingers?"

"You know that I do." Lars held up both hands so his grandfather could see.

"Then your mother has nothing to worry about, does she?"

Lars smiled. Grandpa had a good sense of humor. "Is that what happened to your leg? . . . . The wrong mixture of explosive chemicals?"

"Ah, my leg. No, that was not chemicals. Nor some stupid accident on my part."

"What then?"

"Perhaps you have heard of Ali Salaam Rontana?"

"You know that I have, Grandpa. Everyone has."

"Well, like I said. Before I worked at the Pentagon, I was a soldier in the field. I am not supposed to tell you this. Even your mother doesn't know. But the truth is my team was tasked by the President with assassinating Rontana."

"Oh, Grandpa, don't be silly. You could not harm a hummingbird."

The two were now climbing the second set of steep switchbacks up the mountain trail. As was his nature, Lars liked being up high. He moved, now, to the edge of the trail, peered down the steep slope. Rocks skittered down the side from under the tip of his boot.

"Be careful, Lars."

"But I am not afraid."

"No. But you should be."

"You're not. Why should I be?"

Grandpa Flix stopped on the trail, caught his breath. "You and I, Lars. We are the same. Very little scares us. Not heights. Not speed. Not physical danger. You and I, Lars. We are not like other men. We climb a fence, become desensitized to the risk. Then we take the next rung higher on the stepladder, find that we enjoy it. Then we climb up on the roof, scramble to the second story, find that we are not afraid. People in the military, people who know, call it the Yeager Syndrome."

Lars moved back from the sheer edge of the trail, where he had been standing. He liked the idea that his Grandpa thought them both alike. It was a comforting thought to a boy his age.

Lars turned and they resumed hiking uphill. "That Yeager thing. Such a funny name for a disease."

"Oh, the Yeager Syndrome is no disease. It is named for that man I told you about. Chuck Yeager. A daring, young test pilot who lived nearly four hundred years ago. Set the standard for every airman who followed."

"What is a test pilot?"

"Yeager was the first man to break the sound barrier in an experimental aircraft. Nowadays we use bots to test-fly any new aircraft design. But in those days actual humans did the test-flying. It was amazingly dangerous work. Countless airmen died as new designs were evaluated and put through their paces."

"There was actually a time before robots?"

"Hard to believe, I know. Yeager was a fearless flier. The aircraft designers would commandeer a wartime bomber and strap a rocketplane to its belly. The bomber would take off with the rocketplane strapped beneath it and go up to an altitude several thousand meters in the sky. When they reached the appointed height, the test pilot would have to step down out of the belly of the bomber and lower himself into the open cockpit of the rocketplane while it was hanging there in midair with all hell streaming beneath them. Then someone else would have to lock the canopy into place above the test pilot.

"Yeager had the nerve to risk flying these unproven experimental aircraft not because he had been born to it — for he surely had not been — but because he had worked his way up to it. I should imagine it went in steps. First climbing fences, then probably trees, then likely taller things still. With each step up the ladder of risk, he passed through increasing levels of danger and excitement. But he never really got scared, not like a normal man."

Lars was young. But he thought he understood. Danger did not stir up his grandfather like it did other men. Lars possessed that same mental toughness, even as a young man. That might explain how he later managed to cross Domtar Province alone and on foot after his second rejuv.

Grandpa Flix continued. "Now, Lars. About that hummingbird you think I could not harm. Back in the day, my military unit was called the STAR Team. The Special Target Attack & Recon Team. I am sorry to disappoint you, son. But I am indeed capable of harming a hummingbird, if not a wooly mammoth. We were trained to kill, and to do so quietly and professionally. That is what we did. Me, Tiger Matthews, Tex, Oiler, all of us, even your grandmother. That is what we did. Every last one of us was deadly lethal."

Flix stopped, checked his grandson's reaction, then continued. "Our Team took out Rontana at his lair in the desert. First, we wiped out the troops protecting him. Then we took him out. A year later, we went after his woman. Her name was Cassandra Mubarak. She was a piece of work. Totally deranged. Completely out of her head. More dangerous than him. In fact, the only good thing that happened on that horrendous mission was that I met your grandmother. Krista Leidurmarm. My wife. Your grandmother. She was with me that day when we followed Mubarak to the moon . . ."

"Wow, Grandpa! You have been to the moon?"

"It was not such a big deal at the time . . ."

"Did you get to wear a spacesuit? That is my dream, you know. When I am older. To wear a spacesuit, to travel among the stars."

Lars continued like a runaway train. "Did you get to bounce around on the surface? Huh, Grandpa? Did you?

Could you jump really high in the low grav? Was it fun? Was it?"

"I was not there on vacation, you know. It was a mission, a dangerous mission. No bouncing around on the surface for fun. I got wounded, almost killed. That is how my leg got busted up. That is why I still need a cane to help me get around."

"I thought they could fix things like that. A busted leg, I mean. With pins or Acceleron injections or I don't know what."

"Pins? Acceleron?" Grandpa stopped on the trail. "Call me old-fashioned, Lars. But I do not go in for all that fancy medical techno-garbage. There are few things in this life that scare me. But the meshing of man and machine is surely one of them."

"You would rather be stuck lugging around a cane for the rest of your life?"

"Heh, kid. This is not just any cane. It is a rifle cane."

He showed it to Lars. The inside was hollowed out. A long, sleek, rifled gun barrel ran down the length of the interior. The trigger was in the grip.

"Cool gun. You are the coolest, Grandpa. You ever kill anyone with that thing? Blast them to vapor?"

"I would never kill anyone that did not need killing."

"And who decides that, Grandpa?"

"A moral question, to be sure. And one for which I have no easy answer. All I know for certain is this. As soldiers, as members of the START Team, we tried to do our duty. It was dangerous work. On one particularly brutal firefight, Tiger Matthews and I were the only survivors. He was my buddy and my friend. On that particular occasion, I carried him out of the desert on my back. Our two families have been allies and close friends ever since."

"But what ever became of Grandma? I never hear from her. She never writes, never comes to visit. Why not? Doesn't Grandma love me?"

"It is nothing like that, Lars."

"What then?"

"I guess you are old enough now for the truth. But let us be clear, shall we? Her not visiting you has nothing whatsoever to do with her not loving you. Your grandmother was captured by the enemy while we were still both active in the service. She was tortured to within inches of her life. Krista is now in a Naval Hospital. I see that she is cared for. But the truly sad part is this. Your grandmother — the love of my life — does not even recognize me anymore. That lack of recognition totally crushes my spirit. But there you have it. She is an invalid in a catatonic state . . . And there is not a damn thing I can do about it."

"Don't give up hope, Grandpa. Science is an amazing thing. We learn more and more stuff every day. You said so yourself. Someday it may be possible to fix her."

"Oh, you mean nanotechnology? Neuroprostheses? Skullcaps? Brain-machine interfaces? That kind of technology is a double-edged sword."

"How so?"

"I guess it has a lot to do with how you view God. I know it is out of fashion these days, Lars, what with the *Book of Lore* in wide acceptance. But my thinking on the subject has evolved. I have come to believe in a single God, the sort of God that looks in on us from time to time. But He doesn't control our fate. At the end of the day we still have to play the cards we have been dealt."

"I want to live forever, Grandpa."

"Me too, kid. Me too. But even if I cannot, I sure am glad you and I had today."

Lars smiled. He loved his Grandpa. After that visit, Lars was often at his grandfather's house. They became the sort of fast friends that grandfathers and grandsons often do, forging an enduring bond between generations.

Grandpa Flix taught Lars everything he knew, from how to tie a knot that would hold, to how to construct a safe fuse for his explosives; from how to shoot a gun, to how to survive in the wild. The next day they flew his airchop down to Washington, D.C. It was Lars's first visit to a big city, his first visit to a city hooded by a glass dome.

They toured the Capitol, the branches of the Smithsonian, the New White House, the Underground Mall. Then Grandpa got an urgent call from someone and had to rush Lars back home to Ironwood, cutting short their week together.

Lars was angry for a few days. But the anger passed. Then another package arrived in the mail from his grandfather. It was a new chemistry set with enough potassium nitrate, charcoal, and sulfur to whip up an awesome batch of first-rate gunpowder.

More on that shortly.

CHAPTER SIX

When Lars was a boy, his father was always working — and always at dangerous trades. So, when the boy needed disciplining, which was often, the job usually fell to his mother Eleka.

But even as a young boy, Lars was quick-witted. He learned that sometimes, when he was in trouble, the best thing he could do was try and make his mother laugh. If he could just get his mother to crack a smile, no matter how lame the story, he would usually be home free.

The Cabot family was poor. They owned almost no electronic gadgets. Electricity was expensive; gadgets even more so. They could not easily afford either.

They did possess one labor-saving device, however. A floor-sweeper bot. Eleka absolutely adored it. In the morning, she would plunk the thing down in one corner of the front room and set it to work while she read or tackled the daily bills. Then, as she drank her morning brew, the bot would methodically vacuum the carpet and do the floors.

The sweeper bot was flat on top, barrel-shaped on the bottom. It had six hard-rubber wheels, plus a retractable handle. Add water to an internal tank, along with a cleaning agent, and the sweeper would move on to scrubbing floors and doing toilets.

Is it any wonder Eleka simply loved the thing?

Like any friend of the family, the robotic floor sweeper had a name — Mitzi. But, to paraphrase the ancient sentiment: familiarity breeds nosiness. In the eyes of a budding, young engineer, Mitzi was an attractive nuisance, something to be tinkered with. For Lars, curious lad that he was, the sweeper was nothing if not an intriguing temptation.

How did it work? He wondered.

As any boy knows, the only sure way to find out how something works is to take the thing apart. And that is exactly what Lars did one fine summer's day when he was about twelve.

On the occasion in question, Lars waited for just the right moment, a moment when his mother wasn't looking. Then he spirited Mitzi out the front door and plopped it down in the backyard. There were hills and ravines and forests in every direction as far as the eye could see. The boy had it in his head to use the sweeper bot as a sort of summertime sled.

In the eyes of a twelve-year-old boy looking for adventure, this seemed like an immensely fun thing to do, no matter how foolhardy an enterprise in the eyes of a clear-headed adult. In the wintertime, when there was snow on the ground, his greatest joy was to take his brother's wooden sled and careen down a gulley on nearby Bearcat Mountain. *So why not do the same in summer?*

Lars turned the sweeper over, removed her wheels with an Allen wrench and screwdriver. Then he set the wheels aside and turned the bot right-side up again.

Lars was ripe for adventure. He grabbed hold of Mitzi's handle and sat down on the sweeper's flat top. The bottom was barrel-shaped and exquisitely suited for downhill racing. He pushed off downhill with his hands and almost immediately ran into trouble.

What the thick shroud of snow usually covered in the winter — roots and rocks and fallen logs — were now fully exposed for what they were, sharp-edged hazards. Lars had gone barely five meters down the hill when he struck a nasty looking boulder head-on.

The collision with the boulder dented Mitzi's bottom in a very stern and permanent way. But it got worse.

When Lars hit the big rock, Newton's Laws took over. Gravity is a bitch. The collision sent Lars sailing in one direction, Mitzi in the other. The bot flipped end over end, careened off a tree. Lars landed in a bramble of bushes.

In an instant, Lars knew he was in deep trouble. The scrubber had been flattened by the impact. The handle he had been holding onto for dear life was now broken though still in his hand.

A bolt of panic ripped through his insides. *His mother was going to be mad.* He stooped to gather up the pieces of the busted sweeper and began to drag them one by one up the hill. Tears flowed from his eyes. *What was he going to tell his mother when she saw what he had done?*

When Lars got to the top of the hill with the last piece, she was there, hands planted on her hips, steam blowing from her ears. There was only one way out of this. If Lars wanted to save his skin, he had to get his mother to crack a smile. Then he might have a sporting chance.

"Now Mom, don't be angry. I spotted some great looking blueberries on the opposite ridge. I was going to bring them home to you."

"Is that so?"

"You have to believe me, Mom. I had the best of intentions. I know how much you love blueberry jam. I was going to pick a pint or two of the very best, bring them home, mash them, add in some sugar, and cook the soup into jam."

"And you needed Mitzi's help for this?"

"No, of course not. I told Mitzi to stay home. But you know how she gets. Mitzi has a mind of her own. She always wants to help. That no-good robot followed me out the door. No matter what I said, she absolutely would not behave."

Eleka was not fooled by the boy's story. But she found it hard to swat him in a meaningful way after he had tried so hard to lie convincingly.

"No-good robot," she said, anger subsiding.

When she raised her hand, now, to swat him, it wasn't full force. Once again, he had talked his way out of the worst of it.

That is how it was with Lars. Always. Whatever it took to get himself out of trouble.

Which brings to mind this other time. On that earlier occasion, Lars and a buddy of his named Granite liberated the heating element from his mother's only remaining working kitchen appliance, a toaster oven. He and his buddy Granite were following a set of step-by-step instructions they found in Grandpa Flix's book. The bullet points explained how to string together an electrical system to set off a homemade bomb. We will get to the explosion in just a minute.

Granite Irston was Lars's best friend. Granite was two years his senior and, in Lars's eyes, a whole lot smarter than he was. Granite was also more worldly. He had been with a girl, something Lars certainly had not. Granite had been drunk. He had smoked tobacco. He had swallowed a Delude, purchased a condom, mixed it up with mlorons. Lars had done none of these things. Thus far in his life, he had been too scared to try.

Lars could not remember a time when his mother and father were close. It was not as if they fought regularly, for they did not. Indifference more like. If they were affectionate once, as they certainly must have been, they were no longer, not in Lars's presence anyway. There always seemed to be a certain distance between the two adults, as if they lived in separate time-zones. His father worked hard. When he did come home, which was not every night, it seemed that all his father ever had time for was sleep.

Lars would be cuddled up in bed under his sheets with his lights on. The dark bothered him. Plus, he liked to read his books late at night. Reading relaxed Lars for sleep, especially when the house was quiet and his father was still not home from work.

Lars would be in bed reading, when his father would come in through the front door. Lars's bedroom was upstairs in a sort of loft. He would hear his father enter the house one story below.

His father would go alone down the short hallway to the backroom, not upstairs where his mother slept. The two had separate bedrooms. They slept apart most nights. Lars did not understand why.

Even as a boy, Lars knew this arrangement was unnatural. But he was afraid to ask his mother about it. He had seen her on the verge of tears more times than he cared to remember.

But Granite seemed to understand. The two boys talked about everything. Granite's parents were separated, soon to be divorced. His mother was also lonely. She cried a lot. She blamed her husband, Granite's father, for their ills, said he lied, slept with other women. Lars was not sure, but he thought she was talking about fidelity.

Now, about that explosion. There was a lot of the grandfather in the grandson. The old man was a munitions expert back in the day. Flix had given Lars that book, not to see his grandson get hurt, but to keep the boy safe. Lars was already trying to blow up things long before Flix got involved and sent him that book. Anyway, it was curiosity that killed the cat, not a chemistry set with a book of instructions. That's how he explained it to Eleka. *If the boy was going to try and blow up things anyway, why not show him how to do it safely?* In his mind, the *Primer* was a sort of safety valve to counter the boy's worst inclinations.

Lars had already learned that, when mixed together in the proper proportions, potassium nitrate, sulfur, and charcoal made gunpowder. What he didn't know was that a safer and more powerful explosive could be had by melting sugar into the saltpeter. More powerful still, a blend of Canadian whiskey from across the border, plus a compound of zinc-dust and sulfur. The three could be stirred into a paste, a thick gray composite that could be shaped by hand, much like modeling clay.

On the day in question, Lars squeezed a quantity of gray paste-goop inside an old sock. Then he let it dry under the solar hotwater heater until the next weekend. Saturday morning after raking out the barn, Granite and him decided to test out the new compound. Lars's father had an antediluvian wood-burning stove in his workshop behind the house. On cold days, Hogan kept a fire going in the stove. Now Lars tossed the goop-filled sock into the red-hot stove to see what would happen.

It did not take long, barely three seconds. The stove door was barely half-closed when — *Whoosh!* — the goop ignited.

The two boys had never seen anything like it. The rate of oxygen uptake was so rapid, the goop burned with violent fury. A millisecond later, the explosion of expanding gases flung the stove door off its hinges and blew the top and sides off the stove.

Next thing Lars knew, his father's workshop was on fire, Granite was splayed out on the ground, and his mother was running out the back door screaming at them both. *There would be no laughing this one off.*

His father wasn't home when it happened. That was a good thing. Granite wasn't hurt. That was another good thing. Granite got up off the ground, grabbed a garden hose and began to douse the flames.

Lars looked at his mother. She stood on the hillside, hands still planted on her hips, and glared. He knew she was angry.

Granite stayed at it with the garden hose. He was having some success. The flames were out. In the distance, they heard the blare of a fire truck. Like many rural areas, Ironwood had a volunteer fire department.

News in Ironwood traveled fast. Probably Mr. Jenkins in the next farmhouse over. He was always a little jumpy, ever since Lars ignited his first firecracker three summers before.

The fire truck came and went without spraying so much as one ounce of water. Granite had already managed to put out the fire with the hose.

No fireman likes to be summoned to a false alarm. Nothing makes them angrier. But the anger was short-lived, for they got another call and quickly turned their truck around and headed back the other direction.

Aside from the demolished stove and a good-sized hole blasted in one wall of the workshop, damage to the structure was minimal.

"This time you have really gone and done it," Eleka exclaimed. "I am confiscating that infernal book. And you are grounded for one day longer than your natural life. I will deal with your grandfather later."

CHAPTER SEVEN

That was a bad day. And not just because Lars blew up his father's workshop. There was also a serious accident that day across the valley at the lumber mill where his father worked. One man died and three more were injured, including his father. Sirens blared. Worried wives rushed to the mill. Some had their youngest children in tow. A worn bolt had broken and a rusted chain jammed. A saw blade shattered. It sent shards of metal and wood flying everywhere.

Hogan Cabot's blown-up workshop was soon forgotten. The accident at the mill was much more pressing news. Granite stopped what he was doing, put down the hose, tried to comfort his friend. No one knew yet how badly Lars's father had been hurt.

Lars was afraid for his father. Or maybe he was just afraid for himself. This was a new feeling for Lars, being afraid. He was just a boy. Now, suddenly, he was having adult feelings. His father, once an indestructible superman was mortal after all.

When he saw his mother cry, Lars realized the facts were different from what he first thought. She still loved his father despite whatever distance separated them emotionally.

Eleka ran down the road to learn what had happened. The mill was only half a klom away. Lars took his motorized two-wheeler and followed his mother up to the sawmill. Many of the town's people were already there drifting aimlessly about.

By the time Lars arrived at the main gate, he found himself shaking with a tangled web of emotions. Something about the wind whipping through his hair as he maneuvered his moped up to the fence. There was an ambulance and a medic standing just inside the fence. The gathered townsfolk, many of them simple people, looked frightened.

A neighbor, who knew Lars well, saw the boy at the fenceline. He was just this side of tears. She saw Lars peering onto the grounds of the lumber mill trying to figure out what was going on inside. She came across the broken ground in Lars's direction waving her arms angrily.

"Stop staring, boy!" she screamed. "Show some respect."

Lars was taken aback.

"You have a lot of nerve making a scene here," the woman added.

"But my dad."

"Oh, Lars. Grow up! Don't you know what goes on in there?"

Lars could not answer. He had never once done the math, never once calculated the risks his father accepted every day on the job.

"The men and women of Ironwood go into that sawmill day after day. They go into that sawmill or up into that chute or down by the river. They perform hazardous jobs. It is like taking a single bullet and putting it into the chamber. You spin the cylinder and pull the trigger, a daily game of Russian roulette."

"To what end? Risk death or disability just to earn a buck?"

"Oh, they do it with open eyes. Your father, my husband, the men and women who work here — they all know the risks. Logs are immensely heavy. Sometimes, they roll. Saw blades shatter. People get crushed. Eyes get blinded. Accept it."

Lars stood at the fenceline, hands in his pockets, trying to digest the neighbor woman's words. The last of the injured workers had been loaded onto a stretcher and put in the back of the medi-van, soon to be whisked away.

Lars gazed up the gravel road toward the giant sawmill. A shift change was underway. He saw lumberjacks making their way in small groups toward the main gate. He heard what sounded like normal conversation between men getting off work. The topics varied. Sports. The market. A new pornovid. Someone told a dirty joke. Everyone laughed.

Hearing the boisterous talk made Lars angry. *Had they no feelings?* One man was dead; another three injured. One of the injured was his father. *Did they even care?*

Lars did not know yet how badly his father was hurt. For all Lars knew, his father might have been horribly maimed.

And yet, these men leaving work were acting as if it were an ordinary day. Only one man was dead. *Only one!*

One man was killed or maimed in the sawmills or iron mines of the Mesabi Range every week. But it was amazing. These men leaving the mill after work on their way home to their wives or their girlfriends seemed oblivious to the risk. This was not courage, not in the ordinary sense of the word. It was something else. One part stoicism, one part stupidity. Lars could not reconcile these feelings. He suddenly wanted to grab his things, walk out the front door, leave Ironwood forever.

In the days following the accident at the mill, Lars withdrew totally into himself. He was immobilized by shock and no one could help him, not even his mother. His father had been blinded by a piece of flying shrapnel from the shattered saw blade. The optic nerve had been damaged. A replacement was unlikely.

Lars quit doing everything he loved. He put away his grandfather's book. He quit mixing his chemicals. He quit reading his science fiction adventures. He quit thinking about what sort of hero he could be as a man. He quit hanging out with Granite, would not take his grandfather's calls.

But the day came when Granite cornered him in the parking lot after school. He tried to talk Lars back in off the ledge he was clinging to.

But Lars would not hear of it. He hadn't slept in days. Granite thought he looked like hell. Lars felt as if someone had reached up inside him and ripped out his heart. Had a doctor been called in to examine the boy, he would likely have been diagnosed as being severely depressed.

But Granite persisted. "It is not your fault, Lars. You have to let it go. Your father knew the risks."

"Did he?"

"They all do."

"Am I to grow up and become one of them now?" he asked Granite. His lower jaw was quivering.

"One of them who?"

"You know. *Them.* A hard-ass miner. One of those brain-dead lumberjacks."

"The life of a jack ain't so bad."

"Isn't it? Are you one of them too? One of those axe-wielding chowder-heads? One of those whack-jobs like my father, who take unreasonable risks? All rock-hard and solid, filled to the eyebrows with beer, swimming in God and religion and lore?"

"God is not so bad."

"Which one?"

"Take your pick. I am partial to Aphrodite and Demeter myself, whichever one is the sexiest."

Lars nodded, but did not reply. The only gods he knew were mathematics and chemistry, one chemical in particular. Everything else was just silly poetry.

For Lars Cabot, child of northern Minnesota, mathematics had become his religion. Euclidean geometry. Linear algebra. Differential calculus.

Could anything be more smart or pretty than a Fibonacci series? Here was a series of numbers that described the wondrous spiral of seashells, the breathtaking arrangement of rose petals on a branch, the mystery of how sand came to be arranged a particular way on a wave-tossed beach.

Or what about Euclidean geometry? Could anything be more elegant or more precise than the geometry described by Euclid of Alexandria? His geometry was as beautiful as a sunny day or a gorgeous woman. It spoke to Lars in a language few around him understood.

Euclid of Alexandria, Brahmagupta of India, Isaac Newton, Leonardo Fibonacci, Bernhard Riemann. These men were superheroes in Lars's eyes, actual superheroes, the sort of superhero that breathed life into the adventures of his science fiction, the sort of men who narrowed their eyes, tightened their jaws and dug in their heels when it came time to battle the demons of darkness and evil. And when these men fought evil, they arrived on the battlefield armed with little more than their wits, their intelligence and their reason.

Only, Euclid was not some superhuman god drawn from the pages of the *Book of Lore*. Nor were any of these other men. They were all flesh and blood mortals, people who had actually lived.

Brahmagupta was a brilliant mathematician and astronomer who, in the seventh century AD, was the first to give rules to compute with zero. His texts were composed in elliptic verse, common practice in Indian mathematics. Consequently, when they were read by students, his mathematics sounded with a poetic ring. *Could anything be more beautiful?* Mathematics set to verse.

Then there was Leonardo Fibonacci. He was considered by some to be the most talented western mathematician of the Middle Ages. Best known to the modern world for the number sequence he did not discover but which was named after him, and for helping spread the Hindu–Arabic numeral system throughout Europe. His primary work, written in 1202, was his "Book of Calculation."

Then there was the grandmaster of them all — Euclid of Alexandria. Euclid was a Greek mathematician who lived in the time of Ptolemy I, twenty-seven hundred years ago. He invented plane geometry.

Euclid compiled his thoughts and postulates in a thirteen-volume treatise entitled *Elements*. This work was the earliest known collection of sophisticated, even modern approaches to geometry. In it, Euclid of Alexandria set forth the elements of plane geometry in the form of definitions, postulates, theorems, and mathematical proofs. One volume was an ancient Greek version of elementary number theory.

Euclid's method of reasoning began with a short set of axioms. From these axioms he deduced a series of testable propositions. Then Euclid broke more new ground. He was among the first to demonstrate how these propositions could fit into a comprehensive and logical deductive system.

The *Elements* begins with plane geometry. It states in the language of geometry much of what we now call algebra and number theory. It spoke to Lars loud and clear:

Two planes are either parallel to one another or they intersect in a single line.

A line exists in only one of three states. It is either parallel to a plane. Or it intersects the plane at a single point. Or it is contained wholly within the plane.

Two lines that are perpendicular to the same plane must also be parallel to one other.

Lars found security in a world possessed of square corners and parallel lines, a world where the three corners of a triangle always summed to 180 degrees. In his world — the mathematician's world — things that equal the same thing also equal one another. In this world, if equals are added to equals, then the wholes are equal as well. In this world, this nicely ordered world, the whole never fails to be greater than the part.

This world is a certain world, a world of order and precision and definite length. Circles are round and of known circumference. In a right triangle, the square of the hypotenuse always equals the sum of the square of the other two sides.

In this world, fathers do not become injured by accidents at work. Saw blades do not fail from improper use. Optic nerves do not get severed and then have to be repaired again.

This is a world of black and white but never gray. Angles sum, lines obey rules, axioms are always true. To Lars, such a world was eminently appealing.

Mathematics was his religion. It was the only explanation that made any sense to him, the only lens through which he could view the world.

In the principles and axioms of algebra, in the truths of plane geometry and the hard logic of the calculus, Lars felt the gods of the pantheon had delivered humanity a message, one of order and precision and arrow-straight lines.

Forget Relativity. Forget Chaos Theory and Fractals. Forget Heisenberg's Uncertainty Principle. Forget whatever did not make sense.

Some truths remained true across the Universe, no matter what.

CHAPTER EIGHT

Even after recovering from the ordeal of his second rejuv, Lars still retained two distinct memories of adolescence — the carefree summers he spent at Boy Scout camp and hunting grizzly bear with his father.

In the days following the terrible accident at the sawmill, the doctors from Minnepaul were able to repair Hogan's optic nerve and eye.

Oh, the joy and wonder of modern science!

These were the same technological wonders that led to the development of skullcaps and would eventually lead to whole-body rejuvenation, the same technology that would, in the future, trap Lars as an enslave in the lithium mines of Domtar Province, Venus. — But that future was still many years down a dusty road.

Thinking back, now, Lars remembered one bear hunting trip with his father in particular. It took several days of planning to prepare for their departure. Animals of this size were rare, except in the High Country. They loaded the gtruck with their gear, mostly food and drink, fueled the tanks, entered the driving coordinates into the nav. This was bow and arrow hunting, infinitely more difficult and dangerous than doing the same thing with a rifle or force gun.

Early on the day in question, they swung west out of Minnesota, father and son together, then pushed north, up into the wilds of Montana. Lars was maybe fourteen at the time. It was late fall. Usually by now there would be a sharp chill in the air. But in the lower elevations, the fall weather was still relatively mild.

The roads were poor and the driving slow. Civilization had its automatic roads and its self-driving gcars; but not out here. Out here, where no one lived, driving was still hands-on.

It was a long drive. But the hours on the road were not wasted. They spent much of the time talking about the challenges of hunting big game with a bow and arrow. Aside from the mythical creatures that inhabited his theology, bow hunting was one of the few subjects Hogan would talk about at length.

"A bow is nothing more than a sophisticated spring, Lars. A bit of complex engineering invented by early man."

"I never really thought of it that way. But I guess that makes sense. Kinetic energy is stored in the limbs of the bow as the bowstring is drawn tight."

"Yes. And that stored energy is transformed into rapid motion when the string is released. The string transfers the pent-up force to the waiting arrow. That way, Lars, a bow and arrow can be used for hunting or sport, occasionally even still to make war."

Lars and his father had constructed simple bows together in Hogan's workshop when Lars was young. This was before the boy became infatuated with explosives and other things. Those early bows were made from elm wood. They were crude, ugly-looking weapons. But they did have one saving grace. They were astonishingly large and strong.

"Remember your training, boy. Remember what you learned at summer camp. The bows the two of us used to build together were made from wood — saplings mainly — not the high-tech stuff they use today. And the bowstrings we strung our bows with were made of actual string and gut, not from the fancy polymers bowstrings are made from nowadays."

Lars remembered. There was a certain precision to the mathematics of bow technology. The force required to hold the string stationary at full draw was a measure of the intrinsic power of a bow, so and so many "pounds" in the vernacular of archery. That force in pounds was known as the bow's draw weight. The higher the draw weight, the more powerful the bow. The more powerful the bow, the further and faster it could project a lethal arrow.

Hogan interrupted his son's thoughts. "An archer's size and his strength mean everything when hunting. The bowstring must be held steady and taut."

"But, Dad. It is more than that. Nowadays there are sentry robots. Some of these robots come equipped with high-tech bows and arrows. They are drawn by the bot and held mechanically. That makes the maximum draw weight a matter of engineering not archer size. The mathematics are simple and elegant."

"Shush and bother! Real men do not use mechanical bows. You want to be a real man, don't you Lars?"

"Yes, of course I do."

"Then no mechanical bows for us. Still, you have to admit. The hunting bows we are carting with us today are infinitely more advanced than the simple stuff you and I used to build back in my workshop. That is, before you blew up the damn thing."

"Not my best day."

"Nor mine."

"But you are okay now, right?"

"Good enough to hunt anyway. Which is all that matters. I am tough. Like an old-fashioned bow. I bend. But I do not break."

"I like that image."

Hogan looked up from the steering wheel. "The limbs of a bow must not splinter under the stress of repeated deep bending. There are two basic designs. The limbs may consist of a single curve as in an English longbow or they may bend back upon themselves as in a recurve bow."

"This is a subject I know something about, Dad. As a Boy Scout, I spent a whole summer doing archery merit badge. A good quality bow requires durable materials. Something with high tensile strength for the back of the bow. Something with compressive strength for the belly."

"Mighty fancy talk for a boy."

"Not a boy any longer."

"Using big words don't make you a man."

"Nor does using them make me less of one."

"Fair enough."

"In the old days, they used wood in the core. Maintains dimensional stability. Lessens weight. Plus animal horn to store energy in compression. Plus sinew for its ability to store energy in tension."

"Only certain types of animal horn will suffice, Lars. Water buffalo mainly, or ibex. The horn of a domesticated animal is just too darn soft."

"I did not know that."

"See? The old man still knows a few things you do not."

"I never said different. But a bow is only as good as its string."

"Never were truer words spoken. A good quality string should be able to withstand a strain at least four times the draw weight of the bow. Strong for its mass. Resists stretching. Remains strong after exposure to moisture. The first bowstrings were made from animal byproducts, things like sinew, intestines, even hair. Plant fibers were also common. Linen. Hemp. Stuff like that. When treated with beeswax, plant fibers can resist moisture with the best of them."

"But those were the old days."

"Yes, the old days. But not anymore. Modern strings have no actual string in them nor organic materials of any kind. Most are made from synthetics or spun from steel cable."

•
•

It went like this for hours. Back and forth father and son talked. About bows and arrows and hunting equipment and camping. All the while, Hogan drove west and then north. In the end, the hours passed quickly and soon they were there, in the verdant valley below the ancient hunting grounds.

Gear on their shoulders, the two moved slowly up the slope among high mountain crags and evergreen forests. The lower forests were filled with great stands of blue spruce and Ponderosa Pine. At higher elevations they would find Douglas fir and Lodgepole Pine. In places, the forests were broken by grassy meadows and treeless, sun-washed slopes.

Lars staggered under the weight of his backpack. He wasn't quite a man. He was barely a teenager. The pack was heavy. They carried with them enough food for a week, plus tents, a poly cooking stove, layers of clothing, and their bows and arrows. Oh, and his father's three-day supply of whiskey and drugs.

Lars's father was ten to twelve paces ahead of Lars on the trail. Hogan's long, black hair streamed back across his shoulders, twisting in the wind. Here was a man at one with his environment.

Below them was an ocean of dark pine. The sea of majestic trees flowed for kloms in every direction. It rolled like dark, green waves over the rough topography of craggy mountain peaks and chiseled valleys. Here and there an eddy of black forest would spill into the backwater of a steep, mountain gorge.

Father and son hiked one behind the other in silence, listening to the sounds that occasionally punctuated the air around them. Now and again, the forest and the open spaces would come alive with tiny noises. Unseen creatures scurrying to and fro.

But other than the patterned sounds of their own hard breathing, there were no other sounds to drown out these tiny noises. Not the hum of man's technology. Not the motors or gears of bustling humanity. Not the drone of commerce. Everything else was quiet around them. Not a single community or town of consequence could be found within five hundred kloms of this place. There were no city noises, no snarled traffic, no beeping horns to drown out the quirky symphony of sounds that resonated in the wilderness.

But the music was written in code, and a man had to know the cipher. Otherwise, how could he hope to distinguish one sound from another? — The wind coursing through the pines. Deer munching crab apples. Small mammals, raccoons mainly, crackling through the underbrush. The odd squirrel rustling through thickets of pine cones. Owls hooting in the distance. The occasional howl of a distant wolf.

The sights and sounds of God's Nature were on display everywhere. Lars put Ironwood behind him, forgot his mathematics, put aside his logic, tried to enjoy the time with his father. For the first time in months, he began to feel genuinely happy.

As father and son gained elevation, the air cooled noticeably. The pair was in the Montana wilderness area known as the "River of No Return." Few places in North America could match the sheer ruggedness of this desolate place.

High above them overhead, a cold autumn wind raced over an exposed spine of granite rock. The bracing wind tossed a bank of low, dark clouds from right to left across the mottled sky. Coarse snow stung at their cheeks.

To avoid frostbite, they kept their faces down. Animal tracks were everywhere on the ground. Hogan pointed out the tracks to his son, one by one, as they came upon them. Elk and bighorn sheep. Rabbit and coyote. An older wolf track, frozen in the spill of a marmot hole. The tracks spoke to Lars of wild possibilities.

They were headed, now, toward a cluster of small mountain lakes. Hogan knew the way. He had been in this wild country before.

The cluster of lakes they were climbing toward was tucked beneath the crest of the next range. Along their rocky shorelines and splashed inbetween outcroppings of glacial outwash, a special plant grew in abundance. Biscuit root. The bears loved it. Father and son were looking for bears. Hunting them, actually.

The River-of-No-Return National Wilderness was a land of clear rivers, deep canyons, and rugged mountains. Two whitewater rivers ran through it — the Main Salmon River, which ran west near the northern boundary of the Wilderness, and the Middle Fork of the Salmon, which began near the southern boundary and ran north for about one hundred and fifty kloms until it joined up with the Main.

The canyon carved out by the Main Salmon River was deeper than any other canyon in North America. That included the Grand Canyon of the Colorado River.

But unlike the sheer walls of the Grand Canyon, which ran beneath cactus-topped plateaus of dry desert heat, this river rushed ice-cold below wooded ridges that rose steeply toward the sky and beneath ragged, solitary crags.

A range of mountains dominated the interior of the Wilderness. They flared out in a multitude of minor crests and rose by increments to wide summits.

East of the Middle Fork River were the fabulous Bighorn Crags. The Crags formed a series of jagged summits. Some were several thousand meters in height. As a group, the Crags surrounded fourteen strikingly beautiful, clear-water lakes. Father and son were climbing towards one of them now.

The wind was whipping up the valley with tremendous force. The two hikers drove hard for a grove of big Douglas fir, where they sought temporary shelter from the stinging snow. After a time, the winds subsided and they began to follow a game trail higher up into the wild valley.

A clutch of mature blue spruce occupied the creek bottom. The spruces were majestic trees with an unmatchable blue hue.

Further along, the creek opened up into a half-frozen bog. Lars glanced into the shallow water and felt a sudden paralyzing rush of adrenaline.

In the mud of the lake bottom was the track of a large animal, a bear! More tracks led back into the thicket behind them.

Lars stared down at the bear track. His chest tightened. Suddenly his father was at his side. But, just as quickly, his father turned away, bored and disinterested.

"The paw prints are too small," he said.

Lars was surprised. The prints seemed rather large to him.

"A mere black bear," his father continued, without finishing his thought.

What he failed to say beyond "mere black bear" was that the paw print was too small to belong to the larger, more dangerous grizzly bear they had come in search of.

Lars's moment of excitement passed, and he looked around. He had never seen such wilderness before, such untamed wildness. This was the High Country. Humble and unassuming. A place of legend. An elemental place raw with granite rocks, muddy bogs, and thick stands of gristled pine.

On a map of the United States, the "River of No Return Wilderness" would be but a tiny ink splotch, not large at all. But upon closer inspection it would prove to be a wild ink spot, one that was jagged and rough at the edges, an ink spot filled with sharp mountain crags and dangerous animals.

The higher they climbed into the mountains, the bigger the ink spot became. At this latitude, this far north, the growing season was astonishingly short. The higher elevations were studded with alpine lakes and blue-ice glaciers.

Hogan stopped, pulled off his pack and began to make camp.

"Why are we stopping here?" Lars asked.

"Take a look around. Figure it out for yourself."

Lars took stock of the location. There were fresh bear tracks on the trail in and around the campsite. The tracks zigzagged off into the moss. On the ground at Lar's feet lay fresh scat.

Lars dropped his pack as well. Then he set off to explore. He left his father behind, followed the tracks past overturned rocks and rotting logs. Ants were still swarming beneath the logs where the bear had recently fed for a time. The bear must have lapped up the little critters like an anteater. Lars followed the tracks a short distance further before his father called him back. Hogan pointed to the sky with a crooked finger.

"Heed Pamola," his father said.

Lars knew the story, every Boy Scout did. It was straight from the *Book of Lore*, part of Amerind mythology. Pamola was the vengeful, Amerind storm-god. He lived in the sky, up there among the dark clouds. His angry and resentful spirit caused cold weather.

The father continued. "If Pamola is disturbed late in the day like this, you know what He might do."

"I do not believe in such things, Father. You know that. My gods are not up there among the clouds. My gods are in the pages of a book, a mathematics book."

Hogan laughed. "Forget your books, son. Heed Pamola."

"But father. Why must we be guided by myth and superstition? Hasn't science shown us the way?"

"Who would be your gods then? Euclid and Pythagoras and Archimedes?"

"And why not? They are all brilliant mathematicians, among the smartest people ever born."

"Perhaps. But those men are mere mortals. Pamola is a god. The God of Thunder. The Protector of the High Mountains. Head of a moose, body of a man, wings and feet of an eagle."

"Yes, yes, yes, and again yes. I know the story. Pamola is said to nest on Knife Edge Ridge. I am a Boy Scout, remember? The Pamola Lodge of the Order of the Arrow is the honor camping society of the Boy Scouts of America. But that does not make him real."

"Such colossal disrespect! Let us hope Pamola cannot hear you. We would both be made to suffer! On a night like this, Pamola would surely thunder and rumble and spark in anger. I tell you, son. We should not be on the trail or away from our campfire, not at a time like this. It is far too dangerous. I think we should wait here until morning, when the skies clear."

Lars grumbled and kicked at the dirt. This was not an argument he was going to win. He peeled back the cover protecting the face of his wristwatch and checked to see what time it was. Darkness would be upon them soon.

Grandpa Flix had given him that wristwatch three years earlier, about the time he had given him the *Primer*. Said the watch was very, very old and perhaps quite valuable. Said Lars should use it to time chemical reactions. Said it was safer and more accurate than a digital watch, especially out in the field.

No one Lars knew possessed such a timepiece, not in this day and age. In this day and age, such timepieces were practically unknown. So Lars tried to take good care of it.

"Here, help me with this," his father said, opening the waterproof poly bag that held their tent. "And quit looking at that silly watch."

"Grandpa gave me this watch."

"He is a crazy old man, your mother's father. You be careful of him. Now help me set up camp."

Together the two of them put up their tent, built a fire, laid out their sleeping bags inside, and ate dinner, foil burgers and baked potatoes. When it got dark, a river of stars began to flow overhead. Hogan started drinking whiskey, lit up a cannabis joint. Father and son started talking. Hogan was getting drunk. Every once in a while, he would hand his son the joint and encourage him to smoke.

"You had sex, boy?"

Lars wanted to say yes. But the answer was no. He was only fourteen. Granite was the only boy in his circle who had been with a girl. Granite Irston. Lars admitted as much to his father.

Hogan laughed, tossed his son another burger off the coals. "I thought the definition of a northwoods virgin was any girl who could outrun her brother. What is your excuse? Too slow?"

Lars did not know what to say. His father was stoned, and Lars wasn't much better.

Hogan laughed again. "My two favorite things in the world, hiking and fucking. They are the same, you know? Walking is like sex. Basic, simple, repetitive. And yet both are capable of great sophistication and amplification."

"I would not know about that."

"Ah, but you must learn. Hiking and fucking. Either or both can be completely banal or totally meaningless. It all depends on the woman — and the trail. Yet they can each involve great passion and endless adventure. A good walk is like a good woman. One is as likely as the other to lead a man into strange, perhaps dangerous territory."

"You know, Dad. I was angry at the world for a long time after your accident. It did not seem fair. I could not understand for the life of me why the gods would let such a terrible thing happen to you, to us."

Hogan sighed, looked up at the night sky with his new eye. The aurora borealis shimmered overhead, as it often did this time of year. Ribbons of light danced across the northern sky. Flashes of white, yellow, and indigo violet.

"I am not a religious man, Lars. If you want moral lessons, talk to your mother. If you want parables, get your ass down to church. I admit. I am a bit of a fatalist. I believe there is a plan for each of us, Lars — you, me, your mother, even that grizzly bear we are going to hunt down and kill tomorrow. It doesn't help for you to get mad or to beat yourself up over my accident; I don't. And beating up on Pamola or any of the other gods will not help either. That is just the way it is. You simply must learn to accept that."

Father and son finished eating. Dessert was a bar of chocolate and a final toke on a cannabis pipe. Along with the joy of working fifty stories up on the high steel or in the log chute of a sawmill or deep inside a coal mine, Lars's father liked to get high. Eleka would not allow cannabis around the house. So Hogan did it on the job, when he could. Or on the trail, alone or with Lars. Which made the old man's tent a sort of kiva, or holy place.

"That is just the way it is?" Lars was scornful of his father's statement. "You accept things the way they are? Is that why you drink so much and take such awful chances?"

Hogan turned to face his son. For a second, Lars thought his father was angry. "I drink sometimes or even pop a pill once in a while, so I don't have to think. Other times, just because it feels good. There is nothing wrong with that, you know — feeling good. Maybe you will understand when you are older, when you have more responsibilities. Beating up on yourself all day long is no way to live, son."

Lars thought about what his father had said, about what lay ahead. He didn't mean to say it. The words just popped into his head and then out of his mouth.

"I'm scared of the future."

Father turned to son again, carefully chose his words.

"Who you kidding, boy? Everybody is afraid of that."

"Even you?"

"Son, I want to be able to die at a time and in a place of my choosing. Not in some dismal, sweaty war somewhere, not face-down in the mud."

"But you take such awful risks. What you do is dangerous."

"Oh, I am not afraid to die, Lars. But I want it on my terms."

"Me, I don't want to die at all. I want to live forever. Mars and Venus and places like that. They need men like us. Men willing to take chances. Men possessed of guts and daring. Men who want to be explorers and adventurers."

"Lars, that is your grandfather talking, not you. Or maybe it is your science-fiction writers talking. I am no explorer. And I am certainly no grand adventurer. I like my life just the way it is. I work. I hunt. I enjoy my solitude."

Father and son smoked, and Lars entered a dreamlike state. Maybe he was asleep, maybe not.

He dreamed it was morning, early morning. He was alone beside a lake. He had a canoe paddle in his hand and a Duluth pack on his back. A birch bark canoe lay at his feet.

Lars reached down and gently lowered his canoe into the crystal-blue waters of the lake. Water seeped into his boots. They had been dry up until now. His destination was a smaller, unnamed lake just a dozen kloms away. Lars would camp there, at that second lake, for the night and return to his starting point early the next day.

He stowed his pack in the bow of the canoe and shoved off. The pack fit snugly between the gunnels, as it was designed to do.

This journey would be but one of the many journeys he would take in his mind. Each time he entered his imaginary world he would visit a different place, explore another of the countless lakes and rivers in these seemingly endless woods.

He shoved off, now, in his canoe and within moments was cutting a swath across the mirror-like finish of the water. Fog swirled in his wake.

A family of loons cried out from a nearby shore and was immediately answered by their brethren on a neighboring lake.

A splash of water from his paddle landed on his pack. It did not matter. A Duluth pack was a portage pack. It was made of heavy canvas and was approximately square in shape. That way, the Duluth fit easily into the bottom of a canoe. All his neighbors had one. In fact, everyone who lived in the Boundary Waters used them whenever a wilderness canoe trip beckoned. The pack had a single large compartment. It closed with straps and buckles but never a zipper.

Lars reached a small, shallow stream at the end of the lake, where he got out and dragged his canoe through the shallow water to the next lake on. From there he paddled a couple more kloms to a portage trail.

The overland trail was uncomfortably steep and not well-traveled. It was tough going. The canoe and pack weighed him down. His map showed that halfway up the slope, he would need to turn north, off the trail, to find his magical, unnamed lake.

Lars took a deep breath and dug in. The heavy pack was on his back, the canoe upside down over his shoulders and head.

Despite the weight, he made his way doggedly up through the fern-studded woods. His visibility was limited to a small, V-shaped wedge of light just in front of his canoe. There were tree roots everywhere, as well as loose rocks. The going was rough. By now a hot sun had burned off the fog and he was nearing exhaustion. Then, suddenly, the forest opened onto a small beaver pond.

He dropped the canoe from his shoulders and lowered it to the soft ground. His legs were tired, his back sore. He found a tree and settled down beside it, his backpack still hooked over his shoulders. His eyelids drooped, and he quickly nodded off to sleep.

After a short rest and a small snack, his spirits were renewed. He set his canoe in the water and crossed the beaver pond. When he reached the dam, he got out and dragged his canoe over it.

A small, brackish stream led to yet another beaver dam. Finally, on the other side of the second dam, he caught a glimpse of his unnamed lake through the reeds.

He paddled onward now, his heart pumping. He watched with delight as the bottom of the muddy streambed dropped away beneath him. It was truly amazing.

The lake water was so deep and so pure and clear, he could not see the bottom.

He put his face to the water's surface, cupped his hands and took a drink. It was delicious, like a magical elixir. He splashed the water in his face, took another drink and paddled for shore. *He was here!*

He beached his canoe, stripped for a swim. He found a big rock that stuck out from the shoreline like a diving board, climbed up on it and dove in.

The cool water felt sparkling against his skin, like champagne. He pumped his legs hard and dove down deep. The sunlight fractured and the water became cold, like from a glacier, the cleanest water in the world.

Then he drove for the surface, breaking back into the light and the air, exhilarated by the experience, throwing back his wet hair.

The rest of the day he hung out at the unnamed lake, sleeping, swimming, walking the shores, dipping his line in the water for fish. He ate brook trout for dinner, sat by the fire in the evening, watched the moon and stars tumble out of the darkness.

The aurora borealis performed a symphony overhead. It was draped in shimmering rays of green and white and blue. The rays reflected off the pure waters of the tiny lake, like an eye that was a window onto the soul of the world.

That night he lay in the open without a tent. He lingered on the edge of sleep, eyes still open, deciding what name to bestow upon his lake. Now and again a shooting star blazed a trail across the Milky Way. He felt as if he were on top of the world.

Sleep finally caught him. It ushered his mind and body into peaceful dreams, though at times during the night he awoke thinking he was still asleep and dreaming.

He would call his lake Aurora.

CHAPTER NINE

The next morning, Lars and his father were up early, following tracks and a trail of broken, overturned logs. The air was cold. Lars could see his breath. Hogan said they were maybe half a day behind the bear, but that they would make good time and catch up.

Lars had slept poorly the night before, probably on account of the cannabis. The toxins lodge in the fat tissues of the body, where they can continue to negatively affect a person for up to a month after use. A good lesson to remember the next time someone tries to tell you that smoking pot is no different from imbibing alcohol. Alcohol washes out of your system in under a day; cannabis remains in your body for weeks.

His shoulders hurt as if he had actually made the portage he dreamt about last night while he slept. He had lugged a heavy canoe turned upside down over his head, Duluth pack on his back. His one ankle hurt too, as if he had twisted it on a rock in the trail during his midnight portage.

When Lars told his father about his pains, Hogan was nonplussed. "Your Night Spirit must have wondered from your body while you slept."

Lars asked his father what he meant.

"When a man sleeps, his Spirit can take leave of his body and wander. In its wanderings, the man may encounter an enemy or perhaps hunt dangerous game. If the enemy thrashes him or the prey eludes him, the man may wake up sore the next day. It has happened to me countless times before."

Lars looked at his father as if he found the older man's story farfetched. But Hogan insisted it was true.

Lars's father was always that way. All worldly things had a metaphysical explanation.

It wasn't that the ground he slept on was hard; it was that his Night Spirit had been thrashed by an enemy while he slept.

It wasn't that a pebble had gotten into his boot, causing a blister; it was that he had been irreverent when walking on sacred ground.

It wasn't that he had a runny nose because he was allergic to some offending pollen; it was that he had mistakenly sniffed the flower of a sacred tree.

Science did not exist for Hogan Cabot, only spirits, medicine men and superstition. *Why else hunt a grizzly bear, the most dangerous animal in North America if not for its symbolic meaning?*

Lars was probably too young at the time to fully appreciate the danger. But there was no escaping it. No animal in the North American wilderness inspired more fear or awe than an adult grizzly bear. They were the living, snorting incarnation of the high country. Adult males weighed upwards of 200 klogs at the height of the feeding season in summer. They stood as much as two meters tall when up on their hind legs.

Despite their heft, a grizzly bear could move astonishingly fast, much faster than a man. Their teeth and jaws are amazingly powerful, powerful enough to grind through solid bone like paper through a shredder. A single blow from one of their forepaws can kill a horse or break the neck of a full-grown moose.

And then there is their sense of smell. It is legend. A grizzly can smell carrion from several kloms away, then travel those several kloms over mountain passes, across raging rivers, and through dense forest to find it. An adult bear is so strong, it can drag a five-hundred-klog carcass up a rocky mountainside with little trouble.

Plus, they are smart, one of the smartest animals on the planet. Should one develop an abscessed tooth, they have been observed eating bark they intentionally stripped off a willow shrub. Such bark is packed with salicylic acid, what we mortals refer to as aspirin.

So why hunt one at all, if it is so dangerous?

Because, in the metaphysical world that his father inhabited, hunting unattainable game like the grizzly bear was part of growing up, part of becoming a man.

The bears would not, as a rule, prey on people. But only as a rule. The hard truth was that in the mountains of North America, they killed or maimed backpackers and hunters with stunning regularity, averaging three confirmed kills a year.

Hogan claimed that after mauling a human, an angry bear would feast on the bloody chunks of carcass for as long as it took.

But Lars did not believe him. He thought his father was just trying to scare him with such stories.

Hogan would not let it go. He said that even an experienced outdoorsman was at risk, just as the two of them were now. The Park Service kept records. Aside from those who died, serious injuries from grizzlies ran five to ten a year.

Usually, though, their diet was less red in tooth and claw. During late June or early July, when moths arrived in the high country, some forty percent of a bear's body weight was fat. By late August, which was about the time of their present hunting trip, that proportion had increased to more than seventy percent. Strange as it might seem for city folk who think bears feed only on salmon and big game, bears are actually opportunistic omnivores. Fattened moths were among the richest food in a bear's ecosystem, with more calories per gram than either deer or elk.

The moths would congregate at dozens of lofty, mountaintop sites, from Montana to British Columbia. To get at them, the grizzlies would roll the rock rubble aside and then go to town. A silvertip could eat 2500 moths an hour, up to forty thousand a day. For a boy like Lars, it was an amazing thing to witness. There he would be, a full-grown bear, sitting on his haunches swatting at flying moths and downing them like popcorn at a movie theater.

Not every locale was loaded with huge numbers of winged nougats, of course. But where there were great numbers of moths there were bound to be bears nearby. They were following a big one now.

Father and son tracked this one for two days. A grizzly bear was a tough target, even with a high-powered rifle. They were hunting with bow and arrow.

Their first clear indication that they were getting close was when they came across a large hollow log. The bear had torn it apart, looking for the beehive and honey inside.

Hogan got very quiet, studied the terrain. "Honey can make bears crazy, you know. Some say that is why they attack people, when they are under the influence."

"Because the honey is so sweet?" Lars asked.

"No, because it is dosed with hallucinogens."

Lars thought his father was being metaphysical again. But this time there was strong truth to his tale.

Hogan explained. "Urban dwellers of the modern age, what with their bottles of patented pharmacology and their designer drugs have little appreciation for nature's pharmacy. Psychoactive drugs occur naturally on every continent, in every biosphere, practically every meadow and valley."

Lars knew this to be true. Aside from the cannabis plant, which grew wild in every nook and cranny of the temperate zone, there was also peyote, a small spineless cactus, plus countless mushrooms and fungus that possessed psychedelic properties. And those were just the few he knew of.

His father continued. “Take wild bee honey. Going as far back as Greco-Roman times, there are well-documented stories, stories of soldiers becoming like intoxicated madmen, stories of men collapsing by the thousands after consuming unripened spring honey plundered in the wild.”

“You are serious about this?”

“Very much so. Honey produced by wild bees that have collected nectar from wild azalea blossoms or from mountain laurel or rhododendron can be toxic. It all depends on the when and the where. The when is after a particularly wet spring. The where is in the cool areas of the northern hemisphere where these plants grow, particularly at higher elevations. These areas also happen to be a bear’s habitat. Rhododendrons are vigorous early bloomers. They bear large pink, red, sometimes white, flowers that attract droves of wild bees with their high sugar content and their sweet nectar.”

“How do you know so much about such things?”

“A hunter has to do his homework before he sets out on the trail. What I have learned from my studies is that scientists have identified the active ingredients in toxic honey. They are called grayanotoxins. These complex chemicals act in dramatic fashion on the central nervous system. They can inhibit breathing as well as project a hypnotic effect. A victim can experience anything from tingling sensations to numbness. In larger doses, these toxins can cause dizziness and psychedelic optical effects like whirling lights or tunnel vision, swooning or impaired speech. Just imagine what a grizzly bear might do under the influence? In real bad cases, a victim can experience nausea, vomiting, respiratory distress, even death.”

“Is that why you are whispering? Because it is so dangerous?”

“Damn straight. Eyes sharp.”

They hiked in silence a while longer until finally, they spotted him, the grizzly bear. Again, he was beside a large hollow log. Again, the bear had found an immense beehive inside. Now he was sitting on his haunches, eating the honey with both paws. Each paw was nearly a foot across and ringed with devastatingly sharp claws.

His father dropped his pack silently to the ground, now, and unbundled his bow. The muscles in his arm rippled as he adjusted his armguard, notched an arrow, and drew back the bowstring.

Like all archers, Hogan held the bow in the hand opposite his dominant eye. That arm — his bow arm — was sheathed by an armguard to protect the skin against abrasion from the flashing bowstring. The fingers of his drawing hand were near the tip of his nose and gloved by a leather finger tab as he took careful aim.

Hogan sniffed the air. They were downwind of the bear, maybe seventy-five meters away. The bear had not yet picked up their scent.

The tip of their hunting arrows was pyramidal in shape, with four razor-sharp edges. Hogan was a deadly accurate shot. At this distance, with that bow and arrow in hand, he would have no trouble killing a man. A grizzly bear weighing nearly two hundred klogs was another matter.

The bow was fully extended now, the bowstring taut and poised near the tip of his father's nose. Hogan was an instinctual archer. He did not use a mechanical sight for accuracy.

Instinctual archers like Hogan Cabot used one of two methods for aiming, either split-finger or three-under.

With split-finger aiming, the archer placed his index finger above the nocked arrow to steady it, while placing his middle and ring fingers below.

With three-under aiming, the archer placed his index, middle, and ring fingers beneath the nocked arrow. This technique allowed an archer to better look down the arrow, since the arrow was then closer to the dominant eye.

Lars watched his father closely. *Three-under*, he thought to himself as his father took careful aim.

A tiny leather glovelette protected the fingers of his father's drawing hand from the coarse material of the waxed bowstring. His eyes were focused and intent, his replacement eye steady as a rock. Both eyes were sighting along the shaft of the arrow, past its steel-edged tip, towards the chest of the giant bear. A silent *twang* and the arrow was off.

The muscles of Lars's stomach suddenly tightened. He was prepared for an explosion of blood, a mighty roar of a wounded beast, an earthquake-like tremor as the bear dropped to the ground dead.

But, it was nothing like that at all. The deadly arrow tore into the animal's shoulder, not his chest, knocked off course perhaps by a sudden gust of wind.

The bear stood up on its hind legs and let loose a terrific roar. Then it pulled the embedded arrow from its shoulder with the other paw like the arrow was an errant thorn. The arrow failed to break clean and the bear roared again.

Hogan knocked another arrow, drew back and let it fly. The second arrow struck the bear in the side. Near the wound site its fur looked wet, now, as if he had been swimming. Only, it was not water, it was blood.

The bear's eyes locked with his father's, and the animal charged. To protect Lars, his father stepped between him and the charging bear. A long hunting knife was in his hand, now, the bow and arrow on the ground.

Fearing the worst, Lars retreated to higher ground, where he sought the safety of a big, Douglas fir.

His father crouched into a fighting stance. He moved towards the bear with fury in his eyes. The bear drew closer, blood dripping from its coat.

The two adversaries were about ten meters apart now. Suddenly, a shot rang out, a gunshot. Lars's head spun in the direction of the sound. The holder of the rifle wore a dark green uniform, a Park Ranger. With grim determination, he fired his weapon for a second time.

Lars's head spun back in the other direction, in the direction of the attacking bear. This time there was an explosion of blood, and the bear slumped to the ground only centimeters from his father's feet.

The Park Ranger turned the gun on Hogan, ordered him to drop his knife. Then he took Hogan into custody. Killing a grizzly bear without a permit was a felony.

Because of Lars's age, he got off with a warning. His father spent ten days in jail. He did not kill the bear, after all — even the judge agreed — so he was never officially charged with the crime.

But Hogan was severely fined, money he did not have and could not afford. Mom ripped them both a new one when they got home, and they did not go hunting together again for a great long time, and then only for small game.

Lars guessed it was one of the first rules he ever learned — *Whatever can go wrong, will go wrong.* Only when he was much older would he understand what that fellow Murphy did not — Murphy was actually an optimist.

CHAPTER TEN

Granite Irston constantly disgorged information at a prodigious rate. He was like a fire burning out of control. Granite was older than Lars, old enough to have already been fitted for a skullcap. Now, when they talked, Lars was placed at a severe disadvantage because Granite constantly spewed philosophy. Strange stuff really, stuff Lars barely understood, stuff like —

Intuition is the art, peculiar to mankind, of working out the correct answer to a problem from data that is incomplete, perhaps even misleading.

This was his skullcap talking. But honestly, what fourteen-year-old kid talks like that? Granite Irston, that's who. They mixed dangerous chemicals together, chased girls, learned about time, physics, and the Theory of Relativity.

Lars remembered one day in particular. They had just finished building a humungous pipe bomb, tied it to a big old pine with a length of rope and blown the tree, along with half the adjoining hillside, into sawdust. Afterwards, when they were laying there on the ground crying their eyes out with laughter, things took a more serious turn.

Lars asked Granite about Einstein's famous equation, you know the one, the one where **E** equals **m** times **c** squared. Granite smiled, slipped on his skullcap and began to answer:

"Actually, it was Galileo who first introduced time to the equation."

"What was that, like seven hundred years ago?"

"Yes, yes, something like that. Aristotle had been content to describe what every other ancient knew to be true, that earth and water tend to fall, whereas air and fire tend to rise. Aristotle made this less-than-startling claim without ever once trying to measure how quickly they rose or how swiftly they fell or even why. For Aristotle, time was not a variable, or at least not one worth measuring."

Lars knew a little ancient history himself. So he argued the point. "Not all Greeks were of the same mind as Aristotle. Some Greek physicists considered more pressing matters, like the men who worked in the military-industrial complex of Alexandria. Those fellows were interested in the shapes of trajectories, especially the trajectories of ballistic projectiles. Though for some strange reason, they gave little thought to measuring duration of flight. Had they done so, they might have discovered the calculus."

"Yes, all true," Granite replied, brushing a lock of hair back over his skullcap. "But Galileo was the first to tackle the task of predicting just where a falling body would be at each and every moment of its descent. He was a new kind of scientist, one of a string of like-minded thinkers who tried to bring order to a disorderly world. It is like I always said, Lars. *Nobody asked the orchestra to play Beethoven's Fifth Symphony before he composed it. But after he put his masterpiece to paper, no one could imagine the world without it.*"

"Yes, you have said that before. Even now your meaning eludes me."

"What I mean is this. The dream has always been the same. For three thousand years, the dream has always been the same. For Archimedes and for Roger Bacon. For Isaac Newton and for Albert Einstein. For Pythagoras and for Lyndstrom. For Copernicus and for Adam Smith and for Charles Darwin on his voyage of discovery. For Eduards Durbin and for Arthur C. Clarke and for William of Occam. Each of these great thinkers had the same dream, Lars. Each of them."

"What dream, damnit? You wear that skullcap of yours like it was a crown or a wreath. Can you no longer converse with me at my level?"

"The dream, Lars? The dream of science becoming something more than just telescopes and pulleys, something more than just astronomy and engineering. The dream of civilization breaking free of the shamans and the wizards and the mystical demons that continue to haunt it. The dream of loosening the death grip superstition has held on mankind's soul almost since inception. The dream of all these great thinkers was the same. Someday science would bring order to our lives, to our world. Someday science would quench our thirsts. Someday science would calm our desires, make sense of our accomplishments. Mankind would bask in the bright light of reason. Knowledge would sparkle and illuminate the darkness. Superstition would become a thing of the past. Wizards and demons and elves would beat a hasty retreat back into the caves from whence they came. Religion would grow mute. Faith and science would find common cause."

"You do believe in God, don't you Granite?"

"No more than you."

"And the *Book of Lore*? Is it just whimsy?"

"Your precious *Book of Lore* can go to blazes."

Lars frowned. "That is my mother's book, not mine. I do not pray at that altar."

"Well then, what do you believe in?"

Lars continued pensive. "I am not entirely sure what I believe in, a higher order perhaps. Though I am baffled by that one-god stuff so many people find appealing. There is something to be said for a multi-god system. It seems intuitive."

"That is your father talking. One God is cheaper to believe in than many gods."

"You think that is why modern peoples got rid of all the other gods? — To save money?" Lars laughed.

"Think about it, Lars. Think real hard. Show me just one rich society in the modern era that maintains a full-blown multi-god system. Paying homage to all those many gods is expensive. It impoverishes a society. One god is more efficient, less costly."

"You would have us reduce religion and faith to money and economics?"

"Not faith; religion. Religion is about money, always has been. Faith is about something else, something more fundamental."

"My god is science. Science. Deduction. Experimentation. Hypothesis. Conclusion."

"Yes," Granite nodded. "The steel-edged cutting tools of science. Deduction and experimentation. That is what the dream has always been about. The men of science. They would arm themselves with these sharp-edged weapons. They would arm themselves and then herd the beast of fear and superstition into a cage. There, in that cage, they would wrap the beast in barbwire, fit it with a harness, perhaps domesticate the thing. Beauty and business. Nature and commerce. Faith and religion. All codified into one vast organized thought, one giant Theory of Everything. We humans would then be — if not God — at least godlike. It would be an unholy transformation. From lesser being to omniscient creature. We might gain the power to see the world the way He sees it."

"Humans? God-like? Hah! Do any of us really want that kind of power?"

"Yes, of course, we want it. Is this not the road humanity has been traveling along these past 10,000 years? What the hell do you think a skullcap is all about, Lars, if not the granting of godlike power?"

"Well, it is not as if humanity planned it that way. These people you mentioned — half of whom I have never heard of — Charles Darwin and the rest, they were just following their instincts, their intuition. If they dragged the rest of humanity kicking and screaming along the road with them, that was pure happenstance, an oh-by-the-way."

"They may not have intended it so. But irony rules the world, Lars. Even as these men of science dreamed the dream, the dream itself was being ripped to shreds by other men. Religion was the first discipline to be torn loose from its moorings. You can blame Isaac Newton for that one, what with his calculus and all. Philosophy got left behind in the dust too. — And just when we needed it most."

Lars chuckled. "Since when did any of us need philosophy?"

"Ah, but we do. Philosophy is the glue that holds a civil society together. Philosophy and religion and the rule of law."

"But there have been so many," Lars countered.

"So many what?"

"Philosophies."

"Yes. The Enlightenment. The Romantic period. The Subliminal Age. The Rendition. From darkness into light and back into darkness again."

"You sound cynical."

"Do I? Mankind has fallen more than once into the hands of the nihilists. Lost souls all. Jung. Freud. Nietzsche. Man the Dreamer. Man the Toolmaker. Man the Trader. Now, Man the Existentialist, a tangle of unconscious desires. Rational Man becomes Manipulated Man. Wants become needs. Have to have it. Cannot live without it. Quarterly sales' targets. Advertising. Subliminal appeals. Political correctness. Spin. All rationalized how? Selfish genes. Evolutionary logic. Territorial imperative. Responsibility becomes a thing of the past. Don't blame me. Mother made me do it."

"You are really starting to scare me, Granite."

"And well I should. Nothing has been immune to the disease, not one thing, not religion, not philosophy, not even science. Every discipline swirled and twirled and stirred beyond recognition. Astronomy. Geography. Metallurgy. All the ancient disciplines. Divided and re-divided by smug academics. Men with advanced degrees. Men dressed in fancy purple robes. Men who strut the halls of learning as if they know what is going on."

"I had no idea you held such people in low regard."

"Men of limited intellect. Men who want nothing more than to decipher the meaning of ever-narrower niches of knowledge. Over-educated. Never wanting to get their hands dirty with the truth. Men who have fractured the ancient disciplines into a thousand specialized sub-disciplines, each more narrow than the one before, each possessing its own unintelligible language, each walled off from the other pursuits by value-laden words and professional jealousy."

"Purple robes? Smug academics? University life sounds to me like a Tower of Babel. No wonder you need a skullcap to survive in such a world. Maybe I am not cut out for college."

"The more we appear to know, the less we actually do know. Recent scientific thinking has made it worse. Relativity. Quantum Theory. Chaos. Fractal numbers. Durbin Co-Equivalency. And the most alarming Principle of all — Uncertainty. Thank you Heisenberg."

"So, has the dream you spoke of become unattainable?"

"It is farther away than ever, I fear. Perhaps forever beyond our reach. The pursuit to rationally explain the ways of God and the Universe to Man is in trouble. Thanks to Heisenberg and the rest of the crew, it seems the Universe will never be well-ordered, never be properly tamed, never be fully understood. The noble crusade, the crusade of all scientists for nearly a thousand years, has begun to veer off into unfamiliar territory, into unknown regions that lay beyond common sense, beyond human experience.

How could a particle be in two places at once? How could a shape have infinite edges and thus no shape at all? Why were black swans suddenly everywhere, when before they were nowhere to be found?

"Black swans?"

"They were once thought not to exist. Before the age of exploration, no European had ever seen one. They were thought an impossibility. But then came the arrival of Dutch explorers to Western Australia. The rare and impossible black swan was discovered to be quite common. The term, when spelled with capital letters, came to be synonymous with the unexpected. Nowadays it connotes a perceived impossibility that may later be disproven."

"Yes, I remember now from my statistics class," Lars said. "The far left and far right tails of an ordinary Bell curve. The unlikely event. The rare and improbable event. The Black Swan."

"Yes. The outlier. An event that lies outside the realm of regular expectations. But when Black Swans came to be found elsewhere — in finance, in geopolitical events, in industrial accidents — the landscape changed. Scientists began to actively fear that their entire crusade had been a vast folly. Consider the fragility of any system of thought. Once any of its fundamental postulates is shown to be false, every single conclusion based on those postulates can be undone. Thus, the observation of a single Black Swan can undo the logic of any comprehensive system of thought, be it physics or religion or democracy or finance."

"I see it now. Those great men. Their dream. Their life's work. It is all built on interlocking bricks of logic. Postulates. Axioms. Deductions. Predictions. Now comes Uncertainty. Black Swans. Quantum Mechanics. The logic begins to unravel."

"Yes. And this disintegration produces fear. And the fear is infectious. Once science became infected, the contagion spread like a highly communicable disease across the whole of society. The virus infected the courtroom, the boardroom, the schoolroom, even the family. Suddenly, everything was relative. No longer was anything fixed."

"Contagion? What contagion? What in the world are you and that monstrosity pinned to the top of your head talking about?" Lars was on his feet now, pacing.

"No need to get personal about it, Lars. My skullcap is what it is. And what I have been trying to tell you is no less true just because a skullcap is helping me say it. Euclid, as you say, was among the first. He assembled his mathematics into a logic system. *If this is true, then that is true.* Definitions and axioms. The if-then statements led step by logical step from initial elements to theorem, from postulate to conclusion. All great minds organize their thoughts the same way. Axiom. Postulate. Experimentation. Deduction."

"Ah, but if the logic is flawed, as you say, or if the Black Swans swarm, as you fear, then the fundamental postulate will be shown to be false. The conclusions will prove faulty as well. Nothing is real. Everything is suspect."

"Are you being sarcastic?"

"Of course, I am. I believe in logic. I believe in mathematics and in an orderly world."

"But, Lars. Surely you must see it by now. We no longer live in a deterministic world. Everything is relative. Literature has become self-referential. Government no longer serves the people; it serves only itself. Political comment is no longer a protected right. Free speech is by appointment, and then only if permission is granted. Celebrity no longer has meaning; for these are people whose only accomplishment is their own celebrity."

"You talk in riddles."

"Do I? The very notion of taboo now seems out of place, an anachronism. No longer is anything in life taboo. Not in life, not in sexual habit, not in behavior, not even in marriage. No absolute good. No utter evil. Everything is relative. How can you commit adultery when no one is an adult? If not free love, then how about casual sex? If not eternal life, then how about euthanasia? Abortion. Mercy killing. Assisted suicide. Same-sex marriage. Transgender rights. Blame it on Mom. If not her, then surely Dad."

"But aren't there forces, Granite, tidal forces? Aren't these forces pushing things back the other way? Aren't these forces working to draw the shattered pieces back together again? Behind the uncertainties, behind the chaos, behind the mess you describe, lay a new collection of answers." Lars shook his head. "You are right about the nihilists. They have led us astray. But in the meantime, better minds still have been busy crafting unified theories. These wonderful theories, though strange in many ways, tie together the largest and smallest objects in the universe. Indeed, it is Mankind's final quest. To discover an all-encompassing Theory of Everything. Quantum Mechanics. Gluons. Dark Matter. Quarks. Gravitons."

"But, Lars. These theories are as unprovable and as faith-driven as any religion. Mathematics in twenty dimensions. Multiverses. Dark energy. Hidden matter. Human nature makes us concoct explanations for strange occurrences after the fact, making them explainable and predictable."

"All true. But these strange theories have been shown by later experiment to be true and verifiable. As the results pour in and accumulate, certainty will slowly return to the world. Order will be restored. Soon enough, the nihilists will be driven back and the Light of Reason will again illuminate the darkness. Relax, my old friend, everything will soon be okay."

Even as he said it, Lars was not so sure.

CHAPTER ELEVEN

Lars let loose of his mother's arm, settled uneasily into the doctor's chair. He did not like anything at all about this place. The walls and floors were uncomfortably sterile and Doctor Bernard Feldman, a disagreeable sort. Doctor Feldman was a short man with gray hair and thick, ugly fingers. He was round in the middle, not fit or muscular like Lars's father.

No sooner had Lars settled into the chair than he suddenly felt the chair begin to move beneath him. Startled by the motion, he jumped to his feet and fell back across the room, nearly into his mother's arms.

"There, there," Doctor Feldman said, directing Lars to sit back down. "The boy has heard of a Comfy chair, has he not?"

This brief exchange between the two adults made Lars angry. Not only was Doctor Feldman not addressing Lars directly, he was making him feel the fool.

"We don't have one at home, if that is what you mean," Eleka answered sharply.

Lars sat back down. Now he recognized the doctor's chair for what it was, one of those self-actuated Comfy chairs the commentators crowed so much about. Such a chair was said to be a true marvel of modern technology, although, at the moment, Lars was not sure why.

According to reputation, a Comfy chair sensed the size and shape of its occupant. It remembered whether or not the current occupant had sat in this particular chair before. It remembered the position the occupant preferred, whether they crossed their legs, over what shoulder they preferred their lighting, whether they liked the cushions heated or chilled. In fact, all such chairs were part of a network of chairs. If any chair in the system recognized the occupant, the salient information would be passed along to the current chair.

But Lars could not get comfortable in the chair, no matter how smart or sophisticated the device. He was nervous, and the chair recognized his discomfort. So did his mother, who was hovering nearby.

"Relax, son," Eleka said, hand on his shoulder.

"Yes, relax, son," the gruff doctor said. "This won't hurt."

Lars stiffened at the thought of pain. It had not occurred to him until this moment that the procedure might hurt.

"Okay, maybe it actually will hurt," Doctor Feldman said. "But just a little. The orderly will see you first. She will prep you, shave your head, check your natal contacts."

The idea of natal contacts said it all. These were implants done shortly after birth, when a child was hardly in a position to argue.

Lars had a sense of what was to come. Granite had told him about the Feldman Neurological Institute more than a year ago. Granite had already been here, had already been fitted for a skullcap. He often had misgivings about wearing the thing. Said he preferred to go bare. Made him feel like more of a man.

"The nurse has to shave off all my hair?"

Lars looked at his mother with questioning eyes. How many times as a boy had his mother told him how much she loved his curls?

"You know that she does, son," Eleka answered. "We talked about this."

Lars nodded. Yes, they had talked about it. Everyone had talked about it. Skullcap Day was a rite of passage in a modern society.

Is there a best age for a child to be fitted with a skullcap? The neuroscientists who developed the thing thought the sooner the better. But not everyone agreed, least of all the children who might be forced to wear them.

The youngest children, the ones who might benefit most from a skullcap because of the speed at which young people learned, were also the ones least likely to willingly wear one. *What five-year-old wants to have his head shorn?*

Young children rebelled against the idea, and in droves. It is not as if the young people were in anyway organized, not like a labor union going on strike. They simply rebelled one by one and quite vociferously.

And why shouldn't they? Skullcaps were close-fitting and uncomfortable. They were confining in the worst kind of way.

And what was the point? Did adults aim to steal every last measure of youth from their young? Could children no longer be children? Were children really just proto-adults? — Or were they something else?

Plus, there was a principle involved. Yes, even for children, children who have a tenuous grasp of principles, there was a principle involved. Children are libertarians at heart. Rules are an abstraction. A child is no more likely to willingly don a skullcap for learning than he would willingly wear proper shoes for Sunday school or shin guards for active play. *Simply out of the question!*

But smart parents planned ahead anyway. Minor surgery performed on a newborn within days of birth readied the child for the inevitable. Nine e-nodes, or buttons, implanted in the skull just beneath the dermis. When the time was right for a skullcap — as it was today for Lars, right now in fact — the child's cranium would be ready.

The she-orderly came into the fitting room now. In her hands was an electric hair-shearing tool. She worked with swift dispatch, faster than Lars thought humanly possible. Mounds of Lars's auburn hair gathered between and beneath her feet on the floor.

But something about the woman was strange. She smelled funny, like she had been doused in lemon juice or some strange deodorant. He knew that smell from somewhere but could not quite place it.

Now it was time for the close-in shaving tool. She was closer to him than ever. The smell — while not distasteful — was strong.

"Please hold still," she said calmly.

The scalp had to be shorn to the skin for the initial fitting. The natal contacts, or e-nodes, implanted at birth, had to be fully exposed and made accessible to the doctor's practiced hands. Feldman would soon use an optical scanning computer to completely and accurately map the connections.

For a new skullcap to boot-up properly and then for it to function at highest efficiency, it must fit just so to the head. A rapidly growing child would outgrow his connections in a matter of weeks, which would lead to repeated uncomfortable interfacings. Once again, this spoke in favor of delaying fitting and installation until after a child's final growth spurt, beyond puberty, around age seventeen or so, which, in Lars's case, meant right now.

Doctor Feldman came back into the room, saw the hair clippings still on the floor and lost his temper.

"Clean this up! And I mean now!"

The she-orderly hooked up the vacuum tube and set quietly to work cleaning up the mess. That is when Lars decided the orderly was not human at all, but rather a humanoid bot designed for menial tasks and cleaning.

Doctor Feldman approached holding a small cloth in hand, plus a vial of what appeared to be rubbing alcohol.

"This may feel cold to the touch. I have to clean up your contacts before we move to the next stage, which is the fitting. It is a rite of passage, you know. Skullcap fitting. It says a boy is a man, a girl a woman."

Lars nodded as if he understood. Granite had told him. After the skull was shaved, a poly mold would be fitted to the head. The finished product would be somewhat larger than the head itself. This allowed for normal hair growth, easy removal, and proper hygiene.

The she-robot-orderly completed her task, left the room, then quickly returned pushing a rolling cart in front of her. On top of the cart stood a machine that vaguely resembled a multi-tiered computer with several vid screens and at least two keyboards that Lars could see.

Doctor Feldman grunted his approval and for the first time addressed her by her given name, "Robota."

Feldman took possession of the cart and machine she had delivered. He positioned the cup of the scanning computer over Lars's head, typed a few data strings into the computer and then initiated the scan. There was the purr of a tiny electric motor as the machine made repeated passes over the boy's skull in both directions. Then it was done.

"Now this is going to prick just a little. But the pain should not last long."

In his hand, Feldman now held what looked like a hypodermic needle. He touched it to Lars's scalp in several places and Lars jumped. But then, as the doctor promised, the pain was gone.

"Light sedation of the outer dermis allows me to activate your electronic buttons. You may feel some pressure but no pain."

Lars understood Doctor Feldman's meaning. Buttons, e-nodes, natal contacts. All the same thing. These were the various names for the gold-plated implants set into a baby's cranium just after birth. These nine points of contact were what a properly sized skullcap connected with and to.

"Now I want you to relax, Lars. In fact, I am going to ask you to take this anti-anxiety medicine tonight and every night thereafter for at least a week, maybe two. Eleka, please make sure the boy takes one of these capsules every night before he goes to bed."

Feldman handed a pill bottle to Lars's mother.

"Why must I take those?" Lars asked. "Father says modern pills are the devil."

"Your father is not here. For a skullcap to function properly — and at a high level of efficiency — the host human being, which is to say you, has to voluntarily interface with the device. Please do not fight it. The connection process works best if the patient is relaxed. Neurons are picky that way, in a biochemical sense."

"So, if I refuse . . . ?"

"Well then your mother has just wasted a basketful of her hard-earned money, and I have just wasted two hours of my precious time."

Lars still had a questioning look on his face. Doctor Feldman continued.

"Here is the thing, Lars. Although the science is still not fully understood, a strong-willed person can, in effect, order his brain not to talk to its skullcap — or to do so only reluctantly. A user has to be a willing participant in the symbiotic relationship for the cap to work. Are you going to cooperate or not?"

Lars's mind was racing, sorting through the memories of science fiction stories he had read. They were flashing through his head, now, with great big red warning lights. So many of the stories nowadays were about skullcap technology run amok.

Lars could feel his anxiety levels rising. Skullcaps had a dark side. It was all rooted in the so-called "voluntary" nature of the skullcap's association with one's brain. Should the technology be used improperly or should it be put in the wrong hands, the results could be highly unsatisfactory. Darkened minds and psychotic personalities had found ways to employ skullcaps coercively for purposes of torture or sick pleasure.

"Are you going to cooperate or not?" Doctor Feldman repeated, looking sternly across the room at Eleka Cabot.

Lars put his fears aside. "Yes. Of course," he answered.

"Good. Now let's get on with it, shall we?"

With the scan of his shaven skull complete, the she-robot-orderly named Robota came back into the picture. Under the doctor's direction, she positioned a thin, saran-wrap-like polymer sheet over Lars's shaven skull.

Next would come a spray of hot sintering material that would quickly harden and form the basis of a mold into which the final skullcap material and electronics could be poured. The electronics were an algorithmic self-organizing bio-material — neurofeeds — that, on a micro level, would make contact with and communicate with Lars's neural net. So long as Lars did not fight it, the skullcap would begin to talk to his brain nearly right away. As the doctor said, neurons were "picky" that way.

While Doctor Feldman waited for the bio-gel to set, he continued to talk to Lars.

"Once the mold is complete, we have to synch it up with your neuron signal flow. The quickest way to do a Level One Synch is verbal. Fine-tuning will come in a week or two. If you are ready, I am now going to leave you with my orderly. We are going to give you a sedative and begin immediately with Learning Module One."

•

•

What then is a skullcap?

Lars heard the gravelly voice but he did not hear it. The voice seemed to be speaking to him from out of the ether, not truly human but not actually mechanical. Was he awake? Or was he in some sort of hypnotic sleep? What the hell had Doctor Feldman done to him? And why had his mother permitted this terrible thing to happen?

What then is a skullcap?

Boiled down to its most basic elements, a skullcap is a biomechanical interface device. It performs three functions. First and foremost, it is a search engine and caching device. The user finds himself in a strange city, for instance, or in a strange neighborhood of a known city. He is hungry. He has to go to the bathroom. He requires a bimbooker to service his needs for the night. His skullcap can supply him with the answers within a microsecond. It knows he is hungry for pizza, Chicago style. It will identify the nearest establishment that serves his type of food within his price range and his preferred ambience. It will set his legs in motion walking in that direction if the destination is near and the weather fine or summon him a robo-cab if it is too far to walk or the weather is poor or the bloke is simply in the mood for a ride. The skullcap will place his dinner order remotely, if that is his preference, pay for it from his preferred account, reserve him a table that pods his preferred music. It will do all these things, and more, without the user even being aware of it being done for him.

As the gravelly voice spoke to Lars from beyond the ether, he began to become comfortable with this means of instruction. Was the voice maybe speaking to him through the skullcap, through those nine e-nodes stuck in his brain? He wasn't sure. It was a voice but not a voice. A vid he viewed. But not one he viewed through his eyes; one he viewed directly through his optical cortex.

A skullcap is a storage device. Once it has been synched to the user, everything the user has ever read, every place the user has ever visited, either for real or in his imagination, in his dreams or in his books, every person the user has ever met or thought about meeting, every word ever spoken to him, every song he has ever heard, every vid he has ever seen — it is all there, cross-indexed and subject to instant retrieval. No memory is ever lost, unless, of course, the user orders it abandoned. But even then, delete never means deleted. Even unwanted memories are saved, usually in remote server farms where they can be recalled in an instant longer than an instant. It is here, in this second function, that some skullcaps are more equal than others. Speed of recall separates the better from the less good. A richer man may be able to afford more terabytes of storage. The dataflow may download quicker, be accessible to him in more locations. Thus, the richer man's life experience is made richer still. Moreover, if the rich man's father and grandfather arranged their affairs properly, the user can download their memories and experiences as quickly and easily as his own. Plus, there are memory farms to be had for a price. Want to learn how to stir up a pharmaceutical or mend a broken leg or start a fire or pilot a spaceship or short a stock on the exchange? Simply download the knowhow, memory by memory, module by module.

The gravelly voice became softer, now, more human, less machine-like. It seemed, now, as if the voice was familiar, his voice perhaps. What his voice might sound like to someone else. It was playing in his head, speaking actually, though not to him, through him.

Finally, a skullcap is a highly sophisticated reasoning device. Pure knowledge does not become valuable until it has been organized into cogent thought. Sensible ways of doing things. Rules of thumb. Formulas. Axioms. Best practices. Recipes. Common sense. If a hundred different people wired their homes for electricity and two of them managed to electrocute themselves in the process, the mistakes those two people made are mistakes you would rather not repeat. If a hundred people tried to hang a picture on the wall and eighty-five of them came up with a simple method for doing it correctly, thus making their wives happy, why repeat the mistakes of the fifteen who fouled up the job and did it wrong or poorly? With a skullcap, learning by doing becomes a thing of the past. A man will do it right first time, every time. Here again a richer man might hold the edge. More expensive skullcaps processed information faster, drew on wider experience-databases, reached proper conclusions quicker, committed fewer grievous errors. Money becomes the source of knowledge and knowledge defines success and power.

CHAPTER TWELVE

"You never should have done this, Eleka. I told you the boy wasn't ready."

Hogan Cabot stood near the entranceway to the small house, hand on the doorframe. His cheeks were red, as if whipped raw by a cold wind. He looked past his wife, past his boy, caught a glimpse of the she-bot quietly standing watch behind Lars. Hogan had a keen nose; he could smell her antiseptic stench from across the room.

"The boy only fainted, Hogan. Became disoriented. Doctor Feldman says that happens sometimes. It doesn't mean he wasn't ready." Eleka Cabot was not the sort of woman to easily back down from a position.

"Feldman is a mloron. Our boy does not belong in the techno world. He belongs here, in this world, in my world."

"Your world? My father warned me about you. Your world is filled with demons and mythical beings and god knows what else!"

"You want to bring your father into this? That warmongering throwback from the Middle Ages? — And how dare you make fun of my beliefs!"

Hogan began to approach his wife in a menacing fashion.

"Lars does not believe in such things. And no, I am not trying to make fun of you or your beliefs. But you have to understand, Hogan. Lars finds solace in his mathematics and in his science. He finds comfort in rigorous thinking and sound reason. You should know that better than anyone."

"The boy and I . . . we have smoked together . . . on the mountain. He has been to the dream world. He knows Pamola."

"You let the boy smoke hash with you? How could you!"

Now it was Eleka's turn to approach in a menacing fashion. She raised her hand to strike her husband with the full fury of an angry wife. He stopped her hand mid-air.

"To smoke with another. That is my way."

"But that is not my way."

"Maybe you two ought to quit fighting about me." This was a new voice. This was Lars's voice.

"Lars, we never meant for you to hear us fighting," Eleka said, trying to calm herself.

"Enhanced hearing, Mom. It is one of the many attributes of this fancy new skullcap you bought me. What the techs call an eavesdropping capability. Robota helped configure my ears to their highest setting. I have heard every word the two of you uttered since you first started fighting. If I cared to do so, I could track your conversation up to 500 meters away."

Eleka was white-faced. "I did not realize skullcaps had that capacity."

"You see, woman?" Hogan roared. "You see? Even with all your high-minded ideas, you still fail to grasp what sort of evil menace you have helped unleash upon the world. Just look what you have done to our boy! He has become a Frankenstein monster!"

"Shut up father," Lars screamed. "Shut the hell up!"

"You dare speak to me that way? Have you no respect? Who am I if not your father?"

Lars stood his ground. "What mother did was not evil. And I am not a monster or a freak. Mother tried to do for me what she thought best. The world is changing — and mighty fast. It is right and correct that I should be part of that new world. As I told you when I first arrived home.

I put on the skullcap. I became lightheaded, disoriented. I feel better now. Robota has helped settle my nerves."

"More chemicals?" Eleka flashed.

"You make it sound like a bad thing," Lars said.

Robota came forward now, out of the shadows behind Lars, where she had been standing. "The brain is a chemical factory, Mrs. Cabot. Serotonin. Dopamine. Neurotransmitters of all sorts. Sometimes these chemicals have to be controlled by other chemicals."

"Are you leaving with her?" Eleka asked.

"Yes, Mom. Robota and I will be leaving Ironwood shortly. They want me to try again to interface with the e-world. See if I can manage it without passing out or becoming overwhelmed by the information flow. You hired Doctor Feldman. He assigned his personal assistant to help me assimilate, be my pathway liaison."

"Pathway liaison, my ass. You are leaving us to be with that mongrel robot abomination?" Hogan asked angrily.

"You have no skullcap, Father. You cannot possibly understand."

"Is that what it is then? Without a skullcap I have become an inferior being? Some sort of lesser thing?"

"I did not mean it that way," Lars objected. "All I was trying to say . . ."

"Maybe it is best that you leave after all," Hogan said. "Before you say something grotesquely stupid that we will both regret."

"Where will you go?" Eleka asked. Then, turning to the robot, "Where will you be taking my boy?"

"My programming compels me to answer you truthfully, if you insist. But my programming also compels me to first inform you that at this stage of assimilation, it works out better for the client if you, the parent, not follow the boy where I am taking him. Nor should you try to contact him by any means. Not even by text. If you permit the boy and I to leave without further ado, I will return Lars unharmed to your custody in 30 days."

"You mean after you have had time to brainwash him?"
"Yes, Mr. Cabot. That is precisely what I mean."

•
•

Lars stood, now, in the middle of the giant lakeside park and stared across the narrow beach at the wave-swept lake.

Only twice before had he ever seen such an immense body of water. Once, when he was at his grandfather's home on the Atlantic Ocean; and a second time when he journeyed with his Scout Troop to the shores of Lake Superior not far from his childhood home.

But this lake, this Lake Michigan, seemed in a class all its own. For an inland lake, the waves seemed enormous. Plus, there seemed to be a constant onshore wind. If not for the city dome overhead, this spot might be immensely cold in the winter and uncomfortably warm in the summer. The protective dome moderated the temperature extremes.

Robota spoke. "I take it from the look on your face that you have never been to Chica before?"

"Aside from visiting my grandfather's house in Maine, I have never been anywhere before."

"It was once a wonderful city, you know. In some ways it still is. The only dome in the Midwest. Museums, parks, robo-malls, everything a modern could possibly want."

"But why did you bring me here?"

"Lars, I am to be your pathway liaison."

"It went too fast the first time, my transition. That is how I became disoriented. I plugged in, started to upload data and images, felt lightheaded, passed out."

"I promise you that we will interface slower this time."

"But how? The dataflow was so fast. It made me nauseous, sick to my stomach, almost as if I were seasick. I could not keep up with it."

"A person learns to interface with his skullcap in much the same way that he learns to walk. Mostly instinct. But also need, necessity, and practice. Babies fall down. They hold onto furniture to gain confidence. Running is a voluntary act. So is walking slow, like when one is stalking prey. A person learns to interface more slowly with his skullcap in much the same way that he learns to walk more slowly, he chooses to."

Lars nodded as if he understood. Robota continued. "Like I said. Running is a voluntary act. So is thinking fast. Most people have the capacity to slow their brains down if they want to. Or if they lack that capacity, if they find themselves unable to slow down their thinking, we have chemicals people can take, anti-anxiety meds and the like."

"Chemicals stronger than the anti-anxiety meds I am already taking?"

"Much stronger. Psychedelics. Hallucinogenics. Synthetic neurotransmitters. Powerful neuronal inhibitors. If we have to, we will cross the border into Hedon City to procure the very best."

"I thought Hedon City was off-limits to people my age?"

"Normally it is. — And to robots as well."

"How then?"

"Doctor Feldman knows people. He knows your grandfather. Your grandfather has a flat in Hedon City. We may seek out the old man."

"I find it hard to believe that my grandfather has any connection whatsoever to Hedon City."

"Your grandfather is a most unusual man, a man with many secrets. He has ties to the military and to the intelligence community."

"Yes. I know this to be true." Lars thought back to that day when Flix showed up out of nowhere in Ironwood with his airchop.

"We will go see him if we need to."

"But why am I always so tired, Robota?"

"Pruning. Fatigue is a side effect. Here, sit down on this bench." They were in Grant Park on a grassy knoll below Buckingham Fountain.

"This is a term I am not familiar with. Pruning."

"The skulltechs call it the pruning effect. Picture that word in your mind. Pruning. Instruct your skullcap to access meta files on the subject."

"How do I do that? How do I instruct my skullcap to perform a certain function?"

"Just think about the word, Lars. Picture what it is. Pruning a tree. Cutting back on staff in an office building. Lopping off a dead tree branch."

Lars's forehead furrowed as he sought to willfully drive the thought into his head. He clenched his fists, tightened his jaw.

"Do not force it, Lars. Let the image form of its own free will. Picture it. But let it happen naturally. The skullcap will begin to search."

Lars fell totally silent. He felt the warm air swirl around him, heard the waves crash on the distant beach, saw the glint of sunlight against the glass dome overhead, became dreamy at the sound of water gushing from the nearby fountain.

"Okay, I am beginning to sense something," Lars said. "Pruning. In this context, does it have something to do with neurons?"

"Yes. Now let the data flow. I will synch with you and slow down the rate of dataflow if it threatens to come too fast and overwhelm you. Now relax, Lars, and let it flow."

Lars nodded, closed his eyes, unclenched his fists.

"Okay, that is better."

His jawline grew less tense.

"Now tell me, outloud, what you are hearing."

Lars nodded, began to speak in an unnatural otherworldly voice.

"Beginning even before a child is born, and continuing until about the age of three, there is a huge increase in the number of synapses, which is to say, the number of connections between neurons in the brain. A toddler has roughly one quadrillion synaptic connections, twice as many as an adult. Children have brains that are more active, more connected and more flexible than those of grownups."

". . . good, Lars," Robota said quietly. "Keep going . . ."

"But following this synaptic proliferation comes something new — a significant pruning process. Each human progresses through a series of unique life-experiences. With each succeeding life-experience, the brain changes shape down at the cellular level. Synaptic connections that proved useful are strengthened. Those that stay idle or remain unused soon become pruned, which is to say, sloughed off. Other connections are lost on account of poor diet or exposure to hazardous chemicals. Young children lose on the order of 20 billion synaptic connections each day. This pruning process fine-tunes the brain to survive in the particular environment that it finds itself. By the time a child has become an adult, synaptic selection has uniquely shaped the child's brain to succeed in the world in which that brain finds itself."

". . . good, Lars," Robota said quietly. "I am going to unsynch from you now. Get ready. The dataflow is about to accelerate . . ."

Now the words began to come noticeably faster. "This process of synaptic overproduction followed by strategic pruning may not seem remarkable, at least not until one stops to consider how incredibly expensive a tactic this is in terms of biological constructs and energy cost . . ."

Lars seemed to stutter, as if he were beginning to overload. "There is an inherent paradox here. Nature is pretty smart. But why would evolution allow such a wasteful process to persist? Think of the calories wasted! Think of the doors closing behind you as pathways are destroyed that might later prove useful . . ."

Lars shook his head suddenly and swiftly, as if he were trying to chase away a nettlesome bug. There was a spasm in his cheek. He began to convulse.

". . . and yet, models of neural networks demonstrate what we know to be true — the overproduction-followed-by-pruning approach is very flexible, very plastic. While this process may be inefficient by some definitions of inefficient, starting off life with lots of alternatives and winnowing them down to the most useful ones proves to be a robust process . . ."

Lars fell from the bench to the ground, his entire body in spasm. Robota went white-faced, at least as white-faced as any synthetic human could become.

CHAPTER THIRTEEN

Flix sat alone in his room. There was a drink in his hand. Too often lately that had been the case.

Flix did not drink to forget, though sometimes he wished he could. Men like him had too much to forget. Too many missions. Too many dead bodies. Too many lies told. Too many secrets held.

Loneliness was part of the equation. Not enough women, none that mattered anyway. There had been Krista, of course. But that had not lasted. Oh, how he wished that it had. How he wished that things could have turned out differently for the two of them. *Oh, Krista! Krista!*

Hedon City was no place to spend New Year's Eve. He should have gone to his cabin in Maine. Or to his daughter's place in Ironwood. Or even to Crystal City. Any place but here!

But Flix hated the cold. It reminded him of desperate times. Minnesota this time of year was dark and cold.

So instead he was here, in Hedon City, alone in his flat, drink in hand. Outside, on the street below, the revelers were beginning to party.

Hedon City. In the new century, what began as a few docks jutting out into the foot of Lake Michigan near the site of the once-proud steel mills of Gary, Indiana, had over time become a major metropolis, though of a sort not seen since the days of Sodom and Gomorrah.

A few docks. A handful of gambling boats. An assortment of offshore hotels. Then more hotels, bigger hotels, an airport. Then more hotels, narrow streets, robo-cabs, coffin dormitories. In no time at all, Hedon City was a city-sized mega-dock covering several thousand square kloms of land and open water. It reached up the shores of Lake Michigan as far north as the Chica River on the west and the Indiana-Michigan state border on the east. As a political subdivision it was neither part of Illinois nor Indiana nor Michigan. Enabling legislation between the three states established Hedon City as a quasi-independent anything-goes red-light district. Sort of like the Vatican, only with Satan in charge.

Early successes with gambling boats set the stage. Right on their heels came the brothels, the drug halls, the holo-bars. Then the virtual sex suites and live-ammo parlors. All parked safely offshore, yet within easy reach of the major metroplexes — Chica, Minnepaul, Sane Lou. The curiosity seekers came in from every direction.

In its heyday, Hedon City still retained the character of a wild, colonial station. In those early days the City was a fast-paced district with flash gcars and glamorous hangouts. In the clubs, the standard question was, "Are you a eunuch or do you live in Hedon City?" The men were hard drinking and rough, the women beautiful and loose. The pattern of life was no more predictable than the bloated corpses they dragged out of the live-ammo parlors on a weekly basis.

The three border-states split the tax revenues, which were substantial. Civil order was maintained by a mercenary police force, though there was not a lot for them to do. Crime rates were comparatively low, especially in the arenas that mattered most to people — murder, rape, burglary. The so-called "moral" crimes of the mainland — prostitution, drug-use, gambling — were exempt from prosecution offshore. Only paper scrip was permitted within the walls of Hedon City, no monetary credits. The scrip could be purchased at all ports of entry after payment of the requisite exchange tax. Likewise, to assure anonymity of the sometimes upper-crust clientele, identicards had to be checked at the borders in special failsafe lockers.

The knock came at his door now. Flix looked at his watch. It would be the bio-bimbo. One came with the price of the room. These girls had been genetically engineered for pleasure. Tall, strong, insatiable. Extra ports of entry. For handling two men at once.

Flix laughed. He would never go in for such things.

But some men did. Others preferred octoroons, white prostitutes who were one-eighth AfriAm — very popular with the Christian Fundamentalists. Sometimes they would come by the busload up from Puritan City in Texas.

Flix answered the door. She came in. Asked what he wanted. He said to just sit and talk.

"Too old to get it up?" she teased.

He smiled and reached into his pocket to pay her. "Come back in half an hour," he said. "And bring along a friend. Natch snatch only. No bio-bimbos." Then he was alone again.

A lifetime of walking the wall had cost Flix dearly. Name, rank, and serial number. That is all he had ever given, all he had ever had. It was certainly all he had now. The payoffs could have been anything he desired. Money. Sex. Power. Comfort. Health. Status. Anything. He had gotten none of the above. Oh, there had been power, plenty of that; and status. But sex, money, comfort? Hah!

Flix thought back to that desperate battle in the sand so many long years ago. Some men live, some men die. *But where do honor and duty come from?* Probably from the same corner of the brain as deceit and hate. As humans, we are stuck with a lot of emotional baggage, much of which has been our lot since we first climbed down out of the trees in the jungles of Africa.

Imagine a band of hunters; say a group of five men, back on the savanna twenty-five thousand years ago.

One of the five considers breaking away from the rest of the group to look for an antelope on his own. If that man is successful, he will gain for himself and his kin a large quantity of meat and hide — five times as much as if he stays with the band and the group is successful.

But that would-be loner knows something else. He knows from experience — and from tales he has heard around the campfire — that his chances for success are low, much lower than the five's chances if they work together. In addition, if that would-be-loner goes off on his own — whether he be successful or not — he will suffer anger and animosity from the other hunters in the clan for intentionally lessening *their* prospects for a successful hunt.

So, cooperation is born, soon to be hardwired by genetics into human nature. Better to remain together and share equitably the animals they kill, than to split up and fend for themselves. Not at all times, to be sure, but at least at times where the odds are long and the dangers high.

Reciprocity, which is to say, cooperative behavior, soon spreads throughout the species, and along with it moral sentiment. Conscience. Self-respect. Remorse. Shame. Humility. Moral outrage. All of it.

And standing firmly atop this tower of emotions? — A moral code. No robot could ever be born with these things. Honor. Patriotism. Altruism. Justice. Mercy. Redemption. Every last bit of it rooted in simple cooperative behavior. None of it requiring divine intervention or fancy computer programming.

But there is also a darker side to cooperation, something the Greeks called xenophobia. The Fear of Outsiders.

Consider again our band of hunters, five strong. They take down an antelope. Then, as they are about to divide up the spoils, along comes a stranger, asking for a share, even a small one.

Except under the most extraordinary of circumstances, the stranger will not get one. Personal familiarity and common interest are powerful motivators in a social transaction. Moral sentiments evolved to be selective. People give trust to strangers only with effort. Tribes cooperate with other tribes only through carefully crafted treaties and other conventions. They are quick to imagine themselves victims of conspiracy by competing groups. And they are prone to dehumanize and murder their rivals during periods of severe conflict or stress. They cement their own group loyalties by means of sacred symbols and complex ceremonies. Their mythologies are filled with epic adventures that end in victory over menacing, even dangerous enemies. Their heroes are those that have put group above self.

But with the coming of the modern era, something changes. Sheer growth in numbers alters group dynamics. It changes the nature of leadership and of cooperation. From the need-driven cooperative stance of the hunter-gatherer society comes the power-driven authoritative stance of the pre-industrial era.

The instincts of morality and tribalism, already complementary, are easily manipulated. The trappings of Civilization make them more so.

Rising agricultural societies become increasingly hierarchal and territorial. Families settle on small plots of land. Villages proliferate. Labor becomes finely divided. A growing minority of the population specializes. Some as craftsmen. Some as traders. Some as soldiers. Chiefdoms begin to take shape. They thrive on agricultural surpluses. Khans are born, as well as serfs. Hereditary rulers and priestly castes grab power. They usurp the old ethical codes of cooperative hunting. They sometimes maliciously transform these codes into coercive regulations, always to the advantage of the ruling class. Then, to solidify their position, the rulers author the idea of a law-giving god who, in return for their obedience, gives them divine commandments they can use to obtain overpowering authority. Only late in the process do some of the chiefdoms relinquish their power. This voluntary surrender leads to the rise of cooperative government, what we have come to call democracy. To this day, the tug of war continues.

But in every society that ever arose, from the first organized band of hunter-gatherers to the most technologically-advanced of modern city-dwellers, someone had to walk the wall. Someone had to stand guard at the edge of the clearing, or along the ramparts, or on the forward-most part of the deck. Someone had to stand watch for the enemy. The constant throughout history was the need for the soldier-class. To keep order. To thwart invasion. To conquer their neighbor.

To be a soldier was the ultimate sacrifice, the ultimate form of cooperative behavior.

I keep you safe; you share with me the proceeds of the hunt. I risk my life to protect you; you do not ask too many questions how I manage it.

But it was lonely out there, standing on the ramparts, walking the walls night after night, day after day. Eventually there comes a time, a time like now, a time when a lonely man, even an honorable one, needs companionship.

For Felix “Flix” Weinger, soldier and statesman, grandfather and gentleman, that day had now come. After a long life of sacrifice, Flix was in desperate need of companionship. Tomorrow he would deal with Lars. But today, right now, this instant, he wanted a woman. Any woman.

Flix stirred his drink, stared blindly at the cubes of ice that were floating there in the caramel-colored liquid.

He thought again of Krista, the woman he had let slip between his fingers. Then the knock came at his door.

This time, giggles in the hallway. She had brought a friend, like he asked.

Flix got to his feet to let them in.

Even an old man has his needs.

CHAPTER FOURTEEN

Gritty.

That is about the only word to describe the life of a bimbooker in Hedon City. Gritty.

For a woman of the streets — an AfriAm woman like Violet Vickers — nothing in Hedon City was ever clean. Not the streets, not the air, not the gaming halls, not the restaurants, certainly not the johns. These men, they came to the City to be serviced. They came from everywhere, from all across the country, especially the Bible Belt. They came to be fucked or sucked or just simply jerked off by a gentle hand. The more a woman was willing to do, the better she would get paid. Looks were rarely at issue.

For the women that serviced these men — women like Violet Vickers — disease was always a consideration, had been since that day long ago when the first female parted her hairy legs in the grasses of the savanna to entice a man to feed her starving children.

But it was not just the disease. Some of these men smelled, had not showered since God knows when. They would blow into town, fresh from their white-bread world, go on a seventy-two-hour binge, then prowl the streets until they found a girl willing to let them jam their smelly, uncircumcised zibb up her snatch or in her mouth. It was not pretty. But then nothing about Hedon City ever was.

And if that were not enough, there were those men who were violent, which was pretty much all of them.

Violet could never understand it. The mystery was not in why a man would pay for sex; that part was easy. He may think himself ugly, perhaps inadequate, maybe afraid of commitment, pressed for time, terribly lonely. There were many possibilities.

But where was all that rage coming from? What would possess a man to reach in his pocket to pay a woman for sex then mess all that up with a fist to the jaw or a punch in the face? It did not make any sense. But then nothing in Hedon City ever did.

Actually, that was not entirely true. Certain things about the place made sense, but only once you understood what Hedon City was really all about. This place was a no-holds-barred sin city born of tax-starved municipal budgets and moralistic grandstanding, a byproduct of corrupt politicians and shortsighted compromise. Rather than try and ban strip clubs one by one in a hundred different jurisdictions, why not restrict them all to a single, economically depressed spot on the outskirts of a major metro area? The same goes for every other sin of the body, soul or mind. Sex, booze, porn, drugs — all for sale in a single megalopolis parked at the foot of Lake Michigan.

Mired in this sewer called Hedon City was Violet Vickers, an AfriAm prostitute working the gritty streets. Violet was a runaway. Dark-skinned. Short, kinky black hair. Sparkling white teeth. Wide hips. Thick thighs. IV tracks on her arms.

As a husky teenager, Violet had been violently raped. The man beat her. He slashed her abdomen with a knife, tore her vagina with a stick, damaged her anus. Biometric surgery repaired her body. But the nightmares never ended. Now, wherever she went, she carried with her a pulse blaster to protect herself.

People cope with anger in different ways. Booze, drugs, gambling, pain. To help Violet cope with the anger of her attack, she developed a nasty addiction to Blue Devils. Her supplier in Hedon City was a junkie priest, Father

Joseph McDermott. He was a quirky, little man. Rumor had it that Father Joseph was the estranged son of a big city mayor with the same last name.

Violet saw Father Joseph now, at the next street corner. He was swaying gently with the breeze, his collar hanging askew. She hurried to his side.

"Well, if it isn't my girl, Violet Vickers. Come to fill that little glass vial of yours with Blue Devils?" The man reeked of alcohol and sweat.

"Father. I be buying if you be supplying."

"Addiction! All those happy neurotransmitters bouncing awkwardly around the brain. Does a body good, you know, that dopamine stuff. Helps make a body complete."

"Next week's sermon?"

"Never underestimate the needs of the flock, child. People like to be preached at. Some insist upon it. Just another form of addiction."

"So, tell me, Father. How does a man of the cloth become a drug dealer anyway?"

McDermott became incensed. "You? A bitch of the streets? You mean to stand in judgment of me? A Catholic priest?"

"Some priest you are. From where I stand it looks to me as if they took the 'h' clean out of hypocrite and stuck it right smack in the middle of Catholic. Not all street people are stupid, you know."

Violet scratched her butt, straightened her skirt, tried not to slouch. The last stop in the bathroom had been sans toilet paper. She was still damp.

"And just how smart can a Blue Devil addict really be?" Father Joseph chuckled imperceptibly as another customer approached.

"Drugs are my way of coping. You know that."

"What does a nigger whore like you have to cope with?"

"No need to get snotty about it. Back in the day, before you dealt drugs, you heard confession. You know very well my pain. My father was strict, too strict for a free spirit like me. I ran away from home at a young age. My first week on the streets, I was beaten and raped."

"They do not let me hear confession no more. Truth is, I never met a black woman who did not deserve to be beaten." He turned to sell a bag of goodies to another junkie. Money quickly changed hands.

"Your father teach you to be a bigot? — Or did you learn that one on your own in the priesthood?"

"Leave my father out of this."

"The Mayor actually queer, like they say in the coffins?"

McDermott punched her in the face. "I warned you, woman!"

Violet Vickers touched her fingers to her cheek, where he struck her. She came away with a drop of blood. "You queer like your father? My mama says all Catholic priests are. Pedophiles or fags. — Or both."

McDermott punched her again, harder than before. Blood dripped from her mouth.

"You best not do that again," she said.

"What is a whore junkie like you gonna do about it?"

"I was just a kid when I was beaten and raped. Now I carry protection."

"Condom?"

"Smith & Wesson." She drew the pulse blaster from her purse. It had a silver grip.

"You threatening me?"

"Touch me again and I will kill you."

"No one murders the son of an influential mayor and gets away with it."

"Estranged son, don't you mean? Fag son of a fag Mayor."

Father Joseph McDermott's eyes shone red. He reached for the woman with both hands, as if he meant to throttle her.

Violet stepped out of his reach, gun arm extended. "I warned you."

He laughed and lunged again.

She pulled the contact twice, at pointblank range. Father Joseph staggered backward and fell to the concrete in a widening pool of dark blood. The junkies that had gathered nearby to watch the fracas now scattered into the streets and alleys.

Violet took McDermott's stash from his coat pocket. Then she took his paper money from his trousers. It was mostly government-issue scrip. Then she started across town to the coffin dormitory, where she often slept at night, a place called The Last Resort. Like every day since her rape, she somehow managed from trick to trick and from meal to meal.

But she didn't get far, only one block. A friend stopped her on the street, asked if she wanted to party, make a quick buck.

"A man at the hotel wants two girls."

"Bugger off. I have no need. I just came into some money."

"Come on," the girl said. "How much money could you possibly have? The man wants two bitches with natch snatch. You are not modified, are you?"

"Biometric repairs only. But otherwise natch."

"You will do."

"Will I?"

"The man said to bring a friend. I have to be back at his door inside fifteen minutes. You in or not?"

Violet thought a moment, scratched her butt. "You trust this bloke?"

"No guarantees. But he looks okay. An older guy. Seems harmless."

"Don't they all?"

"I got no time for a philosophy lesson."

"Okay. I'm in. Let me take a pee and I will be right with you."

CHAPTER FIFTEEN

Hedon City never closed, not at night, not in the middle of the week, not in the dead of winter. On certain holidays it was especially raucous, like it was now. BeHolden Day weekend. Seventy-two hours of nonstop partying, whoremongering, and drinking. In other words, very nearly the perfect time and place for two people in their situation to meet. Lars, by virtue of his age, was not permitted in Hedon City. Flix, by virtue of his government post, was not supposed to be there. Robota was considered contraband in any case.

There are several low-tech ways to prevent a well-known face from being recognized. Felix “Flix” Weinger was no stranger to such things. He knew them all.

The simplest method was misdirection. Put a high-profile civilian in an army uniform and his face is unlikely to be noticed. People see the uniform not the person in it. Dress that same civilian in ordinary street clothes and he will pass unnoticed through a crowd.

Equally effective is the opposite, an attention-getting device. Equip a man with an enormous nose, disfigured perhaps by a blot of skin cancer or a severe facial burn. The louts will stare at the nose in fascination. The polite will turn away. — But neither will see the face behind the nose. That is a fact, like gravity.

Flix’s favorite get-up — the one he was dressed in now — was that of an old, broken-down beggar. He had it down to a tee. Ratty clothes. Unkempt hair. Two-day-old beard. Thick glasses. Yellow teeth. When he spoke, it was with a hoarse whisper. When he walked, it was with a limp. He always leaned heavily on his cane.

"That is him coming now," Robota said. She pointed with a stiff humanoid finger across the street in the direction of a vagrant on the opposite corner. The grifter was making his way from garbage can to garbage can as he worked his way down the litter-strewn alley and into the covered plaza.

"Who? That street person? That is not my grandfather," Lars said. "I know my grandfather. He is a soldier. He is a gentleman. He would never scrounge through trash cans like that."

"It is him. I assure you. That is your grandfather."

Lars watched as the beggar drew closer. Recognition dawned. "And what shall I say to him?"

"Let us first see what your grandfather has to say to you."

Flix approached slowly. Like a true beggar, he meandered aimlessly through the giant indoor mall. Places to sit were few and far between. Twice he was solicited by roving packs of bio-whores. Twice, Flix shooed them away.

But the girls kept coming back. They tugged at his dirty clothes, pulled at his arms, touched his legs in an all-too-familiar way, spoke of unspeakable things.

"Anything for a price," one of the girls said.

Finally, Robota stepped forward out of the shadows. She slipped the two biggest girls a one-hundred scrip note each and sent them off in search of another mark.

Without saying a word, Flix nodded with his head towards a nearby holo-bar, a place called Perdition's Cup. Drunken men were everywhere in the street and alongside the sidewalk.

"You expect us to go in here?" Lars asked, pausing at the giant swinging doors that were the entrance.

Flix said nothing to his grandson, but pushed forward past him toward the entryway.

Lars looked nervously around. The three of them were in an unsavory corner of Hedon City near the docks. This place they were about to enter — Perdition's Cup — was lodged between two dilapidated tenements, one of which was clearly a house of ill-repute.

Perdition's Cup had very little to recommend it. Its gaudy décor and unwholesome reputation as a cowboy-tough bar catering to the roughnecks of the Great Lakes was legend from Duluth to Buffalo. The Cup — as the locals liked to call it — was like an oversized bug-light. It attracted every breed of pleasure-seeking vermin one could possibly suppose.

Everything about the place told Lars to stay away. It quite literally reeked of danger. *But which danger was the gravest?*

Was it the naked feeling a man got when he was bathed by the glow of red come-hither lights that emanated from the doorway of the bimbooker house next door?

Was it the tightness that gathered in a man's throat when forced to breath in the appalling stench of fire-brewed tortan intoxicated by the night's muggy air?

Was it the nausea that collected in a man's gut when he stood, frozen in fear, by the snarl of an unseen bio-canine hidden from sight somewhere in the shadows nearby? Stories of these animals abounded. Genetically altered beasts. They could rip out a man's throat without working up so much as a sweat.

Lars swallowed hard. His heart was filled with trepidation. The place smelled. The sense of danger ran deep. The sounds were unfamiliar and scary. The people were base and disgusting.

Danger! Stay away! The words seemed to scream at him from out of the darkness.

But Lars gathered his courage, took a deep breath and shoved open the massive set of swinging doors. They hung across the entranceway in the fashion of an American Wild West saloon. He followed his grandfather into the dark recesses within.

As Lars crossed the threshold into the jam-packed tavern, he was knocked back by a heavy nauseating odor. It hung like deadweight in the air. Smoldering tobacco. The distinctive sweet smell of cannabis. The deafening roar of cack music. Strobe lights. Holo people.

It was quite a spectacle for a young man to behold. Smoke. Commotion. Confusion. Pandemonium.

In the murky shadows, Lars could scarcely make out the grand, twenty-meter-long bar and counter that dominated the room along one wall. Nor could he see the collection of poker tables that were scattered haphazardly throughout the rest of the establishment.

Adjacent to the long bar was a row of tall stools. They provided seating for a lucky few. The rest, drunken patrons all, had to be content to lean against the brass rail and bang on the tabletop for service. Behind the counter, half a dozen scantily clad bartenders struggled feverishly to keep up with the incessant demands of the delirious holiday crowd.

BeHolden Day was the bastard son of Thanksgiving, which was itself a descendant of English harvest festivals dating back more than one thousand years. The fringe elements that had been driven out of Europe on account of their religion discovered a cornucopia in the New World. The immigrants' Day of Thanksgiving was an acknowledgment of their good fortune, considered by them to be a day of grace as well.

Sadly, over the passing centuries, the holiday had devolved into something much more crude, an orgy rather than a celebration. By Lars's time, BeHolden Day was little more than an ugly caricature of its former self. The carved turkey was still there, along with all the trimmings. That much was a constant. But now it was a carnival of engorgement marked by bouts of excessive eating and drinking.

Like the Saturnalia festivals of ancient Rome, the BeHolden Day celebration of present-day was a period of orgiastic revelry. And, like any pagan holiday, it was possessed with peculiar rituals all its own. The over-consumption was often remedied with a round of chemically induced regurgitation. In some circles, this latter event was a matter of some pride. Would-be throwers-up would line the streets, chemical cocktail in hand, to compete for distance or volume.

And if that were not enough to mar the solemnity of this once holy festival, by nightfall on this, the fourth Thursday of November, widespread brawling would erupt in pubs all across the land.

Lars processed the entire history of BeHolden Day in under a millisecond as he pressed ever deeper into the dark bowels of the saloon. His eyes darted nervously from left to right and back again as he warily searched the faces in the crowd for the first hint of trouble. His skullcap had done the research, run the numbers. If it was going to happen anywhere, it was going to happen here. Places like this were primed for trouble. It often came in the form of an uncontrollable outbreak of violent behavior.

Perdition's Cup. Lars stood there, mouth agape. The place was in a complete uproar. Absolute pandemonium.

Drunken rabble-rousers. They jostled one another sloshing tortan-ale everywhere.

Bawdy bimbookers. They hustled the room trying to sell their bodies for a good price.

Macho revelers. They kept busy shouting gross obscenities and boisterous challenges at one another.

Never once in his life had Lars been in such a place!

Lars had no experience with such things. Raucous holiday atmosphere. Riotous, strobe-lit tavern.

Lars carefully negotiated his way across the floor towards the center of the room. He took a seat near one end of the grand bar. Robota stood beside him, ever watchful, the patient pathway liaison.

Lars could barely make out a thing, the cigarette smoke was so thick. The ceiling of the pub was high, easily twice the height of a man. It was splattered with restless shadows.

Then, suddenly, Lars spied his grandfather only meters away. Flix had stayed in character, a bum of the streets. He acted rude, now, rapped his cane against the tavern floor for service.

From out of the blue, someone handed Lars a cold mug. Tortan-ale. A bar stool opened up and Lars sat down. He took a moment, sipped the froth off the mug of ale.

From where he sat astride the bar stool, Lars could see the bulge of a weapon beneath the tattered shirt of his grandfather's street-beggar get-up. Robota saw it too.

She stepped forward, put her hand on Flix's shoulder and spoke to him.

"Sir? You are aware of my programming, are you not?" Robota asked.

It was difficult for the three of them to talk. Their eyes were blinded by the annoying flash of a strobe. Then there was the mind-numbing blast of cack music from the speakers in the center of the room. Plus the commotion caused by the throngs of holo-people. Conversation was a near impossibility.

The holo-people were the most distracting. Tech had come such a long way these past years. It was all but impossible to distinguish a virtual image from an actual one. That is, until you reached out to squeeze a cute one on the behind. A virtual woman might give you an electric shock; a real one, a jab in the ribs. It was anybody's guess how many of which were in this crowd.

Flix leaned in closer to talk. "And what of your programming?"

"I think she means the Three Laws," Lars said. He was beginning to reel from the dizzying first effects of the potent drink he had been handed.

"Yes, I do mean the Three Laws," Robota said. "First Law requires me to intervene whenever I need to prevent another human being from being harmed. Please hand me the weapon you are carrying."

"I do not take orders from some bucket of bolts. Plus, in a place like this we might all be better off if I were armed. As for you, you best not make a scene, not here."

"Sir. You cannot hurt me. You cannot outmaneuver me. I am faster than you are. And I am stronger than you are. I can disarm you forcibly, if you do not comply immediately and voluntarily surrender your weapon to me."

"It is never going to happen."

"It's okay, Grandpa. Robota can be trusted."

"You are drunk," Flix said. "Toasters can be trusted. Coffeemakers can be trusted. Robots? They cannot be trusted."

It was true. Lars was drunk. He could feel the room spinning. An instant later, a festively-clad Hedon City nymph came up to him from behind and began to rub her lithe body against his. Lars shortly forgot all about his grandfather and his gun.

The temptress was real, no holo-image at all. She laced her arms about his waist, baited him with her wares. She took hold, probed him with her powerful hands. Lars never saw her face. But her firm breasts left an indentation in his back. Her perfume splashed an indelible imprint on his brain.

Before Lars could turn in his place and begin to take advantage of his sudden good fortune, a fracas broke out at the opposite end of the bar.

The muscles in his abdomen instinctively tightened. His eyes narrowed. A sixth sense told him that the woman was a contrivance, something to distract him. The fisticuffs were a cover for something much more sinister.

His survival reflex was suddenly triggered. Lars broke free of the woman's arms. The scuffle soon became a fight and the fight, a free-for-all. The fracas rapidly engulfed the entire tavern in a blizzard of flying bottles, crashing chairs, and pummeling fists.

Now Lars saw a man, a skagaway. He was seated just meters away at a table. The man was staring nervously about, a wild look of terror in his eyes. Still, he remained obediently seated. It was as if the man were expecting someone — anyone — to come help rescue him from the midst of this mayhem.

Flix saw the man too. It seemed to Lars that his grandfather recognized the man, as if they might be acquainted.

Flix moved in the direction of the seated man. When he had approached to within perhaps three meters of where the man was seated, Lars saw it — the glint of an upraised blade!

The knife appeared to have come out of nowhere. For a second, Lars thought it might be a holo-image, nothing to worry about at all. Then he changed his mind.

Lars shouted a warning to his grandfather's friend. But the place was so loud, the sound of his voice was lost in the din.

There was nothing Lars could do to stop the assassin's attack.

In the next fraction of a second, it happened. The killer's approach was silent and practiced. He assaulted the seated man from behind, grabbed the man's head, locked it firmly in the crook of one arm.

Then, as if the assailant were thoroughly enjoying himself, he snorted out a staccato laugh before moving to brutally slash the man's throat.

The cut to the man's neck was deep, so deep his head flopped to one side like a slab of meat. A bloodstained ear came to rest on the dead man's otherwise untouched shoulder.

Then, without making another sound, the killer tossed the murderous knife on the table in front of him and melted into the chaotic throng.

Lars was gripped by horror. The killing had happened so fast, Lars never saw the thug's face nor how he was dressed.

All he saw now was blood. — Lots and lots of blood.

And all he smelled was perfume. That same unusual perfume worn by the wench who had been working her magic on him only seconds earlier.

Lars spun to face the woman. But she too had vanished into the crowd without a trace.

Positive, now, that he would be ill, Lars stared in disbelief at the drunken faces around him.

No one in the pub seemed to care. To the people gathered here in Perdition's Cup, this man's murder was unremarkable. In this neighborhood, at this time of day, people were murdered with stunning regularity. Stabbings and killings were a nightly event. *Why should tonight be any different?* One more patron or one less, what did it matter?

As Lars stood there, stomach doing somersaults, he realized that the BeHolden Day festivities would carry on with scant notice being given to the corpse or to the widening pool of blood collecting on the creaky wooden floor.

Eventually the Hedon City police would be summoned, of course. But it would be more of a courtesy call than a serious attempt to solve a capital crime. No policeman in his right mind would take the time to investigate the death of a lowly skagaway, and certainly not in a place as notorious as the Cup. The authorities would tag the assassination as an "accidental homicide" and it would soon be forgotten like all the rest.

Lars smothered the urge to scream. He covered his mouth with one hand and marched stiffly from the saloon. By now he was in a panic. *Could there be any doubt that he or his grandfather would be the next to die?*

Lars looked both ways, stumbled out into the middle of the moonlit street. Instinct told him to run. But his feet were like clay. He was just about to bolt when, all of a sudden, from out of the darkness, a hand clamped down on his shoulder.

Lars drew a sharp breath. He felt the adrenaline surge through his veins. *This is it*, he thought. *The killer is right behind me.*

Lars acted to defend himself.

He summoned every last ounce of courage, grabbed for the man's wrist with one hand, fumbled for what he thought was a blade with the other. Clamping down hard, Lars spun to confront his attacker.

He was jolted by the face that stared back at him. *It was his grandfather.* Robota stood calmly next to him.

"We need to get out of here," Flix said. "And I mean now." His gun was in his hand.

"What just happened?" Lars asked, suddenly quite sober.

"That man was tailing me. Now he is dead and can no longer report on my whereabouts."

"You had that man killed? Why, for Pamola's sake?"

"To protect you and me both, Lars."

"I have to report your illegal actions to the authorities," Robota said mechanically.

"Lars. Could you perhaps explain to this abomination of technology that First Law does not mean jack in the real world. Say this robot goes to the local authorities. Long before they believe her lame story about me and what I am up to, they disconnect her batteries and shut her down for the crime of her even being here in Hedon City. Robots are forbidden. As for the gun in my hand, until I know we are completely safe, the gun stays with me and pointed in the direction of travel. There is nothing either of you can do or say that will make me surrender my weapon. Are we clear?"

"Perfectly."

"Okay then, let's go. Being out in the open like this makes me especially nervous."

"Agreed."

"We need to go someplace quiet where we can talk," Flix said, no longer the beggar. "There is a place I know a few blocks from here. It is none too elegant. But it will do. Follow me. But at a respectable distance."

Robota agreed and Flix hobbled off, leading the way. It did not take long, even at this speed, and they were at the waterfront. Lars let his eyes roam. They were standing in front of one of those ramshackle Hedon City apartment buildings that should have been torn down long ago.

One side of the building faced out onto Richard Daley Boulevard from across a vacant lot littered with broken glass and trash of unknown origin. The other side of the building looked out over Lake Michigan, a big plus once but no longer.

On top of the building was a large metal sign. It still read MARK TWAIN HOTEL in huge faded letters. And below that, GAMBLERS WELCOME.

But the Mark Twain was a hotel like Brooklyn was a city or Madison Square Garden, a garden. Once perhaps but no longer. Now the place was a jumble of God knows how many tiny apartments. Most of them were one-room kitchenettes. Stove, sink, refrigerator, maybe a clothes dresser. Rented by the week, adults only, mostly men.

The lobby was dimly-lit, deserted. The foyer, tiled and smelling of urine. The elevators — no longer operable — sat idle, their doors propped open with bricks. Inside, the gold-colored carpet was threadbare and stained. Off to the left, beyond what used to be a reception desk, was a wall of mailboxes, mostly without doors.

Straight ahead, across the lobby, was a door. Beyond the door, a stairway. Flix's room was on the third floor, a long climb for a street beggar with a cane. At the top of the stairs was a world most civilized people would just as soon have avoided. Lars had no choice. He followed Flix up the three flights. Robota trailed behind.

The first thing that hit Lars when they reached the third-floor landing was the smell. It was as if the air inside had not been recycled since before the war.

Then there were the hallways, perpetually dark and filled with evil unseen spirits. Lars was ready for that, in a way, because his skullcap had prepared him mentally.

But it was the stink that slapped him in the face. This happened not once but repeatedly, over and over again throughout his entire visit to his grandfather's crummy hideout.

There was the urine, of course, and the vomit. But that was only half the story. There were other smells. Layer upon layer of them. Cooking oil. Overheated and re-used. Sweat. Animal and otherwise. Unwashed dishes. Soapy water. Tobacco smoke. Feces.

There were other odors. Hundreds of them, largely unidentifiable. Curry. Cannabis. Beetle dung. Rat urine. Rotting carcasses, mostly animal.

The slurry of smells mingled — always, it seemed — with the charred stench of burning tires that wafted across the lake waters from Chica.

Once his nose adjusted a bit, Lars began to hear the noise. It was insane. Vids. Music pods. Some in Spanish, some in Terrish. Periodic bursts of staccato laughter, most of it vulgar. Constant hacking coughs from behind closed doors. Snoring, burping, farting. The sounds of unspeakable acts. Between men and women. Between men and men. Women and women. Grunting. Panting. Moaning.

It was all so gross. Lars could not figure it out. Then his skullcap ran the grid and spit out an answer.

If this terrible place did not exist, where would all the skagaways of the world live anyway? Surely not in the white-bread world that was Ironwood, Minnesota.

Unable to stand the noise any longer, Lars instructed his skullcap to exit enhanced hearing mode. Now things quieted and he could breathe more easily.

But then something else jarred his thoughts. A man like his grandfather. An important man of the world. Such a man would have to be truly desperate to hole up in a place like this. *What was really going on?*

Lars kept those thoughts to himself as he settled into a rickety-looking chair. *If his grandfather felt safe here, who was he to argue?*

Finally, Flix spoke. "You both realize, don't you? I am a high-level government official. I cannot be seen here in Hedon City, not in the company of a robot, certainly not in the company of a child. That would be a felony. I could be arrested. Put in jail. Perhaps hung."

"That is the reason for the disguise? To avoid being seen?"

"Yes, of course."

"But then why come at all, if it is so dangerous?" Robota asked.

"Lars is family. My daughter Eleka called. She was having second thoughts about this whole skullcap thing. Said she thought you two might be coming here to Hedon City to acquire contraband neuro-chemicals. I had you both followed."

"The man who followed us was the same man who did the killing in the Cup?"

"Yes. He picked up your trail when you passed through security at the gateway to the Chica dome."

Robota became agitated. "I do not understand you, Sir. You are an educated man. Certainly you must know that each generation of young people needs to have the tech of their time to compete. When the first pencils became available, what student did not come to class with a sharpened one in hand? When slide rules became affordable, what engineer of the time did not show up at work with one in his pocket? A skullcap is no different. The last generation of young people had handheld computers; this one has neural interfaces."

Flix shook his head. "The analogy goes only so far. A man with a slide rule in his pocket did not need to take a brain altering chemical to use it."

"Didn't he?" Robota countered. "How many hours can the average man sit squinting at the tiny lines on a slide rule before he needs to take an aspirin to cure a pounding headache?"

"That is not quite the same, is it?" Flix snapped.

"I think the differences are narrower than you care to admit."

"Actually, you do not think at all. You are a robot. You run programs. Programs written by mortals, people like me."

"Well then view me as a seeing-eye-dog, if you must. But General. In the modern world, without a skullcap, your grandson is literally a blind man living among men with perfect vision. He will not be able to keep up with his peers. He will become a failure and an outcast."

"Heh, you two. I am standing right here," Lars barked. You can see that, can't you?"

The room became quiet. The hum of smog filters droned in the background. Robota stood guard at the door of Flix's tiny third-floor flat as grandfather and grandson sat facing one another across the room. An uneasy silence filled the air.

It was late. The room was dark. There was but a single window, a small one. It looked out over the street. The drapes were two-thirds drawn. The few lights of Hedon City cast an eerie glow on the floor. Finally, Flix spoke.

"The modern world. Is that what this is about? My grandson not being able to compete in the modern world?"

"That is precisely what his mother is worried about," Robota said. "The very reason she brought the boy to the Feldman Institute."

"Yes, I know that. And yet, she was the very one who asked me to intervene. My worry is something else. Lars lacks a foundation. He has no sense of heritage. I intend to see that he gets one."

CHAPTER SIXTEEN

"What does having a better understanding of his heritage have to do with the boy's skullcap training?" Robota demanded to know.

"It is a moot point anyway," Lars said. "I already know my heritage. I was in the Boy Scouts, Grandpa. We studied the flag. We memorized the National Anthem. We studied American history in school. Father talked about it all the time. History was always a thing with him."

"Do you honestly believe that memorizing the words to the National Anthem tells you what you need to know about your heritage?"

"But father said . . ."

"I have no doubts your father taught you well. But you still have much to learn, Lars. The history of America is a convoluted and complex story."

"But once Robota teaches me how to control my skullcap, my skullcap can teach me all there is to learn. — And I can learn every bit of it in an instant."

"Yes, perhaps if you ask that contraption the right questions. But are you even smart enough to know what questions to ask? Do you even know what America is all about?"

"Of course I do. Capitalism. Freedom of religion. Right of assembly. All that good stuff."

"Nice start. Straight out of a textbook, no doubt. But you are really only scratching the surface here, like reciting the Ten Commandments when you really do not believe in God."

"What does God have to do with it?"

"Everything."

"Okay then, Grandpa. I give in. Please tell me. What is America really all about?"

"Persecution."

The word hung in the air like a cancer.

"I do not understand your meaning."

"More precisely, the *avoidance* of persecution. That is what drove people to pull up stakes elsewhere and immigrate to this country to begin with. That influx of people is what originally made America great."

Flix spoke now as if he were a rabbi ministering to his flock. "The history of freedom and democracy. It has always been one of crafting systems of law to prevent the ruling elite from crushing its subjects. Sometimes this crushing extends to the point of enslavement. The Founders drew on the lessons of the past. The lessons of the prototype democracies of ancient Greece. They drew on the lessons of the Magna Carta from the thirteenth century. But they also drew on the lessons of the Iroquois Great Law of Peace, something that was contemporary to them."

"The same Iroquois my father descends from?"

"Ah, do I spy a light bulb coming on?"

"Yes, sir."

"Okay, then let us get down to cases, shall we? Have you ever heard this line before: *We, the people, to form a union . . .*?"

"Sure. It is the first sentence from our Constitution."

"Ah, but it isn't. It is actually the first line from the Treaty of 1520 that formed the Iroquois Confederacy. But you are close. The first sentence of our Constitution goes like this: *We, the people of the United States, in order to form a more perfect Union . . .*"

"What an amazing coincidence."

"Coincidence? I hardly think so."

"What then?"

"Historians have long attributed the central tenets of the Constitution to the likes of Thomas Jefferson and Benjamin Franklin. But few realize that the League of the Iroquois also greatly influenced the thinking of the colonial Founders. The Great Law of the Iroquois embraced the basic ideas of both federalism and democracy. It also gave equal voice to each of the half-dozen tribes comprising the League. On top of that, it included a guarantee of religious expression. Also a mechanism for the impeachment of top leaders. Plus a formula for amending the centuries' old constitution. Benjamin Franklin, in particular, saw the Iroquois system as a model on which to base the American Union."

"If what you say is true, how come this is the first I have ever heard of it? Was my father unaware of the truth? He was descended from Iroquois."

"I cannot speak for your father. But this much I do know. Each time in our history, when democracy was reinvented — by the Greeks, by the Romans, by the English of the late Middle Ages, and finally, by us — a new layer of protections were built in by the founders to safeguard the rights of their citizens."

"That is, I suppose, until now," Lars interrupted. He could see the direction his grandfather was going with this. "Is that what you are trying to say?"

"Yes. Ever since the Laborites made it exceptionally easy to amend the Constitution, we have been backsliding. The hole we have been digging for ourselves is getting deeper each year. By granting every splinter group the unfettered right to assemble and speak their mind, by giving voice to every fringe element, every angry mother who dredges up two others who agree with her — by doing all these senseless things, our priceless franchises are being needlessly squandered. The fact of the matter is this. These rights have now been diluted to such a degree, no one any longer has the right to say anything at all for fear of offending someone. There are no universal truths if every trifle is given voice."

"Eloquently put, Grandpa. But what does that have to do with me?"

"Must I spoon-feed you, boy?"

"It is a spoon, isn't it? — and not a shovel?"

"Just for that, you are going to get the long version. — And the long version begins in 490 B.C. with the Battle of Marathon."

Even as his grandfather spoke, Lars had his skullcap run a search. The results came back fast. He mouthed the words quietly —

The Battle of Marathon. 490 B.C. A watershed event. The first in a series of wars that pitted the Greeks — principally Athens — against the Persians under King Darius I. The victory by the Greeks at the Battle of Marathon demonstrated to both parties that the Persians could be beaten. It has been said by some that the Battle at Marathon was the single most important military event in European history.

"You sound like a textbook, Lars. Can that abominable thing on top your head do more than spout facts? Does that contraption know why some have said the Battle of Marathon was the single most important military event in European history?"

Lars narrowed his eyes but said nothing. Flix continued.

"The reason some have said that the Battle of Marathon was the single most important military event in European history is because in the two hundred years following that battle we saw the rise of Classical Greek civilization. This is the same civilization that has been enduringly influential in western society. The Greeks won the battle. After that, Greek culture took control of civilization. Our ideals and our love of liberty descend from them. They applied their intellect to politics and to economics. They invented democracy. They established a highly-evolved system of capitalism. What set the Greeks apart from the Persians was their love of property, more precisely their love of private property. Low taxes. Safe sea-lanes. Sound money. Sensible laws that protected property. These were the foundations of Greek posterity and liberty."

"Low taxes? How low?"

"Extremely low. And never on people. The Greeks considered any form of direct taxation to be humiliating. The poll tax was considered the most degrading of all. When the Greek city-states did have to raise money, they preferred to employ either a use-tax or else a tax on commercial activity, like a harvest tax. This led, by the way, to the development of something you love, something we now all take for granted. — Plane geometry."

"How is that?"

"In order to calculate a farmer's harvest tax, the tax collector had to determine the extent of the farmer's landholdings. There were complications. Rivers and floods constantly changed the natural boundaries of a man's farmland. These changes gave rise to irregular shapes. Plane geometry of the sort you are familiar with was needed to properly calculate land area."

"Now you have hit on something I actually understand. But I thought the subject was methods of taxation, not geometry?"

"The subject is methods of taxation. Since Athens was primarily a trading nation and since direct taxation was taboo, commerce bore the brunt of most taxation."

"But if taxes were so low, how could they afford to build all those wonderful temples?"

"Not with public taxes," Flix said. "With voluntary contributions."

"You expect me to believe that the Parthenon was built by passing around a cup?"

"Believe what you will. But the answer is yes. And other temples too. Whenever a city needed a new public improvement — a bridge, a temple, even a festival — the leading citizens were called upon to underwrite what was needed. The donation was not a tax or confiscation of any kind. It was a voluntary contribution to the city-state. And it was enforced by nothing more than tradition. That, plus public sentiment. Public amusements, athletic games, even military equipment were purchased by rich citizens and then donated to the city in their name."

Lars shook his head. "I fail to see the difference between compulsory taxes and compulsory donations."

"A tax is owed because a government orders that it should be paid. This order involves coercion. To assure itself of all the revenues it believes it deserves, that government must then introduce surveillance as an integral part of its revenue-collection system. Every taxable transaction must be recorded and made subject to examination. Before long, individuals are forced to submit every aspect of their lives to the tax inquisition. Privacy and liberty give way in short order."

Flix continued. "Now, contrast what I just described with voluntary donation. Under a voluntary system, the extent of one's wealth and the size of his income remain a private matter. Then too, there is the related problem of bureaucratic control over state assets. This was the Greeks' brilliant alternative to government ownership. They figured out something very basic: *Ownership of property involves duties as well as rights.*

"Their rationale was that property, by the natural order of things, was bestowed upon those best able to acquire and manage it. But those very same people, the ones best able to manage and acquire property, acquired a communal obligation along with it. They were obligated to hold that property for the community at large if and when it was needed. Thus, the private donor who made the contribution also had a responsibility to manage the public improvement or activity that his generosity bought."

"But what if the donor fell on hard times and could not keep up the property? What then?"

"Others would step in. Pride is a huge motivator in a small circle. If the community needed a bridge, wealthy citizens would get together and have it built. For their hard work and money, the donors would be publicly honored. The government had little or nothing to do with it."

"Are you suggesting that we try and adopt such a system today, here in the United States? Who among us would give?"

"Some people are selfish, of course, and will not give. Plus, it takes time for attitudes to change. But one thing is for certain. Private wealth will always seek to hide from predatory taxation. We could begin the transition to a Greek-style system by having government service carry little or no pay. Begin at the top, as it were, and work our way down from there."

"The army?"

"Absolutely. The early Roman Republic required little in the way of taxation because it operated with free labor. The army, which is always society's most expensive operation, was strictly a citizens' army. It was composed entirely of property owners who served for one year without pay. The citizen soldiers of the time even provided their own uniforms and equipment. I ask you, Lars. In today's world, can you show me even one citizen who would be willing to lift so much as a finger for government without a fat paycheck?"

Lars made no attempt to answer.

"I thought not. The first casualty of predatory taxation has always been liberty. Then wealth. Then the strength of the nation. Business and trade are drawn to peace and stability. Did you know that the world's first stock market was organized in the Forum in Rome?"

"Yes, my skullcap confirms that. But if your thesis is correct, that business and trade are drawn to stability and peace, then why did it end?"

"The empire?"

Lars nodded. "More importantly. How did it end?"

"Ah, now we get to the meat of the matter. The Decline of Empire. It always ends the same way. The revenue system becomes unable to support the empire after it has been acquired. There is no better example of this than the fall of Athens. The Athenians used their muscle to force smaller and weaker city-states to pay them tribute. Then later, in a devastating war with Sparta, these so-called allies rebelled. And why not? They were already seething with anger over excessive taxation. Athens lost a war she should have won."

"My skullcap informs me that you are speaking of the Peloponnesian Wars. But what makes you so sure the Athenians should have prevailed over their enemies in those wars?"

"I am a general, a soldier, a student of war. Athens possessed every ingredient necessary for victory, save one. She held superiority in numbers. A larger population. More wealth. Greater naval power.

"But what Athens lacked was loyal support of her empire. She lost that loyalty as a consequence of oppressive taxation. That, plus the bondage required for its enforcement. Then too, the Athenians mismanaged their currency. What we now call inflation. It is caused by printing too much money. Currency devaluation wiped out the merchant class on which Athenian wealth was based. This led to civil unrest and riots. These riots led, in turn, to the imposition of martial law, the last refuge for governing an unruly state."

Flix continued. "But unrest means more armies. More armies mean more pay. More pay means more taxes. More taxes mean more unrest. Enforcement becomes a matter of life or death for the state. Taxes must be collected or else the soldiers will rebel, and the countryside will be plundered. Anarchy follows."

Lars was confused. "So why not just cut taxes?"

"Rulers do not reduce taxes without a reason. Normally, it takes an actual or an impending catastrophe to bring down taxes. To a Greek of the time, the assassination of a tyrant was always justifiable. A virtuous act. And not one of them had a skullcap."

"Are you saying that increased intellect will not prevent us from making the same mistakes again in the future?"

"You think people with skullcaps make better soldiers than people without? I hardly think so. If the Roman government of two thousand years ago had had sufficient revenues to maintain an adequate military, we would all be speaking Latin today. That marauding band of barbarians would never have been able to penetrate the Italian peninsula the way they did. There likely would never have been a Middle Ages."

"But Grandpa! Aren't you being overly dramatic?"

"Am I? Our own civilization, when it collapses, will likely do so as much under the weight of predatory taxes as from anything else."

"But heavy taxes only fall on the rich," Lars objected. "Anyway, we live in a democracy. Taxes are not collected without consent. We have taxation *along with* representation."

"In that respect, our democracy is a farce. Majority rule is not the same as consent. In the days of the Magna Carta, a majority could not bind a minority. Consent had to be unanimous."

"You want to talk farce? How can you possibly hope to govern a country the size of this one by unanimous consent? America is not a series of agrarian villages on the shores of some inland sea, as Ancient Greece was."

"Juries require unanimous consent, don't they?"

"But surely you can see how that is different. Sending someone to prison for breaking the law is serious stuff."

"You have never filed a tax return, have you?"

"No."

"Refusing to pay one's taxes is a serious crime. It can get you sent to jail, cost you thousands in fines and penalties. No juries involved here. A bureaucrat says you are guilty; end of story."

At first silence. Then, after a long pause, Lars said, "Are you suggesting we put all revenue matters to a direct vote of the people?"

"No, not all revenue matters, just the ones that change tax rates. And why not? With today's technology, it could work. It has worked for the Swiss. Everyone goes online at the appointed time, puts in their password and votes. What could be simpler?"

"A backward country, if ever there was one."

"You know this for a fact? Or is that your skullcap talking? Or is it perhaps the bias of whoever programmed that thing?"

"How does bias enter into the equation?"

CHAPTER SEVENTEEN

"This is your question, Lars? How does bias enter in the equation?" Flix shook his head with irritation. "Honestly, Lars! Has it not occurred to you that someone — a human being with agendas of his own — programmed your skullcap? That someone instructed your skullcap which databases to concentrate its efforts when it performs a search? That someone taught your skullcap in what order to rank its search results? That someone caused those results to be skewed in whatever fashion best suits him?"

"I admit. That had not occurred to me."

"Okay, then do not be so quick to disparage the Swiss. They believe that to be real, liberty requires the right to privacy, especially financial privacy."

"You mean secret banking?" Lars asked, an edge of incredulity in his voice.

"Call it secret banking, if that makes you feel better. I mean financial privacy. Must we all have sex in public, as it were?"

"I do not understand."

"I know you don't, Lars. But consider this. Every withdrawal of cash. Every deposit of interest. Every sale of stock. Every purchase of a home. All wages. Every gift. Every trip into or out of the country. Every birth. Every death. Every adoption. Every marriage or divorce. — They must all be reported. *And to whom?* Our Federal government. *And should you fail to, or fail to do so within the allotted time?* You could go to jail. No trial by jury here; simply by fiat. Our tax system is a pocket of tyranny in an otherwise free society. In the end, fear and compulsion sustain our tax laws, not honor or duty."

"We seem to be going in circles, Grandpa. If lower taxes mean faster growth, then why not just cut taxes like I said before?"

"Cutting taxes is part of it, to be sure. But there is more to this than just cutting taxes. What I have been trying to lay out for you here is an entire philosophy. Yes, by all means, keep taxes low. If you do, the pie will get bigger. People are spurred to work, to save, to take risks. But economic freedom requires more. Freedom of trade. Zero tariffs. No monopolies. Low and simple taxes."

"Go on."

"Liberty is something we have inherited, not something we earned or achieved on our own. We take liberty for granted, because it has been given to us by our forebears. We do not seem to realize or appreciate how hard it will be to get liberty and freedom back should we let them slip through our hands."

"This philosophy you speak of. What is it called? Does it have a name?"

"I give it a name, then your skullcap looks it up in some silly compendium or encyclopedia, then you parse it into trite little phrases. Is that it?"

"I promise you I will not do that."

Here Flix stopped, and his demeanor changed. "You are going to take notes, aren't you? Please do not tell me that I am going to do all this for nothing. That I am going to have to go through all this with you again someday. Here I am trying to lay out for you the entire legacy of the Enlightenment point by point, and you are not even going to write any of it down? At least humor the old man. Pretend to be interested. You do have a recording pod, don't you?"

"My skullcap has perfect recall, Grandpa. I do not need to write any of it down. Plus, Robota keeps a log of everything I say or hear as a backup. She downloads to a cloud server every fifteen minutes or so. Nothing you tell me will be lost, I assure you."

Flix scowled. "Somehow that seems to me like cheating. People remember best what they write down. It is part of our evolution. Fingers to eyes, eyes to brain. People remember to a lesser degree what they read or what they see on a vid screen. They do not remember what they hear with their ears alone."

"You are going to have to trust me on this one, Grandpa."

Flix scowled again, peeved by the interruption. It was already past midnight and he was becoming tired.

"Let's start with something simple. Tax evasion is not a criminal act."

"That cannot possibly be true." Lars was aghast. "Since when can breaking the law not be against the law?"

"Laws are written by men, not handed down to us by gods."

"I do not understand."

"Tax laws are made-up laws. Tax evasion does not violate any of the Natural Laws."

"You are making a subtle point here, I know."

"Subtle like a sandstorm. Certain crimes violate the Laws of Nature. Murder. Terrorism. Robbery. Rape. Treason. These crimes violate what we all agree are our most fundamental rights."

"And which rights are those?"

"Life, Liberty, and the Pursuit of Happiness, for starters. We have a right to feel safe in our home. To not be assaulted on the street. To not have our possessions taken from us by force. Tax laws are not Natural Laws. They are manmade. They are rules made by men for other men. Violating arbitrary rules is not a crime. If you do not follow the logic on this, read John Locke's *Second Treatise on Civil Government*. Or Stuart Mill. Or Montesquieu. Or Alexander Hamilton. Or William Blackstone. Or . . ."

"All right, already! I get your point!"

"Don't be a mloron. You do not get even half my point! If a government can criminalize a manmade rule, all hope of liberty is forever lost."

Flix's explanation was greeted with silence.

"Arbitrary taxation is liberty's biggest foe. Thus, arbitrary taxation justifies every form of recourse — Evasion. Defiance. Violence. Treason. Armed insurrection. Even the overthrow of government by force."

Suddenly Robota spoke up after having been silent all this time. "Sir, I could have you arrested for sedition."

"You see, Lars? Even freedom of speech evaporates when one takes an unpopular philosophical stand."

Robota drew closer. "Condoning the overthrow of government by force is sedition. I could have you arrested, Sir, for making such a statement. Retract that threat of armed insurrection or I will immediately contact the authorities. I can do it in an instant simply by instructing my positronic brain to connect electronically to the security net. They will be here in minutes."

Flix drew his weapon. "I dare you to try it. This room may look like nothing. But it is maximum secure. That is why I brought the two of you here. If you should try to connect electronically to the security net, the capacitor hidden in these walls will discharge. The electronic surge will burn out your positronic brain in less than a millisecond. You will have committed suicide."

"I do not believe you," Robota said sternly.

"Fine. Then do it. Connect electronically to the security net."

Robota hesitated. "I cannot knowingly commit suicide."

"Run the calculation, you bag of bolts. What do you think the odds are that a man with my background and training is not telling the truth?"

Robota hesitated.

"Okay, then. Sit down. Shut up. And do not ever threaten me again."

"Have you lost your mind?" Lars exclaimed, as Robota retreated to the far corner of the room.

"Stay on topic. What makes a tax arbitrary?"

"Lay it out for me."

"First. Taxation must be with consent. Whatsoever is a man's own is absolutely his. No man hath a right to take it from him without his consent. Whosoever does so, commits a robbery. So sayeth British Law."

"That sounds made up. Are you making all this up as you go along?"

"No fiction here, Lars. If you do not believe me, have your skullcap do a history search. Run British history all the way back to the Magna Carta. You will see that I am telling you the truth. Now moving on to Principle Two. Taxes must be apportioned according to a definite rule. Any discretionary power invites corruption. Prejudice leads to persecution, even extortion."

"And Principle Three?"

"Equality; which is to say, uniformity. Ability to pay is no principle at all. Progressivity in taxation — that Karl Marxian idea of *from each according to his ability* — is the death knoll to liberty. Who is to judge what the relative burdens should be?"

"The Congress, of course. That is what the legislators are elected to do."

"Think what you are saying. If, by definition, the rich represent a small segment of society, and if Congress apportions taxes by majority rule, who represents the interests of the rich?"

"The rich can take care of themselves," Lars replied.

"Can they?"

"They always have."

"Is that the bias of your skullcap speaking? Or have you thought this one through? If the many tax the few, who protects the few? No one. Non-uniform rates are inevitable."

"So what?"

"So — it is not only immoral, it is unconstitutional."

Lars nodded as if he understood the moral distinctions. "What about the constitutional issue."

"Ah, yes, that dusty old document. The very first power granted Congress under the Constitution was the power to lay and collect taxes. But Congress was only granted the right to lay and collect taxes that were uniform throughout the land. If you go back now and check an Oxford English Dictionary of the time, you will find that to the Founding Fathers the word uniform meant *the same* — the same in different places, the same at different times, the same under varying circumstances. It is what present-day peoples now call *equal*. Thus, a flat tax of some fixed percentage of income, applied equally to everyone, would be considered by them to be uniform. A progressive tax with higher rates on higher income would not be. Ability to pay is no principle at all."

"Is it even possible at this late date to get away from the graduated tax?"

"Is any date too late to correct a moral wrong?"

"I suppose not."

Flix shook his head. "If an income tax must be levied, it must be uniform. All taxpayers must pay the same rate, no exceptions. And the rate must not be too high."

"How high is too high?"

"It is hard to answer that question with precision. But the principle is clear. When you tax too much all you get is rebellion. That, plus flight to avoid the tax, fraud to evade the tax, and an underground economy to hide from the tax. Flight is the number one device used by the wealthy to avoid heavy taxation. Indeed, back in the colonial days, more people emigrated to the New World to avoid taxes back home than for any other reason except perhaps religion. The loss their native countries suffered by driving out that much wealth and talent was considerable. Remember, Lars, money has no allegiance except to safety and profitability."

"So, how do we remedy matters?"

Flix smiled. “Cut taxes. Then cut them again. Then cut them once more. Cut spending. Cut taxes. Then cut them both further. With each new cut in marginal tax rates, the country will grow faster. Even at lower nominal tax rates, tax collections will rise if GNP grows. The deficit will actually fall. We know this to be true for a fact. We have seen it happen before in our history. Lower taxes lead to faster growth.”

“That will do it? That will fix America?”

Flix nodded with dead seriousness. “Cut taxes. Make them uniform throughout the land. Cut spending. Reinstate financial privacy. Decriminalize the tax code. Reduce tariffs . . .”

“The sun is coming up,” Robota suddenly interrupted. “You and your grandfather have been talking all night.”

“Maybe that is a sign,” Lars said.

“Yes, enough is enough. At least now you know something of your heritage.”

“I have learned a lot, Grandpa. But if you had to sum it all up in a few words, what would you say?”

Flix turned thoughtful. “A man’s home is his castle. That includes his treasury. If you want to make a fresh start in this country, if you want to witness the rebirth of liberty, reinstate financial privacy. Put in place a Bank Secrecy Act. All the rest must surely follow.”

CHAPTER EIGHTEEN

Sunrise can be a beautiful thing.

But some sunrises are more beautiful than others. Sadly, a Hedon City sunrise was not among the world's loveliest. Something about the airborne particulates inside the sealed atmosphere of the dome that scattered the natural light. Whatever vibrant colors were in the palette to begin with were washed away.

Now, when Lars looked out the window of his grandfather's apartment, everything outside looked drab and gray.

"Time for pancakes before you leave?" Flix asked. Lars loved pancakes.

"Sir," Robota said. "Lars and I might be well advised to leave the City before the morning patrols. Neither the boy nor I are legal inside the dome."

"You are right, of course. But where do you mean to go after you leave here?"

"Lars's assimilation program is not complete. Our next stop is the Neurological Center in Ypsilanti."

"Getting out of the dome is more difficult than getting in. Is all your paperwork in order?"

"How can an illegal — someone who should not be here in the first place — possibly have all their paperwork in order?"

"No paperwork then. I see. Maybe you should follow me. I know people who know people. I have a pre-arranged escape route already in place."

"There are police downstairs," Lars said, still at the window. "They seem to be preparing to come into the building."

"Robota, I want you to connect electronically with the Hedon City security net. Find out what the police are looking for."

"But you said . . ."

"Yeah. Well, I lied. Humans will do that sometimes." Even as Flix spoke, he rolled an antediluvian wheelchair out of the closet and pushed it in her direction.

Robota nodded as she spoke. "Okay, checking now . . . Wait . . . Wait . . . They are looking for you, General. On account of that dead body. From last night in Perdition's Cup. They have somehow tied it back to you. The manager of this building gave you up."

Flix grabbed his kit. "Backstairs for me then. Lars, sit down in this wheelchair. Cover yourself with this blanket. Put on this hat. Robota, you drive. Take him down the elevator. Meet me across the alley. Go. Now. Both of you!"

With official vehicles of all sorts converging on the Mark Twain, scant attention was paid to the beggar working his way down the backstairs and into the street beyond or to the cripple being led out through the lobby by his nurse.

By the time the three of them hit the street, the sun had just crept above the horizon. The early morning air was still.

They quickly dumped the wheelchair and walked hurriedly into the next block. Even though Flix was hobbled by his cane and his kit, he was moving fast. Lars and Robota had to hustle to keep up.

They passed yet another police gcar as it pulled up to the curb, klaxon wailing. Had they waited in the room any longer, they would have surely been caught and arrested.

Like Chica next door, Hedon City was a domed city, had been for nearly a century. Doming was expensive. But it offered a city many advantages — controlled weather, reduced pollution, tighter security. This last — tighter security — was one of the driving forces that led to the construction of the Hedon City dome.

With a limited number of entrances and exits, controlling access to America's version of Sodom and Gomorrah was just that much simpler. All airchop pads were outside the dome, as were all but one of the metro stations.

There were a few people, though — and Flix was one of them — who knew the "alternate" routes into and out of the City — the sewers, the viaducts, the grease traps. The old city, pre-dome, was crisscrossed with such routes, many of them hazardous. Flix was headed for one of them now.

Hedon City began life in the early 1900s as something completely different from what it is today, a company town controlled by a giant industrial complex. The city of Gary, Indiana, was named for its founder, Elbert H. Gary, the first Chairman of the United States Steel Company.

U.S. Steel dredged a harbor in the picturesque sand dunes that dotted the southern shores of Lake Michigan. Then, to transport coal and iron ore into his steel mill and to ship finished product out, Elbert Gary also built an inland shipping canal that ran from his manmade harbor to his mill. The area nearby was riddled by train lines that served much the same purposes.

Now, with the old city mostly covered over by the new city, some of its history had been lost to posterity. There was one place, though, where Flix knew the original Gary Harbor River Canal ran underground through a tunnel for 2000 meters or so until it resurfaced again between two giant floating casino complexes. There, where the old river canal resurfaced, it might be passable.

Flix opened his kit, checked his gps. He knew that a catwalk ran along the ceiling of the manmade river-tunnel. The tunnel itself should not be full with water just now as the spring rains had been light this year and the waters of Lake Michigan were lower than usual.

Sirens could still be heard screaming in the distance as Flix, Lars, and Robota made their way across the grassy dune that ringed the entire inner circumference of the dome. The sand and grass were wet, products perhaps of seepage from the lakefront or sprinklers that had run overnight.

Flix ignored the wet ground and led the three of them down a slope towards the old river canal. He checked their position on his instrument again. Somewhere down here was a long forgotten manhole cover that would allow them entrance to the viaduct and down into the canal. All he need do was follow the signals of the pencil-thin metal detector he now held out in front of him.

No one said a word.

From the one-bedroom apartment in the Mark Twain Hotel, across the streets and onto the wet lawn, down the slope to the manhole cover — not a word.

What was there to say? They were the object of a manhunt — him, an underage youth and a robot. One man was dead. They would be dead too if they did not keep moving.

The metal detector beeped, and Flix pushed aside the tuft of grass with the tip of his cane. *There it was!*

With Robota's help, Flix lifted the manhole cover from the dirt and started down the ladder built into the wall of the descending pipe.

It was just past dawn outside. But inside the descending pipe it was nearly dark as night. With the lid pulled back into place, darker still.

Flix hooked his cane over his wrist and turned on his penlight. He handed a second one down to Lars. Together the three went down the ladder, hand over hand, rung by rung.

Within a few meters, the situation got dicey. The rungs on the ladder had become wet and slippery, the walls of the descending tube, a forest of mold and lichen. To keep from slipping, Flix threw on a pair of gloves.

He dropped his kit and his cane. They clattered to the concrete twenty meters below.

Hanging on for dear life, the three continued down. Robota seemed to have no fear, no difficulty descending the ladder. Not so for Lars. He was definitely scared.

Suddenly, there was a blast of cold air and the sound of rushing water. *They were at the river canal.*

The river-tunnel was not completely dark. They could make out the catwalk and the river beneath.

The catwalk hung from the ceiling on thin metal straps. Every fifty meters or so, a single light bulb hung down over the center of the catwalk. The bulbs were suspended from the ceiling by a series of old-style electrical cords, many of which were broken or frayed.

Like a big dotted line, the catwalk snaked off into the distance, long stretches of dark interrupted by short patches of illumination. The lights threw weird shadows onto the churning water, making the whole scene wildly surrealistic.

Following the catwalk downstream should have been a relatively simple matter. But it surely was not. In places, the wrought iron scaffolding that held the catwalk in place had rusted through. In other spots, the walk itself was jammed tight with logs and branches that had been deposited there when the waters of the canal were running high, then left behind in a knotted mess when the water level subsided.

Picking their way through these logjams proved both dangerous and time-consuming. An axe or saw would have come in handy. But they had neither. Instead, they had to pull apart the branches with their bare hands as best they could. In some cases they had to climb over or through the worst of the jams.

For hours the three of them slugged their way downstream. They finally reached open air again near the lakeshore around 2 p.m. that afternoon.

A light rain was falling as they dragged themselves, muddy and cold, up the slippery riverbank. They had covered all of two kilometers in the past seven hours and were now nearly at the point of exhaustion.

Their faces and hands were bloody, their clothes caked in mud and sweat. But they *were* outside the city. The Hedon City dome rose up behind them like a giant beach ball.

Everyone knew a price was still to be paid for last night's acts. — But for now they were safe.

•
•

The sun was settling below the horizon when they arrived at the doorstep of Flix's house in Maine. The hike along the catwalk north and east to where the tunnel ended and Lake Michigan began, had taken them all morning and into the early afternoon. Another forty minutes were consumed getting to the airchop pad. They arrived there cold and wet. Thirty minutes later they were in Maine, courtesy of Flix's expert piloting.

PART II

CHAPTER NINETEEN

The three laws of robotics.

When, at age 11, Lars was first introduced to them, the laws of robotics seemed almost romantic in their simplicity. Laws written down even before the first robots had been assembled. Laws conjured up by a brilliant mind, the mind of Isaac Asimov.

- A robot may not injure a human being or, through inaction, allow a human being to come to harm.
- A robot must obey any orders given to it by a human being, except where such orders would conflict with First Law.
- A robot must protect its own existence so long as such protection does not conflict with the First or Second Laws.

Now, though, those three laws did not seem so damn brilliant. The skullcap changed everything for Lars, hardly any of it good.

What use was there in reading a book when your enhanced mind could simply race ahead and figure out the mystery before the hero had a chance to solve it?

Where was the fun in reading a book when your enhanced mind could race ahead and finish reading the book — and the sequel — and the sequel to the sequel

— before your "ordinary" mind could even savor reading the first page of the first chapter the old-fashioned way?

With a skullcap affixed to the top of his head, so much of what used to give Lars great joy, no longer did; so much of what used to be great fun for him, no longer was.

Why run an experiment? Why test out a new mixture of explosive chemicals or a new way of blending compounds? Why do any of these things when your enhanced mind can race out, check the world's databases, see who else has run the identical experiment before and report the results back to you before you even have a chance to break out a pipette or heat up the first test tube?

With such frustrations thwarting Lars at every turn, the only avenue that remained open to him was escape. *But how?* Drugs to drown out the noise? Chemicals to quiet the nerves? *What a devastating thought.*

Drugs and danger. What a perfect aphrodisiac! Drugs and danger and alcohol. Take chances you never would have taken before. Recapture every last ounce of vicarious pleasure the skullcap had robbed you of.

Steal a candy bar from a shop. Revel in getting away with it. Or get caught instead. It does not matter. Blame it on the skullcap. Blame it on society. Blame it on your parents for making you wear the damn thing.

Drink alcohol until your mind turns to mush, until you puke up your guts, until every word spoken to you becomes a jumble of noise. Drink and keep on drinking. There is no downside. You know that no matter how much alcohol you consume, no matter how many ounces of the evil drink you down, your enhanced mind can never get drunk, can never stop thinking for you even after you have stopped thinking for yourself.

Smoke pot, inject yourself with dangerous drugs, swallow pills. It is all the same. Drive too fast. Rock climb. Leap with a parachute from an airplane. It does not matter. You will always cheat death. *And if you do not, so what?* At least the pain would end.

And so the downward spiral accelerates. Had it not been for his grandfather, Lars might have ended up in the morgue. As it was, he was in a juvenile detention center when Flix arrived on the scene.

At first, Lars was angry, angry that his grandfather had to see him like this. Lars was ashamed of what he had done, ashamed that he had been caught.

"The officer tells me you defaced public property."

"I would hardly call a church sanctuary public property."

"A case of semantics then?"

"If it pleases the court."

"Do you honestly believe that I am too old and too enfeebled to swat your adolescent butt?" Flix was getting steamed.

"Yes. By all means. I am sure that hitting me will solve everything."

Flix's eyes shone anger. "I have never been fitted for a skullcap, you little shit — not like yours anyway. I simply do not believe in them. They do not suit my character, never have. So Lars, if it satisfies some inner need, you will be happy to know that with that thing fitted to your head, you can outthink me each and every day of the week, from sunrise to way past dusk. You can outsmart me, shave fine slices of meaning off any word I use and lose me in the distinctions. — But mark my words, boy. You cannot outrun me. — So I will ask you one last time. Do you honestly think I am too old and too enfeebled to swat your miserable butt?"

"No, Grandpa." Lars was respectful now.

"Okay then. Tell me what the hell is going on here, Lars. The police officer tells me that you defaced public property. — And none of this horse hockey about a church sanctuary not being public property."

"It is true . . . I did it . . . And I am sorry."

"You can make your apologies to the church deacon when you go there this weekend to clean up the mess."

"I will."

"Now explain yourself. Why did you do it?"

"I feel so trapped, Grandpa. All sense of wonder has been taken from me."

"Trapped? Trapped by what?"

"By this . . . this . . . thing." Lars touched his fingers to his skullcap.

"So take the goddamn thing off and rejoin the living."

"I cannot."

"For God's sake, why not?"

"I cannot let Mom down. She says that it is important. That I will need a high-quality skullcap to compete in the modern world. She spent everything she had on it. Even sold her *Book of Lore* to raise enough money. I do not want to disappoint her."

"Then be a man and learn to live with it."

"I am not sure that I can."

"You think I like this bum leg? Hell no! But I have learned to live with it. You think I enjoy seeing your grandmother in that bed, a complete vegetable? Hell no! But I have learned to live with it. Grow up, kid. Grow up, go to college, join the military, get a job, quit belly aching!"

"But, Grandpa. These skullcaps change everything. What makes a man a man, but makes a robot something else?"

"More word games?"

"Not at all. You have met Robota. What makes a man a man but makes a robot something else?"

"You tell me."

"It cannot be intelligence, for there are precious few cognitive differences between robot and man."

"I disagree, Lars. The differences are not cognitive. The differences between robot and man lay in their respective moral codes. People acquire their moral codes from upbringing, from genetics, from religion, from the people with whom they associate."

"Yes, and robots get theirs from programming, from a sequence of behavioral laws hardwired into their positronic brains."

"Unless, of course, they do not."

"What do you mean?" Lars was crestfallen, as if his grandfather had just slain a sacred cow.

"Evil people can write evil computer code. Or did this not occur to you? Robots can just as easily be programmed to be immoral — or amoral — as they can be to obey that famous sequence of behavioral laws. Whatever limits those three laws are supposed to place on robot behavior can just as easily be neutered or done away with by someone smarter or meaner. The Three Laws can be rendered moot."

"Maybe that is why I feel trapped, Grandpa. Does a man become a robot the moment he dons a skullcap? My best friend Granite seemed to."

"I do not know, son. Can a robot deceive itself into believing it is a human being?"

"I suppose that is possible."

"In that event, consider this. Any robot that has deceived itself into believing it is a human being will no longer feel bound by the Three Laws. He can willfully violate any or all of the Laws and not give the violation a second thought."

"I get your point, Grandpa. Any robot that believes it is human will find it has no obligation to obey the Laws of Robotics. Thus, in contravention of those laws, it could harm another human being, no questions asked, and do so with a clear conscience."

"Exactly."

"Thus, to remedy this inherent loophole in their programming, we need a fourth behavioral law, don't we? One law that overrides the other three."

"Have you a solution to offer?"

"Yes, I believe that I do. We shall call it the Fourth Law of Robotics. *A robot must know at all times that it actually is a robot.*"

"That is brilliant, Lars."

"You think so?"

"I do," Flix said. "But that still does not solve our most pressing problem, does it?"

"And what is our most pressing problem?"

"You. What to do about you. You have broken the law."

"Yes. Me. I almost forgot."

"You are the reason why I am here today, Lars."

"Yes, Grandpa. And I thank you for coming."

"What will it be then, Lars? Some people I have spoken to would say that a year in military school would do you a world of good. Teach you some discipline; maybe develop your skills as a mathematician or scientist. Military school could become a springboard to something grander, perhaps a commission to the Space Academy."

"We are talking at cross-purposes here, Grandpa. I have already told you how trapped I feel. Now you want to trap me even further, stick me in a prison, warehouse me in some military school?"

"A military school is not a prison. Nor is it a warehouse. Plus, this is not just any military school we are talking about here. This is Anaconda Military School. It has graduated some of the very best. Viscount Henry. President Bartholomew. Many others."

"I will not stand for it, Grandpa. If you force me to go to that bloody school, I will simply walk away from the place, melt into the fabric. If I have to, I will live on the streets of Hedon City. You will never see or hear from me again."

"Threatening me is not the way for you to go on this, Lars. You need help, help that neither your mother nor I nor even Robota can give you. The police are not going to release you into my custody without some assurances. I would like very much to walk you out of here a free man this evening. But that is not likely to happen unless

I sign an affidavit. I must agree to either place you in protective custody at a detention facility for recalcitrant boys or else enroll you in one of a short list of military schools. Anaconda in the Hawaii Free State is one of the very best."

"The Hawaii Free State? That bug infested cesspool? The islands seceded from the Union, what two hundred years ago? Now it is nothing but a rain-drenched chemical toilet."

"Rain during the rainy season, sure. But otherwise, quite nice. Parts of the Hawaii Free State are quite lush and very tech. The Big Island is home to the Space Elevator Depot. In fact, Camp Anaconda is headquartered only minutes away from the Depot by airchop."

"So, not only am I being exiled to a military school, I am also being expelled from the land of my birth? Hawaii is no longer part of the United States. How is any of this supposed to help me?"

"You remember what I told you about Chuck Yeager?"

"The flyer?"

"Yes. If you have any hopes of becoming an airman like him or flying an airchop for real or, better still, getting to outer space, there is no better way. After a year at Anaconda, you will have the chops to enroll as a cadet at the Space Academy. I will help smooth the road for you."

"I guess I am afraid."

"Pish posh. The people at Anaconda will toss that silly skullcap in a closet, train you physically, toughen you mentally, make you stronger. They will teach you straight-as-an-arrow thinking. Common sense. Duty. Honor. Sacrifice. Country. You will go in there a boy, and come out of there a man. Trust me. You will see."

CHAPTER TWENTY

Boot camp. Plebe cadet. Greenhorn rook. Anaconda Military School. This was Lars's new life. It boiled down to just two words. Order and Discipline. It was also about something else. Loss of Self.

Indeed, that is the first goal of all military training. Loss of Self. Hard physical training; yes, of course. Discipline, certainly. Order, yes. Uniforms, of course.

But Loss of Self; that is the key. Forget self. Remember unit. *None of us is as important as all of us.*

An army runs on a clock. 0500 hours. Time for the cadets to wake up. 0520 hours. Time to gather in the yard for roll call. 0530 hours. Line up in front of the messhall. 0600 hours. Breakfast is over. Back to the barracks. Tidy your bunk. 0630 hours. Back in the yard. Time for calisthenics. The entire day programmed like that, every minute scheduled. Every day for nine weeks, the same.

The first stop on the road to loss of self is Loss of Privacy. Eighty men sleeping in the same room. No walls. Under four square meters of personal space. A single footlocker. No lock. Group bathroom. Single row of twenty porcelain stools. Twenty toilet paper dispensers. No walls between the stalls. Thirty shower heads. Thirty soap dishes. Eight wooden benches to change at or on. Open wall lockers. Two hooks. Two shelves. No door.

And so it began. Basic Training. Hard physical regimen executed under the harshest of conditions, the tropical environs of Hawaii. Bugs, lizards, snakes, spiders. Skullcaps had to be left at the curb. They were not permitted on the grounds of the school, not to cadets, not during Basic. The only exception to the rule? Rudimentary skullcaps were occasionally used to speed instruction. Otherwise, the physicality of training — the very nature of preparing a man for combat — would almost certainly damage a skullcap's delicate neuronal contacts. Plus, there was one further benefit. Stripping every cadet of his skullcap helped achieve another admirable end. It helped ensure Loss of Self.

Deprived now of his skullcap and restricted to barracks, Lars never felt so alone or lost. No mother to make laugh when he did wrong. No mother to salve his wounds when he was hurt. No loyal and obedient Robota to help point him in the right direction or repair his damaged psyche. No skullcap to make him feel superior or invincible or all-knowing. No support network. No Granite Irston. No grandfather Flix. No Pamola to fear. No mathematics. No Primer on Explosives to worship. Adolescence stripped to its fearful, tentative core.

Basic Training. The object was the subject. Obey orders. Learn how to become fearless in the face of mortal danger. Yield ground to no man. Become a more lethal killer.

Lars's mind was filled with doubt. Could he learn how to be brave? Could he learn how to face danger without shirking?

Lars thought of the storybook heroes from his science fiction. Were they brave men? *Of course they were.* What could be more lethal than Outer Space? Radiation that could fry a man's brains. Cold that could, in an instant, freeze a man solid. Oxygen in such short supply you might have to wait eons between breaths just to find enough. Water buried deep in frozen rock or not present at all.

No, surviving out beyond the protective cocoon of Earth's atmosphere took more than courage and tenacity, more than being afflicted with Yeager Syndrome, more guts than simple soldiering.

But there had to be a Step One and this was it: Basic Training to become qualified as an infantryman. Then would come Scorpion School to toughen up the body, tighten up the skills. Then, if he graduated from Scorpion, the Space Academy, like Grandpa Flix said. Only then would he be allowed to land a post on a supply ship or at the Station.

The Induction Center. First stop for all incoming cadets. A stark and drafty place that had seen better days in another lifetime as a National Guard Armory when Hawaii was still part of the United States. Now it was just old and poorly lit, a perfect home to Kona's bugs and humidity.

The incoming class, of which Lars was a member, numbered three hundred. For hours, the three hundred young cadets — some male, some female — looped their way from table to table in the roomy drill hall. It would not have been such a bad experience, except for one thing. Aside from their street shoes, every last one of them was stripped completely naked and carrying their clothing rolled up into a ball beneath their arm.

What a sight! Three hundred young people, boys and girls alike, naked and standing in a long, snakelike line. A virtual cross-section of the human anatomy. All sizes. All shapes. Small breasts, large ones. Big men, small men. All in line and inching their way slowly around the giant hall, moving from station to station — registration, physical examination, bio-med examination, full panel vaccinations, genetic markers.

Turn your head and cough.

Hold out your arm and make a fist.

This will not hurt a bit.

Piss in this cup.

They followed instructions, did what they were told. But the very act was embarrassing. Any young man, naked from the floor to the ceiling aside from his shoes, would hardly be able to carry out his instructions. To be forced to stand there in the open and piss in a cup in front of a naked woman, a perfect stranger.

What could be more humiliating?

But then again, humiliation was part of the plan. Loss of Self.

After a while in line, Lars came to know the few cadets directly in front of him and directly behind him. One of the men had enrolled at Anaconda even though he could neither read nor write. His name was Jinnaro. He was a charity case. Another man had never owned a new pair of boots before today. His tag was Bonker, or so he said. Lars wasn't sure whether that was his actual name or his nickname. One of the women in line nearby had never worn a skullcap before. She had large breasts. Her name was Sansofia.

Despite all these shortcomings, molding all these many disparate souls into a single cohesive unit was a possibility. As his grandfather said to him the night before, when he dropped Lars off at the gate:

From such rough tinder, a blazing fire can often be built.

The series of examinations inside the old National Guard Armory took half a day. Nothing unusual. This was the first of many lines Lars would stand in, in the days ahead, as a cadet soldier.

Uniforms came next, what the Anaconda Training Cadre called OD's, a designation for olive drab. The OD's were issued by the Company Quartermaster. As the weather in the islands was warm year-round, summer-weight gear was the order of the day: olive-drab poly shirt, olive-drab safari fatigues, field jacket with Velcro flap pockets, olive-drab poly raincoat, fatigue hat, olive-drab cap, socks, underwear, toilet articles, two-pair of waterproof, steel-toed boots that came above the ankle, one pair low-cut boots, as well as a canvas barracks bag to carry it all in. The females got the same. It was all standard issue down to a pair of olive-drab colored handkerchiefs, toothbrush, and set of towels.

Now they separated the men from the women. The men formed up outside the QM, gear in hand. The women were marched off in a different direction. It was raining, a humid damp rain.

The Commissioned Officer in charge ordered that roll be called. Then he divided the men into three groups of approximately eighty men each. He turned Lars's group over to one of three Staff Sergeants standing nearby. The Staff Sergeant was backed up by a humaniform robot named Soldata Fifteen. It was outfitted with the latest in battle armor and military tech gear.

Now, with full barracks bags slung over their shoulders, the Staff Sergeant — his name was Esterhaus — marched his eighty or so men along a gravel road to a barracks area. Here, each man was assigned a bunk. Lars's bunk was near the center of the big room. Industrial grade bug-wrap covered the mesh windows.

Each barrack in the cadet training area was identical. On the ground floor were two private rooms, a multi-hole latrine, a showering space, and a large squad room. Upstairs was a second squad room outfitted as a holo gallery, plus three more private rooms. Sergeant Esterhaus slept in one of the private rooms downstairs; Soldata Fifteen slept in the other. A Master Sergeant or junior officer would normally sleep in one of the three private rooms upstairs.

Inside the barracks the men received their first instruction. Esterhaus demonstrated how a bunk was to be made up, Anaconda-style. Soldata Fifteen handed out bedrolls, and the men made up their bunks according to pattern.

By now Lars was tired. He yawned as unobtrusively as he could and was immediately made fun of.

"Little boy need his nap?" It was Bonker who had earlier been next to him in line.

"Yeah maybe," Lars admitted. "It has already been a long day and I am exhausted. What I wouldn't give to stretch out on this bunk and drop to sleep."

"Quite bellyaching, my pretties," Sergeant Esterhaus bellowed. "Finish making up your bunks. Secure your barracks bag. Form up outside. Soldata will call roll as soon as you have fallen in. Now move it!"

Lars sighed. This latest calling of roll was like the fourth time in the last two hours. It seemed to Lars as if there was going to be a lot of that here at Anaconda — standing at attention and counting off. Soldata Fifteen did not seem to mind or tire of the sport. But then Soldata Fifteen was a robot, an "it," not a human being that could get bored.

Just great. Lars thought. *How is standing in a straight line and repeatedly counting off going to make me a better man?*

The answer would have to wait. So would a nap on one of those freshly made-up bunks. After calling roll, Soldata Fifteen led them in a half-hour of calisthenics and marching around the yard. The only thing Lars learned from the exercise was that the robot preferred being called Soldata rather than Soldata Fifteen. Apparently the thing had feelings.

Finally, though, came time for a hot meal and shower. The food tasted like paste. No home cooking, this. But the shower felt damn good. Then the men were ordered to hit the sack.

This was an order that Lars gladly obeyed. No one complained. It was late. Everyone was tired.

As the men settled into their beds, the wind began to blow outside. These were the so-called Kona winds. They came out of the west and blew onshore hard.

The wind brought forth a noisy rain. Somehow, though, the noise did not seem to bother a soul. The men were so tired their ears went to sleep along with their brains.

Only minutes passed before every cadet was fast asleep. Soon the walls of the barracks began to tremble with every manner of snore. High, low, stuttering, whistling, even booming sounds arose from the sleeping troops.

But no matter how random or annoying the sounds, no one seemed to care. Ears do not transmit muted sounds to sleeping brains.

Thus ended Lars Cabot's first day in boot camp at the Anaconda Military School located near the base of the Hualālai Volcanic Mountain, Kona District, Hawaii.

CHAPTER TWENTY-ONE

Suddenly, the plebes were awakened by emphatic yelling.

"Rise and shine, my pretties! Mess Call in fifteen! Put on your OD's! Form up outside in Company Street! We will march as a unit to the messhall. Snap to!"

At the sound of Sergeant Esterhaus's voice, Lars sat straight up in bed. He tried to remember where he was. The man in the bunk next to him, Bonker, swore loudly. Then Lars looked outside. It was still dark. Last night's rain was still coming down. His wristwatch, the wristwatch his grandfather had given him, said it all. Five forty-five a.m. 0545 hours. They had had about four hours' sleep.

Confusion reigned. Eighty-plus men had to jump from their beds, make a quick stop at the latrine, wash up, and get dressed. The men had been so tired last night when they sacked out, no one had given much thought to how their barracks bags were packed or even where they had been set down. Now clothes flew everywhere. Somehow, though, the men managed to make it out the door within the allotted fifteen minute timeframe.

They stood in the cold rain, now, waiting for the inevitable. Lars could see it coming even before his lungs breathed in the tropical humidity or his feet hit the gravel road of Company Street out front. *Morning roll call.*

Lars shivered. The locals called it Kona rain. In the language of the ancient Hawaiians, kona meant leeward or dry side of the island. For much of the year, moisture laden winds would blow in from the east, where they would reach the windward side of the island leading to rain. As the winds traveled further inland, they would lose their moisture and be nearly dry by the time they reached the leeward or kona side of the island.

But during certain months of the year, like now, the wind pattern would reverse. That reversal would produce a kona storm that would arrive from the west. It was always a cold, unwelcome downpour.

They stood in the rain, now, and the first thing Esterhaus did was call roll. Then off they marched, this time to a different messhall, one closer to their barracks than the one they ate in last night.

Much to Lars's surprise, the food tasted much better than last night's grub. But then, breakfast is a little harder to muck up than supper.

After eating, the men formed up outside the messhall and — you guessed it — roll was called again. Last night's rain was still coming down. The cadets were instructed to return to their barracks where they would be granted free time until 0800 hours.

But the offer of free time was more an illusion than fact. For most of the men, almost every minute of that free time was consumed making up their bunks and organizing their uniforms. Unlike the previous night, this time all clothing was folded neatly and barracks bags repacked in a more sensible fashion, then lashed to the bedframe.

At 0800 hours, they formed up in Company Street. After Esterhaus again called roll, they got their first instruction of the day. Esterhaus taught them how to stand at attention and the proper way to deliver a salute. He lectured them on military courtesy then spent the balance of the morning instructing them on close-order drill, learning how to march. They practiced the routines over and over again.

Sergeant Esterhaus was good. He knew how to get results. After the midday meal, the cadets spent another two hours marching in formation. They got progressively better each time they practiced. Still, Lars could not fathom how this boring protocol would make him a better soldier, much less a better man like his grandfather promised. This place was a cesspool, just like he thought, a steaming jungle thick with bugs, lizards, snakes, rain and humidity.

Finally, about three o'clock on that second afternoon, they were given the balance of the day off. They were given strict warnings to remain in the immediate area. For most of the men, a warning made no difference. They were so tired, they sacked out almost immediately. Getting under covers before lights-out was against protocol. So the exhausted men slept on top of their bunks. Once a bunk was made-up in the morning, it had to remain that way all day until lights-out at 2200 hours.

Then, just before five o'clock that afternoon, Esterhaus came in, blew his whistle and yelled, "Form up outside for *Retreat!* Hop to!"

Lars had been a Boy Scout. He knew what *Retreat* was. But most men did not. A few were scratching their heads with confusion. In their minds, the word retreat had something to do with a setback on the battlefield.

On a military installation, just as at most Boy Scout camps, bugle calls were used to indicate changes in the daily routine. They were usually centered on *Mess Call* or the raising and lowering of the flag. At the start of each day, before breakfast, *Reveille* is sounded and the flag is raised. At the end of the day, before supper, the flag is lowered and *Retreat* is sounded.

The men stood, now, in formation outside their barracks. Once again, Esterhaus called roll. Then, at his word, the men fell totally silent. From off in the distance, hundreds of meters away, came a sound. It was the sound of a single, solitary bugle. It was ringing out its solemn and lonely call. They could not see the bugler.

But if they could, they would be amazed. He stood on the high ground alone. Just the bugler and his instrument. A man standing alone, proud and confident and sure. First, *Call to Retreat*, followed by *Retreat*.

Lars felt right at home, hearing that bugle call. A bugle call was a beautiful thing. There was something so desperately wholesome and pure about its simple brassy sound. It consists only of notes from a single overtone series. This is a requirement, for the call must be played on a trumpet or bugle without moving or depressing any valves.

Once the flag was down, the cadets had a short time to clean up before supper. Following supper, they were off for the rest of the day. Sergeant Esterhaus told them that *Tattoo* (Army talk for lights-out) would be at 2100 hours and that *Taps* would sound thirty minutes later. Everyone was to be in bed by then. Soldata would do bed check.

As evening drew to a close that night, the men talked and milled around. A few played cards. A few others tapped out e-notes home.

But Lars had a different agenda for the evening. The sounding of *Retreat* on a bugle had brought back memories, memories of two summers earlier at Scout Camp. That summer was when he first heard the term "Tattoo" to describe the last bugle call of the day. Such a strange term, Tattoo. A strange term for such an important moment in the day. Lars wondered. *Where did it come from, this strange term?*

Lars instinctively reached for his skullcap to find the answer. But then he remembered. He had been forced to surrender his skullcap to the school administrator upon enrolling at Anaconda. Now, for the first time, he missed the cursed thing. He would have to research the question the old-fashioned way, online with a computer.

A few minutes of clicking through and he was there —

The term "Tattoo" dates back hundreds of years, to the seventeenth century. At the time, the British Army was fighting in the Low Countries of Belgium and the Netherlands. Each evening, drummers from the garrison were sent out into the surrounding towns at 2130 hours to inform the soldiers that it was time to quit drinking and return to barracks. The process was known as *doe den tap toe* (Dutch for "turn off the tap"), an instruction to innkeepers to stop serving the soldiers beer and to send them home for the night. The drummers continued to play until curfew at 2200 hours. Some bastardization of the Dutch term by the English and "Tattoo" was born.

Funny what a man learns as he goes through life. — And Lars didn't even need the services of his skullcap to learn it.

•
•

The next morning was a carbon copy repeat of the previous morning. Again awakened by Sergeant Esterhaus at 0545 hours. Again formed up in Company Street by Soldata Fifteen. Again roll was called. Again they stood *Reveille.*

But the new day did bring certain subtle changes. After breakfast, the men had to completely clean the barracks from floor to rafter, leaving out no detail. Mop the floors. Do the windows. Clean the latrine. Make up beds. Lash barracks bags to the foot of each bunk. Then form up to begin two days of testing in the Reception Station area adjacent to the Induction Center, where this all began.

There were two tests to be taken. The first was the Anaconda General Aptitude Test — what amounted to a sophisticated IQ test. The second, a day later, was the Mechanical Aptitude Test — a variant of the how-handy-are-you-with-your-hands sort of test. Both tests would help determine which training squadron a man would eventually be assigned to. No skullcaps here.

Lars did well on both examinations, near the top of his class. His extensive camping and Boy Scout experiences — not to mention his work with explosives — demonstrated him to be quite adept with his hands. The differences would matter later in his next training segment.

Men in Lars's age group differed greatly in many respects, some tall, some short, some mature, some awkward and fearful, some natural leaders, others more of the bookworm kind.

But in at least one way, these boys were all quite similar. Pride was everything with these lads. No matter how much they may have missed their families, men his age rarely admitted to being homesick.

Even so, as their first week in boot camp morphed to a close, there was no denying that everything about their lives had dramatically changed from the week before. Last week's petty larcenist was this week's model cadet. Last week's lazy slacker mloron was this week's latrine manager.

Now, as a greenhorn rook, there would be no more dragging oneself off the couch midafternoon to saunter over to the refrigerator for something cold to drink. Luxuries like these were things of the past. There was no refrigerator in the barracks, and certainly nothing cold to drink, save tepid water from the tap.

Now, from the moment these men woke at 0545 hours until the moment their heads hit the pillows at *Taps*, their lives were under complete control of someone else.

Loss of Self. The first objective of Anaconda military training.

CHAPTER TWENTY-TWO

"Ah, new digs," Jinnaro said, dropping his barracks bag to the ground. He stood in front of a large, pyramidal-shaped tent. With the two aptitude tests now behind them and the scores tallied, the next phase of their training would begin.

"Not as nice as we had before," Lars said. Bonker and Lognasto were there as well. Soldata had said it would be four men to a tent.

"Yeah, we at least got to sleep indoors before," Bonker said. "What is this crap?"

Compared to the relatively new wood-frame barracks they were previously assigned to, these lodgings were downright primitive. Large, four-man wall-tents mounted on a stable wooden base. The tents had physical sidewalls made of plywood which stood approximately waist-high. Mounted above the sidewalls was a four-piece wooden framework. Draped over the skeletal-like framework was a sheath of waterproof canvas plus mosquito netting. The netting kept out most of the flying bugs. But, no amount of netting could keep out the everpresent spiders and lizards.

Ned Lognasto sneered his disdain. "This place don't even have central heating or air. How we supposed to survive the heat during the day and the cold at night?"

"It's not all bad. There is an HVAC unit in the wall." Lars pointed to the left sidewall where a small apparatus vented to the outside.

"A lot of good that will do us."

"I promise you, we will manage," Lars said. "My father used a similar gizmo to heat and cool his workshop when I was a kid."

Lars had taken his father's heating unit apart once. He knew exactly how it worked. The apparatus gathered and later dispensed radiant heat from a chemical reservoir. During the day, tiny hydraulic coils imbedded in the tent canvas would absorb the photonic energy of the sun's light and capture that energy in the reservoir. At night, the process would reverse and the chemical reservoir would shed the day's stored energy to keep the tent at a livable temperature.

But it was primitive technology and hardly up to the task. The unit could get very, very hot when it was running, thus making it a constant fire hazard. At least one tent caught fire each training cycle. The cadets detested these clunky units, which became the subject of frequent jokes and ridicule.

"Well let's stow our gear and get to the messhall," Lars said. "I'm hungry."

"It's a long hike," Lognasto complained.

"Bitching about it won't make it any shorter."

"No, but it might make me feel better."

Anaconda Military School was an enormous place. Lars had no idea of its scale until he and the others got their orders earlier in the day and were told to move out.

The camp covered thousands of square meters of open and wooded ground. Much of it was harsh jungle. Much of it stretched across the steep, treacherous slopes of the dormant Hualālai volcano. The cantonment area — which is to say, the training camp — was possessed of a flat plain in the center. The plain was cut by several large streams and small rivers. Because it rained almost on a daily basis in the uplands, those streams were kept full and flowing year-round.

The Training Regiment was made up of four Training Battalions. Each Training Battalion was laid out in squares, grid-fashion. At their center was a large parade ground. The arrangement of Battalions loosely resembled the organization of a functioning active-duty outfit, with each Battalion consisting of four Training Companies.

There were two Post Exchanges in the cantonment area, one at either end of the compound. The PX, as these shops were called, stocked practically anything a cadet might need to purchase, from underarm deodorant to extra socks to vids that had passed muster with the censor. The PX was a military school's version of a modern convenience store.

There were also three enclosed theatres on base. Two of these were tent theatres under canvas. A fourth was open-air. During the day, when training was in session and the men were tasked with running sims, the theatres were used for lectures. Three nights a week, vids were screened.

There was a hospital, a post QM, an athletic field, and an artillery range. Also a number of chapels. Anaconda saw to it that no cadet was ever far from a house of worship. When asked about it, the Chaplains repeated the mantra that God always fought on the side with the heaviest artillery.

Lars was assigned to Second Training Battalion, Company B, along with his newfound buddies, Bonker, Jinnaro and Lognasto. The physical layout of each Training Company was the same. Four, one-story buildings. A messhall. A Day Room. The latrine. The supply room. All four buildings appeared to be carbon copies when viewed from the exterior. Inside, they were vastly different. The buildings were situated at opposite ends of Company Street, the latrine and messhall at one end, the supply room and Day Room at the other.

The messhall was both their kitchen and their dining room. The latrine was their bathroom, an open arrangement, complete with a line of sinks on one wall and a line of toilets on the other. No walls or stalls inbetween. An adjoining room had showerheads placed every meter or so along two perpendicular exterior walls.

Privacy was now a thing of the past. Four men bunked in each wall tent; many times that number shared the open latrine.

Standardization was the fare. Each man slept on a small bed. Identical mattress, identical pillow. Each man was issued the identical equipment — two olive-drab poly blankets, two sheets, two pillowcases. As before, their barracks bags were lashed to the head of the bed. Their shoes, laced up, were placed beneath the bed. The tents had no cabinets or closets to hang clothing. So the men had to become proficient with folding their uniforms carefully to keep them from becoming wrinkled or infected with bugs.

Beginning with *Reveille* the next morning, Lars found himself immersed in basic training. *Reveille* sounded at 0545 hours. It came in the form of a bugle call from atop the nearest hill.

The cadets got up. Before they even dressed or washed their faces, they formed up at the command of a second bugle call. This one sounded *Assembly.*

At this point, they fell out in Company Street and formed up into their new platoon assignments. Then came the reports of each platoon sergeant — *First Platoon, all present or accounted for, Sir!* — and so on down the line with each of the five training platoons.

Then the cadets were dismissed to wash up, shave, and dress. A simple assignment, to be sure. But not as easy as it sounds. Two hundred men all trying to do the same thing at the same time and in the same place — the company latrine.

The next bugle call that sounded was *Mess Call.* The men ate quickly. Then, under the watchful eye of Soldata, they hurried back to camp to clean up their tents, make their beds, and police the area around the tents.

It was the same routine every morning. Wash and scrub the wooden floors of their tent houses. Scrub down the latrine. Sanitize the shower house. Complete all these duties before *First Call* at 0800 hours.

"Our life is not our own. You know that right?" Bonker complained.

"We live, eat, and shit by the bugle. I got that," Ned Lognasto said.

"It is the philosophy of a military school," Jinnaro said. "My dad says Anaconda has been run this way since before the last war. He says it will still be run this way one hundred years from now. The bugle informs us what to do and when."

Lars nodded. During the day, besides telling them when to get up and when to eat, there might be other calls, *Sick Call* or *Mail Call* or *Call To Quarters*. On Sundays, *Church Call*.

About noon each day, the men would hear the call for the noon meal. After lunch, it would be *Assembly* to fall out for an afternoon of training, usually hard and physical.

At the completion of their duty day, the cadets would return to their Company area to wash up and don dress uniforms in preparation for *Retreat*. It was a wonderful ceremony, the daily retiring of the flag.

The bugler would first sound *Assembly*. The men would form up in Company Street wearing their best. At precisely one minute before the scheduled lowering of the Post Flag, the bugler would sound *Call To Colors*. Then the bugler would sound *To The Colors*. The men would stand at attention and hold a salute until the *Call* ended. As always, the bugle set a cadence to their daily lives.

Tents were inspected on a daily basis by Sergeant Esterhaus and Soldata Fifteen. The men hated that robot. It never forgot. Never. And it could never look the other way. This kind of dogmatic adherence to even minor rules made their lives miserable. Every infraction, trivial or otherwise, was recorded for all time in that infernal silicon brain.

On Saturday mornings, the men stood formal inspection. This involved an entire team of inspectors, all senior personnel. The Company Commander, his most senior Captain, the Sergeant, and their platoon leader, Soldata Fifteen.

The formal Saturday morning inspection began precisely at 0900 hours. It lasted sixty minutes. Each cadet stood at attention at the foot of his bunk for the entire hour while the inspection party made its rounds. They would go tent by tent, up one row and down the next, until the entire Company had been reviewed.

These formal inspections were tough and exacting. Everything had to be perfect and in order. Bed corners. Window frames. Floor cracks. Latrine seats. Barracks bags. Everything. Pity the cadet who cut corners or erred. Extra duty was a sure penalty. Often, whole tents would be gigged.

After Saturday inspection, the men were free for the rest of the day. But again the freedom was an illusion. They were still in the early stages of basic training and restricted to Post 24/7.

At first, Lars was disappointed by the restrictions. But it was really not as bad as it sounded. He could take in a vid with Bonker or one of his other buddies. Or visit one of the Service Clubs. Or even hang around the PX. There was a game terminal they could use to amuse themselves. Most Saturdays he would just plain sack out from sheer exhaustion.

Some Saturday nights there was dancing at one of the Service Clubs. Sometimes it would be to a live band made up of cadet musicians, more often to music piped in from an external pod. Ample refreshments of a non-alcoholic nature were provided by the Academy, as well as a small stable of local girls. They were chaperoned by adults and admitted on the honor code. First names only, no touching, no feeling. That last was a rule often broken. Curbing the hormones of young men and women was a formidable task. Cadets were frequently bilged for lewd and lascivious behavior, at least one a term.

To those who enjoyed dancing — and certainly Lars could be counted among their number — Saturday nights were great. It was the perfect mix. Music. Dancing. Fraternity. Lars was dreadfully timid around girls, always had been. But the chance to make new acquaintances and spend time with a real live girl was a refreshing break from the strict routine he lived under the rest of the week.

Here was an instance where he came to better appreciate his upbringing. The Cabot's did not have much back in Ironwood. But they did have music. His mother taught him a love for dance and a love for music. She helped him develop an appreciation for what some would have called "old-fashioned" music, the sort two people could dance to. Plus, she taught him how to dance, a skill most other cadets lacked. This gave him the confidence to step out onto that dance floor and not feel he was making a fool of himself.

Lars found himself out on the dance floor that first night. For the first time in his life, he possessed a skill that members of the opposite sex found desirable. This was exciting in and of itself. As an added bonus, Bonker and Jinnaro were clumsy oafs by comparison.

Sundays were completely theirs. No bugle calls ordered them to line up and count off. No mandatory duty of any sort. For all intents and purposes every minute of the day was theirs to spend as they saw fit. There was only one proviso. They had to remain on Post.

Naturally, there were church services at each chapel. Nearly all denominations were represented by the Camp Chaplains. A cadet had only to select the service that most closely suited his religious calling. But the exceptions were legend. No High Temples here. No *Books of Lore.* No pantheon of gods. Lars did not attend any service.

Even Sunday meals were different from ordinary days. Each Training Company had its own cooks. Very often they would whip up a special baked food that was available to the men at breakfast. Sunday dinner was probably the best meal of the week.

CHAPTER TWENTY-THREE

"I could do this with my eyes closed."

They had been doing close-order drills for nearly an hour. This was the third day of it. One hour each day. The correct way to stand. The correct way to march. The correct way to dress and act. Not much of a challenge, not for a former Boy Scout. Lars was bored to tears with it.

"Shut up, Lars," Bonker said. "If Soldata hears your bellyaching, she will write you up for sure, put you on report."

"She? You call that mechanical drone *she*?"

"It, then."

"Oh, how tough is it to stand at attention?" Lars said. "Or to march in a straight line? Or shoulder an unloaded weapon? Or salute a superior? Military courtesy crap."

"Heh, we didn't all grow up with Tonto for a father or General MacInFart for a grandfather."

"It will not advance your cause one bit to make fun of my family. My grandfather could squash you like a fly if he chose to. And my father could conjure an evil spirit to infect your soul for all eternity."

"Oh, I am so scared," Bonker said.

"Yeah, if the Tonto fits," Jinnaro jeered. "Military discipline may be old hat to you, screwball. But it is new to most of us."

"Quiet in the ranks," Soldata barked from the rear of the line.

The cadets grumbled. The idea of moving in concert with forty other men at the discretion of some silicon-brained overseer with a starter's whistle in its mouth was unnerving. Some of the men had trouble distinguishing their left foot from their right.

"Being made to walk in a straight line is okay," Jinnaro said. "Sure beats the heck out of the many hours of bookwork they make us do."

"Six hours a day behind a desk. Fuck," Bonker said. "Lectures. Interactive vids. Learning modules using those primitive skullcaps they keep hid in the closet."

"A desk isn't that bad. Plus, we get plenty of exercise between lessons," Lars said. "Calisthenics and all that."

"Yeah, running in place is real tough."

"I was sore the first few days," Lars admitted. "Truth is: Sergeant Esterhaus is a pretty good drill instructor."

"Compared to what?"

"I mean it," Lars insisted. "With practice comes achievement."

"Some boneheaded lesson from the *Book of Lore*?" Bonker snickered his disapproval.

"Hardly," Lars replied. "Simple commonsense."

"Ah, you and your dime store Boy Scout morality," Jinnaro gibed.

"You poke fun. But that dime store Boy Scout morality, as you call it, has gotten me pretty far."

"Ah, yes, your big promotion. Esterhaus made you Drill Squad Leader."

"Indeed he did," Lars retorted. "And now we move correctly and with precision whenever the unit transitions between training areas during the day."

"All thanks to you, I suppose. Are you now taking credit for our progress, Mister Adhesive Sergeant?"

"And why shouldn't I?"

"But the elevation in rank is purely ceremonial," Bonker said.

"Yes, but Sergeant Esterhaus did it up right and designated me Adhesive Sergeant."

"All the man did was tape three sergeant's stripes on your uniform with strips of masking tape."

"They do look nice, don't they? Now I am a man among boys."

"Pishaw."

"Quiet in the ranks!" Soldata barked, louder than before. "And Company halt!"

"Why we stopping here?" Jinnaro wondered. The soldiers stood, now, before a red-brick building. It smelled of cordite and sulfur.

"Is it possible? Are we finally going to be given the chance to shoot something?" Bonker asked. The column of cadet soldiers was standing on Company Road near the entrance of the firing range.

After nearly two weeks of marching, two weeks of counting off and saluting and marching some more, the tedium had begun to wear. The men were bored with the drudgery and routine. They ached for something — anything — more exciting.

The truth was uncomplicated. No man since the dawn of time, no man who had signed up to be a soldier wanted to sit for hours behind a desk or be stuck in front of a computer screen. Such a man wants to carry a gun. He wants to carry a gun, feel its weight in his hands, aim it carefully with his eyes, squeeze the trigger with his fingers, feel the recoil against his shoulder.

Such men want to sense their blood pump faster. They want to fire live ammunition and do so under the most exciting of circumstances. The simulators on which the men trained, no matter how sophisticated or well-designed were no match for the real thing. Modern sims were remarkably realistic. They generated sounds and smells and percussion quite like a real gun fight. Still, they lacked one thing, a sense of danger, the adrenaline rush that came with fear and trepidation and pain and suffering. Only an actual weapon fired under actual battle conditions could accomplish that rush.

"Next week maybe," Esterhaus said, reading his men's minds. "You men are not yet ready for the Shoot House."

"Company!" Soldata Fifteen barked. "Right foot. Step off!"

"Damn!" Bonker swore. "Still no gun."

"Let it be," Lars whispered. "We will get our heaters soon enough."

•

•

While the men waited for something more exciting to come along, their physical conditioning accelerated. Twice a week, in addition to their one-hour daily program of calisthenics, they executed a fast-paced, fifteen-klom march across uneven terrain. With the insects and the snakes and the humidity and the intermittent rain, it was a challenging scramble over pockmarked hills and through tropical jungle thick with undergrowth. Soldata set the pace. Adhesive Sergeant Lars Cabot kept track of the stragglers.

Then there was the obstacle course. It was called the Scorpion — and with good reason. Eight hundred meters of pure physical pain. Twenty-five daunting physical obstacles. Here is where the weaker and less experienced men broke down.

The obstacles on the Scorpion Course were built entirely of pine logs. They came in an immense assortment of sizes and shapes, many in vast, towering structures that bore colorful names. Tarzan. Tough Nut. Belly Buster. Depending on its type, these obstacles had to be scaled, crawled through, climbed over, balanced upon, or leapt from.

The water-confidence test. A carnival-act-like event that included a frantic run across a log suspended fifteen meters above a pond, followed by a dive into a shallow bog with full pack.

The distance-swim. A half-klom lake-crossing that included dragging a sixty-five-klog load behind a man after plunging with it into the water from a hovering airchop.

Most rook cadets were expected to fail the course. Yet, they had to pass it in order to graduate.

•
•

After what seemed an eternity — though it was actually only another week — the cadets were finally issued pulse rifles. You would think these guns were made of gold, the way the men cradled them in their arms.

But the gods' honest truth was that these pulse rifles were obsolete, outdated weapons. They bordered on being relics. The guns were Enfield Pulse Rifles with manual bolt, nearly a century old. The blasters had been taken out of storage for this training class. They had been under lock and key since the closing days of the last big land war.

The electronic clips on these old gems held all of five rounds of ammunition. But at the outset, the training officers did not even issue the men charged capacitors. So the weapons were useless, little more than fancy paperweights.

For the first five days after the men were issued these weapons, what they did learn was the Manual of Arms.

The idea of a Manual of Arms dated to before the American Revolution. Such manuals were especially important in the matchlock and flintlock eras, when loading and firing a gun was a complex and cumbersome process that was usually carried out in rapid-fire fashion.

The present-day Manual of Arms, the manual these cadets trained on, had been updated, of course, many times from those early days. The mechanical rifle was no longer standard issue; electronic weapons were now the norm.

But the object of the lesson was the same. Teach a man the proper functioning of his weapon. How to disassemble his rifle. How to put it back together again. How to do so both quickly and efficiently.

"Okay, men. This is it. Break down the gun. Reassemble it. Do it as quickly as you can." Soldata stood before them grim-faced. Or as grim-faced as a robot could be made to look.

"It may not sound like much of a challenge," Soldata added, "especially to the uninitiated. But you best take this exercise seriously, for next week you will have to do it blindfolded and in a space of under two minutes."

Jinnaro grumbled. "Why in Lore's name would someone insist we master such a complicated task blindfolded?"

"You have perhaps heard of the dark?"

"A robot with a sense of humor?" Lars remarked.

"None that I am aware of."

"Is that it then?"

"No, it is not. You boys will have to learn how to clean the Enfield Pulse Rifle properly. How to clean it properly. How to keep it clean. The electronic firing chamber. All the metal parts. The capacitor. How to change it on the fly. The wooden stock. It is what insulates your hands; keeps them from being burnt off. Also, the leather and brass on the sling."

For five long days, four hours a day, they practiced. Their hands became bloodied. But still they practiced. They did these things over and over again. The monotony was beginning to get under their skins.

When would they actually be allowed to load in a capacitor and shoot one of these damn things? Every man asked the same question.

And they asked it again the next week. *When would the trainers issue them charged capacitors so they could begin target practice?*

The entire second week was spent on "dry fire." The cadets had to learn the prescribed firing positions. A pulse gun could be finicky. They had to practice developing a smooth trigger squeeze. They had to learn how to properly sight the weapon for distance shooting. Should a man pick his target poorly, the energy pulse could come whipping right back at him, the so-called bola effect. It killed one or two rook newbies a year.

But what the men really wanted to handle was live ammo. *How long would they be stuck firing dummy loads?*

These lessons, while boring, were invaluable. The cadets had to study the characteristics of different pulse generators. As with all rifles, firing characteristics were a bit of a science. It had become ever more so in the modern era.

In the old days, the issues of long distance shooting were many. Muzzle velocity. Throw-weight. Flight path of a projectile. Line of sight versus actual trajectory. Range limitations. Kinetic energy. Striking power. Energy retention upon impact.

In the current day, the issues were different. Charge levels. Pulse counts. Arc length. Capacitor gradient. Striking power.

But it all had to be learned — and in great detail. And it all had to be learned without firing a single live round, just instruction, simware, and vid time.

Then the big day came. On Monday of the following week, they moved out to the Shoot House.

CHAPTER TWENTY-FOUR

"I finally get to kill something," Bonker gleamed.

"Not so fast, Rambo," Soldata said. "Practice in the Shoot House comes first."

"What exactly is the Shoot House?" Ned Lognasto asked. He was not the brightest stone in the pond.

Soldata answered. "Each room in the house is programmed with a different sim. Here you will soon practice fire with a fully-charged Pulse Gun."

"Yes, finally." Lars exclaimed. He simply loved it, the chance to hold a hot weapon in his hands, the chance to fire it at life-like sim objects. A bit like the virtual patrons at Perdition's Cup. Lars took to it immediately. Quite a step up from a bow and arrow.

"Okay boys. Sim Room One. Login with your password and eigenhead. Take an Enfield from the rack. Step up to the line."

Lars felt at ease in the Sim Room. The pulse gun felt light in his hands. But Lars was surprised by how many men closed their eyes when they pulled the trigger, how many flinched when they fired. It seemed that for the great majority of cadets, handling and firing a weapon was a brand new experience.

"We will move from room to room as you become more proficient. I promise you. Each day your speed and aim will improve."

"Can we get started already?"

"We will move through the house as a team. No one moves on to Room Two until everyone succeeds in Room One. So help your buddies. Practice every chance you get."

For the next hour they practiced shooting in Room One. It was basic stuff. Stationary targets at twenty meters.

Lars was good, better than the other shooters. That first day he scored high on the range, missed Expert by just one point. When they were done for the day, Soldata took them aside.

"Okay boys. Fun time is over. Now that you have fired your weapons, you have to learn how to clean them properly. Every gun ever made is the same, whether it is loaded with bullets or with electronic capacitors. You fire them. They get dirty."

Sergeant Esterhaus added. "Dirty weapons are dangerous weapons. A dirty weapon can lead to a violent discharge and death. Misfires can kill."

Soldata Fifteen resumed its instruction. "The hard part of learning how to shoot is learning how to properly clean the gun after it has been fired. Varnish the contacts. Brush carbon from the filaments. Oil the firing mechanism. The barrel can become pitted by repeated pulse firing."

"Come on, Sarge. We been at this all day long. First the Shoot House, now this. This robot you tagged us with is running us ragged," Jinnaro complained.

"Heh, you knuckleheads, quit bellyaching. You had a good first day in the Shoot House, nothing more."

"But Sarge. We are practically pro shooters. You see Lars's target? Near perfect."

"Don't get a big head, boy. One good target does not an expert make. It takes weeks of determined work to qualify in the Shoot House. And even after you have qualified, your work here is barely half-done. Finally, you should know this one last thing. Once you do qualify on the range, you will no longer be restricted to Post. Think of it as an incentive plan."

Lognasto approved. "Heck of a day. Heck of a first day. Not only are these Anaconda boys teaching us how to kill things. Now I have a fighting chance of getting out of this dump once in a while."

Sergeant Esterhaus explained. "For the right man, one-day passes will be available to get off base on Saturdays or Sundays."

"Just how far do you think I can get on a one-day pass? To see my main squeeze, I will need three days' leave at least."

Sergeant Esterhaus shook his head in disapproval. "Bonker, you will have plenty of free time to pork your girl after you graduate. That is, if you graduate. In the meantime, you meatballs still have much to learn. We are going to make your hands into lethal weapons. Basic knife fighting. Unarmed combat. Garrote. Killing with your hands. Proficient with every weapon in the arsenal. Pulse gun. Bayonet. Metal Storm. Light machine gun."

"Nothing we can't handle, Sarge."

"You are not soldiers yet. First we have to develop your skills as an individual soldier, an infantryman. Then we have to validate your skills as part of a team. Map reading. Small group tactics. Aerial photog analysis. Code breaking. Signaling. That kind of stuff."

•
•

"Okay soldiers, final lesson. Four day-long bivouac in the kona backcountry. We establish a base camp, set up tents and a field kitchen, dig a latrine and fire hole, set out on maneuvers."

At first, Lars was skeptical. But then he thought about it. Perhaps no better place existed for such a vital exercise than the backcountry of Hawaii's big island. Aside from the bugs and humidity and treacherous landscape, it was perfect.

They were presently about two kloms north-northwest of base camp on the leeward side of the island. The trail they were following was steep, up the jagged mountainside, through a series of switchbacks. It began near sea level and climbed to within earshot of the peak 2500 meters above the coastline. The clearing they were now in was about 1000 meters elevation.

"Okay, listen up and pay attention," Sergeant Esterhaus said. "Actual combat is noisy and chaotic. Radios can go on the fritz. Signals can be jammed. Signal lights and the like attract attention. So does barking orders and shouting. So we must have a different way of communicating in the field, a quiet way."

"Some sort of silent comm system, Sarge?"

"Nothing so sophisticated. — Hand signals."

"We give each other the finger in the dark?" Jinnaro quipped.

"Yeah, bend over and kiss your ass goodbye. We're all gonna die," Ned Lognasto taunted.

"Okay, next knucklehead who interrupts me will get down in the brambles and give me one-hundred pushups. Any takers?"

The Sergeant's challenge was met with total silence.

"I thought as much. Moving on then. During actual combat, verbal communications may be impossible and unwise. In the noise and confusion, verbal orders may be misunderstood or misinterpreted. The usual set-up calls for a platoon or other small unit to operate in total silence using hand signals only. Maintaining total operational silence also helps avoid giving away one's position."

Soldata spoke. "To make it realistic, we have set up mobile sim units in the practice field. Sound effects. Holo soldiers. Distracting lights. The sim plateau is about five hundred meters ahead. Stay together now. It is a steep climb."

Lars thought through their earlier briefing. The volcanic slopes of this mountain, Hualālai, and of nearby

Mauna Loa had long possessed ideal microclimes for growing world-class premium coffee.

Mauna Loa was of course much taller than Hualālai at 4205 meters. But both volcanic mountains were home to countless native Hawaiians as well as their very own Camp Anaconda. It was also home to several rare species of amphibians and a few dangerous ones. Hualālai was what they called a dormant shield volcano, though dormant was a relative term. Its last eruption was centuries ago, in 1801.

"Your first test in the sim field will be tonight after sunset," Soldata said. "Adhesive Sergeant Cabot, you will head up Squad One. Ned, you and Jinnaro will head up Squad Two."

Lars spoke out of turn. "Before we get started, I still have one or two questions about these hand signals."

"Yes, Adhesive Sergeant, what is your question?"

"Considering where we are, what is the protocol when visibility is poor? Say in a rainstorm? We get nearly daily cloudbursts around here. Or what about in a thick fog?"

"You are right, kid. The rules change when visibility is poor. Troops have to maintain closer formation or fall back on simple radio codes. Clicking the squelch for instance."

Soldata picked up where Esterhaus left off. "Rough terrain can restrict clear observation. Plus, the enemy might turn visuals to their own advantage. Those visuals can be intercepted. Or the enemy can signal back, creating disinformation."

"Yes, yes, Soldata. But that is a lesson for Day Two," Sergeant Esterhaus said. "Let's stick to the basics on this, our first day, shall we?"

Soldata grew quiet at the rebuke.

Esterhaus continued. "Okay. An easy one first. Anyone know the hand signal for double-time?"

Jinnaro made a fist, pumped it in the air.

"Correct. Make a fist. Raise it to your shoulder. Thrust the fist upward to the full extent of the arm then back to shoulder level. Do this several times rapidly."

"Can we go home now and grab some shuteye?" Jinnaro asked.

"Next one is a little tougher, smart guy. How do you signal 'Danger!' to the other members of your team?"

The Sergeant's question was answered with silence.

"No one?"

Continued silence.

Sergeant Esterhaus explained. "Draw the right hand, palm down, across the neck in a throat-cutting motion from left to right. This is the military's universal hand signal for Danger. Okay, everybody try it once or twice."

Each of the men did as the Sergeant instructed. Some did it several times comically.

"Okay, last one for today. How do you signal the others 'all-stop'?"

Lars raised his closed fist to head level.

"Yes, that's right, Adhesive Sergeant. The raised fist signals freeze or all-stop. Okay, soldiers. That's it for today. This afternoon's feast is military-issue foodtabs. Eat up and get ready for tonight's maneuvers in the sim field."

This should be fun, Lars thought grimly.

He had taken a moment earlier to study topos of the area. They were in an area of the Big Island that once was home to Camp Tarawa, a United States Marine Corps training camp. The camp earned its name from a bloody, ruinous battle that occurred nearly four hundred years ago in the Pacific between the Empire of Japan and the United States during World War Two. The camp was chosen by the Marines for its mountainous terrain, cold conditions, and relative isolation.

Yes, this was certainly going to be fun.

CHAPTER TWENTY-FIVE

No sound is more unsettling than an unexpected shout that wakes you in the middle of the night. It is like a bolt of adrenaline that shoots through your veins like hot fire.

The barracks were dark, though not completely so. Moonlight filtered through the west-facing windows. At the sound, Lars sat bolt upright in his bed. Other men did the same. They had returned only the afternoon before from their four days of maneuvers on the outdoor sim field and had not yet recovered fully from the punishing exercise.

The barracks lights came on. Esterhaus stood at the door. Behind him stood Soldata and the Camp CO.

"I need five volunteers," Sergeant Esterhaus said, his voice booming. "There has been a serious accident. I need five volunteers who are willing to act as a rescue party. Time is short."

The cadets were on their feet, now, ears suddenly alert.

"Cabot. What about you? You are quick-witted. You are a man who can think on his feet. Can I count on you?"

"Due respect, Sergeant. Doesn't sound like you are looking for volunteers. Sounds like you are looking for conscripts. Level with us, Sarge. What has happened?"

"You have heard of the Space Elevator?" Esterhaus asked.

"Who hasn't?" Jinnaro retorted. "Even us uneducated jinks have read the occasional book."

"Well soldier, there has been an accident," Sergeant Esterhaus said. "A terrorist attack, by all accounts. TAT claims responsibility. District Viscount Henry may be among the injured. Details are sketchy."

"TAT? What in blazes is TAT?"

"Terrorists Against Terraforming," Soldata answered. "These people are radicals, zealots. They threaten to destroy years of progress in space. They do not want to see Mars terraformed, something Viscount Henry has been a strong proponent of. They do not want to see any alien environment conquered by tech. They don't want to see Venus terraformed, don't want to see it settled either. And we have already come a long ways along on that one, what with introduction of the trans-comets and all that."

"Sounds like a bunch of wackos, if you ask me. And you want our help to hunt them down and kill them?" Jinnaro asked.

"Nothing so dramatic, I assure you," Esterhaus said. "We have killer robot teams detailed for that task."

"What then?"

"We realize you are not trained for this," the Commandant interrupted. "But there have been multiple attacks tonight, one much earlier this evening. The Depot normally has a certified rescue team on standby to deal with such emergencies. But that team has already been dispatched to another location. It will take us hours, hours we do not have to get another certified team onsite. That is where you men come in."

"Yes, quite right," Esterhaus said, impatient by the Commander's interruption. "The passengers onboard the crippled Space Elevator have only 80 minutes of oxygen remaining before they expire. We are quite pressed for time."

"That's where you are sending us? Up that electrified cable to a half-wrecked Space Car?" Ned Lognasto asked.

"Isn't that what I said?" the Commandant barked. "Sergeant! Is this man deaf and dumb?"

Lars stood up for his friend. "Begging your pardon, Sir. But that is not what you said. For a man arriving here in the middle of the night, hat in hand, asking for volunteers, what is to be gained by impinging another man's intelligence?"

"You would rather be put on report then?"

"I think what my Adhesive Sergeant is trying to say, Commander, is that you have not fully disclosed the nature of the men's mission," Esterhaus interjected.

"Very well. Let me make myself clear. Yes, son, we mean to send you up that electrified cable — as you call it — to a half-wrecked Space Elevator Car. We mean to send you up that electrified cable to rescue the survivors. People onboard will likely be injured or dead. You will take a rapid ascender pod up the cable, a lightcraft we have on standby. We will equip you with spare spacesuits from the secure locker, plus tanks of breathable, water, medical supplies, the whole kit. Are we clear?"

"Crystal," Ned replied tartly.

"Hazardous duty, eh?" Lars seemed to grasp the danger in a way that Ned Lognasto did not. "I would be more than willing to volunteer. But like you said, we are not trained for such an enterprise. Why come to us?"

"You will of course need your skullcaps to prepare for this," Esterhaus said. "We already took them out of lockup. We have them here with us. You will learn on the fly what you need to know. We have instinct modules on standby. The training will take only minutes. We will download everything we have on hand directly into your head. In an instant, you will learn how to be safe in space, how to operate the ascender pod, how to treat the injured and how to get them safely to the Station. Soldata will accompany you."

"Like I said, count me in," Lars said.

"Count me in too," Bonker said.

"Me too," Jinnaro added.

"Okay, the Three Musketeers. Come with me," Esterhaus said.

"Make that four," Ned Lognasto said, stepping forward. "You jinks aren't going up there without me."

"Okay then, boys. Let's saddle up. Grab your skullcaps from the bin. They should be marked. Hook 'em up. Download your learning modules. Get to those people. Save them. Make yourself heroes. We have a jetchop waiting. It's just a short hop across the island to the Depot."

•
•

The data-rush began. It was unnerving, just like the first time. An avalanche of information, a tsunami that drowned out all other thought.

A skullcap was an awesome piece of human engineering. But it could be too much for an unprepared someone.

The four of them plus Soldata were now in a jetchop racing to the Space Elevator Depot where they would board a rapid ascender to vault up the cable to the disabled passenger car.

But Lars was in his own world, an electronic world that was simultaneously real and metaphysical, a world that was topsy-turvy with terabytes of information. He became dizzy and threw up on the floor of the jetchop. No one paid him any attention, as they were all in the same unreal world.

Now, as the skullcap made contact with the e-nodes in his brain, the data-rush was a tidal wave, a flow of information so rapid it became disorienting. In the days since Lars first enrolled at Anaconda, since he uncoupled from his skullcap, he had forgotten how to control the thing, how it made him feel all-powerful, how it made him feel invincible and powerless all at the same time.

Now the feelings came again. The data spun up like a whirlwind —

. . . . The Space Elevator is one of those amazing marvels of human engineering. Skyhook cables constructed from ultra-light carbon nanotubes hang down from a pair of large satellites suspended high above the Earth's surface in geosync orbit. Each cable is attached at one end to a massive counterweight. The pair of orbiting satellites take turns raising and lowering earthbound loads, so as not to disturb their relative positions in the sky. The mathematics are daunting. But the name of the game is the preservation of angular momentum.

Passengers returning to Earth from space, as well as space travelers requiring medical attention stop first at the Space Station. More people crack up on the way home from space than from any other location; thus, the Station houses one of Earth's finest psych wards.

For some, the Station is a stop all its own. Tourists, adventure-seekers, scientists, lovers. To reach the upper post of the Space Elevator from the Station a passenger first has to board one of several small shuttle ships that ferry people back and forth across the short gap that separate the two.

From the upper post of the Elevator to the ground is literally all downhill. While any descent from orbit can be unnerving, the most harrowing return of all is like in the old days, a red-hot drop from orbit, slowed to a jerky stop by parachute.

By comparison, descent by Space Elevator is actually quite pleasant and usually uneventful. Ballast is supplied by ingots processed at the orbiting smelter.

The Skyhook cables that hang from the satellite make the descent more like a rapid, extended

elevator ride than the high-g fall it otherwise would be.

A "steady" line hangs from beneath the floor of the Elevator, like the tail on a kite. Without the steady line, the Space Elevator would swing like a pendulum from orbit, sickening everyone onboard. Plus, the tail is a good way to dispel the potent static charge that naturally builds up on the cable as the Elevator descends through the atmosphere. Motion through a magnetic field generates electricity.

The island they are lowered down onto is the largest chunk of volcanic rock in the Hawaii Free State. The interior of the big island is a topographic mapmaker's nightmare. Tortured rivers, cavernous ravines, lava-belching volcanoes, hidden lakes, sulfur hot springs, intractable jungles. The coastline is more benign: kloms of picturesque beaches; two large modern cities; a myriad of smaller ones.

The landing zone is unmistakably high tech. Viewed from a distance, the landing zone resembles a giant metallic ice-cream cone jammed point-down into a very large hill. The metallic cone is in fact an inverted hollow tower two hundred meters deep, with a gaping maw of a hole up top. The descending Elevator car is lowered into the business end of the cone, still dangling from the Skyhook at the end of a cable that extends all the way to that satellite hanging in geosync orbit and a bit beyond.

If, on the descent from orbit, the dangling Elevator car acquires even the hint of a back and forth rocking motion, it is quickly damped down as the "steady" line beneath the car is secured and the Elevator slips ever deeper into the narrower and narrower recesses of the giant inverted cone.

The "steady" line continues to be reeled in until finally the Elevator comes to rest on a large concrete platform at the bottom of the cone. The end is always the same. After such a long journey, a boisterous cheer will go up from the passengers. *They are home!*

Another hour remains, however, on their trip to terra firma. The passenger compartment has to be separated physically from the descending cable and safely stowed. The cable itself has to be grounded, this to bleed the static electricity that inevitably builds up on the line. Uncoupling the Skyhook cable is a slow process. The kinetic energy of descent — now stored in an orbiting counterweight — will later be transferred to an ascending payload, which can then be hauled up to the Space Station. It is an amazingly modern and efficient system, using simple block-and-tackle physics the Greeks devised nearly three thousand years earlier. Whatever energy is lost to friction in the raising and lowering of loads is reacquired by solar cells, both orbiting and ground-based. No further need for fossil fuels here, or for volatile chemical brews. . . .

Download now complete, the blinding rush of information slowed to a trickle. Today there had been no boisterous cheers at the end of the homebound trip, of course; for no descending Elevator car ever entered that landing cone. It was still dangling precariously from a fractured cable 25,000 meters up. Terrorists had damaged the steady line. Inevitably, static charge built up on the damaged cable. A fire broke out onboard. Cabin pressure collapsed. People died.

Now Lars and three of his cadet brethren were on their way to try and rescue the survivors.

CHAPTER TWENTY-SIX

No matter who sat at the flight controls, a ride onboard a rapid ascender pod was bound to be frightening. *Why should today be any different?*

Today, the pilot was a robot of uncertain origin. Soldata checked the bot's serial number, ran a background check. This particular model had a spotty record. Soldata was not impressed. Smart robots like Soldata had no more interest in dying in a terrible accident than a human did.

The rapid ascender they were riding in was actually a small ship. Some would call it a pod, others an LC, a lightcraft. This particular ship's name was *JumpShip IV.*

Regardless of nomenclature, *JumpShip IV* was something more than a simple pod. It was an enormously sophisticated lightcraft. Such craft were quick and easy to launch. In this instance, the jumpship had been programmed to lock onto the emergency locator beacon of the Space Elevator car and run alongside the connecting cable, a fifth-generation carbon nanotube. The goal was to keep the jumpship flying straight and not overshoot its target.

The ascender pod came equipped with five passenger seats plus a complete complement of emergency gear. Med kit. Pressure suits. Portable life support systems. Umbilicals.

The four men plus Soldata were even now strapped into g-chairs for the short trip skyward. In the next few moments, a full ground-pulse would slam the lightcraft up into the atmosphere. It would be six minutes straight up. Six very intense minutes. Their next stop would be a crippled ship dangling 25,000 meters over their heads.

The launch of a lightcraft was unlike any other.

Had *JumpShip IV* been a solid-fuel rocket like one of those used at the dawn of the space age, there would have been a bright orange flame, followed by a volcano of blinding smoke and a tremendous thundering roar as the big fuel tanks ignited and the towering rocket lumbered slowly skyward picking up speed as it broke its earthly bonds.

But with a lightcraft everything is different. No orange flames. No blinding smoke. No big fuel tanks filled with volatile chemicals. Just raw acceleration. And blinding heat. And ground-rattling vibration. The roar grew exponentially as the lightcraft's acceleration rapidly compressed the air in front of the ship into an increasingly thick wall. Inside, the passengers were compressed into their seats like flattened pancakes.

Then came the air spike. This is where Lars thought he saw the robot pilot flinch. Physics now ruled their destiny. The wall of air that had piled up in front of the vehicle had become superheated by the annular mirror. Now it collapsed in a brilliant flash of white energy. The violent noise abated and the jumpship fairly leapt into space. Only four minutes to low-earth-orbit; two more to docking orbit.

They left Camp Anaconda in a rush. There had been only one delay. The time required to suit-up. Part of the process had been completed onboard the jetchop racing over to the Depot from Camp.

But there was no easy or speedy way to fit a space helmet over a skullcap in a moving aircraft. That had to wait until they reached the Depot. For the moment, the skullcaps bled data into their heads at blinding speed — —

A modern spacesuit is a compound garment. The newest version is called the Mag 10. It has

multiple layers, an inner pressure suit surrounded by a protective outer shell.

Suit technology is a well-established science and has been for nearly one hundred years. For a man to be able to work productively both inside and outside a spacecraft, a suit has to perform several functions —

Maintain stable internal pressure. Higher than normal oxygen levels inside the suit allow for lower overall pressure. The lower the internal pressure, the less mobility is restricted.

Provide a reliable supply of breathable oxygen; eliminate carbon dioxide. These gases are exchanged with the spacecraft through an umbilical or else to a PLSS — a Portable Life Support System. The PLSS is later flushed out and recharged.

Regulate temperature inside the suit. In locations where there is gravity, heat rises. It can be transferred by convection directly to the atmosphere. In space, where there is no gravity, heat can be lost only by thermal radiation or conduction. Advanced suits regulate an astronaut's temperature with an LCVG, a Liquid Cooling and Ventilation Garment. The garment is in continuous contact with the occupant's skin. Heat is dumped into space through an external radiator in the PLSS.

Comm system. Requires an external connection to the umbilical or else the PLSS. The usual method requires that a specialized cap be worn over the head. The caps, which came to be called "Snoopy" caps by early spacemen, have built-in earphones and mic. The name stuck because the color of early caps matched the coloration of a then-popular comic strip character named Snoopy. (For an explanation of the term "comic strip," click here.)

Waste collection. A means for collecting and containing bodily wastes, both solid and liquid. Historically, the solution has involved a MAD, a Maximum Absorbency Diaper. For reasons that ought to be apparent, the diaper is a very unpopular device. The acronym itself was the butt of jokes. Mutually Assured Destruction. A man has to be MAD to use it.

Radiation shielding. A means for protecting the suit-wearer against ultraviolet radiation and micrometeoroids. This protection requires a puncture resistant weave in the shell's outer layers.

Lars learned all of the foregoing in little more than an instant, for that is all the time it took for his skullcap to reach out to the net and inform him. He simultaneously learned about suitports, the breakthrough innovation that revolutionized space travel. It allowed explorers to reach the nearest planets, Venus and Mars.

As far back as the earliest moon landings, it became apparent to Mission Controllers that lunar dust was more than an inconvenient nuisance. In fact, it was a serious hazard that could really muck up a mission. Martian dust is worse. There is more of it, and the dust can be propelled across the Martian landscape at high speed by wind. It blackens solar panels in a matter of hours and often leaves explorers without a source of electricity until the panels can be cleaned.

During exploration, with boots and machinery kicking up a storm of dust, some of that powder inevitably collects on — and sticks to — a man's spacesuit. Later, when the spacesuit is removed upon return to the command module or living quarters that dust can spread like a pathogen throughout the ship. Later still, when the fine dust

settles, it can contaminate and degrade surfaces, not to mention increase the risks of inhalation and skin damage.

Numerous attempts were made over the years to combat the dust problem. One early technique was to wash down the exterior of a suit before a spacejockey disrobed. But this was costly and time-consuming. In an emergency, it was all but impossible to do quickly.

Then one innovative space engineer harvested an idea from science fiction, a novel entry and exit system for exploration spacecraft. That system has come to be known as the Hagarty suitport, after its inventor Walter Hagarty.

Walter Hagarty was an aerospace engineer and visionary. He was also a compulsive tinkerer and habitual user of 3-D printing for developing prototypes. Applying his amazing mind to the problem, Hagarty sat down one day at his drafting table and came up with a solution: the suitport. Nowadays a suitport is considered a practical alternative to the traditional airlock.

A working model of Hagarty's prototype was detailed by his team of space engineers. It was a rigorous invention, one designed for use by astronauts in a hazardous environment and more generally in human spaceflight, especially during planetary surface exploration. The genius of the Hagarty suitport system lay in its design. A rear-entry spacesuit was vacuum sealed and attached against the outside of the spacecraft.

The spacewalking astronaut enters the suitport from inside the craft, then seals up the suit mechanically and goes on EVA. No need for an airlock. No need to de-pressurize the cabin of the spacecraft to exit it.

Space and weight are among the most precious commodities aboard a spaceship. Any device that

consumes less of either is a boon. The Hagarty suitport does both. It requires less mass than a traditional airlock and consumes less overall volume from the spacecraft design.

Because an astronaut returning from a spacewalk in effect leaves his spacesuit "outside" the ship — firmly attached once more to the exterior — his dust-covered spacesuit never actually enters the inside of the spacecraft. Suddenly, dust mitigation becomes a manageable problem. No longer do spacejockeys have to fear cross-contamination of the crew compartment with the outside environment.

Now, as Lars carefully positioned the helmet of his spacesuit over his skullcap and Snoopy cap, he drew a deep breath to flush the adrenaline from his system. What was to come next was bound to be exceptionally dangerous.

CHAPTER TWENTY-SEVEN

Some of what they were about to do had never been done before, not even by the experts. Oh, there were sims and there were failsafes. But sims were programmed in the context of accidents and emergencies that people *expected* to happen, not around those that actually did happen. Those events, the ones no one anticipated, included acts of terrorism. These were in a class by themselves, the Black Swans, a special class of events that included the unknown unknowns.

Plus, every emergency since the dawn of humanity was new in some unexpected way or another. An aerospace engineer cannot plan for a contingency he does not anticipate. Until the *Titanic* sank upon striking an iceberg, no one planned for icebergs. Afterward, everyone did.

Thus today's rescue had to it an element of the heroic. It was literally a trip into the unknown. Its success hinged on untested methods, two in particular.

A lightcraft like their own *JumpShip IV* reached its maximum ascent speed so rapidly, the first problem they faced was how best to slow the craft down in time. If they miscalculated, the jumpship would sail right past the crippled Elevator car, which even now dangled precariously overhead from the shattered cable that still had tenuous hold of it.

Their second challenge was equally daunting. How best to hold the lightcraft stationary and motionless at an altitude of 25,000 meters above the surface. It would take time to effect the rescue of those passengers still alive onboard the broken Elevator car.

The craft had to be held steady and in a fixed position long enough to allow the four adult humans and one robot to make their way from pod to car and back again with the survivors. No chemical rocket could manage such a feat; it could not possibly hover in place for a sustained period.

But a lightcraft could manage it, at least in theory. They would have to lock onto the damaged cable with a gripper, then extend an umbilical between pod and car. No one in the group would give voice to what they each were thinking. To a man they were praying that when the pilot hooked onto the cable, the added weight would not collapse the entire assembly, instantly killing them all.

The solution to both problems lay in the nature of a lightcraft itself. Whereas the spacecraft of yesteryear carried their own source of power, onboard fuel, rocket motors and all the rest — a lightcraft was engineered differently. It rode a beam of high-intensity laser light that was pulsed up to the space vehicle from a transmitter on the ground in Hawaii. It was a complicated arrangement that took a hundred years of tinkering and experimentation to perfect. Though there were accidents along the way, the aerospace engineers working on the project finally came up with an arrangement that actually worked, one that did not malfunction midflight.

The theory behind the revolutionary propulsion system is simple. Light has momentum. Concentrated light has even more. That momentum can be focused by mirrors then imparted to a target. Reflective surfaces at the base of the lightcraft focus the incoming beam of energy into a ring beneath the craft. The focused energy heats the air to a temperature nearly five times hotter than the surface of the sun. This causes the superheated air to expand explosively for thrust.

A fully functional lightcraft has three parts. A forward aeroshell. An annular, ring-shaped cowl. And an aft part consisting of an optic and expansion nozzle.

During atmospheric flight, the forward section compresses the air in front of the craft and directs it to the engine inlet. The annular cowl takes the brunt of the exiting thrust. The aft section serves as a parabolic collection mirror. Think of it like a big magnifying glass, the sort a kid might use to fry bugs on a concrete sidewalk. The mirror concentrates the incoming infrared beam into an annular focus. This provides yet one more surface against which the hot-air exhaust can press. This ingenious design offers the added benefit of automatic steering. If the craft begins to stray outside the diameter of the beam, the thrust inclines and nudges the spacecraft back into line.

We no longer live in a stick-and-rudder world. A mirror inside the craft focuses some of the incoming energy to a location one vehicle-diameter ahead of the spaceship. The intense heat radiated forward creates what aerospace engineers like to call an air spike.

The air spike diverts oncoming air past the vehicle. This reduces drag and practically eliminates unnecessary heating of the craft. By varying the amount of energy the mirror reflects forward, the pilot can control the airflow around the vehicle. This is how mission planners proposed to solve their first problem, how best to slow down the jumpship before it blasted past an altitude of 25,000 meters where the crippled Elevator car dangled from the shattered cable.

Additional beamed-energy spawns a powerful electric field around the rim. This ionizes the surrounding air. The effect is magnified by a superconducting magnet in the fuselage. It forges a powerful magnetic field. The fluid dynamics of an electrically charged plasma dictate that when ionized air moves through an overlapping magnetic and electric field, magnetohydrodynamic forces come into play. These forces accelerate the slipstream to create thrust.

Normally, once the craft reaches an altitude of about fifty kloms, where air becomes scarce, the ship has to switch from riding the laser beam to burning onboard liquid hydrogen propellant. But in this case, the rescue team from Anaconda had to reach barely half that height. The damaged Space Elevator car hung some twenty-five kloms above the ground, not fifty.

At higher altitudes, above fifteen kloms, the mathematics suggested it might be possible to dial down the intensity of the pulsed laser beam in order to balance the force of gravity and allow the craft to hover. This is how they intended to solve Problem Two.

But the solution was both theoretical and temporary, perhaps five minutes at the outside. After three hundred seconds or so, the plasma would begin to break down. Gravity would once again begin to reassert its dominance. The lightcraft, no longer suspended in the upper reaches of the atmosphere by the pinprick of light radiating from its source on the ground, would stall and begin to fall back to Earth. An uncontrolled fall from such a height would likely kill everyone onboard.

So the rescue team had no more than five minutes to make good a rescue and re-engage the laser beam. If mission control re-amped the laser pulse before the ship began to fall off its perch, the craft might yet reach orbit and the Space Station. To keep them from falling to their deaths, the ground-based power station would have to unload its entire energy-pulse in a single, furious blast at the three hundred second mark. A moment later, the pilot onboard the jumpship would have to light up the onboard liquid hydrogen propellant and pray like hell that this thing works.

This rescue method had only been run previously on sims; no actual crew had ever attempted it. Their robot pilot was no more practiced at this maneuver than an ordinary man. Thus, successfully pulling off this stunt was no better than a fifty-fifty proposition.

•
•

Sound waves cannot propagate in an airless vacuum. That is a fact, like gravity.

In practical terms, what this means is that the screams of the surviving passengers were lost on Lars and the others as they made contact. They could of course see their terrified faces. But in terms of hearing anything, they heard nothing across their comm units besides the sounds of their own rhythmic breathing.

Three of the four passengers were clearly terrified out of their minds. The fourth, an older man, was relatively calm. After nearly three hours aloft, waiting and hoping for help, they had maybe thirty minutes of breathable air left in their tanks.

Four survivors. Nineteen dead. TAT's attack had sabotaged the Elevator's steady line, as suspected. Static electricity on the cable had built up to dangerous levels. The violent and sudden discharge of this energy had led to a devastating fire.

The terrible thing about a fire onboard a spaceship is that it may burn for a long time without notice. In space, in the absence of gravity, heat does not rise. Convection is absent. Fires often have no flame. A heat sensor on the ceiling of a compartment, while useful down on Earth when the craft is parked in its lorry, becomes a useless party decoration aloft. Thus, a treacherous fire may be quite hot and quite dangerous, yet remain completely undetected for a long time.

This particular fire started beneath the Elevator floor in the machine works chamber where all the gearing took place. It began more than an hour before the detonation, around the time when the steady line was amputated by the saboteur's explosive device.

When the temperature in the gear chamber rose high enough, the ventilation fans spooled up and fed oxygen to the smoldering flames. Flash fire followed within seconds.

It was only a matter of happenstance and fear that any passengers at all survived the attack. The four survivors were members of the same family recently returned from a stint on Mars. Viscount Morgan Henry was the patriarch of that family. His wife Mary was a bit of a Luddite. Though she would gladly follow her husband anywhere, she had a deep-seated fear of technology. She flatly refused to remove her enviro suit for the Elevator trip home. Moreover, she insisted no member of her family do so either. That insistence saved the lives of the entire clan.

The pressure suits the Henry family wore were insulated. The suits kept the family cool while the other nineteen passengers burnt to death or were smothered by the fumes. Moments later, the intense heat cracked the hull of the ship and the cold vacuum of space breached the interior. The four were now getting by on bottled air, with only half an hour of breathable remaining.

Lars could only imagine the terrible sequence of events. The flash of fire. An instant of bright yellow followed by an instant of horrifying screams. Then a flash of red. Then pitch black dotted by pockets of glowing ambers.

Now, as the lightcraft ascent pod came to a rest beside the charred hull of the Elevator car, the four men from Anaconda scrambled out of their seats.

"Steady the pod," Soldata ordered the robot pilot. "Hold it steady and extend the grabber."

Soldata broke the seal on the airlock, cranked it open. That is when the harsh reality of their situation hit home hard. Two corpses floated lifeless in the chamber. More dead bodies lay in the short corridor beyond. They had died trying to get to their spacesuits.

When Lars saw the first of the dead bodies, revulsion welled up inside him. He thought he would be ill.

Instinctively he brought his hand to his mouth to catch the bile. But the visor on his helmet blocked his hand. Then he remembered. If he threw up inside his suit, he would choke to death on his own vomit. This he had to avoid at all costs.

Lars turned his head, swallowed what he was about to gag on, tried to change the focus of his mind.

"Pull it together," Soldata ordered. "No time for delay."

Lars nodded, tried to slow his breathing. The fire danger had passed. The vacuum of space had zeroed out the remaining fumes. It had extinguished the flames and flushed out the heat.

Lars steeled himself for what had to be done. He grabbed one dead body from where it sat, then another. Ned Lognasto did the same. Jinnaro would not touch the dead.

"Help us, you jink," Lars said.

"Screw off, friend. I'm here to save the living, not dispose of the dead."

Lars was in no mood to argue. There was something exceedingly strange about the corpses, something he had not expected. *The fire had not charred their skin.*

Soldata answered his question before he could ask. One of the benefits of interlocking skullcaps.

"The fire swept through the ship so fast, it consumed every molecule of available oxygen almost instantaneously. The flames burnt themselves out before they had time to do more than singe the hair on their arms."

Lars accepted that answer. It had a certain commonsensical ring of truth.

The singed hair came off, now, like fine dust, as he slid the first two inert bodies out through the airlock and into the vast emptiness of space. The two bodies spun away from the ship and disappeared past the pod into the darkness of space.

But then something happened which changed the urgency of their mission. The Elevator car lurched to the side.

"What the fuck?" Jinnaro yelped, grabbing hold of the bulkhead.

"Steady the pod!" Soldata yelled through the comm at the robot pilot. "Tighten the gripper! If the cable breaks we are all dead!"

The car shuddered for a second time, then seemed to stabilize. "We have to hurry."

Not everyone onboard was dead. The four survivors were in a panic. An older man; a middle-aged woman; a nearly twenty-year-old daughter; and a somewhat younger teenaged boy; all members of the same prominent family. That panic grew sharper with this new development.

"Are you here to save us?" the older man asked, breathing hard.

"We have to move fast. But yes, Sir, that is the plan."

Upon hearing the sound of Lars's voice and getting a better look at the lad through his visor, Viscount Henry judged the boy's age. "Don't tell me they sent a bunch of children to save us instead of a team of seasoned officers? You would think someone of my station would merit more."

"Children dressed in skullcaps," Lars retorted indignantly. "Tall children dressed in skullcaps."

"Struck a chord, did I?"

"I will have you know — we are as well-trained as any seasoned officer. In any event, your station be damned. We were all that was available on short notice. Volunteers to the last. Now stand up, old man. We have less than five minutes to make this thing happen. — Or we all die."

"A skullcap education is no substitute for actual experience," Viscount Henry grumbled, looking around at the other Anaconda cadets.

"If you will permit us, we mean to save you all the same."

"And how do you propose to that, young fellow?" Viscount Henry could just make out the shape of the lightcraft balancing only meters away on a thin arrow of white light.

"We propose to get the four of you onboard our craft just as quickly as we can. Follow orders, old man, and we may all get through this thing alive yet. Keep fencing with me and I guarantee we all die."

"Do you know who you are talking to, boy?"

"As a matter of fact, I do. You are District Viscount Morgan Henry, a very important man. Now can we just skip the exercise in intimidation and get on with today's business?"

"Impertinent child."

"Father, let the boy be." It was a pretty girl speaking now. At least she looked pretty through the fogged visor of his spacesuit. Two things were for certain. She had glowing red hair. And her spacesuit had two well-meaning bulges suitable to house breasts.

"Hurry now," Soldata said. "Only two minutes left before the pulse. I do not know how much longer the pilot can hold the jumpship still."

Soldata grabbed the Viscount's teenage boy and shoved him bodily through the open airlock of the lightcraft. "Quickly. Find a seat." Soldata manhandled the boy's mother the same way.

"Pulse?" Viscount Henry asked breathlessly. "What kind of pulse are we talking about here?"

Lars answered. "This is a lightcraft. At mark five minutes, we will be hit with a mega-pulse from the ground laser unit. The pilot will have to simultaneously ignite the onboard hydrogen fuel. Between the two energy sources we should be vaulted up to the Space Station in a matter of seconds. We have to be strapped in tight by then. Please hurry."

"Good God, no!" the hysterical mother screamed. "Go back to the Space Station? We only just left that horrible place."

"No choice, ma'am. The decision has already been made. Now sit down. Strap in. Shut up. Only 45 seconds."

Viscount Henry's face tightened. "I thought a pulse re-start was still science fiction, a theoretical construct? Has anyone actually done this before?"

"You are about to go down in history as the first," Lars said. "Now shut the fuck up and sit down!"

"Retract gripper!" Soldata yelled at the robot pilot. "Detach from cable!"

"Everyone! Pull your straps tight as you can!" Lars yelled. "Thirty seconds!"

"You volunteered for this mission?" Viscount Henry asked, cinching his restraint. The jumpship shuddered as the gripper was retracted. For an instant, it felt like they were in freefall.

"Something like that," Lars answered. "Anaconda grunt." He turned his head and screamed an order at Soldata. "Seal the hatch! Now!"

"Anaconda. My alma mater." There was a certain admiration in Viscount Henry's voice. "So you really are an amateur."

"I may have been an amateur two hours ago, when we first began. — But not any longer."

"I heartily agree."

"On my mark . . . Five . . . Four . . . Three . . . Two . . . One . . . Mark!"

CHAPTER TWENTY-EIGHT

"A proper lady rewards a man who has saved her life."

Lars liked the direction this was headed. Indeed it was true. He had not only saved her life, he had saved her family's lives as well.

The ride up from the crash site to the Space Station had been eight seconds of pure hell. Every last one of them had passed out on the way up due to the rapid acceleration. Everyone, that is, except for the robot pilot. He had successfully slowed the craft after the pulse-jump and docked it with the umbilical at the Station. Now, three hours had slipped by and she, the young woman he rescued, sat before him in the Station pub.

The girl, Kaleena, had gorgeous red hair and a pretty face. Like the entire complement of crew and passengers onboard the Station, none of them were going any place fast. Until repairs could be made to the cable or a contingent of ordinary shuttles could be dispatched from the ground to pick them up, they were all confined to the Space Station.

"What sort of reward did you have in mind?" Lars asked.

The two sat across from one another, now, in the lounge of the tiny thousand-klom-high pub. The Night Cap Pub, like all the eating establishments up here, was located in the one-g arm of the orbiting Space Station. Food stayed down better with a gravity-assist.

Space Station physics were rather simple. The Station spun slowly on its central tube creating pseudogravity in the outer rim where the living quarters and eateries were housed. The central tube was motionless and gravity-free. Specially machined elevators and stairways linked the two areas.

Lars glanced rapidly about the place and felt a momentary unease. He had no practical experience with bars or with alcohol and certainly not with women. Before today, Perdition's Cup in Hedon City was about the extent of it. That experience had not gone well. He no more fit in here than he had there.

And what if her father saw them together?

Kaleena smiled her best smile, touched his hand from across the table. She had read his mind, seen his furtive looks.

"If we can sneak away from the watchful eye of my father long enough, I can offer you a turn in the sack."

Lars's jaw dropped. He was still a virgin.

"I am not very practiced," he admitted.

"And you think that I am?"

"I am not saying that at all. I just do not want to disappoint you."

"Do I look worried?" she cooed. "We are both adults. But neither of us has ever done it in zero-g. So in that way we are both still virgins."

That made eminent sense to Lars, and he smiled back.

Lars tried to screw up his courage. He looked across the table at this beautiful woman. Kaleena's eyes were unlike any he had ever seen. As he sat there, he felt it happen. The line between love and lust blurred.

"I have been here before," she said, "at the Station. It was our final docking point on the way home from our trip to Mars. That was before we boarded the Space Elevator. I have been told there are zero-g sex rooms in the Station Hotel," she said breathlessly.

"What about your father? The man is a Viscount. Plus, I'm told he graduated from Anaconda. That makes him powerful. And dangerous. If a man like that gets pissed off, he could make big trouble for me at the Academy, have me bilged, get me exiled to some rock in the asteroid belt."

"I can handle my father."

"All daughters think that. Hardly any of them are correct."

The pub was slowly filling with travelers. They were mostly couples on holiday from Earth. Now they were stranded in space for days, perhaps longer. Everyone was bored and nervous. With the Space Elevator out of commission, they had no good way to get back home. The pub was one of only a handful of outlets where the passengers could burn off that nervous energy. That plus the holo-bar one floor up. Inside the Night Cap, the antidote for boredom was a toxic blue-colored drink.

"Some sort of space hooch?" Lars asked as a platter full of them went by riding on a waitress' arm. She was rather lanky and had nice breasts.

"Forget the hooch. And you can forget her. Let's go."

"Go where?"

"To one of those rooms I told you about."

"Are you serious?"

"Do I look like I am kidding?"

"I like the way you think, woman."

"Then you are probably going to like some of the other things I can do."

"Are you talking dirty to me?" Lars asked.

"You are an amateur, aren't you?" Kaleena reached up and undid the top two buttons on her blouse. The crests of her firm breasts greeted his ravenous eyes.

"See anything you like?" she asked.

"Good God, yes." Lars swallowed hard. "Yes, I do."

"Then let's get to it." Kaleena leaned across the small table that separated them and kissed him hard on the lips. Her red-hot tongue searched feverishly for his.

"We need a room." It was everything Lars could do, now, not to lose control.

The Station had a central tube that ran for nearly one full klom from end to end. The tube was not wide — barely forty meters — but wide enough to house (among other things) a bank of zero-g rooms, the kinds with beds, for having sex.

The two lovers moved quickly from the pub to the hotel registration desk. The clerk handed them each a keycard, a Tranquil patch to slap on for nausea while in zero-g, and sent them on their way. They floated down the corridor to the zero-g room, threw open the door and literally flew in the room.

"I want you inside me," she panted. "Make love to me."

Things moved rapidly now. Kaleena's passion had been ignited and she would not be denied satisfaction. She braced herself against the closed door and pressed her body forward against his. Her nipples were hard, like polished stones. They etched out a message of love on his heaving chest.

Kaleena reached down, below his belt, and touched his trousers. The burning heat of his lust was hard, hard against her leg. At its touch, her heart began to race.

Lars found himself swamped by a tremor of hot craving. He had imagined doing such a thing with a girl many times before. The reality was something different from what he expected, something far more scary.

Locked now in tight embrace, the two drifted across the room in zero-g. Like autumn leaves, they settled to the floor in slow motion, a jumble of arms and legs. Weightlessness cushioned their impact.

"This will never work." He panted breathlessly, hands caressing her bosom. "How can we possibly have sex without gravity? As soon as I move on top of you and begin to thrust, my every motion will only serve to push you further away."

"What can we do?" she asked, begging him to hurry. "One of us needs to be fastened down."

"Check the bed. It must be equipped with sleeping tethers."

"Oh, that sounds downright pagan. I cannot remember the last time a man tied me to a bedpost and had his way with me."

"There was a first time?"

Kaleena giggled. Then she tore off her clothes, stripped bare, and launched herself toward the waiting bed. Lars followed in hot pursuit, launching himself along roughly the same trajectory.

The two landed laughing, a spaghetti bowl of arms and legs. "Okay, bub. Tie me up. I am all yours." She lay back, legs up, knees apart.

From where Lars sat, it was a splendid view. Nothing could quite compare with a girl where the cuffs and links matched. Or, as some said, the carpet and drapes. Either way, her red hair and nakedness drove him wild.

For her part, Kaleena executed a quick survey of his nether regions and seemed properly impressed. "Mighty fine kickstand, if you get my meaning."

"Sex by metaphor, is it? Then what say we lengthen that kickstand of mine as far as it will go and see whether or not we can get that motor of yours running?"

"Oh, it is running hot already. Now find those tethers."

Lars fished around and found a set of elastic sleeping tethers attached to each side of the bed. At night, they could be used to prevent a sleeping occupant from floating out of bed.

But the tethers had other uses, more interesting uses. Lars found that by strapping one tether across Kaleena's waist, well below her breasts, he could fix it so she would not float away yet would still have full range of motion with her legs. The idea was slowly forming in his head. Lars was beginning to appreciate why certain adventuresome couples might make their way to the Space Station for purposes of having sex.

The two began to go at it enthusiastically. But no sooner had they begun, than they discovered something new. There were certain wonderful things a lover could do for his mate when unburdened by the evil forces of "up" and "down."

The coupling lasted a surprisingly short time. Something about the setting or the ultra-low gravity or perhaps the fear of being discovered by Kaleena's father made them crest rapidly, almost too rapidly for their own good. Without ever meaning to, they both came almost immediately.

Lars rolled off her, slid a tether across his chest and put a hand on her belly. "Tighten those muscles down there."

"You saying I'm flabby?"

"No, not at all. You have a body that just will not quit, I promise you."

"What then?"

"I'm worried about leakage."

"You cannot be serious."

"Learned it from my skullcap. Everything floats in zero-g. Orange juice, barf, sperm, you name it. It all floats. If you don't want to be combing that stuff out of your hair two days from Sunday, I suggest you tighten those love-muscles of yours real soon."

"Oh, shut up and hand me that blanket. We will keep those floatie things under wraps."

Shortly, Kaleena closed her eyes and fell asleep. A satisfied smile was painted across her moistened lips. Lars stared at her a moment, figured he did pretty good for his first time out, then dozed off himself.

CHAPTER TWENTY-NINE

Lars woke three-quarters of an hour later with an enormous hard-on. At first he was surprised. Then he remembered where he was and what his skullcap had told him about his environment.

Kaleena noticed his erection right off. "Still in need?"

"Ask a man that question and he will always say he is in need. But it isn't me. This place has an awful lot to do with it."

"Space makes you horny?"

"In a manner of speaking. Spacejockeys have a word for it. Extreme morning wood. In zero-g, excess fluids collect in a man's penis while he sleeps. He wakes up this way nearly every day."

"From the size of things, it looks to me more like morning lumber."

"I will take that as a compliment."

"Of course you will. That is how it was given."

"If you think my wooden puppet friend swells with fluids in zero-g, giving me a hard-on, what do you think happens to that cute little button of yours?"

"Button?"

"Yes, you know exactly what button I am talking about, your love-button. Your member swells up just like mine does. — And with pretty much the same result."

"No wonder I am so damn horny," she said.

"That itch of yours is going to need to be scratched over and over again as long as we are here."

“Is that the voice of experience?”

“Not at all. Just stories around the campfire.”

“Well, if the sex up here is so great, why ever leave and go home? Why not stay up here forever, live and fuck in a zero-g environment from now until the end of time?”

“Because weightlessness has it downsides,” Lars said. “Loss of bone mass. Constipation. Upset stomach. Spend too much time in a place without gravity and things will soon start to get dicey. Long-term exposure can be dangerous. That is why they spin the Station. To generate pseudogravity for the safety of its occupants.”

“That is good to know. My father is a space advocate. He does not often speak of such things, bad things. To his mind, space travel is good and can never possibly do any harm.”

“I am sure your father is a smart guy. But prolonged exposure to micro-g is invariably bad. It harms our immune system, for one. Our lymphocytes, which are our body’s self-defense mechanism, can become seriously damaged by weightlessness. Without that army of white-blood cells to help the body fight disease, it doesn’t take long before the immune system begins to break down. At the cellular level, certain elegant signaling systems do not function properly in zero gravity. Just one more reason why a woman must absolutely avoid getting pregnant while in space. Fetuses do not develop properly. Babies born in zero-g lack the strength to thrive once they are returned to a gravity well.”

“I thought you were a preemie cadet? How does a drill bit like yourself come to know so much about medicine and biology?”

“Mate a skullcap from the Feldman Neurological Institute to a nerd with a love for science and mathematics and you get a big dumb know-it-all.”

“A Feldman, eh? That is one of the best. You must come from money.”

“No money in my family. Our only claim to fame is my grandfather.”

"And who might he be?"

"General Felix Weinger. Retired."

"The man who assassinated Rontana?"

"One and the same."

"This man, your grandfather, is in history books. He usually gets the better part of a chapter. War hero and all that."

Lars said nothing.

"And to think I have just had sex with a man that is heir to such a bloodline. Maybe I should not have used protection. Come to think of it, your little wooden puppet friend looks so lonely, like he does not have a friend in the world. Should we do something about that?"

"I admit. The little fellow is lonely. He may need some handholding, maybe a kiss on the forehead for good luck."

"Oh, I just love it when you talk dirty. You simply must have your way with me again."

"If you insist."

"I surely do."

•
•

Lars woke for a second time. He crawled out from beneath the sleeping tether and fairly glided across the room to a small aft alcove. There were windows back there, fairly large ones, where a person might look out into space, as well as handholds so a person could maintain their orientation.

The windows were darkly tinted now, to protect a looker's eyes from the unfiltered sun, but also to prevent voyeurs from catching a glimpse of couples having sex in the zero-g rooms. Voyeurism was a favorite pastime for visitors and staff alike in the lounges of the main part of the Station. The tinting had the added benefit of keeping the small rooms from overheating when the central tube swung into the sun.

Lars steadied himself on the handhold, took a look around. Above him was the main part of the Station, all spokes and girders and struts. He could see it through the dark glass, but just barely. One thing stood out clearly, though — a trans-comet barreling its way through the ether toward its eventual rendezvous with the planet Venus.

The trans-comet was shiny far out of proportion to its size. This because the dirty ball of ice was wrapped in a giant manmade plastic liner. As always and forever, Man was fiddling with his environment, molding and reshaping it more to his liking, just as he had been doing since that morning long ago, when he climbed down out of the trees, stood on two legs and stumbled out onto the African savanna. This constant fiddling is what had set the Terrorists Against Terraforming in motion to begin with. Their act of terrorism is what had, in turn, brought him, Lars, to this very spot. *Curious how the world works.*

Kaleena woke, saw him by the window. She propped herself up on one elbow, said her head hurt and that she was hungry.

Lars signaled for her to come join him. She launched herself out of bed and in his direction. On the way over, she tangled herself up on his trousers still hanging in mid-air. By the time Kaleena arrived on target, she was hurtling across the room in an out-of-control spin. She crashed into him then ricocheted into the wall.

"Damn. That hurt."

Kaleena rubbed her head, shoved his trousers angrily away. "Didn't your mother ever tell you to hang up your clothes before bedding a girl?"

"Sweetheart, my mother would have a cow or other sacred animal if she knew I had bedded a girl."

Kaleena was still spinning. Lars laughed at her antics, grabbed onto her arm to steady her motion. He knew the score, courtesy of his skullcap.

"Girl, what catches most people off-guard in zero-g is how much rotational velocity they can acquire when they push off a wall or stationary object like a bed. A person can pick up a terrific amount of unintentional spin. Plus, you cannot just put anything down, not in a room where there is no gravity, not like you can on Earth."

Lars continued. "There is always a certain amount of inertia remaining when you move about. Whatever you put down — be it a book or an empty milk glass — will inevitably float off, causing you trouble later on. An hour afterward, you get bopped in the head — or your friend does — by the book you set down earlier. Air currents mainly. But also ship movements. They both cause objects to move off slowly from where you left them. That includes clothing you ripped off in the heat of passion."

"How dare you lecture me at a time like this. Do you have any idea how much my head is pounding? I suddenly have a terrible headache."

"The techs call it grav-head. It comes courtesy of the laws of fluid dynamics in micro-g."

"Could you please stop spewing physics and tell me what the hell to do about it?"

Lars reached into his kit and handed her a pill. "When you spend too much time in zero-g, the fluids in your body try to redistribute themselves. The same thing happens to everyone when they are weightless. There is no escaping it. Clogged sinuses. Stuffy nose. The symptoms can make you feel as if you have a real bad head cold. At least until you become accustomed to it. Plus, you may find yourself needing to pee all the time."

"Yeah, now that you mention it. That is what first woke me up. Then came the headache."

"The overwhelming need to pee will get you every time. That is just the body dumping what it considers to be excess fluid. You will be peeing constantly until your body establishes a new equilibrium. But get ready. You are just going to love that zero-g toilet."

Lars pointed to a small alcove adjoining their bedroom. "It is really nothing but an inverted vacuum cleaner with cushioned straps to hold you down. Me? — I find the whole damn thing quite disturbing."

"Maybe a little mood music would help," Kaleena said. "But for the life of me, I cannot seem to find a radio pod in this place, not even a vid."

"Sorry. But there are no electronics in the central tube."

"Not anywhere?"

"Nope. Not in the zero-g rooms anyway."

"Why not?"

"It is the same old problem of containing free liquids. Remember what I told you about those floatie things after we had sex?"

"Okay, nothing to drink, nothing to eat, can't take a pee. I still have a headache and I am still hungry. Can we please go back to the grav part of the Station already?" Kaleena said.

"Yeah, I think we both have had enough zero-g for one day. Tranquil patches don't last more than a couple hours."

"That is why there is a two-hour limit on the room, isn't it? The hotel manager mentioned it when we checked in. But I just could not understand why."

"Yeah, most people don't need long. They just need time enough to get it on with their mate so they can brag to the folks back home, tell them of their achievement. But when they are done doing the deed, they all want to get back to grav as soon as they possibly can."

"It was fun though, wasn't it?" Kaleena said.

"Could it ever be anything but?" Lars asked.

"Now you are talking psychology, not biology."

"Well then let's not talk either. Let's talk physiology instead," he said.

"Now you have really lost me."

"What I am trying to say, Kaleena, is that you are going to need help getting dressed. In a place where there is no gravity, it is not so easy for a person to just sit down on the edge of the bed and slip on his shoes without help. So let me help you, okay?"

"You helped me take them my clothes off. So I guess it is only fair you help me put them back on again."

Together, the two of them floated back to where their clothes hung. Some still dangled like spider webs in mid-air. Others had moved off to nearby locations. Then, with each other's help, the pair dressed and made their way back up to the restaurant level. All the eateries were in one of the outer spokes comprising the Ferris wheel portion of the Station.

The trip included a ride in one of the Station's infamous elevators. Their nasty reputation was well-deserved. As the elevator car journeyed outward from the central tube to the outer rim, the local gravity changed from zero to one-g. The elevators were known to make people sick to their stomach. Fortunately for Lars and Kaleena, today's ride was short and slow. So no harm, no foul.

This second visit to the Space Bar was in many ways a replay of their earlier visit. Lars was still quite the fish out of water. This was a problem. Men are creatures of habit, even young men. They do not care to have their routine disturbed. Men want their favorite chair, their favorite vid, their favorite woman, doing it to them their favorite way. The rest of the time, they like to be left alone.

"This place gives me the creeps," Lars said.

"You haven't seen anything until you have been to Saron's Place at the nexus of the Mars Colony. Now there is a pub to write home about."

"Do tell."

"I snuck into Saron's Place once with my boyfriend."

"You have a boyfriend?"

"You are kidding me, right? I'm cute. I'm smart. I attract boys like a magnet. My family lived on Mars for six months. Do you really think in all that time I had no suitors?"

Lars did not know what to say.

"Now . . ." Kaleena said. "Are you going to let me tell my story or not?"

"Yes. Please go ahead."

"My boyfriend and I snuck in the back. The place was a jungle — hot, sweaty, filled with evil and pungent smells. Everyone in the place was a deranged animal of one sort or other, even the holos. Merc marines. DUMPSTERS. Chem dregs. Coyotes like that. If there had been police, which there was not, they would have traveled in pairs for protection with guns loaded."

"Weren't you scared?"

"Yes, of course. It was a dirty rat-trap. Some merc marine with bad breath and dirty hands tried to make a move on me. I hightailed it out of there."

"And your boyfriend?"

"I didn't see him again until the next day. They beat the crap out of him. After that we never went out again."

"What a great story." Lars laughed. "But this place is different, isn't it? Clean. Nearly antiseptic. No rotten smells. No shady characters. Good lighting. Comfortable chairs."

"It is awful, isn't it?"

"You want to leave?" he asked.

Her hands were on the table, now, reaching for his. "Let's eat something then fly back to that zero-g room to have another go at it. I think we may still have another half-hour left on our room rental."

There was a small loaf of hot bread on the table. She hungrily broke off a piece. Her headache was already starting to melt away.

"I thought you had had enough of zero-g?"

"Can't a girl change her mind?"

"Honestly, had I known the Space Station would make a girl so horny, I would have brought one here ages ago." Lars squeezed out some butter from the tube and spread it on a bread slice of his own. Then he signaled the waiter for a second time to come over.

A minute later, the waiter finally made his way to their table. He had an impertinent, unpleasant air about him.

"I will be with you in a minute," he said.

"What is wrong with right now?" Lars snapped impatiently. "We have already been waiting five minutes for service."

"There is only one pub on this tub, Bub — and this be it. You don't like the service? Feel free to step off any time."

Lars felt a flash of anger. He instinctively tightened the muscles in his jaw. "Feel free to step off? That is how you want to talk to me?"

"It's okay, Lars. Let it go," Kaleena pleaded. "We do not want a scene."

"Yeah, Lars, let it go," the waiter parroted, staying just beyond Lars's reach.

"But you said you were hungry." By then, Lars had decided that he wanted to be anyplace but here.

"We will order in room service," she said.

"Yeah, you do that," the waiter scoffed as he walked haughtily away.

"Now who is stepping off?" Lars shouted after him, fists clenched. But the waiter shrugged his shoulders and headed back to the kitchen.

"Let it go, Lars. I would much rather have another taste of you than eat in this dump."

She grabbed what was left of the loaf of bread and stuffed it in her handbag. Lars pocketed the tube of butter.

"If it is another taste you want, it is another taste you will get."

•
•

It was unhurried lovemaking at its best.

Rather than take another zero-g room, they went straightaway to the hotel located upstairs from the pub.

The room was not much. Unstructured living space was at a premium onboard the Station. But the room did have a bed. One of those plump, oversized affairs with a brass headboard and a nightstand on either side. The floor was covered in a thick blue pseudo-carpet. The windows, which looked out on the verdant Earth below, were dressed only in auto-shades. The room lights were low.

She came to him at the window. He was watching North America go by. The sun had set. The coasts were aglow with light. So were the shores of the Great Lakes, as well as all the major rivers and their tributaries. Mankind loved his water. It made transport cheap and commerce possible. Every civilization, before or since, has set up shop along the shores of some lake or river.

Now came the less populated northern latitudes. Newfoundland. Greenland. Iceland. Such a strange little island, that one. A cold world stripped to its essential. Geography reduced to geometry. No forests. No visible vegetation. Black seas. Elemental landscape.

She pointed out Ireland on the western fringes of the approaching continent. Said it was her family's ancestral home. Then a strip of water and more lights to the east.

Kaleena wrapped her arms around his waist, pressed her head into the small of his back. The muscles of his abdomen rippled beneath his shirt. The tension in his chest brought forth memories of their first time together. She quivered, now, at the thought of the two of them joined again at the hips.

He turned in the circle of her arms to face her. He kissed her on the forehead. She sighed warmly in response.

He worked his lips down to her cheek, then to her neck.

Now Kaleena took control, her hungry mouth devouring his lips and tongue.

Neither of them wanted to rush. It would be over soon enough in any event.

They undressed each other slowly, deliciously, button by button, clasp by clasp. Their clothes fell into two neat little piles on the floor. Panties and underwear remained unshorn.

Still standing, they kissed, tongue on lingering tongue. He pressed her to him, hands on her bottom. She moaned softly, feeling his hard, young body against hers.

They moved to the bed without saying a word. He peeled off his underwear and tossed them to the floor. She did the same.

Kaleena lay back full-length on the sheets, inviting him in. Hips encircled hips, thighs pressed against thighs. It was instinctual lovemaking, the hallmark of inexperience.

A moan escaped her lips. His breath came faster, as did hers.

For several long minutes they were joined together, bodies pressed tightly, as if one.

Then it was over. In a warm explosion of energy, it was over.

Satiated at last, Kaleena rolled off him and they lay apart. Gradually, their heart rates returned to normal, and Kaleena slid blissfully to sleep, a contented smile on her lips.

At that singular moment in time, life seemed awfully sweet.

But the knock on the door changed everything.

CHAPTER THIRTY

"Oh, my God. It's my father. He is standing in the hallway outside our door."

Kaleena was peering at the monitor. There was an IDcam located beside the inner door of their Space Hotel room.

"Open the door, Kaleena. I know you are in there." Viscount Henry's voice was stern and uncompromising.

Kaleena screwed up her courage and opened the door about one-third of the way. She blocked her father's entrance with the full of her body.

"Do you mind telling me what is going on here?"

"How did you find me, Father?" Kaleena was still blocking the door. Inside, Lars was throwing on his clothes, brushing his hair. "Did you have us followed?" she demanded to know.

"Don't be silly, child. Your mother saw the two of you in the Space Bar. Your boyfriend was making some sort of a scene. She called me to come get you. I went to the Front Desk. They know me there by face. Now are you going to let me in or not?"

"Not so fast, Father. I am no longer a child."

"I will be the judge of that. Anyway, your age is not at issue here."

"What then? Keeping up appearances?"

"Is that so much to ask? I am a Viscount after all. My face is known throughout the free world — and much of it that is not free. My reputation is impeccable, beyond reproach. Why must you besmirch it?"

"That was certainly not my intent. But I must be free to live my own life, Father."

"Not yet, my child. Not yet. Now stand aside and let me in."

Kaleena moved out of the doorway and Viscount Henry followed her into the room. He took one look at Lars and harrumphed with disapproval.

"I might have known. Our boy-hero. Have you taken advantage of my daughter?"

"Father . . ."

"Sir. I did no such thing."

"You, young man, are hip deep in sheep manure. What price do you think ought to be paid for your insolence?"

"Price?"

"The question of price is strictly rhetorical. I have already made my decision. Your impertinence has earned you one month hazardous duty doing drill bit work here at the Station. Then we shall see. Maybe six months hard labor on Mars will serve to teach you some manners. As for you, young lady. You have earned yourself two bodyguards round-the-clock for six months. You will not be able to make a move without me knowing."

"That's not fair, Father."

"With respect, sir," Lars said. "What can you possibly have to gain by punishing your daughter? Or me, for that matter? I saved your life, remember? I saved the lives of your entire family. Why not just forget what happened here today between Kaleena and me? Allow me to return to the Academy. Allow me to return to Anaconda. Let me complete my course of basic training. Shouldn't my volunteering for a suicide mission count for something?"

"It counts for plenty, sure. I have spoken with your commander. If not for your heroism, you would be behind bars facing much worse. But rather than having you charged with a crime and jailed. Rather than blemishing your record forever. I am going to give you a chance to work off your egregious mistake. It was a spectacular blunder you made with the wrong woman, my daughter."

"That's it then? You have decided my fate? Judge and jury?"

"Yes, son. Judge and jury."

Lars shook his head, looked at Kaleena, reluctantly accepted his sentence.

Viscount Henry motioned to the door, still ajar. "Follow these men, son. Do whatever they tell you to do and do not resist in any way. That is an order. I expect my orders to be obeyed."

The two uniformed men at the door were of a size that a smaller man like Lars would not dare argue with or fight.

"Am I under arrest?" Lars was incredulous.

"Daddy! You are arresting this sweet boy? I love him!"

"Oh, for goodness sake, child. What does someone your age know about love? Isn't it about time you grew up?" Then he turned to Lars. "Think of it as detention, not arrest."

"Oh, that sounds so much better," Lars jibed.

"I will not ask again," Viscount Henry said sternly. "Follow these men or else."

CHAPTER THIRTY-ONE

"Here's the thing, kid. There are about ten dozen ways to kill yourself working in space. Truth is, we lose a newbie rook to an accident just about every month. They are all young, arrogant, and stupid."

The speaker was a Sergeant Major in the Space Corps. His unit's portfolio was maintenance and repair of the Space Station. He administered a crew of merc marines, roughnecks really, who did much of the heavy lifting. Today's repair was simple by comparison to most of their contracts. So he was even now training rooks on the job.

"You boys have been placed in my custody for 30 days. You are all supreme fuck-ups in one way or another. That is why I am stuck with you. I do not much care whether you go home dead in a box or whether you go home alive in a travel pod. Either way, your ass belongs to me for the next 30 days. So pay attention and don't waste my time with dumb-ass questions."

Aside from Lars and Sergeant Major Grovosky, there were two other team members in the Ready Room, young men both. Lars had just met them, Barley and Oats. The Ready Room was located at one terminus of the zero-g central tube. Exiting the Station from the nearby airlock without the interference of gravity made it easier for spacewalkers to heft the necessary toolbelts and shoulder paks.

"This is the protocol," Sergeant Major Grovosky said. "We move from the Ready Room to the Suit Room to the airlock. Three moves. Once we are suited up and the air is evacuated from the airlock chamber, we move outside. Then we crawl around outside on the skin using the handholds until we locate the node we are looking for, node 22FZ. Outside, on the skin, we use a curvilinear grid system to keep from losing our bearings. Node 22FZ is the grid-mark nearest to where the damaged fuel cell is housed. We pull the fried fuel cell, pop in a new one, check the power couplings, close the compartment, come home."

Grovosky continued. "Each man on the team operates as a self-contained unit. He wears a Portable Life Support System, a PLSS, to maintain suit pressure. The PLSS also handles urine and fecal matter and keeps the internal environment within acceptable limits."

Barley raised his hand. "How much these things weigh, Sergeant Major, these Portable Life Support Thingies?"

"You really are a dim bulb, aren't you? Weightless means weightless, boy. Here in the central tube, the tools and backpaks you wear weigh nothing. Zero. Nada. Nothing. You and everything you wear or carry are weightless when we enter and leave the airlock. But don't get used to it. The Station spins. We spin with it. There is pseudogravity, progressively more of it the further you journey outward toward the rim from the center. You will weigh plenty before we are done. Gravity is earth-normal at the outer ring."

"You mentioned tools and toolbelts." Lars asked the question carefully. He did not want to risk being berated by Grovosky as Barley had been. "I don't know what tools to take. — Or how to use them."

"We will get to that soon enough, newbie. First we need to see the technician in the Suit Room for gear. Once we have suited up and transitioned outside, we will need to swing out chimpanzee-style on the exterior rungs to the busted fuel cell at 22FZ."

Lars found that he was not at all scared by the prospect of exiting the craft to perform a hazardous space job. He harkened back to his grandfather's words to him as a boy, how he could be fearless when others froze, what Flix had described to him as the Yeager Syndrome.

As the spacewalkers entered the domain of the ops man in the Suit Room, he handed them spacesuits. The first three suits he tendered were Mag 10 spacesuits, one to Sergeant Major Grovosky, one each to Barley and Oats. When it came Lars's turn to be handed a suit, the specialist handed him a Mag 8 from the suit locker. It clearly had seen better days.

"I have to settle for old tech?" Lars could not hide his disappointment.

"Get with the program, boy. It is old tech or no tech," Sergeant Major Grovosky barked. "You choose. But I have to warn you. Should you refuse to follow orders. Or should you refuse to do as you are told. You will go straight into lockup. Viscount Henry's orders. I guess you should not have been steaming up the sheets with his daughter."

Barley laughed. Oats snickered.

Lars relented. "You will get no argument from me, Sarge. It has always been my life's ambition to wear old, worn-out tech. Thank you so much for giving me the chance."

"Look, kid. The Mag 8 is easy," Grovosky said. "Step in, lean back. The Mag closes around you automatically. It conforms to your body shape. A tech-shirt is built into the lining. It talks to the life support system. It tells the system how you are doing temp-wise and all. Put on the helmet, strap on the PLSS. It will hook you up to the breathable right away. Now go ahead. And make it quick. You have wasted enough of my time already with your pointless gab."

Lars did as he was told. When the Mag 8 began to close around him, Lars felt pain in his back and thigh muscles. He winced.

"Do not hold your breath," Grovosky ordered. "The suit will misjudge your size. It will get too tight. Relax. Breath normally."

Lars did, and the suit loosened noticeably.

"Never been in a spacesuit before?" Grovosky harrumphed. "The inside of a spacesuit is anything but smooth. In fact, it is quite rough. A latticework of internal stiffness. Bearings. Joints. Seams. After a couple hours battling physics and gravity inside a Mag 8, a man's body becomes a human mountain range of bumps and nasty bruises."

The suit tightened around Lars and his helmet locked into place. When all the lights shone green, the Sergeant Major hit the failsafe. The fans snapped on and the atmosphere was evacuated from the airlock.

"Sixty seconds!" Sergeant Major Grovosky said. "Sixty seconds to space vac."

There was the sound, now, of rushing air. It was followed a moment later by the creak of the airlock's outer door opening. Then, complete and utter silence. It was eerie. The vacuum of space deadened sound like a blanket of freshly fallen snow in winter. From here on out, they would have to use their comm whenever they wanted to talk.

The space beyond the airlock was a vast, star-flecked emptiness. The team was presently in the shadow of the Station's rim. That meant they were in the dark. Neither the Earth nor the Sun was presently visible. But, as the Station turned on its axis, they would spin into the light and then later, back out again. For a short while, crescents of earthshine would become visible and then disappear.

With the Station spinning slowly and g-forces tangential, every direction was "down" — down and out for a million kloms.

"Men. Pay attention. I want no mistakes," Sergeant Major Grovosky said. "As you come out of the airlock, make sure your safety line is snug and secured properly.

Be sure it passes twice through the beryllium copper ring at the outside rim of the airlock."

Grovosky was quoting Space Corps protocol. Yet, even going by the book, with safety lines secure and snug, every space repair remained an inherently dangerous enterprise. Some jobs were like that. The risk came with the territory. Coalminers, policemen, welders on a skyscraper. All dangerous jobs. These four men had to excise a damaged fuel cell and replace it with a brand new one.

Keeping the Station operational was a fundamentally different task from keeping other space vehicles up and running. The Station was immensely more complicated. Plus, it remained aloft and exposed to uncountable space perils for decades, not weeks or months. Damage from micrometeors, radiation exposure, enormous changes in heat and cold, structural stresses resulting from ships constantly docking and departing. The list was long.

To allow for its nearly constant maintenance, the outside skin of the Station was neither sleek nor smooth, certainly not airline-fuselage smooth. Unlike a jetchop or passenger aircraft, which had to contend with the drag caused by air friction, the Station orbited well beyond the thickest portions of the atmosphere.

Instead of having a smooth exterior, the Station was blanketed outside with handholds, thousands of them. They were for the convenience of roughnecks like these men, drill bit types who — at great personal risk — serviced the Station inside and out, as well the ships that docked there from time to time.

Grovosky explained. "When we get over to grid-mark 22FZ, you will find that there is an external protection plate that covers each fuel cell. The plate itself is held in place by a series of large bolts."

The Sergeant Major's voice boomed over the Snoopy cap sewn inside their spacesuit helmets.

"The protection plate needs to be removed carefully. No accidental discharges, folks. An errand spark can make for a very bad day. Fuel cells use volatile chemicals to generate electricity. We do not want a sympathetic explosion."

"Sympathetic?" Barley asked. "Like a soupy Valentine Day's card?"

"Every outfit has to have either a smart-aleck in the mix or an idiot. Now they send me little boys who are both," Grovosky grumbled. "Sympathetic explosion. Where one explosion sets off another that sets off a third, and so on, in a violent chain reaction."

"An outcome we wish to avoid," Lars said.

Grovosky nodded. "I am not even sure why this one blew up. It is quite unusual. They are usually quite stable."

"Which makes this one more dangerous," Lars said.

"Bright boy." Grovosky nodded again. "Onboard the Station we have dozens upon dozens of tanks of compressed oxygen and hydrogen. All these many tanks line the insides of two of the Station's eight main radiating spokes. The tanks are connected to a series of fuel cells. Each fuel cell is outfitted with a panel of catalyzing electrodes. When the two gases flow into the fuel cells, they react with the electrodes. The two gases, oxygen and hydrogen, combine to produce three things the Station needs very badly. — Electricity. Water. Heat."

"Okay, Sergeant Major. We get it. We have to be careful. But your telling us to be careful will not make us more careful."

"You truly are an idiot, Barley, a veritable mloron. In a weightless environment, a man does not use his legs much. He moves himself around with his arms, thus the handholds everywhere. A rook newbie like yourself constantly grabs onto things. It is instinctive. But it is also wrong. When a man works a thousand kloms up on this, the really high steel, he has to break down and re-learn nearly every physical act he once did back on Earth without a second thought. It does not matter whether you are taking a shit or tightening a bolt, nothing is the same."

Sergeant Major Grovosky continued. "Don't get cocky, boys. At first, your tendency up here will be to grab tightly onto things to support your body weight, just like you would back home. But don't. Resist the temptation. Learn instead to grasp things more lightly, maybe with only one or two fingers.

"Now follow me," Grovosky said, and he pointed.

Lars started up then stopped, overcome by a momentary bout of dizziness. It was evolution wreaking havoc with his balance. That monkey we all evolved from does not want to tumble out of his tree. Whether a man likes it or not, his brain quickly decides which way is up and which way is down. It is an amazing feat, especially when you consider that it makes absolutely no difference whatsoever when a man is weightless.

When Sergeant Major Grovosky saw Lars hesitate, he laughed. "Half the spacejockeys that work the Station vomit the first time out. Not a good idea, I can assure you. Plus, most men hurt. Severe back pain is not uncommon. In the absence of gravity, the spine stretches. Not bad if you have arthritis. Otherwise, it sucks."

The team inched their way, now, away from the central tube and out along one of the many struts that held the giant Station together. Their weight increased almost immediately. And it increased more, the further they moved away from the zero-g center. Their legs drifted out, feet pointing away from the center of spin. The additional weight of the toolbelt and PLSS added to the stress on their arms. It became increasingly more difficult for the men to maintain a firm grip on the handholds.

Lars completed a quick inventory of the tools on his external toolbelt. It was quite a list. Standard adjustable wrench, manual ratchet, vise grip, cutter, deadblow hammer, spool of 5th-generation beryllium copper duct tape. Other men carried other tools — an electro-solder gun, a pair of pneumatic pliers, a Pigtail, a Bolt Gun, and a riveter. The Bolt Gun was the same kind of high-powered gun alpine climbers used to secure a climbing bolt to solid rock when making an ascent up the side of a mountain. Parts were carried in either a front or backpak.

"Okay, we have about forty more meters to go," Sergeant Major Grovosky said. "Move slowly. Stay on your safety line. Hold tight to the grips."

There were handholds every meter or so around the circumference of the skin of the Station's superstructure. The handholds ran in both directions, up and down, around both hemispheres of each spoke.

There were footholds too, pads actually, made from strips of magnetic-Velcro. The magVel pads meshed with similar material sewn into the soles of each man's boots. It was also sewn into the palms of his gloves and the material covering his knee. A spacejockey could thus work kneeling, standing, or squatting. There were safety lines, of course, and mechanical ascenders to help them "climb" up the fuselage when the ship's gravity was pulling them the other way.

But nothing substituted for smarts and caution. Lars had an adequate supply of each. Grovosky had more.

"Bring that Pigtail over here, Barley," Sergeant Major Grovosky said. "Unhook it from your belt and bring it over to me right away."

Barley reached for the closest handhold then stopped short. He knew he was supposed to swing hand-over-hand out to the spot where Grovosky had tied off his safety line waiting to yank out the damaged fuel cell.

But for some reason he could not move. All infinity was spinning beneath his toes. The thought crossed his mind. *One wrong move and they were all dead.*

"Ah, the Pigtail," Grovosky said with some admiration, still waiting on Barley to deliver. "My absolute favorite space tool. An overgrown cordless drill on steroids. The Pistol Grip Tool."

"Sergeant Major, it sounds to me like you two are in love. You use that tool with your wife in the bedroom at night?" Oats remarked.

"The Sarge isn't married," Barley said, afraid to let go of the handhold.

"So he uses that Grip Tool on his own self?" Oats cracked.

Oats and Barley broke up laughing. They thought themselves quite clever.

"Knock it off, you two," Grovosky barked. "Now hand me that tool, will you? A Pigtail saves a man's arms."

Barley again began to move in the direction of the Sergeant Major with the Pigtail still attached to his belt. But no sooner did he again begin to move, than he became disoriented and froze into place.

"Let's go, soldier. Move, move, move. We're running short on breathable."

Barley was hanging by both hands from one of the beryllium copper rings. But he was nowhere near the compartment that housed the damaged fuel cell they were here to replace.

"Let me get him," Lars offered.

"Get the tool, not the kid. I need the tool."

Lars nodded his understanding and began to move in Barley's direction. He found that it was no great trick to hang by his hands and wheel himself out to where the petrified soldier clung to the fuselage, stalled.

Once Lars had worked his way over to the other man, he fluidly transferred the Pigtail from Barley's belt to his own.

"Hang tough. You will be okay," Lars said. Barley had succumbed to his instincts. He had looked down, been overcome by an attack of agoraphobia and nearly passed out. A fear of open spaces was another part of our evolutionary past.

"Time's a wasting," Sergeant Major Grovosky barked. The replacement fuel cell, along with the attendant tubes and bushings and other repair gear hung from the sergeant's shoulder in a sort of backpak. He had winched the pack tight back in the airlock before they exited.

Lars removed the tool from Barley's belt, handed it across to Oats, who handed it across to Grovosky. Grovosky took the Pigtail, slowly fitted the grip to the head of the closest bolt on the protection plate. Since ordinary steel turned brittle in the intense cold of space, all their tools were made of a beryllium copper alloy.

Lars grabbed Barley's arm, tried to steady him. The spacesuit impeded him more than he cared to admit. The gloves were clumsy. The knee and elbow joints were stiff. He was already tired. It was hard, exhausting work. He was becoming winded, and he had only been at it fifteen minutes.

Meanwhile, Grovosky was hard at work. He loosened the protection plate that housed the ruptured fuel cell. The bolts were designed not to screw out all the way. This was a failsafe to prevent the bolts from being dropped or lost by a careless man. Up here in space, at orbital speeds, anything not strapped down, anything floating loose, could become an unguided missile that might strike a man or a piece of equipment with devastating results.

Grovosky delivered a short sermon while he worked. "If the business end of a power drill like the Pigtail is spinning clockwise, the tool wants to ignore the bolt and spin you the other way, counterclockwise. A man must learn to adapt. Should there ever come a time when I trust you enough to let you use one of these gizmos, make damn sure the tool isn't pushing against the weak side of your hand. Otherwise, you will exhaust yourself in nothing flat."

Sergeant Major Grovosky loosened the last bolt, popped the protection plate off the panel and studied it closely. He craned his neck, took a gander inside the box.

"Can't see a damn thing. Bring over that light, Oats. Shine it in here." Grovosky pointed.

Oats positioned a lightstick so they could both see better. He drew a sharp breath. The motherboard and microworks were blackened and melted.

"Damn thing is fried. If I did not know better, I would call this a case of sabotage," Grovosky said, his brow creasing.

Lars drew closer to where Oats and Grovosky were working. Barley had settled down. Lars had stayed at Barley's side until the biometric readouts on the man's wristband returned to normal. Oxygen, heart rate, pressure — all greenline.

But the gravity where the two of them were seated was measurably stronger. It tugged at Lars's feet with more vengeance. Holding onto a rung became harder. It taxed his energies; it taxed everyone's energies. They were all getting noticeably more tired.

The Station rotated slowly. The spin was intentional. Its purpose was two-fold, to provide pseudogravity to the occupants and to keep the internal temperature within acceptable limits. The spin kept the Station from frying on one side while simultaneously freezing on the other.

So the giant spacecraft spun, first into the sun, then out of it, then into the sun again. They all turned with it. The slow revolutions imparted tangential velocity to anything not strapped or bolted down.

"We need to quit wasting time and get this job done," Grovosky said, urgency in his voice. "Mag suit or no Mag suit, the radiation hazard out here is real. Like getting a chest x-ray several times a day."

The damaged plate was still in Sergeant Major Grovosky's hand. He bagged it for later inspection. These kinds of malfunctions always led to an official inquiry after the fact. Considering the sabotage done to the Space Elevator, this kind of mishap looked suspicious to him.

The damaged fuel cell was next. Its removal was not as simple or easy as the protection plate's had been. The problem lay in the tubes and bushings and the mesh of surrounding electronics. The explosion of the fuel cell had melted the lot of them into gooey blobs of polymerized wire and semiconductors, blobs that had quickly congealed and frozen solid in the icy chill of space.

Grovosky pulled a laser cutting tool off his belt and began to cut away at the useless material. It was like dissecting an old computer. Motherboards. Silicon chips. Derelict wiring. If it didn't come apart quickly enough, the deadblow hammer would be next. The hammer had a pocket of shot in its head to absorb the recoil. He would bag as many pieces as he could, also for later inspection.

In a flash of activity, Sergeant Major Grovosky cut the old fuel cell loose and slipped the new one out of his backpak and into the receptacle. Securing the replacement fuel cell into place would be orders of magnitude more difficult than pulling out the old one.

"The wiring should be self-threading. The software drives the connections. But we have to manually secure the bushings and tubes. Hand me a bolt wrench and an insulated flange."

The fuel cell, while neither large nor heavy, was impossible for Grovosky to fasten down without help. He needed one hand to cling by, one hand to hold the fuel cell in place, and a third to handle the bolt wrench. That left him shy one hand, no matter how hard he tried to juggle it. Even kneeling did not help. The magVel kneepad was too close to the handhold to allow him to reach the bushing.

"One of you drill bits come over here and lend a hand."

"I will be right there," Lars said.

"Use the ratchet," Grovosky said as Lars got into position. "But torque it slowly."

This was a sensible caution. A manual ratchet was capable of delivering a hundred foot-pounds of torque at the press of a gloved finger. It was also capable of breaking a man's arm if used improperly.

"Fit the ratchet squarely to the bolt head. Set the foot-pounds on the pressure meter to the lowest setting.

Squeeze the trigger of the pistol grip while simultaneously holding down the safety. But brace yourself, kid. The machine will try to spin you in the opposite direction."

Now the job went fairly quickly. Grovosky held the fuel cell in place while Lars ran the ratchet. Meanwhile, the internal circuit connections self-threaded according to the built-in software.

The first three bolts went in easily. But the fourth bolt got hung up.

"There must be some rust or debris in the bolt hole," Sergeant Major Grovosky said. "Torque up the pressure a bit."

"You sure?"

"No choice. We are running low on breathable. Torque it up higher. Set it at about fifty percent."

Lars did as Grovosky instructed. But it was a mistake. Even with the increased torque, the bolt only shimmied from left to right in the hole. It would not go in. Then suddenly, under the added pressure, it shattered and the wrench nearly flew from Lars's hand.

Shards of metal spun off into the darkness. One small piece ricocheted off the Sergeant Major's facemask and helmet. He instinctively recoiled, hands to his face.

"Bloody hell!" Grovosky swore.

"Sarge? You okay?" Lars asked.

"If I weren't okay, I would be dead already. Bloody hell. We cannot leave the job half-done. The new fuel cell is secured only at three points."

"Give me another bolt," Lars instructed Oats. "And make it snappy."

"Who fucking died and put you in charge?" Oats retorted, red fury in his eyes.

"Just do it, lard face," Lars barked. "That is an order."

With anger rising, Oats reached into his kit and fished out a fresh bolt. Then, when he reached across, fresh bolt in hand, he did the unthinkable — he intentionally bumped Lars.

The jolt sent Lars reeling. He grabbed for his safety line with both hands. In doing so, he loosened his grip on the manual ratchet. With the ship slowly spinning — and Lars with it — he lost control of the ratchet. It slipped from his grasp, went flying from his hand, and spun off into space.

"You fool!" Grovosky yelled. But he wasn't yelling at Lars for losing the tool. He was yelling at Oats for intentionally bumping the other man.

"You bloody fool!" Grovosky continued. "You could have gotten us all killed! You are in deep shit now, buddy. Consider yourself on report."

Though the moment of danger had passed, Lars was still holding onto the safety line for dear life. His pulse and breathe were racing. Fear and adrenaline and anger had taken over. Yeager Syndrome or not, almost falling free had shaken him to the core. He could not think or focus. All he could do was stare blindly after the tool.

Like a fool, Lars watched the wrench go — out and out, down and down and down — until the thing was so small it faded from sight, lost among a blanket of stars and distant galaxies.

It had been an amateurish mistake, watching the tool drift away. Until now, Lars had been too busy concentrating on the job at hand to look down.

But now that he had done it, he knew that it had been a mistake of the first order, the same blunder Barley had made earlier.

This was the true mark of an amateur, making dumb mistakes. Now he was dizzy. His head was pounding. He could feel the sweat bead-up on his forehead, the nausea grumble in his belly. Lars was in trouble. Grovosky saw it right away.

"Do not hyperventilate, kid." Sergeant Major Grovosky grabbed Lars's arm, tried to calm him. "I need you alive. You are the brightest stone in this somewhat murky pond."

For some reason, that made Lars feel good. He began to relax. He swallowed the bile that had come into his mouth. It burned going back down. But it stayed down.

"Okay, boys," Grovosky said. "That's it for today. We are way low on breathable. Hand me that socket."

Oats did so and Grovosky moved swiftly to twist the final bushing into place by hand and tweak the beryllium copper hoses a final notch tighter. He tapped twice on the glass of the external dials and waited. After a moment's hesitation, the lights inside the device came on. They were all green-line. He smiled and breathed easier.

"One final climb left, boys."

"Come again?" Lars asked.

Grovosky pointed back towards the airlock. It suddenly seemed a long distance away.

"Gravity is a heartless bitch," Grovosky said. "It is all uphill."

Finally, Lars understood. Having climbed out on the superstructure to grid-mark 22FZ, they were now deep into the pit of the local gravity well.

Grovosky continued. "We actually have to climb back up to the airlock. It is hard work, like scaling a wall. You are all tired, and we are out of time. Use the mechanical ascender attached to your belt. Fasten it to your safety line. The ascender will pull you up along your own safety line to the entrance of the airlock. Do it and do it now."

CHAPTER THIRTY-TWO

"I may have to keep you working indoors for a while."

"Sarge?"

The two men sat at a long table in the crew messhall. The permanent staff of the Space Station numbered under 200, both men and women, men mostly. They had their own sleeping quarters, messhall, and exercise facilities.

Sergeant Major Grovosky continued. He had a plate of hot food in front of him, actual food grown in a garden, not food of the sim variety. It smelled good. Rank had its privileges.

"Sit down, Lars. Have something to eat. Everybody needs a warm meal to start the day."

"Thank you, sir. Don't mind if I do. Are these actual eggs?"

Grovosky nodded. "Believe it or not, chickens will lay in space."

"Cold milk too? We have cows up here?"

"No, the milk is imported." Grovosky paused to enjoy a bite, then continued.

"Lars, you seem brighter than the usual drill bits I get in here. If you worked at it, if you got yourself some advanced book-learning and a dose of enlightened mentorship, you might be able to elevate yourself into a first-rate space monkey."

"Frankly, Sarge, I am at a loss. I was actually in school getting me some book-learning — as you put it — before Viscount Henry got pissed off and had me bilged."

"Yes, Anaconda Military School. Good place, so I have been told. But here is the thing, kid. Every girl on the planet began life as some man's daughter."

"You don't think I know that?"

"Based on the way you acted, I wonder. Clearly you have forgotten the corollary."

"I don't follow."

"Every girl on the planet began life as some man's daughter. Thus, every girl on the planet has a father. When you bang the daughter you also bang the father. Some fathers take offense, especially if you fail to clear it with them first."

"Do I even have a future? Is there any way out of this for me?"

"Anaconda will never take you back, if that's what you mean. Viscount Henry will see to that."

"I may yet have one card to play," Lars said.

"Yes? Is it a deuce or an ace?" Grovosky asked.

"My grandfather happens to be a retired general."

"You think I don't know that?"

"He is held in the highest regard."

"You think I didn't know that as well? General Flix Weinger. They still teach his infiltration techniques at the US Army School. I know the whole story. Everyone does. The man is a textbook hero. He took out Rontana. And he took out that Cassandra Mubarak bitch as well. But the sad truth is that dropping your grandfather's name will not help your case. He is already on the hook for bailing your sorry ass out of jail back on Earth. In this matter, he has no juice left."

"So what do I do?"

Grovosky answered. "My mother, bless her soul, always said that when opportunity knocks, you should answer it."

"Good advice. But what is a fellow to do when all the doors in his life have slammed shut in his face?"

"Well, one thing you cannot do is wait on God to open another one. If the door is shut and you still want to escape, you must find yourself a window and climb like hell through the damn thing."

"And I take it you are opening a window for me?" Lars asked, enjoying his breakfast.

"A window of sorts. Allow me to take you under my wing for a spell, perhaps train you a mite. I will keep you indoors for awhile, where it is safer, away from the dangers of spacework. My next assignment will be on Mars. I am to be part of an investigative team assigned to identify TAT members, perhaps hunt them down and kill them. You know what TAT is, don't you?"

"I do now. Terrorists Against Terraforming. They are the crazies who blew up the Space Elevator. That act of lunacy is what got me sent here in the first place."

"That is not the half of it," Grovosky said. "The bastards may have also sabotaged the fuel cell we had to replace. Those fuel cells are made from some rather sturdy stuff. They rarely fail on their own."

"Seriously?"

"Seriously. I gave the ruptured fuel cell to Lex Wheeler in the Engineering Department. He put two of his top people to work on it. They are taking the thing apart bit by bit and studying the pieces. I already have their preliminary findings. Sabotage seems likely. How the bad guys got access is still a bit of a mystery. Inside job for sure. Maybe some sort of remotely controlled drone. I will have the Engineering Department's final report in hand when I set out in a couple weeks for Mars with the others."

"You are leaving that soon?" Lars asked, still munching on a piece of toast.

"Like I said, I am to be part of the TAT investigation. Care to join me on the team as a junior member? I could arrange for you to be posted on the Red Planet as part of the team for one year as well. I leave in about two weeks' time by solar sailship. This is no luxury cruise, mind you. But it is sure to be interesting. Might look good on your resume someday."

"Two weeks, eh? I think I can manage two weeks on this hulk."

"Two weeks on the Station is a snap. There is plenty for a man to do and plenty for him to learn. The challenge is the three plus weeks it takes to get to Mars and the six or more weeks it takes to return. Even the largest ships can feel rather small after seven or eight days onboard. People have problems coping."

"That is a long time to be alone."

"No man makes a trip like that alone. It simply isn't allowed. The company, Trans-Comet, employs dozens of trip companions — of both sexes — to attend to the passengers. Which way do you swing, by the way? Oh, it doesn't matter. There are plenty of diversions onboard, holo-clubs and the like. Even so, psychological problems are legend. It is the Old West all over again." Grovosky frowned.

"On second thought, maybe I am not cut out for such a thing," Lars said.

"No shame in that. But should you decide to go, there will be no turning back. Minimum trip length is twelve months, one month out, two months back, nine months outland. It all depends on the relative positions of the two planets when we clear spacedock here. Plus, there is all kinds of paperwork to be done ahead of time. — Background check. Med exam. Vaccinations. Psych eval. The whole nine yards. — So I need to know soon. If you decide to go with me, you go as part of the crew, a maintenance crank perhaps. There are repairs to be made and maintenance to perform enroute. We run the 3-D printers day and night to make replacement parts for broken gizmos. You will sign on as a grease monkey."

"Let me think about it, Sarge."

"You do that. In the meantime, I am going to turn you over to Lex Wheeler."

"The engineering guy?"

"Grovosky nodded. "He will teach you everything a man needs to know to perform your duties here and prepare you for a trip to Mars, should you decide to come along."

The two men finished eating, got up from the table, and began to walk. They dropped their dirty dishes and tray at the kitchen window, put them on the conveyor belt.

"Lexus has a crib tucked away upstairs in Strut Seven."

"Crib?"

"Apartment. Man-cave, actually. But do not let the name fool you. His flat is no cave and certainly no dive. It is large and very tech, the largest crib on the Station."

"Is Mr. Wheeler important?"

"Lex. Or Lexus. Or Chief. But never Mr. Wheeler. And yes, Chief Wheeler is important, perhaps the most important person you will ever meet onboard. Chief Engineer. Head of Station Security. Retired Marine. Not a man to fuck with or take lightly. Lex Wheeler is strong, freakishly strong. And he is mean. Or can be. Do not piss the man off unless you want to have the crap kicked out of you."

Their walk had brought them amidships in Strut Seven, though some said spindle or spoke instead of strut. The Station was a big Ferris-type wheel, with a dozen or more radiating spokes.

They stood, now, before a large door, a wooden door. This was absolutely the only wooden door on the Station. All the other doors onboard were either metal-clad or metal-fiber. This was a wooden door, the door of an important man.

Sergeant Major Grovosky pressed the contact on the wall beside the door. He spoke into the intercom. There was a security cam mounted prominently overhead.

"Chief Wheeler? Grovosky here. Do you have a minute?"

"What the fritz do you want?" came the answer through the mic. "And who the fritz is that with you?"

"I know it's early, Chief. But do you have a minute?" They were still in the corridor and the big, wooden door was still closed.

"Have you brought me another one then?" Chief Wheeler answered through the intercom. "The last one did not work out so well."

"This one is different. May we come in?"

The electronic lock disengaged and the door opened.

"Lexus, I want you to meet Lars Cabot, general fuck-up and first-class reprobate."

Lars reached out his hand to shake with Chief Wheeler. But the big man ignored him completely and continued about his business. He was finishing getting dressed for the day while simultaneously checking messages and returning comm. His apartment was a bit of a shambles. But it was large, as large as Sergeant Major Grovosky had said, larger than the home Lars grew up in.

"This the boy that donked District Viscount Henry's daughter?"

"This be the one."

Lexus Wheeler stopped what he was doing, studied Lars's face. "Well son, I have only one question. Was she worth it?"

Lars got very red in the face. He did not know what to say.

Chief Wheeler was enjoying himself. "Question too complicated for your simple mind? What say we break it down for you? Put it in terms even your simple mind can understand. Five minutes of pleasure nets you five months in purgatory. What I want to know is this, boy. Was she worth the price?"

"No, I guess not." Lars could not look Wheeler in the eye.

"Sarge, I thought you said this boy was smart. He doesn't even know whether donking the Henry girl was worth the sperm he expended."

"No," Lars said firmly. "No, it was definitely not worth it."

"Ah. Now we are getting somewhere. Okay Sarge, go home. I will look after the boy for a turn. Come with me, Lars. Down this corridor, up those stairs. I have some repairs to oversee. Which brings us to our very first lesson."

"Already with the lessons?" They were now at the end of the corridor, ready to bound up the flight of stairs.

"When you start up this staircase, this will literally be your first step. Figuratively as well. Today's lesson. — Elevators. Ladders. Stairs."

"You have got to be kidding me," Lars said, grasping the railing. "This is why Sergeant Major Grovosky put me in your capable hands? To learn about chutes and ladders? How downright mundane."

"Arrogant shit. You are quite mistaken. This is no children's game. How one gets around inside the Station is actually one of the more interesting aspects of living here. And also one of the more dangerous."

"Convince me," Lars said defiantly.

"Run these stairs," Chief Wheeler said. "Run them up two steps at a time. Then turn around at the top and come back down them fast as you can. — Go!"

Lars took the challenge. He bounded up the stairs two at a time. Almost immediately he stumbled and bounced off the banister on the right.

Undeterred, he pressed on. When he hit the landing at the top of the flight of stairs, he again lurched uncontrollably to the right banging his head against the wall.

"What the hell?" he swore, picking himself back up.

"Turn around. Get your ass back down here just as fast as you can."

Lars turned around and started quickly down the stairs. He immediately lost his footing and started to fall headlong down the stairway.

Chief Wheeler moved to catch him before he hit the bottom rung or hurt himself further. Wheeler knew exactly what was going to happen to Lars even before it happened.

"What the hell?" Lars swore again, once Chief Wheeler had steadied him.

"Chutes and ladders, my boy. Chutes and ladders. Are you ready to listen now?"

"Okay Chief, I stand corrected. No children's game these lifts and ladders and stairways. So tell me. What the hell just happened to me?"

"Coriolis pseudoforce. It is at work whenever you move vertically inside the Station."

Lars rubbed the bump on his head.

Lexus smiled a knowing smile. "Climbing stairs inside the Station is a matter of simple physics compared with riding an elevator. Elevators inside the Station do not work like they do inside a skyscraper back home. If they did, passengers would experience a wild, even dangerous ride every time they stepped aboard."

"I'm not sure I follow. Aside from falling off its cable, how can an elevator ride be dangerous?"

"It has to do with that same Coriolis pseudoforce."

"You understand I have no background in physics, right?"

"But you do have a skullcap," Chief Wheeler said. "I thought all you space nerds used their caps to keep up?"

"I am actually trying to cut back. Teach me the old-fashioned way, Chief. Why are all the forces up here pseudo?"

"Oh, the forces are real enough. It is just that these forces are generated under contrived circumstances, like the spinning of the Station."

"Yes, Sergeant Major Grovosky already took me out on a spacewalk. I now know a little something about the pseudogravity caused by the Station's spin, how it varies with one's distance from the central tube."

"That's right, you donked Kaleena Henry in one of the zero-g sex rooms."

"Again you have to remind me?"

Chief Lexus Wheeler laughed with delight. "Okay, let's climb these stairs again. But this time step slowly and hold tight to the banister. The Coriolis pseudoforce works its magic on any vertical travel within the Station: elevators, stairs, what have you. Consider an earth-elevator on the top floor at a dead-stop. When the elevator begins to descend, it accelerates downward. This change in velocity briefly lessens your body weight. Later, when the elevator terminates its descent, that deceleration and eventual halt is — in vector terms — mathematically equivalent to an acceleration upward. Your body weight increases. Anyone who has ridden an earth-elevator is familiar with these effects, even if they are rather mild.

"But aboard the Space Station, things are quite different. This is especially true near the central axis, where the elevator's rate of acceleration can easily exceed the local centrifugal force."

"In English, please. Or at least Terrish."

"That's right. Today's young cannot think without a skullcap bolted on and powered up. Let me dumb it down for you. When the local gravity field is but a fraction of one-g, any sudden change in motion will be quite noticeable."

"Yes, I see now."

Lexus Wheeler continued. "If a space-elevator worked like an earth-elevator, the ride would not be at all pleasant. As soon as the car begins its descent, you would instantly be lifted off your feet, as if the car had been turned upside down. You would fall against the ceiling lamps. Then, because of the Station's spin, the elevator car would seem to tumble crazily until it was tilted nearly on its side. You would fall against the anti-spinward wall and slide down along that wall until you hit the floor . . ."

"Whoa, whoa, whoa . . ." Lars interrupted. "Anti-spinward? What in the world?"

"Moving in the same direction as the Station's direction of spin is considered spinward. Moving in the direction opposite the spin is considered anti-spinward. You sound like a boy asking what one does with his hands when the rollercoaster car leaves the track."

"Okay, I think I got it," Lars said. "The g-forces inside the Station vary from high to low as you travel from rim to center. Thus, an elevator ride that traverses different gradients of g-force will feel more like a tilt-a-whirl than a smooth ride."

"Yes, that is precisely what I am trying to say."

"I sense that this discussion has become rhetorical. This tilt-a-whirl problem has been solved long ago and you now know the solution."

Chief Wheeler shook his head. "Actually, there are two solutions, neither of which is optimal. Slow down the elevator. Or, if you must keep it running fast, secure everyone in it, passengers and cargo alike, before getting underway. Either way, it is slow and a pain in the ass."

"How so?"

"In order to keep a space-elevator ride from feeling like that tilt-a-whirl you are so fond of, you have to triple the transit time. You have to make the elevator begin very slowly and accelerate at a steady, slow rate. The other option takes even longer, strapping everyone and everything inside it down."

"Lousy choices, to be sure."

"No worse than the problems we face every day in the stairwells."

"Like what almost just happened to me? I could have broken my neck."

"Oh, quit whining. I caught you, didn't I? All the stairs on the Space Station seem to lean one direction or the other when you try to climb them."

"Let me guess," Lars said. "It is on account of the Station's direction of spin. That's why the stairs seem to lean."

"See? You are indeed learning your physics. When you climb to spinward, staircase steps will seem to lean forward. When you climb to anti-spinward, those same staircase steps will seem to lean backward. Either way, the results can be dangerous. The apparent slope of a set of stairs will change depending on its location inside the Station. After your recent experience, the safety implications ought to be obvious."

"I have not forgotten my lesson, Chief. I nearly slipped and fell when you made me run those steps."

"Three rules, kid. Always keep a firm grip on the railings. Always climb stair steps slowly and deliberately. Finally, if the stair steps ever do seem to be suddenly leaning out too much, come to a complete standstill until the stairs obey and quit leaning. Then resume climbing, only slower. Oh, and one more thing. Never run the steps, no matter who dares you. Near the zero-g tube, the pseudogravity is so low there isn't enough friction between your feet and the floor to keep you grounded."

"You might have told me that before."

"What would have been the fun in that?" Chief Wheeler asked.

"What if I had hurt myself?"

"I would have felt bad, of course. Doc already has plenty to do. In the opening days of space travel, thinking back to the first Station, accidents were legend. In those early days, there were no standard protocols about staircase orientation or steepness. Aerospace engineers holding blueprints in their hands when that first Station was still on the drawing board, stuck staircases in the plan helter-skelter, wherever they seemed to fit. As a result, no two staircases behaved the same way. Even old-timers on that first Station had to be extra careful climbing stairs they seldom used. After a few accidents, one serious, a new set of rules came into play. From that day forward, all staircases were to be anti-spinward up."

Lars replied. "Reminds me of a story my grandfather once told me. When the Germans built some of the earliest dirigibles, everyone knew hydrogen gas was explosive. Yet, the Germans filled airships like the Hindenburg with hydrogen gas anyway. Only later, when the Hindenburg blew sky-high, killing hundreds, did they switch to filling their lighter-than-air craft with an inert gas, helium, to make them fly."

"Nice history lesson. What the hell does that have to do with dangerous staircases onboard the Station?"

"Nothing like a bad accident to improve safety."

"Fair point. Following that first bad accident, like I said, all staircases became anti-spinward up. After that, Station stairways had a much better safety record. Now, after the change, if a man were to fall on such a staircase, he would fall *against* the stairs rather than away from them. The other sort of stairs, the spinward up sort, would tend to get out of the way if a man fell. This would cause him to fall further and faster, making injuries worse."

Lars was thoughtful. "Maybe going to Mars isn't such a bad idea after all."

"You going to Mars with Sergeant Major Grovosky on his snipe hunt?"

"Come again?"

"Snipe hunt. It is what detractors call the solar-system-wide hunt for the bad-guy terrorists. Kill teams have been dispatched to Venus, to Mars, to the Moon."

"You make it sound like a wild goose chase," Lars said. "Are we — I mean, they — wasting their time?"

"No, not at all. When I called it a snipe hunt, I was just poking fun. Snipes are wading birds with a long straight beak. They are native to the marshes and riverbanks of the northern hemisphere. They are also impossibly difficult to hunt."

Lars still seemed confused.

"Son. There will always be terrorists. And there will always be people whose job it is to hunt down the terrorists and kill them. It often means standing dead still for a very long time in the cold waters of some swamp and waiting silently. Not everyone has the stones for such work. It is cold and it is nasty. Be sure of yourself before you sign on for such a mission."

"I haven't decided yet. But Mars does have something this place lacks."

"Oh, what is that?" Wheeler asked.

"Gravity. A planet has gravity. Up is actually up, and down is actually down. Not like here on the Station. What about you, Chief? Are you going on the snipe hunt as well?"

"Cannot slip much past you, can I? Yes. I am scheduled to be part of the team. Actually, I am to be the head tech and munitions guy."

"Explosives? I like explosives."

"Yes?"

"I spent much of my youth studying a *Primer on Nitrate Compounds*."

"I know this book. It contains classified material. How did you get your hands on such a thing?"

"My grandfather."

"Ah. Now it is all beginning to make sense. You were made for this job, weren't you Lars?"

CHAPTER THIRTY-THREE

"So, Chief, what is the verdict?"

"I will need more than that to go on, Lars." They were in Strut Six headed for the shuttle docking bay.

"I am talking about the damaged fuel cell, the one Sergeant Major Grovosky gave you to study. What is the verdict?"

"The damage was not accidental, if that is what you mean. It was not a system failure nor was it the result of natural degradation. The damage was almost certainly the result of deliberate sabotage."

"You know that now for a fact?" Lars was intrigued. When they arrived at the shuttle docking bay, he was to accompany Chief Wheeler on a short flight to visually inspect the outer skin of the parked sailship.

"Yes, I do now know that for a fact," Chief Wheeler replied. "The meltdown of the fuel cell was an act of terrorism, just like the blitz attack on the Space Elevator."

"These TAT bastards are keeping lots of good people up late at night, aren't they?"

"Oh, these people are the enemy okay. But the real enemy on Mars is the environment, specifically the dust. In the long run, dust will likely kill far more people on Mars than the terrorists."

"That is interesting. I have already had some skullcap instruction on the havoc dust can play with spacesuits. But why is it such a risk to the colonists?"

"They prefer to be called colonials. But let me lay it out for you, kid. Free flowing liquid water is practically nonexistent on the Red Planet. Oh, there is plenty of the wet stuff lurking about. But in its natural state, it is all frozen, every last drop of it. On Earth, liquid water in the form of falling rain mops up and sweeps away the world's fine dust particles. Our planet is fairly dust-free. But on Mars, there is no such cleaning agent. The planet is covered with tiny particles. They gum up damn near everything."

"How tiny is tiny?"

"On a par with cigarette smoke. Very tiny grain size."

"Most filters cannot process stuff that small, at least not very well or for very long."

"Precisely why there is a problem. Martian dust causes a lot of damage. It gums up spacesuits. It scratches helmet visors, causes electrical shorts, clogs motors, sandblasts instruments, degrades equipment. The particles are coated with corrosive chemicals like hydrogen peroxide. This makes them even worse. These toxins eat slowly away at manmade materials like rubber seals and other plastics. Mag 10 suits last under one week before beginning to leak."

Lars interrupted. "But wasn't terraforming supposed to change all that?"

"No lie there. And terraforming is already beginning to change things for the better. But it will take centuries. Lightning fast by geological standards; but still damn slow. In time, more liquid water will accumulate on the surface, mostly as a result of rainfall. By then, of course, mud will be the problem. It will be slick, like drilling muds, a carpet of a billion tiny ball bearings."

"If spacesuits degrade that rapidly, what happens to people who breathe-in unfiltered air?"

"Unprotected lungs definitely suffer. Some of the dust particles are quartz. If those particles are inhaled, they pose a major health hazard, something the medicos call silicosis."

"I think my father once told me about this. Men in the field, men who regularly use jackhammers to break up concrete suffer from this disease."

"Silicosis is an incurable lung condition. And you are correct. Even today, the condition kills several thousand construction workers and earthminers every year. Colonials have no choice but to keep their habitat spotless and dust-free. They need to thoroughly clean themselves off before entering the facility, something that is exceptionally difficult and time-consuming."

"Why so hard?"

"Hold that thought a minute, we are here."

The two men were now at the end of a long corridor. Chief Wheeler reached out and placed his palm on a security pad beside the locked door. It flashed a moment, scanned his finger and palm print. The door slid slowly open.

"Okay," he said. "Let's suit up. Then we will take a spin in the maintenance shuttle. What I want to do is take a look at the skin of the *S.S. Ticonderoga*. It is one of only three sailships in the fleet."

They entered the tech room and sat down. An ops man approached and helped them step into a Mag suit.

"Now about that Martian dust," Chief Wheeler said. "The dust is magnetized. It is electrically charged. It sticks to damn near everything. With water in constant short supply, colonials have to settle for scrubbing themselves clean using dry-ice condensed out of the atmosphere. Cold stuff, this dry-ice. But even with all that scrubbing, the problem is mitigated only for a short time. Whenever the colonials go outside, they must wear twin-layer spacesuits. Later, when they return to base, the outer layer must be left in a special airlock outside the main habitat, where it is scrupulously cleaned by robotic scrubbers."

"If exposure to Martian dust is life-threatening, am I risking my life by going there?"

"No more than I."

"I am younger than you are. Silicosis takes time to kill."

"You are not wrong about that. But breathing in quartz dust is only one of the many dangers," Wheeler said. "The dust wreaks havoc with the Colony's electrical output. This is not a trivial problem."

"Please explain."

"Like I said, the dust is sticky. It settles onto the solar panels in a constant rain. Left untreated, the output from the solar panels declines one percent every three days. That is an amazing number, if you think about it. The grainy powder accumulates on the panels like nobody's business. When a dust storm darkens the skies, power generation is cut in half. That is why, when the second wave of colonials arrived about eighty years ago and the facility was tripled in size, the Trans-Comet Company erected a Gen Five 800-megawatt nuclear reactor to supply electricity. The Space Council now considers it — the reactor — one of the terrorists' chief targets. Should the reactor go down, the colony will cease to exist. Elements of our team are trying to protect the power plant at all costs."

By now the two men had completely suited up, all but their helmets. "Follow me, Lars. When we get to the airlock, secure your helmet. We will step into the chamber and stabilize the atmosphere inside the shuttle to match the air mix of the Station. Once the shuttle has cleared the umbilical, we can remove our helmets and operate inside normally. But the suits stay on. Kapische?"

"Got it."

While they waited for the air mix to stabilize, they continued to talk.

"How do you defend a nuclear reactor against attack?" Lars asked.

"No easy thing, I grant you. Reactors are highly vulnerable to attack. For a man with evil intent, it is no great shakes to disrupt a nuclear reactor and cause it to meltdown. Containment vessels can be cracked. These

TAT bastards are armed. They have access to weapons of every sort. As a result, we have on the one hand half of humanity hard at work terraforming Earth's two closest neighbors, while these outlaws from TAT simultaneously threaten to destroy everything the others have created in a brilliant flash of white light. Can you imagine a bio attack on the Venusian colony? Or a missile attack on the Martian power plant? Catastrophic."

"But how will killing a room full of colonials prevent either planet from being terraformed? That process has been underway for a long time. It transcends the lives of just a few dozen people."

"Every generation has its Luddites. But there is more than a little bit at stake here, Lars. Billions of public and private credits have been expended to transform these planets into livable spheres. Venus has been the beneficiary of an especially large private investment, a truly mammoth engineering feat, if you ask me."

"Every school boy knows the story, Chief. The terraforming of Venus is far and away the largest engineering achievement in the history of mankind. Bigger than the building of the Pyramids or the digging of the second Panama Canal. Space engineers haul the trans-comets out of the Kuiper Belt, wrap them in big plastic baggies so the water doesn't boil off during the trip through the inner solar system, then crash them into the Venusian cloud cover. These giant snowballs arrive onsite at roughly sixty-day intervals. I am told they detonate an avalanche of sonic booms in the atmosphere when they hit."

"Not everyone is a fan of loud noises, Lars. The local Venusian strongman — a fellow named Uday bin Hassan — hates the noise. He hates the sonic booms. He hates the torrential rainfalls that follow even more. Hassan has vowed to put a stop to all inbound trans-comet traffic."

"That makes no sense to me. The trans-comets are the only way to cool down the planet and make it livable."

"Sense or no sense, Hassan hates the noise. He hates the constant rainfall even more. To try to put a stop to it, he has linked up with these outlaws from TAT. Hassan is quite sympathetic to their cause."

"So why not cut the head off the snake?"

"Lars? You don't think we thought of that? We are not utter morons, you know. It just is not that easy."

Lars was about to ask why, when Chief Wheeler motioned for him to be quiet. "Okay, move forward inside the shuttle. Watch your head. Clearance is not as high as inside the Station. Move forward. Sit down in the co-pilot's seat there on the right. Strap yourself in, so we can shove off. We have a long day of work ahead of us."

Lars did as he was told, and a few minutes later they had gracefully unhitched from the Station.

"We still need to detach from the umbilical. When I tell you, press down hard on that big red button beside you. You must press it down really hard. There will be resistance. Okay .... now .... press ...."

Lars closed his fist and pounded down hard on the large button.

"No! Don't hit it, you fool! Press it down. With the flat of your hand. Steady downward pressure."

"Sorry, Chief."

Now the plunger went down smoothly. There was a distant hiss of pneumatics as the umbilical detached, and the shuttle floated free.

"Let me tell you about this Uday bin Hassan fellow. He is the quintessential tyrant. He rules the lithium mines and the two principal settlements of Venus with an iron hand. The rest of the planet is unpopulated. Heavy heat. Heavy humidity. Overpressure of eighteen pounds per square inch. Permanent thermal inversion. People tire easily. Tropical undergrowth. Bugs. Bacteria. Fungi. You break bin Hassan's rules, you go to prison. Only it is no ordinary prison. No tall walls to scale, no beefy guards to elude, no electric fences to avoid. No need for any of these impediments. Escape means death. It is a thousand kloms of dense, dangerous jungle in every direction. No prisoner who wants to live dares escape."

"So I guess if I go there, I will not be breaking any rules."

"You better hope to hell you never go there. This guy Hassan: you don't want to be messing around with him. He is a tyrant and completely crazy. We avoid him, if we can. But I will tell you about him, because you need to know."

Chief Wheeler had his hands on the joystick as he eased the shuttle out into the shipping lanes. He would steer a large graceful arc away from the Station, then angle back in on the opposite side where the *Ticonderoga* was parked.

"Uday is a loner by nature. But power increases isolation. Walls define the tyrant's world. These walls keep his enemies out. But they also block off the tyrant from the people he rules. In time, he can no longer see out himself. He loses touch with what is real and what is unreal, with what is possible and what is not possible. His perceptions of what his power can accomplish and the value of his own importance bleed into fantasy."

"If the man lives behind such thick walls, how do you know so much about him?"

Even as Lars spoke, his eyes were drawn to the starboard window now filled with a longitudinal view of Struts Six, Seven and Eight. The struts were basked in sunlight, gleaming tubes of a beryllium cupronickel aluminum alloy. Beyond it, the zero-g central tube and a cluster of docked space vehicles.

"Our people, some of whom are inside those walls, have compiled a dossier on this lunatic. Consider a young man without money or power. Such a man is completely free. He possesses nothing. But he also lacks for nothing. Thus, in a sense, he has everything. He can travel. He can drift. He can make new acquaintances whenever he pleases. He can try out new things; try to soak up the rich variety of life. He can seduce or be seduced, start an enterprise or abandon it, join an army or flee a nation, fight to preserve the status quo or plot a revolution. He can reinvent himself on a daily basis, change his stripes to accommodate the discoveries he makes about the world and himself."

Chief Wheeler continued. "But if the young man prospers through the choices he makes, if he acquires a wife, children, wealth, land, power — if he acquires all these things, his options do not expand, they diminish. Responsibility and commitment limit his moves. While one might think that the most powerful men have the most choices, they actually have the fewest. Too much depends on their every move. The tyrant's choices are the narrowest of all. He can no longer drift or explore, no longer join or flee. He can no longer reinvent himself, because so many others have come to depend on him. He, in turn, must now depend on so many others.

"He stops learning because he is walled in, walled in by fortresses and palaces, by generals and ministers none of whom dare tell him what he does not want to hear. The accumulation of power gradually shuts the tyrant off from the world. Everything comes to him second or third hand. He is deceived daily. He becomes ignorant of his land, of his people, even of his own family. He exists, finally, only to preserve his own wealth and power, to build his legacy. Survival becomes his one overriding concern. So he regulates his diet, tests his food for poison, exercises his limbs behind well-patrolled walls, trusts no one, and tries to control everything."

"Sorry to interrupt, Chief. But there is a view out this starboard window that will not quit. I have never seen such a thing close-up."

"It is a big mother, isn't it?"

"The Station?"

"That too. But look at the size of that sailship. For now it is docked. That is the ship we will be taking when we ride the solar wind to Mars. The *Ticonderoga*."

Lars studied the ship and the Station closely while Chief Wheeler continued to explain about Uday bin Hassan.

"Cruelty is the tyrant's art. He studies and embraces it. His dictatorship is based on fear. But fear is not enough to stop everyone. Some men and women have great courage. They are willing to brave death to oppose him. But the tyrant has ways of countering even this. Among those who do not fear death, some fear torture, others disgrace, some humiliation. And even those who do not fear these things for themselves may fear them for their fathers or their mothers, for their brothers or sisters or wives or children. The tyrant uses every tool at his disposal. He commands not just acts of cruelty, but spectacle, cruel spectacle. So we have Uday hanging fourteen alleged plotters in a public square; leaving their dangling bodies on display until they have been consumed by gelatinous fungi. So, we have top party leaders forced to witness and even participate in the executions of their colleagues. Pain and death and humiliation become public theater. Ultimately, of course, guilt or innocence play no part in this spectacle. There is no law or value beyond the tyrant's will. If he wants someone arrested or tortured or tried and executed, his mere saying so is sufficient. The exercise serves not only as punishment, but also as a warning to his subjects, to his potential rivals, to his enemies, that he is strong, that he is invincible. Compassion, fairness, concern for due process or the law, are all signs of weakness. Cruelty asserts strength."

"My gods, Chief, you do like to go on about things, don't you? Have you made a study of this man?"

"We all have. Everyone on the team. To defeat your enemy you must first understand him."

"Well then, tell me. Where is this monster from? How did he come to power?"

"Hassan is from Persia, the same godforsaken land that brought the world Ali Salaam Rontana. You remember that beast, don't you?"

"My grandfather had a hand in putting him down. So, yes, I have heard of Rontana."

"Imagine a village in the remote mountains near the Turkmenistan border. There are houses and tents and camps. Large unoccupied spaces separate each simple homestead from the next. Each family has its own house. Each house is sometimes as much as several kloms from the next. The family-units are self-contained. Each family grows its own food, makes its own clothes, provide for their own protection. Those who grow up in these remote villages are frightened of everything — and I mean everything. There is no real law enforcement or civil society. Each family is frightened of every other family. And all of them are frightened of outsiders. This is the tribal mind. The only loyalty it knows is to its own family or village."

Chief Wheeler continued. "Each family-unit is ruled by a patriarch and the village is ruled by the strongest of them. This intense loyalty to tribe comes before everything else. There are no moral values beyond power. You can lie, cheat, steal, even kill. It is all acceptable behavior so long as you are a loyal son of the village or tribe to which you owe allegiance. Politics for these people is a bloody game. It is all about obtaining and holding onto power. Uday bin Hassan is the very embodiment of the tribal mentality, the ultimate patriarch, the village leader who has seized and terrorized a nation."

"You mean a planet, don't you?"

"Yeah, I do mean a planet. Venus. All but one sector, where a small band of rebels maintain a tenuous existence outside of the tyrant's control."

"Chief, I am not very smart about such things. But from what little I know and learned in school, terrorism has never been very effective as a political weapon. It generally motivates the very enemy it was supposed to defeat."

"It is true. Throughout history, terrorism has failed to achieve its ends at least as often as it has succeeded."

"Then why devote so many resources to defeating these outlaws?"

"Humankind has but a toehold on the two planets. This is not like some megalomaniac who controls some useless corner of central Asia. Such a man can be safely ignored. That is hardly the case here. No sane person will emigrate to these far-off lands — bring their families, risk their lives and their livelihood — if they do not believe them to be safe."

"I got that, Chief."

"Okay, good. Now pay attention. We are here."

CHAPTER THIRTY-FOUR

"Physics enables. Policies dictate. Profits sustain."

"Chief?"

"It is a statement of principle, a Behavioral Law. This Law has guided the progress of mankind since we first became self-aware hundreds of thousands of years ago. The operation of this Law is what dragged us kicking and screaming out of the Stone Age and into the age of machines and still drives our species forward today."

"Goodness, Chief. I had no idea you were a philosopher. I thought we were out here today in the shuttle to run diagnostics and examine the skin of the *Ticonderoga* for bruises and damages from micrometeorites."

"Oh, that is our job okay. But it is borderline boring. Plus, we have all kinds of time to kill while the survey bots spool up and load their programming. Physics enables. Policies dictate. Profits sustain. Take the first Stone Age idiot who picked up a rock and smashed open a nut. How did he manage this? The fellow needed an opposable thumb. He needed a strong arm and good aim. He needed to grasp the fact that the rock was hard, harder at least than the shell of the nut. He needed to understand that there was delicious food inside, enough to make the effort worthwhile. These are all examples of the physics that enables."

Chief Wheeler continued. "Now let's say our Stone Age idiot smashes the nut with the rock and a shard of shell puts out his neighbor's eye. The village chieftain may get really angry. If one of his best hunters loses an eye, the entire village may starve. So, in a safety move, the chieftain might forbid all future nut-smashing. Or he might mandate that all future nut-smashing take place away from the village. Both strictures are examples of how policy dictates."

Chief Wheeler continued. "Finally, profits sustain. If the smashed nut fails to yield enough meat to make the gathering and smashing of the nut worthwhile, nut smashing will cease regardless of physics or policy."

"I am truly sorry, Chief. But I really do not understand what any of this has to do with space?"

"It has everything to do with space, Lars. This Behavioral Law I have just described to you explains how the American West was settled. It explains how rich countries decline and become poor under the weight of bureaucracy and rules and regulation. It explains the entire trans-comet enterprise, from start to finish. And it explains why we must hunt down and kill these bastard terrorists.

"Physics enables. The lever and fulcrum. The mechanical screw. The wheel. The windmill. The internal combustion engine. The gas turbine. The solar sail. We never make it out of the trees and onto the savanna, until we master the physics of motion and harness them to our benefit.

"Policies dictate. — Free markets. Property rights. The rule of law. Trial by jury. Uniform weights and measures. Low taxes. — If government interferes with commerce, progress ceases. Civilization stagnates, people starve, war ensues.

"Profits sustain. Whether a technology comes into use, whether a resource gets extracted from the ground, whether a man takes a risk to start a new company or expand into a new market — all of these happy-making things will not occur unless there is an opportunity for profit. Raise taxes, interfere with commerce, profits decline, development slows, incomes decline. This is rudimentary economics."

"My grandfather believed much the same thing as you do. I think I am now beginning to better grasp what you and he are saying."

"Okay then. Today's lesson is over. Time for us to get to work. The survey bots should have spooled up by now. What we actually have here is a sophisticated mapping tool. It employs the same tech a landsat uses when it compiles a 3-D topo map of the terrain below. What we will be looking for are tiny valleys or imperfections on what otherwise should be the smooth skin of the ship. A valley on the topo map is actually a 3-D representation of a ding. Deeper dings require visual inspection, maybe a pressure test, perhaps a ceramic patch."

"So how does this mapping tool work?"

"Laser technology. The *Ticonderoga* is a big mother of a ship. We release hundreds of survey bots from the shuttle cargo bay. The bots revolve slowly round and round outside of the big ship running a high-intensity laser scan. The mapping computer digests uncountable reams of survey data from the bots and relays to our screen the gridpoint coordinates of any potential hotspots. We come back later with torque jets and hot patch."

"So what do we do until then?" Lars asked. "Sit and wait?"

"That is about the size of it. We can expect to wait twenty minutes or so before the computer spits out our first hit. But we can use the time productively, if you wish. You did have a point, you know."

"I did?" Lars was surprised.

"Sure. The point you were trying to make earlier. It had an element of truth. All the great monsters of history were convinced of terror's power to force submission. Hitler, Stalin, Rontana. All were proponents of mass public slaughter as a means of inducing fear to achieve political aims. Hitler thought the London blitz would drive the British to their begging knees. Stalin thought his purges would strike fear into the Russian people, convince them to never again challenge their masters. Rontana thought his mass murders would drive the West into hiding, bend Westerners to his will."

"But the monsters were wrong," Lars broke in excitedly. "Anarchist, fascist, communist — all wrong. Terrorism terrifies; that part is true. But people are tough. They do not easily submit. Evolution is a harsh mistress. It has armed us with a certain mental toughness. Hurt and pain are the natural order of things. We know this instinctively. Bad things happen to innocent people all the time. We are surrounded every day by death and suffering. The news is filled with stories of barbarism and cruelty. Murder and rape. Famine and disease. Lives cut short for no good reason. For some people, the pain and suffering is too much to bear; they break. For many others, they take a deep breath, blot out the pain, push through the horror, focus their minds on a brighter tomorrow."

Lars continued. "I think this is the real reason why terror campaigns often fail. The campaigns inoculate people. They make them immune, provide them with their own antidote. Terrorists provide the people being terrorized with a stupendous duty — to save themselves, to fight back and destroy the very people who mean to ruin their lives."

Chief Wheeler interrupted. "Hold that thought. Computer shows a hotspot in Sector Two that needs to be patched. We need to swing in for a closer look." He pushed the joystick gently to the left and the small ship banked in that direction. "Okay, back to what you were saying."

"You say to me that we must hunt down and kill the terrorists. But where do we draw the line?" Lars asked. "Do we consider a terrorist an enemy soldier or a misbehaving citizen?"

"What does it matter? They are a blight on society and need to be put down like rabid dogs."

Lars disagreed. "If a terrorist is an enemy soldier, we have to punish him according to military law and the Geneva Convention. If he is a civilian, a whole different set of rules apply. You know, trial by jury and all that."

Chief Wheeler chuckled. "I think you are being naïve. This battle is not about justice. Terrorists do not have rights. We don't punish a terrorist or a saboteur like a common criminal. We kill them dead. Anyway, our justice system is a joke. Everyone knows that."

"You don't mean that."

"Don't I? Lars, the human mind is a subtle mechanism. It is devoted more often to the concealment of truth than to its discovery. This is the direct result of our evolution. Take our Stone Age idiot. He happens upon a patch of fresh berries. The berries must be eaten right away or else stored for later use. If he stuffs his face and walks contently back to the village, the first thing he will do when asked where he has been is to lie to his neighbor about the berries' very existence."

"Now you are talking about self-preservation, not criminal behavior. The guy is hungry, perhaps starving. When given a choice between lying and going hungry, no one is going to tell the truth if it means dying of starvation."

"Think it through, boy. Once the brain has evolved a mechanism for successfully lying about a food-source, that same mechanism can be adapted to any use. I'm sorry, Lars, but the capacity for deception is central to our evolution. I learned this at the Schauffhausen Institute as part of my training. Humans had to succeed against other humans to survive, not just against lions and tigers. When your opponent is as smart as you are, you have to be a better liar. To tell a good lie, to keep all the false stories straight in your head, you have to convince yourself first. The principal target of the mind's obfuscation is itself."

"Yes, but now we are no longer talking about the location of a strawberry patch, are we?"

"Criminals are the worst. I worked in the criminal justice system when I first graduated university. Nowhere is the tendency for self-deception greater than among those who have committed a violent crime."

"Criminals may lie to themselves. But the facts never lie."

"Outright denial of a homicide in the face of overwhelming evidence is rare. I will grant you that much. But few criminals who are caught are faced with overwhelming evidence against them. Most cases are circumstantial and most thieves and murderers are pathological liars. A successful liar will likely go free."

"How come you know so much about these things, Chief?"

"In my younger days, before I was made Chief, I worked military intelligence. Before that, I worked in the criminal justice system, like I said. I was a psychologist. I was trained by the best. Dr. Emil Schauffhausen. My specialty was investigations. When a spy had to be turned, when he had to be persuaded to switch sides, we applied the standard techniques of behavior modification, some of which clearly fell into the aberrant category."

"What you call persuasion, others call torture."

"That is one word for it. I began my studies with criminals. In the courtroom, after conviction, at parole, and upon release. At the time, I was not much older than you are now. I remember this one guy. He had been accused of both rape and murder, of two different victims. He admitted to the rapes, but not the murders. In our interview, he told me angrily: *The police are trying to pin a murder on me. But I'm no murderer. They're saying that just to save their own skins.* His impersonation of innocence was certainly a good one, and I was inclined to believe him.

"*But you are a rapist*, I said, trying to twist his mind back to reality, away from what he had not done and back to what he had.

"He looked at me with puzzlement. *Well, yeah,* he answered, as if to say: 'So what?'.

"*Rape is a serious crime,* I continued.

"He looked genuinely puzzled. I repeated to him that rape was a serious crime.

"*I was nice to her,* he said.

"His callous indifference was revolting. Nevertheless, his continued denial of the murder retained its dramatic force. I was starting to believe him.

"A few months later, he was convicted by a jury on both counts. Standing before the judge at sentencing, he calmly confessed to the murder in the most minute detail, entirely forsaking the denial and rage he had expressed in my presence only weeks before. I was left to puzzle out whether the man was a simple liar — albeit, a great actor — or whether he actually believed his own performance."

Lars interjected. "So criminals are liars. This is not news."

"It runs deeper than that, Lars. Another murderer came back from court after having been sentenced to life in prison. He was red with rage. *That wasn't no justice,* he said. *It was a kangaroo court. They didn't listen to me, to nothing I said. They didn't call no medical evidence.*

"*Medical evidence about what?* I asked.

"*About what she died of.*

"*And what did she die of?*

"*Hemorrhage.*

"*And how did she get the hemorrhage?* I asked.

"*Them ER docs pulled out the knife.*"

Lars wore the face of disbelief as he listened to Chief Wheeler's tale. Could people really be that unfeeling?

Suddenly Chief Wheeler spoke up, broke his reverie. "We are here. At the hotspot. Bring up the scope. Set it to ten times magnification."

Lars reached for the instrument Wheeler had pointed out to him earlier. He clicked the dial one notch. The picture on the screen got bigger, with more detail, the surface no longer smooth but pocked with imperfections. It was like looking at a human face under a magnifying glass. All the imperfections, freckles, and dirty pores now clearly visible.

"Click it again. One hundred times mag."

Now the picture got even larger, even rougher, less smooth than before. Myriad details at nearly a microscopic level became clear.

"Good. Hold it there. Now switch it to 3-D. Good."

In the center of the picture was a clearly visible, irregularly shaped valley or rut carved into the spaceship's skin. It had the same rough edges and markings a granite boulder might leave behind in an alpine meadow after a landslide. This was the image of gouge markings etched in metal of a micrometeorite impact magnified one hundred times.

"Do a gridlock," Wheeler said. "Then pass the coordinates onto the patch-bot. The bot has onboard two tubes of hot ceramic paste. The paste bonds almost instantly with the metal alloy on the skin of the ship, like plaster slapped on with a big ole putty knife. Seals the skin and any possible micro-hole against possible leak."

"I have a green light on the board, Chief."

"Okay. Flip the lever just below and to the left of the green light. That launches the patch-bot from the chute. A survey bot will follow immediately afterward and re-survey the spot to be sure it is sealed."

Chief Wheeler waited while Lars carried out his instructions. Then he settled back into his seat and prepared to move on to the next hotspot. "Okay, now back to liars and criminals. I told you about that rapist and murderer. In an altogether different case, two men convicted of murder stoutly maintained their innocence to me and to anyone else who would listen. This went on for many years, both of them always fervently claiming their innocence. After a time, even prison officials began to have their doubts. I saw these murderers every three months, as part of my studies for the Schauffhausen

Institute. Later, after I had left the Institute and moved on to other things, I learned that they had both confessed their guilt in their eighth year of imprisonment. At first, this shocked me no end. Then one of my coworkers reminded me that lifers often become eligible for parole after eight years. Unless they acknowledge their crimes and express remorse, they will never be granted parole."

"Maybe they were innocent and only confessed so that they could be set free."

"That is a possibility, of course. The more likely possibility is that they were always guilty but expert liars. For these kinds of people, denial blends into amnesia. More than one-third of all murderers claim to not recall their homicidal deed. Their brain has blotted out the truth. This is evolution hard at work, a natural defense against the horror of what they have done. Remember: a liar must lie first to himself. He must fervently believe that a man who cannot remember a crime must not have committed it. Therefore, such a man cannot be tried and sent to jail for it."

Chief Wheeler continued. "I will give you a perfect example of this phenomenon. I was interviewing an alleged rapist. He had climbed into a woman's bed after a few drinks and a panel of Deludes. He was furious with me for not being able to see things his way. *How can you expect me to defend myself when I cannot remember nothing?* He asked in a menacing tone.

"I snapped right back at him. *If you cannot remember anything, then you are not in a very strong position to refute the charges, are you?*

"He looked at me like I was a fool. His amnesia allowed him to believe, even after his conviction, that he was the victim of a gross injustice."

"Listen, Chief, I am certainly not going to defend these characters. But are we not all guilty of a certain amount of self-delusion? Like you said before about evolution and all that?"

"In amnesia's house are many rooms. Most of them are filled with mirrors. Others are filled with cluttered closets and blind corners. The mind will willingly distort memories in order to produce whatever mental record is required to ensure the body's self-esteem. The man who has committed an act of violence may remember only a slight contretemps."

Chief Wheeler continued. "I remember this one fellow. He had been brought in on a charge of murder. He swore to me. *I only gave the man a slight tap on the head.* Me, I tried not to react. I had seen the pathologist's report. It described a badly fragmented skull that had received a crushing blow from a blunt instrument. *It couldn't have been me*, he said. *It must'a been someone else. I only gave him a small tap on the head. The bastards are trying to frame me for a crime I didn't commit.*

"Believe me, Lars. They are all like that, every last one of them. All liars. A man who killed a woman after he raped her told me he had gone a bit too far. I always wondered what he meant by that. Did he mean that the rape was acceptable and that it was just bad luck the pressure on her neck killed her? I think that is what he meant. Bad luck like that often strikes murderers. They walk about with a knife, and then, perversely, someone comes along and impales himself on it. So sorry you stabbed yourself with my knife. Personal responsibility evaporates. Mommy made me do it. No one is guilty. Lies become the truth."

"You sound bitter, Chief."

"No. Just old."

"May I ask you a question?"

"Sure, Lars. Shoot."

"Let's go back a step and let me repeat my question from earlier. — Is there a line to be drawn here?"

"What do you mean?"

"Is a terrorist a soldier or is he a civilian? How do we punish the sons of bitches? I mean aside from just hunting them down and killing them?"

"I sort it out this way, Lars. If a man is acting on orders — whether they be from a military man in uniform or from some syndicate crime boss — or if that man is acting on behalf of some group — whether it be TAT or the anti-abortion league — that man should be treated as a soldier not a civilian. He should not be afforded any of the rights a civilian court might grant him. Those civil rights are reserved only for individuals not acting in concert with others."

"What about the other side of the equation?" Lars asked.

"Other side of what equation?"

"We are debating how the enemy ought to be treated, as soldier or civilian. But what about the people who prosecute and capture the enemy? In what capacity are they acting? As soldier or policeman? And under whose authority? When you, Chief, go in to hunt down these people and possibly kill them, in what capacity are you acting? Are you acting as a soldier obeying orders from some military man in uniform? Or are you acting as a member of the law enforcement community under orders from a civilian judge?"

"This makes a difference?"

"It does to me."

"Perhaps I can put your mind at ease."

"What is our legal standing in this TAT business?" Lars asked. "Are we policemen pursuing a fugitive? Or are we soldiers trying to quash an enemy unit? Do we cuff these people and read them their rights? Or do we drag them kicking and screaming behind a truck until they confess?"

"We are under civilian authority," Chief Wheeler answered. "But our mandate is broad. This sabotage business is not a simple either or proposition."

"Who has civilian authority over the team?" Lars asked.

"Viscount Morgan Henry. The Space Elevator is still out of commission. He and his family will board a jumpship for the Station in about ten days' time. He will assume command authority over the kill team and provide us with political cover for what has to be done."

"She will be there as well?"

"His daughter Kaleena? Oh, yes."

"Then I cannot possibly join the team in any capacity."

"Oh, but you will. He asked for you specifically."

"Viscount Henry? I cannot imagine why. You must have misunderstood."

"Son, I do not make those sorts of mistakes."

"No, I suppose not."

"Henry will arrive at the Station flanked by a security detail. Soldata Fifteen will head the detail. This is the same mech you worked with back at Anaconda. After the Space Elevator incident, District Viscount Henry is still considered a prime target for the terrorists."

Lars fell quiet, tried to digest the news.

"Listen, Lars," Chief Wheeler said. "We have to break off this discussion for a spell. Computer shows a hotspot and a possible micro-hole in Sector Four that we may need to seal. Bring up the scope. Set it to ten times magnification. I will swing us over in that direction."

Chief Wheeler leaned the joystick to the left this time. Again, the shuttle began to bank under his steady hand. They still had a long day ahead of them.

CHAPTER THIRTY-FIVE

The solar sailship *S.S. Ticonderoga* unfurled its giant, titanium-ribbed sail and turned into the sun. Its destination was Mars Station, a voyage of about three weeks' duration.

The unfurling of the sails was neither a quick nor a quiet thing. The two halves of the immense sail were stored in a pair of footlocker-like compartments, one on either side of the massive ship. The compartment doors, made from the highest grade of beryllium copper, rode on a series of huge hydraulic pistons. The pistons performed two functions. They also drew out the guide wires on which the sail's titanium ribs were suspended.

Lars settled back into his acceleration couch. Seated next to him was Soldata Fifteen, as much his guard as his instructor. The entire team was onboard, Sergeant Major Buster Grovosky, Chief Engineer Lexus Wheeler, Viscount Morgan Henry, his family, a swarm of techs, several colonials, and an armed echelon of merc marines.

She was there too, Kaleena. Plus countless klogs of heavy equipment, machinery, matériel and assorted gear, mostly 3-D printers, along with their metal inks. Mars Station was nearly self-sufficient when it came to foodstuffs, so little had to be imported. Most everything the colonials ate was homegrown and harvested locally. Martian soil was decent enough so long as you added enough nitrogen, phosphorous, and water.

But heavy equipment was different. It was in perennial short supply. Every last bit of it had to be imported from Earth, which made it impossibly expensive.

Lars looked out the closest window. It was small and oval-shaped, not big at all, more on the scale of a porthole on an ocean liner. He could see part of the solar sail being slowly unfurled. The sail was a mammoth thing, one-half-klom long in every direction from center to edge, a circumference in excess of three-and-one-half-kloms, with the giant ship at its center.

When completely unfurled and set at the proper angle to the sun, the thin filaments that lined the body of the sail would catch the solar wind and fill, just like a canvas sail back home when stretching tight against the wind. Think of a large-masted sailing ship before the age of steam or coal or diesel. Fully extended, the solar sail was slightly egg-shaped, a giant ellipse more than one full klom from tip to tail, with the big ship at its focal point.

The technology that made this all possible was rudimentary. It was the engineering that was difficult almost beyond comprehension. Solar sail technology had first been proven feasible in the 21st century by the Planetary Society. They built small unmanned prototypes that rode the solar wind into the asteroid belt.

But with increased size came increased technological challenges. Untold megavolts of static electricity built up on the sail's surface each minute as it billowed. Crafts as large as the *Ticonderoga* would come much later.

Under the pressure of all that kinetic energy, the ship would begin to lurch forward. Velocity would be slow at first. But acceleration would be nearly constant.

Lars blinked at a sudden flash of light, blanched at an explosion of noise. An unfortunate side effect of the massive energy build-up on the sail and subsequent discharge was the din, a nearly constant crackling, practically a roar, as the charge on the surface of the solar sail was bled off every few seconds with a loud pop and a flash of white light. — But the big ship itself would keep right on accelerating.

The ship was heavily insulated. But the noise made talking difficult. And the jarring flashes of light took a bit of getting used to. Both annoyances lessened after a few days' time, once the accelerating ship reached a velocity of about one percent of light speed.

Lars reached for the shade on the small window, tried to pull it down. Other passengers did the same for windows near them.

But the shade would not budge. It was electronically controlled from another location. Outside, the solar sail seemed to be on fire. But the man in the next row, an experienced tech, said everything was as it should be. Soldata nodded its agreement.

Lars turned his head from the window. The crackling of static electricity worsened. For the moment anyway, talk was all but impossible.

Who would he talk to anyway? Soldata? Hah! What a laugh.

The last ten days onboard the Station before they left had seen a whirlwind of activity. There had been a lot for Lars to learn and he had been Chief Wheeler's shadow nearly the entire time. The ship's manifest ran into the hundreds of pages, from the mundane to the spectacularly arcane, everything from medicine to manure, from tractors to tracheal needles, from photography equipment to pornographic vids. Chief Wheeler was responsible for every last detail.

Two days before the *Ticonderoga* was scheduled to depart, Viscount Henry arrived from Earth with his daughter in tow. The Viscount's wife Mary had stayed behind on Earth. After the terrorist attack on the Space Elevator and her near-death experience, Mary's spacefaring days were over.

For Lars, it had been an awkward reunion. Kaleena was still off-limits. Viscount Henry had been very specific about that. Until the *Ticonderoga* broke anchor and pulled away from the Station, Lars was to keep his distance. Lars hoped to soon speak with her alone onboard. For the moment, the noise of acceleration made that impossible.

Ten days ago, after that long day of sealing micro-holes on the exterior of the *Ticonderoga*, there remained many lessons and protocols for Lars to learn. Weapons, materials, medical care, comm nodes, dress code, that sort of thing. His skullcap buzzed with information for hours.

Chief Wheeler spent that same afternoon giving Lars an overview of what he might expect upon touchdown on Mars three weeks hence. He was wistful when he spoke:

"I have only been to Mars once before, Lars. The truth is I had a tough time adjusting to being away. I could not wait to get back home. I was in a ship much like this one, not the *Ticonderoga* but an older model, the *Alexander Hamilton*.

"On the day I finally sailed for home, I stood at the window, watched Mars slip away beneath my feet. Let me tell you, Lars. The two planets, Earth and Mars, are superficially alike. But the actual truth is that they could not be more different. Earth is green. It is vibrantly alive. Fish and birds and antelope. Lakes and rivers and oceans. Cold winter mornings, hot summer days. Mars is none of these things. Mars is dry. It almost never rains, though terraforming is slowly beginning to change that. Its gravity is much weaker than Earth's own, barely one-third as much. You will notice the difference right off, from your very first step. Walking on the surface will be a completely new experience for you, more like swinging a pendulum than engaging in a casual saunter. People tend to walk about sixty percent faster on the Red Planet than at home, and burn up half as many calories doing so. A man has to watch his pizza intake; it is easy to get fat on Mars. Women are prone to forgetting; probably the estrogen. They all eat like horses, swell up like balloons and soon look hideous. Watch that girlfriend of yours. Keep her away from the buffet table."

"She is not my girlfriend."

"Yeah, Lars. You keep telling yourself that."

"Her father hates me."

"Some things trump hate."

"What do you know that I do not?"

"It is not my place to say," Wheeler replied. "But one thing I can tell you for sure. Mars is an unforgiving place. The atmosphere is thin. Temperatures fluctuate wildly and rapidly. So does air pressure. Winds can be wild. Gusts up to one hundred kloms per hour are not uncommon."

"How do the colonials survive against storms of that magnitude?"

"For openers, these people have tough constitutions. Plus, the winds lack Earth's destructive power, even when they are blowing fast. The force the winds exert is comparatively low. Dust is the real problem, like I told you before."

Lars nodded and Chief Wheeler continued. "In the morning, a man might see fog or frost or wispy blue clouds. Depending on which direction he looks — and at what time of day — the sky will have a different color. At noon, if you look towards the horizon, dust scattering makes the sky appear red. The rising and setting sun is blue. In every other direction and at every other time of day, the sky is butterscotch. The sun always throws weird shadows across the landscape. The ground never looks the same. Even footpaths you are accustomed to look different. A simple hike can become treacherous."

Chief Wheeler continued. "Mars is boringly flat. Even Olympus Mons, the largest mountain in the solar system, is comparatively flat."

"Seriously? I have seen pictures. It looks hellishly steep."

"Pictures are a matter of perspective. Olympus Mons is steep in certain places; that much is true. But overall, it has an average grade of only a few percent. The only place on Mars where the topography gets interesting is on the rim of Valles Marineris. There, it is a bit like Canyonlands in Utah. Perhaps you have been?"

"Never had the pleasure. My family did not have much money. We never traveled much. But again, I have seen pictures."

"That is too bad. Young people should travel. They ought to throw on a rucksack and hit the road. The Valles Marineris rift system of Mars is one of the larger canyon systems in the solar system. It is surpassed in size only by the rift valleys of Earth and in length by the Baltis Vallis of Venus."

"Will we get to see it?"

"The Baltis Vallis rift valley on Venus? Pray you never set foot in that hellhole. Baltis Vallis is nearly seven thousand kloms long and up to three kloms wide in places. That sinuous channel is longer than the Nile River. It is the longest known channel of any kind in the solar system. It is thought to have once held a river of lava. Some people say it still does."

"I did not mean the lava channel on Venus. I meant the Canyonlands of Mars. Will we get to see that?"

"Perhaps," Wheeler said. "But let me tell you something else queer about Mars. The planet has no ionosphere."

"So?"

"So . . . think about it. Radios are useless. Except for point-to-point communication, radios are of no value. Line-of-sight only. Never more than seven kloms apart, the approximate distance to the horizon. It is one of those instances where physics, not policies, wreak havoc with profits. Without a fortune in relay satellites or tens of thousands of microwave towers, the planet can never be settled in a big way. This is a real drawback. Humanity depends on radio comm in everything from weather prediction to emergency vehicles."

It had been ten days, now, since that conversation. They were now onboard the ship, the *Ticonderoga*, with solar sails unfurled. They were already five thousand kloms out and picking up speed quickly. The buzz from the solar sails remained deafening, all that static electricity being harnessed and sloughed off, crackle and pop and flashes of bright white light.

Lars stepped away from the window and moved further back in thc ship. Any number of passengers were doing the same, relocating to the rear. The ship was better insulated and quieter back there. People could talk.

The *Ticonderoga* was a big ship, twelve levels in all. On Level Eight, at the rear — the so-called Entertainment Deck — was a large aft lounge. There were windows back there, fairly large ones, where a person might look safely outside at space without risking damage to his corneas.

The windows were darkly tinted now, on one side of the ship, to protect a passenger's eyes from the harmful rays of the unfiltered sun.

But no amount of tinting could blot out the glimmering visage of a trans-comet hurtling through space from its origin in the outer reaches of the solar system to its eventual rendezvous with Venus.

Lars thought back to that first day with her. He and Kaleena had just finished having sex. They were in the zero-g room staring out the window, exactly as he was now. There it was, the trans-comet, gleaming and shiny, far out of proportion to its size. Man fiddling with his environment. This was the crux of the problem. For every man who wanted to change the environment to better suit Man's needs, there was another who thought it wiser to leave it alone, even if leaving it alone meant others might suffer a lower of standard of living as a result or have a shortened lifespan.

As if the Garden of Eden were an actual place and every bite of the apple since that idyllic time had distanced us somehow from a world of plenty, a world of grace where we all lived in perfect harmony with nature. Hah! What crap!

Lars found a seat, now, at the bar located towards the rear of Level Eight. He sat down, ordered himself a beer. Unlike some bars earthside, no bot or other hardwired marvel of technology stood behind this counter. Here, service was doled out by a real live bartender, one trained to be a good listener or to mind his own business and smart enough to know which was which.

Nor was this place sterile, not like the Night Cap Pub onboard the Station. It was quite homey, actually, quite warm and friendly with an emote wall at the far end.

Nor did this place feel dangerous, not like Perdition's Cup deep inside Hedon City. This place was crowded, crawling with people, most of them happy and laughing.

Besides the bartender, an older man was already sitting at the counter nursing a blue-colored drink. The man was distinguished looking, like a college professor or a diplomat. Lars recognized him right off. It was Viscount Henry. Here, in the center of the ship, the crackling of the solar sails was barely audible. The two men could have a conversation.

"What is your poison, old-timer?" Lars asked, sucking the head off his beer.

"Such enduring arrogance. And from such a young man too."

"Tell me, old-timer. Just how far up your ass can you get that golden thumb of yours anyway?"

Lars was in a mood. *Out here in the middle of space on a ship destined for Mars, what could Viscount Henry do to him?* Throw him off the ship? Toss him in the brig? Not very damn likely. Lars suddenly felt himself on a level playing field with this much more powerful man. He was ready for some payback after the way Viscount Henry had spoken to him weeks before.

"You are a piece of work, aren't you kid?"

"No more than you. I know a Korinthenkacker when I see one," Lars said, downing his beer and ordering another. The bartender, if he had any opinion at all, kept it to himself.

"Ah, the arrogant young lout seeks to impress," the older man said, studying the contents of his glass. "Dare I ask what that foul-sounding word means?"

"Korinthenkacker. Translated from the German. It literally means *raisin-crapper.* An anally retentive person. One who is bossy and overly concerned with trivial details."

"And from what virtuoso did you learn this little gem? It seems a bit advanced for a washout from the Anaconda Military Academy."

"Chief Wheeler, that's who. And I did not washout. You had me bilged. After which, I became Chief Wheeler's charge. He took me under his wing. The man is brilliant. He has taught me a great many things."

"And learning how to call someone a raisin-crapper in German was one of those brilliant things the man taught you?"

Lars threw back the beer, ordered a third. "What exactly do you want from me, old-timer?" He was getting drunk.

"I don't know which I like better, raisin-crapper or old-timer."

"What exactly do you want from me?"

Viscount Henry pushed back his drink, got up from the bar, and stood very close behind Lars, who was still seated, practically brushing the younger man's shoulder.

Lars turned slowly on his barstool. Viscount Henry looked the younger man sternly in the eye. The bartender had his finger on the crisis button, half-expecting a fight and a need to alert security.

"My daughter is pregnant. You are the father. I expect you to make an honest woman of the girl. There will be no wedding. But you will propose marriage to my daughter and she will accept. You will execute a legally binding contract that provides financial support for her child and you will execute this contract in front of witnesses.

I expect this nuptial to take place before a magistrate while you are both still onboard the *Ticonderoga* and before we put down on Mars. Is that understood?"

Lars was suddenly very sober. All the fight was out of him. The bartender relaxed his finger and moved on to the next patron further down the counter.

"What will it be, bub?"

CHAPTER THIRTY-SIX

The bar was crowded now. Some of the patrons were not even actually there. They were holo-people, designed to entertain. Highly sophisticated fictions programmed to help lonely people pass the time or make them laugh or cry depending on mood.

But there were others, genuine people built of flesh and blood, both male and female, travel companions hired by the company, who were also there to entertain. Some were very well paid. Montera Cantina was one of those women. She was tall, leggy, and knock down gorgeous.

Viscount Henry smiled widely as Montera approached the brass rail of the ship's watering hole. His wife Mary was home on Earth. He was free to roam. Viscount Henry was a powerful man. He could have nearly any woman he wanted. When it came to shipboard travel, Montera was his favorite.

Lars, still at the bar, saw Viscount Henry smile. It made him think.

"Is that how it is then?" Lars asked. "You can step out on your wife any time you please? But I have to pay dearly for a moment's indiscretion?"

"Yes, son. That is exactly how it is. Now step off without making a scene and leave me alone. Montera and I have a lot of catching up to do."

Lars grumbled and excused himself. Montera took his seat at the bar. She crossed her legs and hiked up her skirt. Viscount Henry signaled the barkeep to bring her a drink.

"Is that the boy who was with your daughter?"

"Yes, that is him."

"What do you intend to do about it? Grapevine says she is pregnant."

"Make him sign a marriage contract, of course."

"What is to be gained by that? She is just a child and he has no money."

"Montera, this really is none of your concern. You are a travel companion, not a marriage counselor or legal consultant. Please remember your place."

"I know my place. Do you know yours?"

"Montera, please . . ."

"Does your daughter even want to marry this man?"

"Kaleena does not have a say in this."

"Of course she does! And even if she didn't, what could that boy possibly have that Kaleena does not already have? That boy has nothing to offer her. Pay the boy off and be done with him."

"A man in my position cannot have a grandchild born out of wedlock. Besides, the boy is disrespectful, calls me a raisin-crapper."

Montera chuckled. "At least the little shit has a sense of humor. But let's face it. Kaleena is no different from me."

"That is an insanely rude comment. Kaleena is a Viscount's daughter, you are a . . ."

"I am a what? .... A whore? ... Is that what you are calling me?"

"I did not say that."

"No. But that is what you meant."

"Montera, please let's not argue."

"Every woman is different. That is, until you get them horizontal. Then every woman is the same."

"Okay, girl. You have made your point. Now, can we get to it? I have certain needs that are presently going unmet."

"Yes, I know. You like to watch. Then you like to do."

"Yes. In that order."

•
•

Travel companions had some of the largest and most luxurious accommodations onboard the *Ticonderoga*. This was by design. They were among the most important crew members, with important work to do. Turmoil onboard a commercial spaceship was perhaps the most virulent disease a fixed human population could possibly face in an enclosed space. The travel companions were the release valve on what might otherwise become an uncontrollable pressure cooker.

Montera Cantina took Viscount Henry's hand, now, and led him across the threshold into her quarters. The interior wall colors were subtle and inviting, the floors carpeted and soft. In the corner was a Comfy Chair. The onboard apartment of every travel companion featured at least one such Chair. It reset, inventoried, and remembered its shape according to each new occupant.

The first order of business tonight, indeed in all such liaisons, was an offer to use the shower. Hot water was perennially in short supply onboard a sailship, sold at a premium, timed and metered to the last deciliter.

But travel companions had an overlarge water allotment, more than anyone else onboard, including the captain. A man in the company of a travel companion could stand beneath the pounding water for up to twenty minutes and let it flow down hot over his body.

"Shower first?" she cooed. "Or a drink?"

"Shower after," he said.

Montera opened her liquor cabinet, poured him a drink, dropped in three ice cubes. He liked ice cubes, but never two or four, always three. She knew that about him.

He smiled. "How is that travel companions always have the best hooch?"

"For medicinal purposes, I assure you."

"Of course, Doctor."

"And how is it with your wife?"

"If you and I are to have sex together, you best not bring up my wife again. Or my daughter, for that matter."

"Sorry."

"Let's get started then," Viscount Henry said, swallowing the last of the potent elixir.

Montera smiled, undid the buttons of her white cotton blouse. She dropped her bra to the floor, let her breasts hang free.

This was one good-looking woman. Montera admired her reflection in the glass of her full-length mirror. It hung on the back of the bathroom door.

Viscount Henry stood behind her, enjoyed the view from the mirror as much as she did. He got off watching a beautiful woman pleasure herself. Montera knew that about him. It was the essence of her power over this man.

Montera's breasts were taut and high, her nipples thick and hard. Being young and fit was important to this woman. Getting old was for someone else. Her time, if it came at all, was far in the future. By then, rejuvenation would be commonplace and she could misspend another youth.

Now Montera undid the clasp at her waist, dropped her skirt to the floor. Her underwear was shear. The dark triangle of feminine hair was visible beneath the fabric. Henry felt himself getting hard inside his trousers.

Montera was still in front of the mirror. She placed her hands on her hips, tightened the muscles of her buttocks and abdomen. She was firm in the right places, soft everywhere else. No bodybuilding for this woman, just hard physical labor, cleaning house, chopping wood at her father's cabin when she was home, scrubbing bulkheads and decks when the ship was docked.

Montera equated hard work with femininity. This is where she felt the modern woman had gone wrong. By seeking equal opportunity in the workplace, today's woman had abandoned the home. Washing dishes and scrubbing floors and raising children was beneath the modern woman. *Could refusing to service their husbands be far behind?*

Montera Cantina was all about sex. More delicious than food, she would say. More fulfilling than a career. An act of physicality more rewarding than any other.

The tight-fitting panties were next to go. Now she stood naked before her mirror dressed only in her tennis shoes. They hardly ever came off.

Viscount Henry was out of his pants as well, holding himself ramrod hard in his right hand. The man needed no encouragement for what he was about to do.

Montera turned to face him in all her glory. His manhood was rigid in his hand. It was reaching out to her. Montera took great satisfaction in knowing she held that kind of power over a man.

But now, every last restraint had to go. It wasn't as if she had a choice in the matter. There was important business to be accomplished here. If she were to achieve the heart-pounding orgasm she so desperately sought, all restraints had to go, the physical as well as the spiritual.

From the mirror, Montera moved now to the emote wall. Only the rich or the well-placed could afford such a wall. It was one of those inventions that had been three thousand years in the making, a technological marvel, a stepchild of the first cave painting, a direct descendant of the first fresco ever daubed onto wet plaster by an ancient Greek. Practically the entirety of human evolution had been invested in escaping the dangers of outside and perfecting the comforts of inside. An emote wall of such calibre was the culmination of that long evolutionary process.

The emote wall was screen and vid, game and hologram, sound and light. It was governed by a learning program. With repeated use, the wall would come to know its owner, what music they liked when their mood was such, what colors they preferred, what sounds they found most appealing, what images they liked displayed before them on the wall. A pedophile might want pictures of little boys. A masochist, images of pain. A hiker, towering mountains. A space jockey, images of ring-laced planets. Montera liked pornography, hard pounding scenes of women with men, sensual moaning, blue colors, the smell of rain, a gentle wind.

As the naked Montera approached the emote wall, she rubbed her breasts. The wall sensed her presence. It instantly began to search its database for the things that turned her on. She stood before the wall, watching, feeling the warmth grow between her legs. This was sex taken to a higher level. Pleasant music. Enchanting smells. Bewitching images. All programmed to make its owner happy.

Viscount Henry watched Montera Cantina's every movement closely. The curve of her neck, the swell of her breasts, the roundness of her behind, the crease behind her knee. He had his hands on his manhood, stroking it gently.

She went to her nightstand. In the top drawer was a receptacle. In the receptacle was a small mechanical device. It was the size of a small flashlight. In an earlier age the device might have been called a vibrator. In fact, it was much more, a pneumatic drill in an age of ordinary hammers.

The business end of the Autoclit featured a small, rotating head. A woman could brush or press the spinning head against her privates or any erogenous zone she preferred. Rapidly moving microfilaments would give her a buzz like no man ever could, not with his rather blunt instrument or finger or tongue.

But the Autoclit was more than just a simple battery-powered mechanical device. It was a sophisticated electronic device with a tiny brain. It employed harmonic motion accompanied by low-volume sonic waves that heightened the experience, plus biologic agents that accentuated the engorgement of her female parts. The sonic waves were pulsed to match the tempo of her internal contractions.

Autoclit in hand, Montera settled into the nearest Comfy Chair to begin her self-administered therapy.

The Chair softened and changed its contours as it recognized its master. It spread and flattened to the position that afforded her the most access. She gently touched the apparatus to its intended spot and began to softly moan.

The emote wall sensed her sounds. It exchanged data with the whirring machine between her legs. Then, suddenly, the visual imagery changed. It was more raw now. Female mouths. Male parts. Women stroking themselves. Harsher lighting. Erotic sounds.

The vibrator changed shape in her hand. It had built-in protocols, standard ways to respond. Now it conformed to her carnal needs according to its programming. It changed its shape in ways she had, on previous occasions, found most satisfying.

Now came a spray of potent, bio-engineered hormones, a delicate mist applied to the spot where it would do the most good.

Montera was losing control. Viscount Henry already had. With one final stroke, he came hard and fast. It splashed across her upper chest and arms.

Montera arched her back, now, and in a great rush let it happen. She let go of the Autoclit and gripped the rounded arms of the Comfy Chair with both hands. The mechanical device could operate on its own, without anyone directing its movements. It was an e-tool, a smart tool. It could be guided by lasers built into the arms of the Chair. The tool knew what she wanted, for it had learned from previous use. It knew how to pleasure her better than she knew herself.

Then finally it was done. She screamed but then caught herself. Wave after wave of tumultuous pleasure pounded through her pelvis until she could take no more.

Then slowly, everything powered down. The emote wall darkened. Viscount Henry sat down exhausted. The vibrator guided itself to the nearest power receptacle and shut itself off.

A blanket rolled out of one side of the Comfy Chair and covered her naked body. Little by little, the Chair altered its shape until she was cradled in its arms.

Montera drifted off to sleep, a look of remarkable, everlasting contentment on her face.

Viscount Henry got to his feet, stepped into the shower, turned on the hot water. It would be a long time before he turned it off again. Travel companions could use as much hot water as they liked, and this travel companion belonged exclusively to him.

CHAPTER THIRTY-SEVEN

"It was the best of times, it was the worst of times."

"Come again?" Lars said. The two young people were sitting in one of the ship's public lounges not far from the aft messhall.

"The opening lines from *A Tale of Two Cities*," Kaleena replied, waving the electronic reader in front of him.

"This is the name of a book?"

"Yes, and a very old one at that," Kaleena answered. "French Revolution. Jacobin Reign of Terror. Written by Charles Dickens in the late 1800s."

"And you are reading it?"

"Why not? The outbound trip is three weeks minimum. Then six months on the ground with the colonials. I will have plenty of time on my hands with nothing much to do. Why not read?"

"Honestly, Kaleena."

"No, listen. This is good stuff — *It was the best of times, it was the worst of times, it was the age of wisdom, it was the age of foolishness, it was the epoch of belief, it was the epoch of incredulity, it was the season of Light, it was the season of Darkness, it was the spring of hope, it was the winter of despair, we had everything before us, we had nothing before us, we were all going direct to Heaven, we were all going direct the other way . . .*"

"Honestly, why read such a nonsense if the author cannot make up his mind? Which is it? The best of times or the worst of times? The age of foolishness or the age of wisdom?"

"Have you no imagination?" she grumbled.

"Are you actually pregnant?"

"Way to change the subject."

"Well, are you?"

"Do you actually think I would make up a story like that?"

"No, I suppose not."

"Then what?"

"You really want to be my wife? You really want me to be your husband?"

"God no. We hardly know one another."

"My very point," Lars said. "We have no business being married. We haven't even been on a first date yet."

"Hah. What a pair we two are."

"Yes. Mother and Father from hell."

Kaleena grinned. "So what about that first date?"

"Are you asking me out?"

"Turnabout is fair play," Kaleena replied, powering down her reader. "Yes, I am asking you out. What do you say?"

"You are really not my kind . . . But I accept."

"Good. The *Ticonderoga* has a nice dance club onboard. I remember it from my recent trip home. Good music. Cheap drinks. Some holos. But mostly just good people looking for a good time."

"Sounds trig to me. Let's go."

•
•

Chief Engineer Lexus Wheeler and District Viscount Morgan Henry sat across from one another on the flight deck of the *Ticonderoga*. It was an enormous area filled with instruments and control modules. The nearby nav screen was lit up like a Christmas tree, lights and vid screens purring. Captain Nathanial Reynolds was at the wheel. Sergeant Major Grovosky was standing in for the pilot, who was below resting. First Watch was nearly over.

"The solar system runs on data," Chief Wheeler said, eyeing Captain Reynolds carefully. An armed soldier bot stood either side of the flight deck doorway.

"A rather bold if incomprehensible statement," Viscount Henry replied. After being with Montera, his only interest was in retiring for the day.

"But true nevertheless," Wheeler snapped.

"If you say so."

"I do say so. And so should you," Wheeler retorted, still casting a wary eye at Captain Reynolds. Reynolds had come onboard at nearly the last minute. Wheeler had not been able to properly vet the man. He didn't know the Captain's background or his credentials. That bothered him.

Chief Wheeler continued. "More to the point. That data is quite valuable to our business, to our company, Trans-Comet Incorporated."

"Listen, Chief. I am tired. If I nod my head and say that I agree with every last word you say, can we end this discussion quickly and you let me grab some shuteye?"

Chief Wheeler ignored the other man completely. "Please tell me that you understand. We take every precaution to safeguard and vouchsafe every scrap of data we collect. You understand that, right?"

"I have every confidence in you, Chief. But you know very well that I am no tech. Why are you bringing this to me?"

"How much do you know about our data storage systems?"

"Not much. I do know that the volume of data we collect each trip is gargantuan. It is measured in petabytes or terabytes or some such big number like that. But I have no clue how we protect all that great volume of data or even what is being collected."

"Let me give you a quick primer."

"Must you?"

"Magnetic tape is the oldest data storage medium still in use. It dates back to the infancy of computing, to the very earliest days, a UNIVAC computer circa mid-1900s."

"Damn, a history lesson." Viscount Henry swore.

"In those days de-bugging a program referred to removing actual bugs, sometimes spiders, sometimes insects. The first bug removed from a computer was a night moth. Only later did the term come to refer to mistakes in programming."

"Good night, Chief. I am going to bed." Viscount Henry got up from the table to leave.

"Sit down!"

Henry was surprised by the Chief's insistence. But he sat back down quietly.

"Take a stim, if you have to," Chief Wheeler said, signaling to one of the robot soldiers to come over. "But stay awake and hear me out."

Chief Wheeler continued. "Magnetic tape is long outdated. Hard disks and flash memory and bubble chips have become ever more popular and less expensive. But tape is what we use onboard. For the long-term preservation of large amounts of data, magnetic tape has certain advantages.

"The first is speed. Tape can be read four times as fast as reading from a hard disk, twice as fast as from a bubble drive.

"The second advantage is reliability. When a tape snaps, which is not often, it can be spliced back together easily and quickly with ordinary adhesive. The data loss is rarely more than a few hundred megabytes, small potatoes in information technology circles. But when a hard disk fails, a terabyte of data may be lost in an instant.

"A third and very big benefit of using magnetic tape is that it doesn't need a constant input of power to preserve the data. But temporarily turning off the power to a spinning disk increases the likelihood the disk will fail causing a catastrophic loss of data."

Viscount Henry was beginning to grasp the importance of what Wheeler was trying to tell him. He had swallowed the stim Wheeler had instructed the mech bot to give him. The pill was having its desired effect. Wheeler continued:

"Better security. That is a fourth benefit. A hacker with a grudge can delete 50 petabytes of disk-based data in a matter of minutes. To erase that same amount of data from magnetic tape would take years.

"Finally, tape is cheaper. And it lasts longer. Kept under the right conditions, magnetic tape can still be read reliably after three decades, against five years for a disk."

"Chief, you make a very good case for tape, I admit. But I still do not see how this concerns me. Data collection and retention is not part of my mandate."

"Data collection is first to short-term media, flash memory and the like. Every six hours or so the data is purged and transferred to magnetic tape. We keep the originals onboard. Duplicate tapes are generated each time the ship docks at the Station."

"I'm no tech, like I said. But what kind of data do we collect on these long trips to and from Mars?"

"Direction and speed of the solar wind. Gravity wave distribution. Ion concentration. Density of micrometeor swarms. The really valuable stuff is what we gather while we sit in parking orbit above Mars."

"Yes, I know a little something about that," Viscount Henry said. "Beryllium mining data, isn't it?"

"Yes. It is one among several valuable ores. The space industry is in desperate need of beryllium ore to manufacture aerospace-grade beryllium copper alloy. But this stuff is dangerous for people to handle. It presents technical challenges. Beryllium-dust is toxic. If inhaled, beryllium is corrosive to living tissue. It can cause a chronic life-threatening form of pneumonia, an allergic disease called berylliosis that results in severe lung damage. Since the colonials already wear spacesuits pretty much 'round the clock and since they already have dust mitigation protocols in place, mining the stuff on Mars and bringing it home to Earth is cheaper and less dangerous than doing the same thing back on Earth."

"Which makes your data tapes valuable stuff," Henry agreed. "Mining companies, maybe other governments, would be willing to pay big sums of money for access to your data runs."

"Valuable booty to pirates as well," Wheeler observed. "A set of tapes like ours would bring a healthy ransom."

"Now I see where you are going with this, Chief. Permit me to guess what you are going to say next."

"You have the floor, Viscount."

"A complete set of data tapes like the ones you collect would likewise make an attractive target for a terrorist attack. Destroy that archive of tapes and you destroy decades of work and trillions of invested credits."

"Nail on head," Wheeler replied. "Nail square on head."

"So, Chief, in your estimation the *Ticonderoga* along with its cache of tapes and perhaps its cargo of heavy equipment is now a target?"

"I believe them to be."

"In which case, the ship is less likely to be blown up than hijacked."

"My thoughts exactly."

"In which case we need to buck up security," Viscount Henry said.

"I don't want to pop your balloon, Viscount. But there is little we can do from out here in space to improve security onboard. When I spoke of pirates stealing our data tapes, I meant when we were docked, not when we were in motion. There are no pirate ships out here trolling the netherworld for booty. Plus, I cannot imagine another ship, no matter how sophisticated, pulling up alongside and boarding us, not without help anyway."

"A month ago, no one could have imagined saboteurs blowing up the Space Elevator and nearly killing me and my family. But that happened, did it not?"

"Point taken," Wheeler replied. "But that does not change the parameters one wit. A sailship is not a battleship. It is not equipped for combat. It does not have armor plating. It carries no offensive weapons. Who expects an attack on a sailship? They move fast, faster with each passing minute. All we have onboard to fight back with against an enemy is a single, fixed laser. Oh, and a trash compacter that forcibly ejects all our non-recyclables out the garbage chute once a week. It is mainly filled with sanitary napkins and rotting potato skins."

"Forget about being boarded," Viscount Henry intoned. "Couldn't an incoming missile or an explosive charge destroy the sail? Wouldn't that slow down the *Ticonderoga* appreciably, maybe bring it to a dead stop?"

"You are forgetting about the laws of inertia. Blasting a hole in the solar sail would more likely send the ship into a deadly spin. The ship would lurch out of control and be destroyed. We would all die. Any data or valuable cargo would be destroyed along with us."

"So we are no longer talking pirates. We are again talking terrorists."

Chief Wheeler nodded, sat back in his chair, and let the words hang in the air. He noticed, now, that Captain Reynolds had left his post while they talked and had drifted closer to where they sat, perhaps close enough to hear the last few minutes of heated discussion. This was troubling.

"Okay, Chief. You have convinced me . . ."

"Lower your voice," Wheeler said.

Viscount Henry began to look around, when the Chief suddenly said, "Don't."

Henry froze. Chief Wheeler nodded, as if they were still talking. He watched the goings on closely. Captain Reynolds began to drift further away from the two, afraid he had been made.

"Okay," Chief Wheeler said. "Coast is clear."

"What the hell was that all about? Don't you trust the Captain?"

"I do not actually know the Captain. Until I can complete a background check on the man, what we say must remain between the two of us."

"We cannot keep this a secret, not for long anyway. As I was about to say. You have convinced me. We have to call a meeting. The entire security team, including Captain Reynolds. You, me, Grovosky, Soldata, Reynolds, everyone. We need to work out a defense strategy in case the ship comes under attack."

"If terrorists were to make a play for the ship, they would need someone on the inside, possibly multiple someones. If we were to have that meeting, everyone at the table would be a suspect. You cannot ignore that fact. No one onboard the ship is above reproach until I say they are above reproach."

"Okay," Viscount Henry said. "I will begin on the Q.T."

"And I will run some sim scenarios to see if there is any possible way for someone to board or otherwise slow this ship while the sail is furled."

"Good. You do that and get back to me."

•
•

"Have you ever danced with a hologram before?" Lars asked as they entered the holo-club. The music was subdued, as if the band were between numbers.

"Oh yes, indeed I have," Kaleena answered. "But I would hardly classify it as a rewarding experience."

"And how could it be? No touching, no physical intimacy?"

"But a holo won't step on your foot when you are out on the dance floor doing the waltz. It will not turn you in the wrong direction when you are doing the tango."

"It won't make love to you afterwards either," Lars said.

"Ah, now I see where this is going."

"And why not?" he asked.

"Can we dance first?"

"Yes, by all means," he replied. "But I have to warn you. My waltz is a lot better than my tango. So I hope you are wearing your steel-toed sneakers."

The music began, he took her by the hand, led her out onto the floor. The band was a troupe of holos made to look real enough. It was a retro look, closely cropped hair with full beards.

The music drew them close. He pressed his body against hers. She cooed, then her body tightened, as if she had something important to ask.

"What did my father say to you?" Kaleena trembled as she spoke.

Lars looked her in the eye, afraid to answer. "He said I am the father of your baby. Is that true?"

"Maybe. Maybe not."

"Maybe you are not pregnant? Or maybe I am not the father?"

Kaleena considered her reply. But Lars had it already figured out.

"That boy on Mars? Is that who?"

"It is possible," Kaleena said.

"How possible?"

"Very possible."

"You might have told me this before now."

"I didn't know how. Plus, we were not allowed to talk, remember?"

"You never heard of email?" Lars said. "Never heard of text messages? Of students passing folded notes in class? If you had cared, you could have found a way."

"I am sorry. I only just did the math myself. I was with that boy only a week before I was with you. He and I took the same sailship home from Mars, this ship."

"Your father is a son-of-a-bitch. You know that, right?"

"I am aware."

“Are you also aware that he keeps company with an onboard bim named Montera?”

“Crude term. You mean travel companion, don’t you?”

“Travel companion then. So you knew?”

“Of course, I knew,” Kaleena said. “Mother will no longer get it on with Father. So he gets what he can on the outside. Montera Cantina is mostly discrete.”

“So, if your father can be so open-minded when it comes to his own sexual needs, why is he breaking my balls over what has happened between you and me?”

“A father getting upset by his daughter having unwed sex and getting pregnant with a boy she hardly knows? Yeah, that is really unusual. I cannot think of any other father who would react that way.”

“It is more than that.”

Kaleena nodded as if she understood. “I think he knows the truth about the other boy. My guess is that he thinks more highly of you than the other boy.”

“The man sure has a funny way of showing it.”

“What would you have me say, Lars?”

“For starters, let me off the hook with your father. Tell him about the other boy.”

“If I agree to that, then what? I am a pregnant girl with no husband and no visible means of support.”

Lars stared at Kaleena hard. By now the music had stopped and they had stepped apart.

“I guess our dance is over,” he said.

“Wasn’t sex next up on the agenda?” she asked hopefully.

“Not tonight, Kaleena. My heart is no longer in it.”

“That’s it, then? You are going to hang me out to dry?”

“Girl, you hung yourself out to dry. I am nothing more than a clothespin for the line.”

CHAPTER THIRTY-EIGHT

"Chief, the Captain would like to see you."

Lars found Chief Wheeler in his usual spot, his office one deck below the flight deck. From this command center, he attended to the ship's business. One wall was a large window. It looked forward out over the bow of the ship.

"Why the hell didn't he just come down here himself?" Wheeler grumbled. "The man works and lives just one deck above me." He pointed to the ceiling with obvious disgust.

"Do not shoot the messenger, Boss. One of his bots cornered me outside the galley, asked me to personally deliver you the message. I do not know what is going on. Though I will say this. Those bots of his give me the creeps. They are not like Soldata Fifteen at all."

"I will tell you what is going on. Captain Reynolds did not want the logs to reflect an official record of my visit. That is why he avoided the comm. He did not want his request or a record of my visit put through the ship's electronic mail. So he did the next best thing. He sent the request by carrier pigeon instead."

Chief Wheeler was already suspicious of Captain Reynolds. He did not like the way the man had been lurking about when he and Viscount Henry had their conversation. Wheeler had since sent a secure communiqué to Central for a comprehensive background packet. But no answer had come back yet. Now this.

"Come with me upstairs," Wheeler said.

"Am I in trouble?" Lars asked, suddenly worried.

"Not in the least. I want to see if Reynolds throws you out when we meet."

"Something not kosher?"

"Indulge me," Chief Wheeler said as he picked up a pair of two-ways from off his desk. He fiddled with one, put it in his pocket, handed the other to Lars. Then he closed the door to his office and locked it securely.

"What is this?" Lars asked, palming the two-way.

"You know exactly what it is. Put it in your pocket. Mine is set to broadcast only. It cannot receive. Yours is set to receive only. You cannot speak into it. But you will be able to hear every word. Plus, I have set yours to record. When Captain Reynolds throws you out of the meeting, as I am sure he will, I want you to go someplace quiet, listen to our conversation. Leave the settings where I placed them. That way I will be able to playback the conversation again later. Understood?"

"Yes sir. But what is going down?"

"Shut up and leave it be."

The two walked silently aft to the first set of stairs, went up one level, then forward again to the flight deck and nav suite. Captain Reynolds was there, along with two uniformed men, the pilot, and the Captain's usual pair of soldier bots. The uniformed men, a comm officer and a junior engineer, were studying flight maps and grav projections.

"The boy is not cleared to be up here," Captain Nathanial Reynolds barked the second he saw Lars enter the nav suite.

"The boy does not need clearance. He is with me," Chief Wheeler retorted.

"This is my flight deck. Damn straight he needs clearance. Now get out of here, boy. Before I have you forcibly removed."

Chief Wheeler nodded to Lars that it was okay, and Lars left the way he had come in, the two-way in his pocket.

"What is so damn important that you have to interrupt my morning routine?" Chief Wheeler barked. He was more suspicious of the man than ever.

"Chief, we have a big problem," Reynolds said, pulling Chief Wheeler aside.

"What kind of problem?" They were now out of earshot of the other men on the flight deck.

"The kind of problem that wrecks this ship and kills everyone aboard."

Chief Wheeler screwed up his forehead. "Funny that you should mention something that puts our ship at risk. Just yesterday Viscount Henry and I were discussing whether we had overlooked any possible terrorist threats to the ship."

"Oh, is that what you two were talking about yesterday in such hushed tones? I might have known."

Chief Wheeler was evasive. "Our business is just that, Captain. — Our business. Now what has got you so corked up?"

"This dispatch from Central." Captain Reynolds handed Wheeler a comm printout with supporting jpegs.

Wheeler sat down, scratched his head, tightened his jaw. "Have you verified these telemetry readings?"

"Working on that now." Captain Reynolds said stiffly. "Confirmation requires three separate readings in order to triangulate in 3-space. The three reference points are Mars Station, the L5 telescope, and the orbiting Space Station. That should give us a wide enough baseline."

"What are our options? I mean if the triangulation confirms that a collision is imminent?"

"Not many," Captain Reynolds replied. "A trans-comet can be guided remotely. In fact, it has to be. There is no other safe way. All trans-comets work the same way. After the comet is first captured, robot miners attach an electromagnetic mass driver to the comet's tail. The

EMD is constantly fed directional and guidance data by controllers camped out in the Ground Control Tower near Hilo."

Wheeler was incredulous. "Are you saying that someone may have hijacked the controls? That they are planning to use the trans-comet as some sort of ballistic missile to bring down this ship? Is that even possible?"

"Their objective may be different."

"I am listening."

"What if their aim is to hijack the *Ticonderoga* rather than bring her down?"

"And how would hijacking a trans-comet advance their crazy agenda? There is no possible way to board a sailship going as fast as we are traveling. I had my people runs sims last night. It is statistically impossible."

"So this is what you and Henry were talking about yesterday?"

"Fuck off, Reynolds."

"Well here is a sim I bet you did not run. The terrorists threaten to ram our ship unless we furl the sails and slow the ship down. Then, once we are becalmed, we become vulnerable to being boarded."

"An angle I had not considered. What would they want with our ship? To extract a ransom?"

"How the hell would I know?" Captain Reynolds bellowed. "What if they simply want to steal it?"

"Steal it? Why?"

"What if this isn't TAT? What if it is Uday?"

"That crazy Arab? What would that barbecue chip want with a sailship on Venus?" Then, as if to answer his own question, Chief Wheeler suddenly fell silent.

Captain Reynolds said, "If Hassan wants to put a stop to the incoming traffic of trans-comets, what better way? A fully operational sailship like the *Ticonderoga* is worth trillions. Besides, I think he is Persian, not Arab."

"Persian? Arab? What is the difference? The *Ticonderoga* is not just precious in money terms, it can also be turned into a weapon," Chief Wheeler observed.

"A sailship is not armed. That would be contrary to the Space Treaty, which is itself based on maritime law."

"The ship itself is a weapon. Uday can turn it around. Aim it at Earth. Kick in the sails. An asteroid moving a whole lot slower and packing a whole lot less mass wiped out the dinosaurs sixty-five million years ago. Think what the *Ticonderoga* could do to life on Earth if it were intentionally crashed into the atmosphere."

"I get it," Captain Reynolds said. "The ship becomes a bargaining chip in an all-out effort to put a halt to the trans-comet trade. Brilliant plan. So what can we do to counter the threat?"

"For the moment, I have no idea. No idea whatsoever. Clearly, we need to notify Hilo Ground Control right away."

"Will you handle that?" Captain Reynolds asked.

"Straightaway."

•
•

"Did you get it all on tape?" Wheeler asked once he caught up with Lars after the meeting.

"Chief, I did what you asked," Lars replied, handing Wheeler the two-way. "But I did not playback the recording to verify. I really do not know how this gizmo works."

"No time for that now. Take my two-way down to Viscount Henry. He is familiar with the equipment. Henry ought to be in his suite or else on the TC deck. Find him. Give him the two-way. Tell him it is from me."

"TC deck?"

"TC. Travel Companion."

"Okay, got it. Montera Cantina."

"You had a taste of that one?"

"I am just a boy, remember?"

"No need for sarcasm. Take the tape to Henry. Ask him to listen to it. Then both of you come to my office after chow tonight. Pack your thinking cap, Lars. Oh, and one more thing. Grab Sergeant Major Grovosky while you are at it. I want him there as well."

"Honestly, Chief. Couldn't you ask someone else to take this damn thing to Henry? The Viscount and I are not on the best of terms."

"Cannot be helped. You shouldn't have donked his daughter. But that is now yesterday's news. Take it to Henry. If he gives you any gump, tell him he will have to answer to me. I have to contact Hilo Ground Control, see if they are having any control issues with the EMD on the incoming trans-comet."

•
•

"Is there any way to untie this Gordian knot? Anyway at all?" Viscount Henry asked.

Dinner was over, and they were together now in Chief Wheeler's office, five people in all — Wheeler himself, Lars Cabot, Viscount Henry, Sergeant Major Grovosky, and Soldata Fifteen.

"Are we even certain that someone of malicious intent has taken control of the trans-comet?" Sergeant Major Grovosky asked. "Where is Captain Reynolds anyway? Why isn't he present at this meeting?"

"Chief Wheeler thinks the man cannot be trusted," Viscount Henry said. "But we have no hard evidence either way."

"If Chief Wheeler says the man cannot be trusted, the man cannot be trusted. It is as simple as that," Sergeant Major Grovosky said. "I trust the Chief's instincts implicitly. But that still does not answer my question. — Has anyone spoken yet to Ground Control? Is this a real problem or still a hypothetical?"

Chief Wheeler answered. "Oh, it is real enough. Ground Control shows the trans-comet to be more than three percent off prime trajectory. This path, while wide, is still within tolerable limits. Or so they say. But they are bound to lie. The truth might panic the public. So they say it is still within the margin of error, still within the safe corridor. They have dispatched instructions to the EMD to pivot the driver jets ever so slightly and to alter course by three-quarters of one degree along the y-axis. But these comets are big. They do not turn on a dime. Thus far, the controllers have not declared an emergency."

"Have the telemetry readings been confirmed?" Grovosky asked.

"Yes, the preliminary triangulation data Captain Reynolds gave me confirms that we and the comet are on paths that cross. Whether that crossing leads to a collision is unknown and will remain so until the very last minute."

"Even if this thing is aimed at us, can we not outrun it? We are moving pretty damn fast, faster all the time. Plus, we have hands-on controls."

"No place to run; no place to hide. If someone is guiding it remotely, or if the trans-comet has already locked onto us by some mechanical means or electronic signature, the EMD can change course as quickly as we can."

"We could hide behind the moon," Lars suddenly said. The words were out of his mouth before he knew he said them.

Chief Wheeler seemed to like the idea. He cautiously nodded his approval. So did Sergeant Major Grovosky.

"Don't tell me we are actually going to take advice from a boy?" Viscount Henry guffawed.

"Let the boy talk," Chief Wheeler said. "He may be on to something."

"I used to hunt bear with my father," Lars began.

"Now you have resorted to making up crazy stories about your childhood?" Viscount Henry ridiculed.

"No, it's true," Lars insisted. "I am not making up a story. But the principle is sound. We should change course now. Turn the ship back into the sun. Tack across the solar wind. Put the moon between us and the incoming trans-comet. We can use the moon as cover, just like my father and I used to use boulders and trees as cover when we hunted grizzly bear."

"Don't listen to him," Viscount Henry said emphatically. "The boy is pulling your leg. No one hunts big game anymore."

Chief Wheeler said, "Whether or not Lars is telling the truth about hunting bear is irrelevant. Turning tail to hide behind the moon is a brilliant idea. Henry, where did you dig up this smart young man anyway?"

Sergeant Major Grovosky interrupted before Viscount Henry could answer. "Hell, everyone knows the story. Lars helped rescue the Viscount's family after the attack on the Space Elevator. Then Henry's daughter thanked Lars for saving their lives by spreading her legs for him. Then Henry had the boy bilged from Anaconda before later reversing course and trying to force the boy to marry his girl. — Did I get all the salient facts straight, Lars?"

Lars shook his head in the negative. "I wasn't the first."

"The first what?" Henry demanded to know.

"The first one to be with your daughter."

"You liar," Henry shouted, grabbing for Lars with outstretched arms. "You fucking liar."

"Ask her yourself. Kaleena just told me. She is pregnant by another man, some man she slept with coming home from Mars."

Viscount Henry fell quiet. He looked as if he were about to cry.

Chief Wheeler returned to topic. "If we are going to change course, we will need a nav officer working with us."

"And a comm officer too."

"Are you absolutely certain Captain Reynolds cannot be trusted? This whole run-and-hide maneuver would be a lot easier with him running the show, instead of us piecing together a makeshift nav team."

Before Chief Wheeler could answer, Viscount Henry interrupted. "Wait a minute. Think this through. If we run and hide behind the moon, they could just as easily threaten to crash the comet into Earth instead."

"Kill all of humanity just to make a point?" Wheeler interjected. "They could make that threat now. No, I do not think so. This ship — or something on this ship — is what they are after. They have no reason to target Earth."

For the first time, Soldata spoke up. "Gentlemen. In point of fact, we do not know what they are after — or even if there is actually a 'they'. No actual threats have been leveled. This entire discussion is based on a supposition."

"Bot has a point," Grovosky conceded.

"The entire argument is moot," Wheeler said. "My people have already run sims. From its present position, no alternate trajectory can bring the comet onto a collision course with Earth. A trans-comet is not a powered craft. It is not a heat-seeking missile that can dodge and turn. A trans-comet operates on simple billiard ball physics. The only source of inertial guidance is the directional jets on the rear of the electromagnetic mass driver. The only source of propulsion is gravity, the Sun's pull. That plus the smaller gravity wells of the Moon plus the three innermost planets."

Wheeler continued. "Earth is not at risk from this comet. But the *Ticonderoga* is. We either change course now and make a run for the moon as Lars suggested. Or we prepare ourselves for a possible collision in several days' time."

"I absolutely disagree on all counts," Soldata said. "There will be no collision, not now, not ever. For two objects separated by millions of kloms to be guided by clumsy ballistic mechanics to the exact same spot in 3-space at the exact same moment in time is a mathematical equation so difficult it cannot be solved by any computer in anything other than years not days. The rendezvous point is constantly in motion, as are all the planets and the sun. Our speed is constantly changing. No computer can plot a course that complicated. It cannot be done. No, if this ship is under any threat at all, it is under threat from within. Either someone at this table is behind the plot or, as you said, Captain Reynolds is the threat. There are no other possibilities. The trans-comet is a distraction, a misdirect. Whoever gave you that telemetry information is probably the inside man."

Chief Wheeler did not say the man's name. But he thought it — *Captain Nathanial Reynolds*. He was the fly in this ointment.

CHAPTER THIRTY-NINE

Lars woke suddenly. Something had changed. Lars could feel it in his belly. The ship had slowed.

Under the pressure of the solar wind, an outbound sailship accelerated at more or less a constant rate. Passengers became accustomed to that acceleration, always pressed back in their seats, always pressed down when they used the potty.

But now, something had changed, something fundamental. That pressure of acceleration had evaporated. It was gone. The ship had slowed down — or had at least stopped accelerating. Something was definitely wrong.

Lars dressed quickly. His legs were shaky. The ship was definitely slowing.

He checked his comm for messages. There were none. He made a quick scan of shipboard alerts on his device. There were none.

Lars moved quickly into the corridor, pushed amidships until he could find a window to look out.

Damn!

He half-expected to see what he saw. But it still came as somewhat of a surprise. The solar sail was no longer taut; it was being furled. There were two giant footlocker-type compartments, one on either side of the ship, where the sails were stored. The compartment doors were made of beryllium copper. They were open now and the titanium-ribbed sail was being slowly retracted.

Lars could hear the whine of the giant hydraulic pistons. The pistons drew open the compartment doors and hauled in and out the guide wires for the titanium ribs that gave the sails their distinctive shape.

The intercom crackled. "All team members are to report to the armory on the double." The announcement repeated two more times.

Lars started in that direction. The armory was aft on Level Ten, two floors below the Entertainment Deck.

He met Chief Wheeler on the stairway. The Chief was red-faced and fuming. "It was Reynolds, fucking Reynolds. I have been suspicious of that bastard since I first got onboard."

Lars already had an inkling but kept his thoughts to himself.

"The fucker locked himself in the wheelhouse, melted the locks with a blowtorch, fused the door shut. He is in control of the ship and has retracted the sails. At least one of those silicon mechs is in there with him, one of those soldier bots that is always at his side."

By now Viscount Henry had caught up with them. They were on Level Ten and moving rapidly aft toward the armory.

"It is just as you said." Viscount Henry was breathing fast. "The fucker is hijacking the ship. Why didn't I listen to you?"

"Because you are an arrogant prick."

"Yes, a lot of good that is going to do, calling me names."

"Fuck you. Who hired this Reynolds slug anyway?" Wheeler said with accusing eyes. "How the hell did he get onboard? Who did his background check? Who gave the asshole security clearance?"

"We will get to the bottom of this, I assure you," Viscount Henry said. "But this is no time for recriminations. We have to blow that door and regain control of the ship. Who is the best man onboard to lead an assault against the flight deck?"

"That job would fall to me," Sergeant Major Grovosky said. They were now at the door of the armory and Grovosky was running his keycard through the lock. "Me and my crew."

Suddenly the ship banked. The scene outside changed, and they could feel the shift in acceleration in their boots.

"Where the fuck is Reynolds taking us?" Grovosky demanded to know as he threw open the armory door.

"This matters how?" Chief Wheeler replied. He and Sergeant Major Grovosky began handing out weapons as more crewmembers came on the scene. Force guns, contact pistols, electronic whips. Two of his corporals strapped on blaster shields.

"To be perfectly blunt, it doesn't matter where he is taking us," Grovosky replied. "But I would still like to know."

"Wouldn't we all?" Viscount Henry snapped. "If we knew the man's intentions, it might be easier to talk him down. Has anyone spoken to the bastard yet?"

"Who? Reynolds? He refuses to answer the comm. We have been trying to raise him on the two-way since this first began half an hour ago," Wheeler said.

Soldata arrived at the door of the armory. Without being told, the bot picked up a satchel of communications gear, radios and such. He strapped it over his shoulder, prepared to do battle.

Sergeant Major Grovosky began to give out orders. "Pick someone, Chief. Wire him up to a skullcap. Lash him to a database. Have him begin a comprehensive search of all our datafiles. Figure out who this Reynolds character really is. Figure out what his loyalties are, who he is working for."

"I will get someone on it right away."

The ship banked further and the sun came into view. Suddenly the whirr of the hydraulic pistons revved up and the sails again began to be unfurled.

"Where the fuck is he taking us?" Grovosky asked again.

"Isn't it obvious?"

"Not to me."

"He is taking us back," Viscount Henry said. "He is turning us around."

"What do you mean back?" Grovosky asked. "Back home to Earth? To the Space Station? To the moon? Maybe crash us into the sun?"

"Venus." The words popped out of Lars's mouth before he even knew what he was saying.

"Venus? How in blazes did you arrive at that conclusion, boy?" Viscount Henry demanded.

"I do not know from politics, Sir. But Chief Wheeler explained some of it to me before we left the Station. This Uday fellow fits the profile. He lives on Venus. He controls everything on the planet. He wants to put a stop to all the inbound trans-comet traffic. The Chief tells me the noise bothers him or something like that. What better way to get Space Command's attention and put a stop to it than to hijack a valuable piece of State property?"

Chief Wheeler agreed. "Plus, do not forget, the bastard can harvest a king's ransom for our data tapes, if he wants to."

"Explain."

Wheeler brushed off Sergeant Major Grovosky. "A subject for another day perhaps."

"Okay, Sergeant Major," Viscount Henry said in a take-charge voice. "Here is where you begin to earn your pay. Develop an assault plan to re-take this ship by force or by any means possible. And do it mighty quick. By my reckoning, we have three days tops to put a stop to this insanity."

"On it, Sir."

Faces grim, each man looked at the other. The techniques for sailing into the solar wind were identical to tacking against the wind on a lake back home. The course would be oblique, diagonally across the airstream. Inbound velocity would be slow at first. But acceleration would be constant. The whole thing might be idyllic, even faintly reminiscent of the old schooner days on Earth, if it were not so very dangerous.

Outside, the crackling of violent amounts of static electricity began to buzz as the solar sails tightened in the wind and the *Ticonderoga* began to move back towards the center of the solar system.

CHAPTER FORTY

"This assault has to take place on two fronts, from the outside as well as from within."

It was two hours later, and they had gathered again, this time in Chief Wheeler's office just below the flight deck. Sergeant Major Buster Grovosky had the floor. Viscount Henry was being his usual difficult self.

"Outside? You expect men to risk their lives and try to break into the ship from outside?"

"Yes, Viscount, one team will attempt to gain access from outside the ship. The other, which I am about to discuss, will attempt to gain access from within. Now are you going to let me talk or not? You put me in charge of this, remember? Now shut up and pay attention."

Henry thought to raise an indignant objection but then thought better of it. Sergeant Major Grovosky continued:

"The nav deck is designed to be impregnable. The watchwords have always been denial of access. The security risk has always been the same, to prevent a hijacking by a passenger or member of the crew. It will not be easy to break into the flight deck from the corridor outside the bulkhead door. Neither gunfire, nor acetylene torch, nor electronic laser is going to punch much of a hole in that door or in the adjoining wall. None of the usual stuff will work."

"What then?" Viscount Henry barked.

"We will need to drill bore holes, push in tubes of fresh Comp 6, step back and blow the tubes. I am not even sure this will work. When the C6 ignites, there will be a lot of damage to the corridor outside, even perhaps to the deck below. If we do break through the bulkhead door, we risk inflicting irreparable damage to the ship's controls."

"This is what you call a plan?" Viscount Henry ridiculed.

"It isn't much of one, I admit."

"What then?"

"The assault from outside."

"That sounds like a suicide mission," Chief Wheeler said.

"It may very well be," Sergeant Major Grovosky admitted. "That is why it has to be me who does it."

"Oh, that is so very brave of you, Sergeant Major. It is also so very stupid," Viscount Henry said. "Would someone please talk some sense into this man?"

Chief Wheeler spoke. "I'm sorry, Sergeant Major. I cannot risk losing you on a suicide mission. Anyway, we cannot send a man outside. The ship is moving much too fast. Plus, there is the issue of the solar sails. They are sparking like mad. You would not make it ten meters before you got fried like bacon."

Grovosky shook his head. "The ship's speed is irrelevant. There is no hurricane-force wind outside to tear off my flightsuit. It is not like I would be on top of a boxcar being pulled along by a moving train. I will not be swept aside. I will be moving in the same direction as the ship, and at the same speed.

"But you are right about the solar sails," Grovosky continued. "They are hot and they are dangerous. The only safe route I have been able to chart out in my mind is down and out the garbage chute, up the perimeter of the ship to the nav deck. I place explosives on the canopy, move off to a safe distance, blow the charges. As soon as the glass gives way, everyone inside dies and we regain control of the ship."

"You cannot do this alone," Lars said.

"No, I do not think that I can. But I am unwilling to risk a second man's life on what we all agree is an extremely dangerous mission with long odds of success."

"Why risk a man at all?" Viscount Henry asked. "Isn't this exactly the kind of risk bots were designed for? If not, why the hell even bring them along?"

"I thought about that," Sergeant Major Grovosky said. "There are only three robots onboard. Two are locked in there with Reynolds on the nav deck. The third is right here with us in this room, Soldata Fifteen from Anaconda. But even he cannot do this alone. At least one human will have to be involved."

"Can't we use some of the simpler bots?" Henry asked. "We have countless small bots onboard. They serve all kinds of servile tasks, clean toilets, do spot welds, drain dangerous chemicals, stuff like that."

Lars interrupted. "I do not think that will work. The smaller bots have no radiation shielding. They would fry in an instant out there."

"Lars is right," Grovosky said. "And there are other problems. The smaller bots all operate on radio commands, even the autonomous ones. Some use microwave signals. We have no reliable way to exchange data with a mini-bot when it is outside the ship, not for a task this complicated. The ship is shielded and the static discharge off the sails makes comm unreliable. Plus, that same lack of shielding poses a genuine risk to Soldata. If his positronic brain was fried, the shock would render him inoperable. No, we absolutely require human involvement if we have any hope of successfully pulling this off."

"Have you asked yet for volunteers?" Henry asked.

"Not yet . . . But I was about to."

•
•

Ten Hours Later

Lars had volunteered. So had Sergeant Major Buster Grovosky. After running some diagnostics and a complete system check, it was determined that Soldata would likely malfunction when working in such close proximity to the solar sails, especially when they were charged with such high volumes of static electricity. If this was going to happen, it would be up to the humans to make it happen.

The *Ticonderoga* was moving inward, towards the inner planets of the solar system with rapidly increasing velocity. Captain Nathanial Reynolds was at the helm, and he was expertly tacking back and forth across the solar wind. Their likely destination was Venus.

For six hours, now, the Chief and his assistants had been trying to raise Reynolds on the comm. They had tried everything, music, alarms, electronic mail, banging on the door, everything. Reynolds had ignored all attempts at communication. He would not acknowledge their messages, and he had not changed course.

Two hours ago they had begun drilling holes into the bulkhead to place explosive charges. It was hard, demanding work. The drill team had already burned out one drill and three bits. At the time the ship was built, the metal surrounding the nav deck had been hardened to prevent such an entry.

Detonating the charges was actually Plan B. The explosion, even if successful at gaining entry, could damage the ship, perhaps irreparably. The preferred agenda was an assault on the flight deck from outside the ship, the assault Grovosky and Lars were preparing for at this very instant.

The garbage chute had been cleared of debris, and the maintenance crew had depressurized the shaft in preparation for their exit. They would leave the ship just as any flotsam would, then make their way up to the canopy. The spacewalk they were about to engage in would be among the most dangerous EVA's ever attempted in the history of the world. No one in his right mind journeys on a spacewalk carrying high-density explosives in his backpak.

Buster and Lars were suiting up now in the Ready Room. Lars had the lower portion of his Mag 10 suit on, ready to proceed into the airlock. The lock was little more than a small cylindrical closet. A man shimmies into the upper half of the suit on his own. Then comes a one-hour wait. A man has to breathe pure oxygen for approximately sixty minutes to flush all the nitrogen out of his blood. That is to prevent the bends. Then comes the final suit and tether checks before exiting the craft.

Lars was suited up, now, and waiting when Chief Wheeler began to speak to him over the comm. The Chief was in a philosophical mood. He was worried about Lars's safety.

"This is crazy. You know that, right?"

"Someone has to do it," Lars answered.

"But why you? This stunt is like asking the Wolf Man to take a scalpel in his hand and operate on a patient during a full moon."

"Are you trying to scare me?"

"Yes."

"Well you are doing a pretty good job of it."

Chief Wheeler spoke. "For years, we have soothed ourselves into believing that sudden change is something that happens outside the normal order of things. But the truth is different. Events are unpredictable."

"What are you trying to say, Chief?"

"Vehicle crashes are accidents. Fatal illnesses are beyond our control. Financial panics are unforeseen. Most scientific breakthroughs have been fortuitous. — Random chance that involves the right person in the right place at the right time. Pure luck. A bloody accident."

Chief Wheeler continued. "But nobody likes to admit this. We all think we are in control, that events can be determined. We fail to accept the fact that sudden, radical change is built into the very fabric of our existence. And yet it is. Accidents do happen. Luck can be bad. Straight line motion is an aberration. Planned outcomes are unlikely. We are programmed to think otherwise, but it is true. Linearity simply does not exist, not in the context of events. Real life is not a series of interconnected events that occur sequentially, one after the other like so many pearls on a string. From physics to science fiction, it is the same. Life is more typically a series of encounters, many of them random, but each one capable of changing those that follow in a wholly, unpredictable, even devastating manner."

Chief Wheeler concluded. "You get that, right?"

"Are you trying to tell me to be careful?"

"Yes, that is precisely what I am trying to tell you. Be careful."

Then the Chief turned away and let Lars finish his preparations for the spacewalk. Sergeant Major Grovosky was doing the same in the adjoining closet, breathing in pure oxygen to flush out the nitrogen from his blood. Then it was time to go.

As soon as they exited the garbage chute, Lars's heart began to race. *This was a mistake*, he immediately thought to himself. *We should not be out here*.

As if to add emphasis to his thought, a sudden flash of yellow and white light popped off the solar sail and buzzed past their position. The solar wind was electrically charged. Every few seconds, millions of volts of static electricity built up on the sail above their heads and then had to be bled off. Clearly, no place for a man. And certainly not for a man weighed down by a satchel filled with high explosives. Everyone agreed. This spacewalk was going to be extremely dangerous.

Lars was serving in the capacity of assistant. Sergeant Major Grovosky was proficient with munitions; Lars was not. Sergeant Major Grovosky was the experienced spacewalker; Lars was a veritable rook. He had been out only once before, that first time back at the Station.

But Grovosky needed more than two hands to accomplish this task. Lars was those extra hands.

Another bolt of lightning whizzed by the Sergeant Major's ears. Grovosky was beginning to grasp the enormity of the problem.

"Piss. If one of those energy bolts hits me or hits the satchel — or even comes close — that will be all she wrote. We will both be blown to Kingdom Come."

"Maybe we shouldn't be out here, Sarge."

"Fiddlesticks."

"What do you suggest we do?"

"Remain as far apart as possible. No need for both of us to die."

"Then why am I even out here?"

"I miscalculated the risk, Lars. Before this day, no one has ever attempted a spacewalk on a solar sailship with sails fully furled. I think you should go back inside. This is too damn dangerous."

"I think we both should go back indoors, Sarge."

"This was my fool idea. I will figure out a way to finish it alone."

"I am here for a reason. You said so yourself," Lars replied. "I am staying."

"Then remain where you are. That is an order. Stay put. And absolutely do not forget to snug up your safety line in case something goes wrong."

"Got it." Lars reached down and pulled the line tighter. Overhead, the sails were sparking like there was no tomorrow.

Sergeant Major Grovosky edged out further along the hull. He was now maybe fifty meters away from Lars, maybe one hundred meters from the nav canopy. The area around him was lit up with white lightning.

Grovosky edged out further, maybe another fifteen meters. Lars could feel his breath coming faster. That is when it happened. It took only a fraction of a second. A bright white spot erupted on the surface of the solar sail. A bolt of incandescent energy. A glowing electric arc of unimaginable intensity. A flash of brilliance. Then a huge explosion.

The shockwave knocked Lars from his perch, snapped tight his safety line. His arm slammed against the hull. His head crashed against the inside of his helmet bruising him badly. Blood gushed from his forehead. He dangled unconscious from the hull of the ship like a fish on the line.

The blast killed Sergeant Major Grovosky instantly. It blew a gargantuan hole in the hull and the breach immediately began to vent atmosphere from inside the ship.

Alarms went off in every part of the ship. Emergency protocols went automatically into effect. These safety protocols were hardwired into the ship's programming.

Large, bulkhead pressure doors slid rapidly into place. They were designed to stop the atmospheric bleeding and seal off the damaged section of the ship. Anyone trapped on the wrong side of the pressure doors when they closed would shortly pass out and die from lack of oxygen.

But the protocols were designed to save the ship, not individual lives. Such losses of life, while regrettable, were the price of everyone else's survival. Everyone onboard knew the protocols the day they signed on. It could not be helped. Death would come fast.

Lars was still out cold when the pressure doors closed. His head was bleeding. His arm was either broken or badly sprained.

But his Snoopy cap was alive with sound. Chief Wheeler was yelling at him through his comm. Viscount Henry was beside him yelling as well. There were no backup teams. No one was suited up inside, ready to descend out the garbage chute and into space to help him.

Viscount Henry was standing nearby. "So much for Plan A," he said coldly.

Chief Wheeler turned on his heels, closed his fist, and walloped Viscount Henry in the face. "You bastard! You fucking bastard! Lars Cabot is not a Plan! He is a living, breathing human being. So fuck your Plan A. Fuck your Plan B. Fuck all your fucking plans. Get the hell out of my way and let me try and rescue this kid if he is still alive."

Now Chief Wheeler turned to Soldata Fifteen. "The safety line is attached to the mech winch. Reel him in. Now! Go, go, go!"

Viscount Henry, still prone on the deck, rubbed his chin. Soldata grabbed the handle of the electric winch, punched the POWER button. The line shimmied then tightened as the slack began to be taken up.

"Can't that thing go any faster?" Chief Wheeler barked.

"All due respect, Sir. If we reel him in any faster, the cable might get wrapped around his leg or his arm. Then he would be dead for sure. Patience please."

Chief Wheeler turned to Viscount Henry, who was now on his knees and about to get up.

"Make yourself useful, asshole," Wheeler said. "But stay out of my way."

Henry nodded. "I need a damage report. What deck was that explosion on?"

"Check the board," Soldata said, eyes fixed on the incoming safety line. "It will tell what systems have been compromised, if any. Hit the personnel button and you may get a report on who was hurt."

"Yeah," Wheeler said. "Buzz my engineering staff. Get them down here on the double. Alert medical that there may be casualties."

Wheeler continued. "Soldata, can you connect wirelessly to the ship's brain? If you can, send ship schematics to my screen. Search the blueprints. Find the exact location of the blast. I need to know exactly which blast doors closed and who was trapped on the other side."

The safety line was still moving. Suddenly, out on the line, the motion stirred Lars to partial consciousness. He mumbled. "What . . . what . . . God, my head hurts."

"He is alive!" Wheeler said as he touched the comm. "Lars, we are hauling you in. Stay with us, boy."

Lars sensed the motion, began to throw up inside his helmet. Wheeler could hear the sounds of him gagging.

"Reel him in faster! I order it! Reel him in faster! He will suffocate on his own vomit in that suit. Do it, Soldata!"

Soldata obeyed and the line began to spool in faster.

Every second counted now.

CHAPTER FORTY-ONE

"Are you okay, Lars?" Chief Wheeler was anxious and worried.

They had his helmet off, and Lars was splayed out on the floor of the Ready Room beside the airlock. Blood was caked on his forehead.

". . . I . . . where am I . . . what . . . happened . . ."

"You are okay now, son. Soldata hauled you in from outside. Your helmet is off. Breath normally, if you can."

"My arm . . . hurts . . . my head . . ."

"Doc is going to look at that arm. But first we have to get you out of that suit. And that is going to hurt like bloody hell. You have bruises all over your body. So we are going to administer a painkiller first."

Lars nodded as if he understood. "The suit. It shielded me . . . But Sergeant Major Grovosky . . ."

"Sergeant Major Grovosky is dead, Lars. He was killed in the blast."

"Blast? What blast?" Lars choked on the words.

"Doc, he is delirious," Chief Wheeler said. "What can you give him?"

"The painkiller may make him groggy. Get him out of the top half of the suit. He will probably pass out from the pain. The bottom half of the suit will be easy."

"There was an explosion . . ."

"Lars, your suit shielded you from the blast. But Sergeant Major Grovosky is dead. He was carrying high-explosives in his pak. A bolt of static electricity . . ."

"Oh, God. Is that what happened?" Lars said. "He is dead, isn't he?"

"You are covered with bruises, Lars. How did you get all these bumps and bruises?"

Lars looked down at his mostly naked body now. They had him out of the suit, were moving him to a medbed for examination.

"The inside of the suit," Lars said. "It is not smooth. The inside is filled with bearings and joints and seams. Very rough. I must have gotten bumped around in there real good."

"Chief, he's right," Soldata said. "The upper torso is a stiff fiberglass shell. Even on a good day, a man gets bumped up pretty well. He is lucky that only his arm broke."

"My arm is broken?"

Chief Wheeler shook his head. "We do not know that yet for sure. Doc is checking. He may need to give you a shot of Acceleron. Hold still."

"Oh, no. No shots. I hate shots. Keep that needle away from me."

Chief Wheeler laughed. The laugh broke the tension. "The boy is getting mouthy, has started giving orders. He must be okay."

"I want payback," Lars said suddenly. "How are we going to avenge the Sergeant Major's death?"

"You are not going anywhere until Doc clears you. So get comfortable."

Lars ignored the Chief and sat up on the medbed. "What about Plan B?"

"We broke our last drill bit an hour ago. Plan B is officially now a bust."

"What then? Is there a Plan C?"

"Yes. There is a Plan C. We have had it in the works for several hours now."

"Spill."

"Starve him out."

"That could take weeks."

"That is precisely why it wasn't Plan A or B. But no, Lars, it will not take weeks. People can go without water for just a few days. If we can find a way to muddy up their air supply, it might take only a matter of minutes."

Lars shook his head. "These people aren't stupid, Chief. They would have stored up water and provisions ahead of time. You must know that."

"Shush. Let me finish. They can only go a few hours without fresh air. Turn off the fans and they will eventually pass out as the carbon dioxide levels rise."

"This you have done?"

"Two hours ago, when you were suiting up to go outside. Turned up the temperature as well. They should be sweating bullets by now."

"Can we see inside?" Lars asked. "Do we have vid and comm?"

"Yes, both. But the comm has been dead quiet since this first began. I have been away from the vid feed since being down here with you. But I have two men watching the feed closely."

Lars swung his feet out over the side of the hospital bed. "I want to see the vid."

"We need to go up to my office for that." Chief Wheeler turned to address the doctor. "Doc, is he good to go?"

"That arm needs to be immobilized."

"So do it already."

The doctor nodded, then began to fit an auto-sling to Lars's wrist. The auto-sling unrolled slowly and wrapped around his lower arm. A tentacle slithered out of one side of the sling and gradually became firmer around his shoulder and upper arm. He could immediately feel the heat from inside the sling. It felt good.

"Keep it on for forty hours. After that time the sling will loosen itself and fall off. In the meantime, it will feed Acceleron to your bone and muscle. Then you should be good to go. Now get out of here kid, and don't you ever come back."

Lars jumped to the floor, slipped on his trousers with some difficulty. The Chief wrapped a shirt around his torso, helped him put his good arm into the armhole. “Okay, let’s go to my office.”

Ten minutes later, the Chief and Lars were at the door to his office. Inside, two men sat hunched over a large vid screen. They straightened up the instant they saw Chief Wheeler come through the door.

“What is going on inside that room?” Chief Wheeler asked. “Catch me up fast.”

The older of the two men answered. “No change. The players remain the same. Captain Reynolds. Two soldier bots. All three seem completely unfazed by the heat.”

“How long have the fans been off?”

“About thirty minutes.”

“Any reaction?”

“They looked up at the air duct the instant the fans went off. But they shrugged it off. The three do not seem to care one way or the other.”

Lars cleared his throat, began to speak. “Can you square up Captain Reynolds in the frame?”

“Sure, kid,” one of the men answered.

“What are you thinking, Lars?” Chief Wheeler asked.

“Square up Reynolds in the frame . . . Good . . . Now magnify. Let me see a close-up of the Captain’s face.”

The man at the controls fiddled with the knobs. Suddenly Captain Reynolds’ face filled the screen.

Chief Wheeler was beginning to understand. “By God. He’s not sweating either. I can understand the bots not sweating. But Reynolds? He should be sweating like a pig from the heat.”

Lars kept giving instructions. “Re-set magnification to normal. Pan the camera across the room.”

Chief Wheeler nodded to his man that it was okay, and he fiddled again with the knobs.

“What are you looking for?” This was a new voice, Viscount Henry’s voice. He had just now arrived at the door to Chief Wheeler’s office.

"Water bottles." Lars answered as if it ought to be obvious. "If these hijackers had planned ahead, they would have stored up provisions ahead of time. The Captain would have broken out water bottles by now . . ."

"Pan across all the countertops," Wheeler said. "Give me ten times mag on that trash can over there. I want to see what kind of garbage is in there."

The camera moved and generated a close-up of the trash can beside the nav console.

"Good God," Wheeler exclaimed. "No half-empty water bottles on any countertop? A trash can that is completely empty? In all this time they haven't eaten anything, haven't had anything to drink, haven't thrown away any garbage? How can that be?"

"There can be only one conclusion," Lars said.

"Let's not go there just yet," Chief Wheeler said.

"Wheeler, didn't you order a background check on this drill bit?" Viscount Henry asked in that ornery tone of his. "Have you heard back yet from Central about this?"

"Let me go to my computer and check. Crank the temperature five more degrees. See how they react. We will turn off the lights next."

Chief Wheeler walked across the room, sat down at his machine. "Yes, here it is." Silently he read the report. "Nothing. Not a damn thing. He is a ghost."

"How can that be?" Viscount Henry exploded. "Everyone has a past. How in blazes did that man land a berth as a sailship captain without a full book of creds?"

"Sergeant Major Grovosky cleared the crew," Wheeler said. "He was in charge of security, not me."

"And now he is dead," Viscount Henry said. "So we may never know the truth."

"Maybe we are asking the wrong people," Lars said.

"Or the wrong questions," Wheeler said.

"What do you mean?" Henry asked.

"Let's look again at the vid," Chief Wheeler said. He turned to his man at the controls. "Check the archives. Go back six hours."

“What are you looking for?” Lars asked.

“Food.”

“First water, now food?” Henry asked confused.

“I want to know if Reynolds eats or drinks anything at all, even an energy bar. He may have pocketed the trash for all I know. Go back six hours. Run it forward at three or four times normal speed. Watch it closely. Tell me what the man eats or drinks. I need to know for sure. Get to it straightaway.”

“Yes, sir.”

“What do you intend to do, Chief?” Lars asked.

“If I have been asking the wrong questions, I need to figure out what the right questions to ask are.”

“You have an idea where to start?”

“I do now. I need to send a secure packet. Lars, I need you to get me an IP address plus an encryption key. Soldata can get you the key.”

“I’m on it, Chief. What IP address are you looking for?”

“A place you ought to be familiar with. The Feldman Neurological Institute.”

“The skullcap place? What does Doctor Feldman have to do with this hijacking?”

“That remains to be seen. Now get to it. We are running out of time.”

CHAPTER FORTY-TWO

"Is it true that you once hunted grizzly bear with your father?" Chief Wheeler asked. It was just the two of them alone in his office. "Or were you pulling Viscount Henry's leg when you said that?"

"Who could make up a story like that?" Lars chuckled.

"So it is true?"

"Yep. Every word. When I was a kid, my father and I would hike with full pack up into the mountains of Montana, bow and arrow in hand."

"Old school, eh?" Wheeler remarked.

"It did not seem so at the time. I loved that country where we hiked. It was a wilderness area called the River of No Return. Very rugged, very elemental."

"Reminds me of my younger days."

"Where you from?"

Chief Wheeler's face tightened as he contemplated his answer. "My mother raised me. I never knew my father. Mom and I lived in a clapboard cabin on the high desert mesa of New Mexico. The closest town was Las Cruces, half a day's ride away."

"That seems like a hard way to grow up, Chief. Not much for a kid to do in a place like that. I myself lived on the far edge of nowhere as a kid. I am guessing you were pretty bored growing up. I know I was."

"Bored? Not at all. The high desert is really quite a fascinating place to grow up, especially if you have an agile mind. I learned a lot of history growing up. A lot about myself too. The pioneers. The Amerinds. The Spanish. The ranchers. The bandits of the Old West. I was an avid hiker. Like you with your father. Out on the trail, every day was an adventure. My mom just let me run free."

"I suppose you found fossils and stuff like that," Lars said.

"Fossils, yes. Artifacts. Other stuff too. Skeletons of horses, sometimes even people. The desert can be unforgiving."

"I don't know if I could handle finding a human skeleton in the sand. I think that would really weird me out."

"That skeleton, that human skeleton, was not even close to the weirdest thing I found. Hikers in the desert southwest sometimes come upon a puzzle in the shape of a concrete arrow on the ground. We are talking big hulking pieces of concrete, twenty-five meters long, poured like a slab foundation for a house."

"Alien artifacts? Like invaders from outer space?"

"Not hardly."

"So what were these concrete monoliths doing scattered about the desert in the middle of nowhere?"

"Interesting story, Lars. Those concrete slabs are relics of the earliest days of American aviation. When the first coast-to-coast airmail service began operating in the early 1900s, radar had not yet been invented. Pilots had no aeronautical charts. Radio beacons were not yet in regular use. Pilots had to eyeball it all the way. Navigation was difficult by daylight. It was all but impossible by night."

"These concrete things were manmade markers of some sort?"

Wheeler nodded. "Like coastal lighthouses. The concrete arrows were built to point the way for pilots. Within a matter of years, there was a concrete arrow every seven kloms, from New York City to San Francisco. Each was painted bright yellow and capped by a twenty-meter-tall tower. On the top of the tower was a rotating beacon visible from fifteen kloms away."

"Amazingly low tech."

"From our lofty perch perhaps. We are as far away from that tech as the inventors of the internal combustion engine were from the discovery of fire. Within another decade, radar had been perfected and radio beacons were coming into wider use. The concrete arrows were already becoming obsolete."

"And yet, two hundred years later, you were still finding these abandoned slabs in the desert?"

"Roman viaducts were still in use 1000 years after the fall of Rome. Telephone poles were still standing long after the last landline had been dug up and disconnected. You were still hunting with bow and arrow in an age of force guns."

"Okay," Lars said, "so how does this journey into the past help us in the present?"

"Today we are cavemen crowded around our first cooking fire. Someone has just handed us an internal combustion engine and we have two hours to figure out how the damn thing works."

Lars was stunned into silence. Chief Wheeler continued. "In thinking about who has hijacked this ship, we have no choice now but to contemplate the existence of some very cutting edge stuff."

"As a kid I learned to pray at the altar of mathematics. My heroes were guys like Gottfried Leibniz and Alan Turing. I dined on scientific principles like Asimov's Three Laws of Robotics. There was a time when I did not think it was possible to build a humaniform robot, certainly not one lifelike enough to fool ordinary people and pass for the captain of a sailship. But I have worked with such a robot before."

"When? Where?" Chief Wheeler was astonished.

"When I was first fitted for a skullcap as a child. I was at that same Feldman Institute. There was a very lifelike orderly — a woman — that helped me, helped me a lot. She went by the name Robota. But she certainly was not as lifelike as our Captain Reynolds. Plus she smelled funny."

"Smelled funny how?"

"A chemical smell."

"I knew they had been working for years on a project like this at the Neurological Institute. At other labs too. But I had no idea it had advanced to this level of sophistication. Maybe one of these research teams finally had a breakthrough, one the Defense Department has kept under wraps."

"You cannot be serious, Chief. A development of this magnitude would count as more than a simple breakthrough. No way does the Defense Department or anyone else keep this amazing breakthrough under wraps for long. I would venture to say that a humaniform robot of such quality would be of unimaginable value. Every corporation in the world would want to get ahold of it, not to mention every government and every criminal syndicate."

"I would agree," Chief Wheeler said. "Plus, if this is DOD tech, how the hell did it fall into the hands of someone like Uday bin Hassan? That bothers me in a very serious way. Hassan is a bully, a thug, nothing more. To get his hands on something like this would require he have an ally with high-level clearance at the Neurological Institute or else in the research wing of the Defense Department. No other explanation is possible."

"Maybe Hassan developed this tech on his own. Maybe he did not need to steal it."

"That hardly seems likely, Lars. I doubt if the man had the resources or the technical knowhow to develop such a thing. Anyway, why make just one of them?"

"Well maybe it is not Hassan at all. Maybe we are jumping to the wrong conclusion. Maybe it is someone from our side who is trying to slip Captain Reynolds past Hassan's security?"

"For what purpose? To assassinate Hassan? Then why not let us in on the secret? No, I still think Reynolds is under Hassan's control."

"Have you heard back yet from the Neurological Institute? I know you sent them a secure packet. I assume that is what you are asking them, whether Reynolds is one of theirs."

"No, I have not heard back yet. It is too soon to expect a reply. But at the end of the day, it doesn't matter how they answer. Hassan somehow got his hands on this tech. After looking at the tapes, we have nearly incontrovertible evidence. Captain Reynolds is not human. He is some sort of sophisticated machine, a synthetic. He doesn't eat, he doesn't drink, he doesn't sweat. He is as unaffected by the heat in that room as those soldier bots locked up in there with him. And now it would seem that he doesn't breathe much oxygen either. We have had the fans turned off for more than sixty minutes now."

"Okay, let's say for the sake of argument that you are correct. Let's say that Captain Reynolds is indeed some sort of advanced robot. We need to be specific about what we are saying here. Would he still bound by the Three Laws?"

"Who can say? We are in uncharted territory here. All we know for certain is that he will not voluntarily yield the ship's controls. Nor can we break down the door or safely penetrate the hull from the outside. Unless something radical changes soon, we are going wherever the man — or should I say robot? — decides to take us. Presumably Venus, like you said earlier."

Lars nodded as if he understood. "I had this discussion once before, with my grandfather. At the time, I devised a Fourth Law of Robotics. It may even be applicable here."

"I'm game. Go ahead."

"The Fourth Law of Robotics. *A robot must know at all times that it actually is a robot.* Without such a law, a robot would be able to violate the three previous laws.

Which brings me to a question. Are the Laws of Robotics sacrosanct? Or can they be tampered with?"

"Excellent question, Lars. And I do not really know the answer. I have learned over the years more than most people about robots and their programming. It comes with the job. On the Station and also onboard the *Ticonderoga* we are constantly having to tweak the programming of the small, helper bots to get various jobs accomplished. But in all my years, I have never known of a Law of Robotics that would allow a synthetic to endanger a human life. That includes Captain Reynolds."

"That would be a statement of First Law," Lars said. "*A robot may not injure a human being or, through inaction, allow a human being to come to harm.*"

"So," Chief Wheeler said. "Either that Law can be violated or else the Captain is not a robot."

"Or, like I said, his programming has been tampered with."

"Or, he is obeying a higher-order Law, one we know nothing about," Chief Wheeler said.

"Or he believes that he is still operating within First Law, that he is not endangering lives. Even Asimov himself speculated that there might be a Zeroth Law that superseded even First Law. *A robot may not harm humanity, or, by inaction, allow humanity to come to harm.* Asimov used this Law to circumscribe the behavior of benign overlord-type robots."

"But that was science fiction, Lars. You and I have to make actual decisions within the real world. The Three Laws only apply to higher-level robots capable of thought. The Laws are a bottleneck in terms of brain sophistication. For years, engineers have used simpler constructs to control the behavior of simpler bots."

"Explain."

Chief Wheeler nodded. "Under specific conditions, the Three Laws can be obviated. The Laws are modified depending on a robot's actual design and intended use. Robots of low enough value can have Third Law deleted.

Those sorts of bots do not need to protect themselves from harm; thus, brain size can be greatly reduced. Other robots, those that are designed to operate autonomously and without specific human command, may safely have Second Law deleted. So long as these sorts of bots do not require Third Law as part of their programming, they can be built with smaller brains still. Finally, robots that are both disposable and designed to operate autonomously, without ever receiving orders from a human being, do not require even First Law, not so long as they operate in places where no human being can come to harm. For an extremely simple bot, the sophistication of positronic circuitry can render a brain so small, it can fit comfortably within the skull of an insect."

Lars pressed his case. "I find no argument with what you have said. But that still does not preclude Captain Reynolds from still operating within the confines of the Three Laws. He may reason that the course of action he has chosen by hijacking the ship endangers fewer lives than any other course of action open to him."

"Thus, by maximizing the number of lives saved — even if some are lost — that keeps him safely within the confines of First Law," Chief Wheeler said. "I get that."

"The problem we have in understanding his behavior is a new one. When a robot starts making judgment calls, we step hip deep into a river of goo," Lars said.

"I could not agree more. Predictability is a cornerstone of expected robotic behavior. Without it, robots lose their reliability, their entire purpose for being."

"One of the foundational principles of science, one that goes back to the days of the first proto-human watching the first nut falling out of the first tree, is that the same experiment always yields the same result, no matter who performs the experiment. This is the key to understanding robotic behavior. Predictability."

"Lars, we have always given science more credit than it is due. The scientific method lacks precision in ways that are not always obvious."

"Trial and error. The experimental method."

"No, it is more than that. The scientific method, even double-blind studies, produces two types of errors," Chief Wheeler said. "A type I error is the mistake of thinking that something is true when it is not."

"The so-called false positive."

"Yes, but there is a second type of error, Lars, a type II error. The mistake here is in thinking that something is not true when in fact it is true. What we call a false negative.

"And which do you think we are dealing with here?" Lars asked.

"Some unknowns are known to be unknown. But some unknowns are just that — unknown. We do not suspect them because we are not even smart enough or informed enough to look for them. I would say that Captain Reynolds and Uday bin Hassan fall into that second category."

CHAPTER FORTY-THREE

"You realize we are now prisoners held captive on a ghost ship?" Chief Wheeler said.

"I don't know about the ghost ship part," Lars said. "But I do get the part about us being prisoners."

The two were in the forward lounge talking. They had resigned themselves to the truth. Sergeant Major Buster Grovosky was dead. Three separate attempts to re-take the ship by force had failed. The ship's crew and her passengers were now prisoners, perhaps hostages.

Lars was troubled. "What do you think they are going to do with us once the ship gets to Venus?"

"I guess it all depends on how reasonable we are willing to be." Chief Wheeler looked up from the table. "Some of the crew want to fight. Others want to surrender peaceably. A ship like this cannot land on the ground. If there is powered transport to the surface, our captors will probably off-load us that way. They may have built some sort of orbiting space elevator like on Earth. I cannot say for certain. After Uday assumed power, the quality of our intell declined sharply. I am not actually current on the status of the Venus colony."

"But why go to all this trouble?" Lars asked. "I can understand stealing the *Ticonderoga*. It is an extremely valuable piece of equipment. But why steal us, the crew? Of what possible value are we to them, the passengers and the crew?"

"If they wanted us dead, Lars, we would already be dead."

"For some reason, I do not find that very reassuring."

"Nor should it be."

"What then?"

"Slaves."

"Slaves?" Lars was aghast.

"To work in the lithium mines."

"We are to be put to work as slaves in the lithium mines of Venus? What the hell?"

"Robots corrode quickly in the harsh atmosphere. Even humans do not last long. But lithium is an extraordinarily valuable mineral. Highly reactive. The single most valuable commodity Uday possesses. He can profitably export it in quantity to Earth in exchange for a whole host of things his colony badly needs, drugs and the like, also food."

"And this lithium stuff needs to be mined by hand?"

"And he is short of labor. Lithium is valuable because its compounds have several industrial applications. Heat-resistant glass. Ceramics. High strength-to-weight alloys used in aircraft. Lithium-ion batteries."

"And the only reasonable source of this stuff is from slave mines on Venus? How can that be?"

"Lithium is an alkali metal, very lightweight. Like all alkali metals, it is highly reactive and flammable. Dangerous stuff. It has to be stored where it cannot come in contact with oxygen or water, typically large tanks of mineral oil. Because the stuff is so highly reactive, it never exists in nature in its pure form. Instead, it only appears in compounds. Certain types of coarse-grained igneous rock are a source. Also seawater. Brines. Clays. It has to be isolated from the surrounding material using electrolysis."

"I see," Lars said. "Expensive to extract, but cheap and easy to ship because it is lightweight. Since outer space is inert, what better container to hold the stuff in than a spaceship? It cannot accidentally react with anything enroute causing an explosion."

"That is about the size of it."

"And you are just now telling me about this? How could you, Chief?"

"I only just figured out what our likely fate is going to be. Venus has an extreme labor shortage, like I said. You need to prepare yourself. Life there is hard, brutal even. People die much too fast and far too easily. Any outsiders Uday gets his hands on usually become slaves or soldiers or both. There is constant warfare. When the workers get old or when a good soldier gets wounded, they rejuv these unfortunates in some sort of antediluvian medical center he has set up down there. It is somewhere in Domtar Province. The medicos rejuvenate the slave workers, use them up over and over again until finally the enslaves drop dead from exhaustion."

Lars gulped hard. "Enslaves?"

"That is what they call them; do not ask me why. They get barcoded and numbered, like some toy from off the shelf. I cannot think of a more horrible way to die."

"You mean live, don't you?"

"If you want to call it that, then yes. Some they torture just for sport. The women, they rent out as whores or give them away as gifts to loyals."

Lars shook his head. "Torture as sport?"

"A poor choice of words. Warfare is ugly. The threat of torture, the application of pain, these may be the only means of obtaining vital information."

"You condone torture?"

Chief Wheeler chose his words. "I do not condone it, Lars. But soldiers die in battle, sometimes by bullet, sometimes by knife, sometimes by having been caught by shrapnel. If a soldier is captured alive and his captor believes the soldier possesses vital information that he refuses to divulge, then coercion may be the only way to obtain that information."

"You have done this to others?"

"Yes. I have had to torture people in my line of work."

"I don't know, Chief. You hardly seem the type."

"I am not a sadist, if that is what you mean. But gathering good intell from a terrorist or from an enemy soldier is an inherently brutish experience. I told you about my background. I worked military intelligence in my younger days. Before that, I worked in the criminal justice system. As a professional, I was trained as a psychologist. Investigations were my specialty. Our job was to modify behavior, turn spies when we had to, use whatever means necessary."

"I do not really come from that world," Lars said. "My brother used to beat me up when I was a kid. It did not make me like him any better. I cannot see how beating up someone gets him to cooperate."

"Torture can sometimes get physical," Chief Wheeler said. "That is a fact. But physical beatings and torture are not the same thing. Torture is about getting information, information we need, information the enemy does not want us to have. This requires interrogation. Here, the ends always justify the means."

"Always?"

"Yes, always. Torture inflicts suffering, sometimes physical, most times psychological. In the old days, they used truth-serum drugs. Sodium pentothal. Amobarbital. Things like that. These old-school drugs are actually sedatives or powerful painkillers, not truth serums. They were originally used as general anesthetics during surgery. They do not hurt the person being tortured. But in the right doses, they do tend to make him feel giddy. In the hands of a professional, they can produce a tongue-loosening effect akin to alcohol. Cruel and unusual punishment, this is not."

"Manipulating someone's mind with drugs hardly seems kosher."

Chief Wheeler laughed. "Getting someone intoxicated to spill their guts may not be sporting. But it certainly does not fall into the category of brutal. Nowadays, we use them all — vasodilators, serotonin stimulators, psychedelics like lysergic acid, ketamine, EEC traces, all of them. You must remember: Terrorists are accomplished liars. Their handlers have used chemical means to alter their memories, to convince them that certain lies are in fact the truth. After a time, the terrorist can no longer distinguish between the two himself. No amount of chemical manipulation on our part can reverse the distortion."

Chief Wheeler continued. "Most times we are standing knee-deep in quicksand. The moral question of lengths — and the broader issue of ends versus means — these questions are neither new nor unique. You were not the first young man to ask them. Inflicting pain and discomfort on another human being is always a questionable act."

"Then why do it?"

"Civilized society has to find a way to protect itself from these evil men. The only way to accomplish this is for us — the good guys — to be armed with good information. Terrorists are schooled to withstand harsh questioning. We have no choice but to press them for answers. The softies of the world complain about our methods. But they are dim bulbs. Would you not agree that discomfiting a few psychopaths is preferable to inflicting pain and suffering on millions?"

"I wish I had your strength of character, Chief. I don't think I would have the stones to do what you have done."

"Don't be a democrat, Lars. The world does not divide neatly into good people and bad people; only good circumstances and bad circumstances. Sometimes people — good people — find themselves in bad circumstances. Then these good people have to do bad things."

"But how do you tell the good guys from the bad guys?"

"How do you tell pornography from art? Take a classical Greek sculpture. A nude woman in the heat of passion, her firm breasts heaving with desire. Or a Greek warrior, nude, muscled, with his glorious manhood on display for everyone to see. Is this art or pornography?"

Lars hesitated to answer.

"The difference lies in intent," Chief Wheeler said. "Pornography is meant to arouse. Sculpture is meant to inspire."

"A good person who means well but is forced by circumstance to do evil. Okay, I get that. But I am a little nervous about the lack of due process when you subject a prisoner to harsh questioning."

"Back again to this argument about terrorists and civil rights? You and I fought this battle weeks ago. There is no room here, Lars, for rules of evidence or stuff like innocent until proven guilty."

"No room?"

"None whatsoever." The Chief spoke, now, as a parent or teacher might to a bright, yet uncomprehending child. "Terrorism can only be fought by terrorizing the terrorists."

"And how does one do that?"

"Put three of the motherfuckers in a room. Shoot one of them through the head with a gun. Or set one of them on fire with gasoline. The others will talk, I promise you."

"Will he?" Lars asked, with defiance in his voice. "If you hang one man, it may loosen the tongue of the friend who watches. But it may also harden that friend's resolve. He may prefer to honor his friend's death by refusing to answer your questions."

"Not in my experience. Gasoline works every time."

"You have done this?"

"I have seen it done."

"And you did not step in to stop it? How could you, Chief?" Lars was glum.

"Torture does not always involve physical abuse. And gathering intell does not always involve torture."

"If you say so."

"Use your imagination, kid. There is brainwashing and then there is persuasion. Both are designed to get a man to change his mind. The difference is that when no coercion is involved, this more properly comes under the heading of salesmanship or perhaps propaganda."

Chief Wheeler continued. "Let's start with something simple. One party makes a request of another party. The second party considers whether or not to comply with the first party's request. The level of compliance depends on several factors. There is an art to persuasion, Lars — and a science. I will teach you them both."

"I am in class now?"

"Someplace else you would rather be?"

Lars shook his head. "No, I guess not."

"Consider this example. The Red Cross mails out requests for contributions. When they do this with no other accompanying information, the appeal succeeds with only about fifteen percent of the recipients. But when the mailing includes a set of free personalized address labels, the success rate more than doubles, to thirty-five percent. This is what we in the trade call Reciprocity. You give me something for free; I feel obligated to give you something back."

"Honestly, Chief. People do not fall for such gimmicks."

"Don't they? It is human nature. It is in our genes. People from every society do the same. It is part of our behavior module handed down to us by natural selection, our behavior gene, if you will. *An individual is obligated to repay in kind what he has received.* Acting in this way makes us more fit, more able to survive in a dangerous and unpredictable world. We do not have claws. We cannot run fast. Our bite is not poisonous. But we can overcome adversity by cooperating. Receiving a gift — unsolicited and perhaps even unwanted — can often convince potential donors to return the favor."

"I guess, now that I think about it, lots of places offer free samples to drum-up business — free in-home inspections by repairmen, free food samples at grocery stores, things like that."

"You bet. And women do it too. I let you cop a free feel today; you promise to buy me dinner tomorrow. Ring a bell? It ought to. Think that young girl you were with recently. What did that free sample cost?"

"I had forgotten what a hopeless romantic you were."

"It is no different from the food store offering a free sample. The customer is exposed to the product; he becomes indebted to the salesman. In the interrogation game, we play on the same behavior module. The impulse to reward reciprocity has a further reach than to just gifts and favors. It applies equally well to the concessions one makes when bargaining. In the trade, we call it the Only-Through-Extremism-Do-We-Achieve-Moderation rule. It works like this:

"I make a large request of you, which you reject. I then make a concession to you by retreating to a smaller request. You acknowledge my concession by reciprocating with a concession of your own. In a series of such exchanges, you may eventually agree to my lesser request, even if it is significantly more than you originally intended before negotiations began."

"I have never been much into dickering over price for things."

"Okay, fair enough. Let me give you an example. I offer to sell you my house for 100,000 credits. But you reject my price as being too high. You counter my asking price with an offer of 80,000 credits. I reject your offer as being too low. But in response, I reduce my asking price to 90,000. Seeing that I have made a significant concession, you raise your offer to 90,000 credits and we strike a deal. Reciprocity in the guise of bidding and counteroffer is the very essence of our economic system. It is also the basis for interrogation and for brainwashing. The interviewer threatens an extreme action. Then, through a series of concessions, he delivers a softer blow in exchange for important information."

"When you put it that way, it doesn't sound so bad," Lars said. Things were beginning to make sense to him now.

"The next rung on the ladder of behavior modification is what we call Commitment. Consider the owner of a well-known restaurant. He is struggling with a costly problem that afflicts many restaurant owners. A patron will call to reserve a table. Then later, without notice, the patron will fail to show up for dinner. The table sits empty. Behavioral science tells us that there may be a way for the restaurant owner to solve the problem."

"How?"

"He can have his receptionist change two words in her spiel when a patron calls to make a reservation. It is usually quite successful. No-show rates often drop by more than one-half."

"What two words?"

"Will you."

"Will you?"

"Yes. Will you? Those two words are designed to elicit a public commitment. If she modifies her request from a statement to a question, she forces the patron to answer yes or no. If she used to say: *Please call if you have a change in plans*, she can now say: *Will you please call if you have a change in plans?* Then she can politely pause and wait for the patron to answer. The wait is pivotal, because it induces the customer to fill the pause with a public commitment. Science teaches us that public commitments, even minor ones, direct future action. Back on the savanna, where we evolved, a liar could always be called out. The change in wording is effective because it commissions the force of a potent human compulsion, the desire to appear consistent. This is as much about genetics as Reciprocity is. Getting someone to say yes makes it that much harder for them to later say no."

When Lars looked as if he might argue with him, Wheeler said, "Do you love your country? *Yes*. Are you willing to come to its aid in a time of need? *Yes.* Can I count on your support if we are attacked? *Of course.* Will you authorize a check right now to help the Disabled Veterans Association? *Yes, of course, let me get my voucher.*"

"A subtle form of brainwashing?"

"The point is that after so many yeses, who can say no? Every salesman does it. — It is part of the persuasion process. Also part of the interrogation process. Get the bad guy to say yes, even to something small — accepting a sandwich perhaps — and then build rapport from there."

"You really have made a science of this, haven't you?"

"It is a science, Lars, complete with test subjects and sophisticated research methods. I was taught by the best. Dr. Emil Schauffhausen. I already told you about him. Which brings me to our next topic. Social Validation. If a great many individuals have decided in favor of a particular idea, others are more likely to follow suit."

"Ah, the old herd instinct."

"A non-scientist might put it that way. Humans are social animals. We have an innate desire to belong to a group. We often seek acceptance by imitating the behavior of other members of our group. As humans, we constantly seek Social Validation. When others in our group agree with a certain point of view, we perceive the idea in question to be more correct, more valid."

"Even if that idea is false?"

"Yes, even if that idea is false. There was a time when we all thought the Earth was flat. There was a time when the very notion of evolution by natural selection was blasphemy. There was a time when the idea of robots and computers and skullcaps was still in the realm of magic."

"So people are lemmings. What of it?"

"Lemmings indeed. What better way to understand a financial panic, the unnatural fear that stampedes people into a run on a bank? Or a bull market that leads to unsustainable prices? Or people storming the doors of a sold-out concert to obtain a seat? Social Validation. It is the key to understanding so much about human behavior. Propaganda is a form of mass brainwashing. Adolf Hitler was a megalomaniac. But he understood the herd instinct. *Tell the same lie loud enough and often enough and people will believe.* That was the method to his madness. By simply implying that others, just like you, are going along with the lie makes it easier for you to go along with it too."

"I think you are scaring me now. People are not robots. They can think for themselves."

"Most days, yes. But not all days. Here is another factor to consider. People prefer to say yes to people they like, something we call Rapport."

"Honestly, Chief. That is so obvious. Why even mention it?"

"It may be obvious. But there is more than one business model that has employed Rapport as the foundation for their success. An old company that still exists today, the Tupperware Corporation, built its entire business that way. The home party concept. Familiar faces sell products. Friends are people you already know, like, and trust. Friends can be powerful salesmen to other friends."

"True. But nowadays, most commercial transactions take place outside the home. The lion's share take place in faceless transactions like on the net. How do you explain that?"

"It is still Rapport, Lars. But at a more subtle level. The websites you choose to frequent for buying and selling things are websites you trust. And why do you trust these websites? Mostly because someone you share rapport with has recommended them to you. Rapport is a chair with four legs. Physical attractiveness. Similarity. Compliments. Cooperation."

"A chair with four legs?"

"Let me explain. People often claim that good looks have nothing at all to do with trust or friendship. But that is a crock. Good-looking salesmen outsell ugly ones. Physically attractive political candidates get more votes than ugly ones. Good-looking actresses out-earn ugly ones. The list goes on. Pretty girls get more dates. Being physically attractive helps one establish Rapport."

Chief Wheeler continued. "The same goes for similarity. Salespeople often look for, even fabricate, a connection between themselves and their customer. *Well, no kidding,* he says, *you are from Chica? I went to school in Illinois.* Stuff like that."

Chief Wheeler continued. "Then there are Compliments. These simple niceties are arguably the most important of the four legs. Salespeople are trained in the use of praise. *My, but you look nice today. Please have a seat so I can explain this investment to you.* The same goes for Cooperation. What top salesman isn't known by his clients for how helpful he can be?"

"One that has lost his job."

"You are still the same smart ass you were the day I met you."

"That may be, but aren't you feeding me a bunch of blarney? Before you torture a man, first you try to get him to like you? You praise him, then try to pretend you are his buddy?"

"We do what we have to, Lars. Deception is part of persuasion. So is Authority. People with actual authority — policemen, doctors, etc. — as well as those people who are not actually policemen but are dressed to look like one — or people who act authoritative — a well-dressed man in a business, say, or a well-liked actor who has played a heroic part in a drama — such people can influence the actions and decisions of those around them. Such people can rally support. They can quiet a mob. Or lead an insurrection. Authority is Social Validation and Rapport, all wrapped up in one neat, explosive package. We did not question the true identity of our Captain Reynolds because he acted like a captain, dressed like a captain, and took charge like a captain. When confronted by an authority symbol who is hiding behind a phony claim, people often fail to use their head. I was hoodwinked as badly as anyone onboard, and I am trained to be on the lookout for such things. Under the banner of Authority, we can be easily steered in the wrong direction by an erstwhile expert or even by someone who presents the aura of legitimacy."

"But when you are interrogating someone, you turn Authority to your advantage."

"And why not? If we have to turn a source, we use every means at our disposal. Even terrorists fear Authority."

"What else do they fear?"

"Scarcity. It is the final step in forcing compliance. The less available an item or an opportunity is, the more desirable it becomes. We always want what we cannot have. Marketers trumpet unique benefits. Salesmen tell us about one-of-kind offerings or limited-time-only promotions. And it is not just applicable to sales campaigns. Scarcity affects the value of information as well. Information perceived as being exclusive is considered more persuasive than information known by all. As interrogators, we use one-time offers as a tool to prod people into giving us more information or making a confession."

"What do you mean, like — *Hello, shoppers, pizza ovens are on sale for the next five minutes only* — something like that?"

"Yeah, just like that. Only in the context of an interrogation the limited offer might be reduced jail time or a more pleasant way to die."

"Chief, much of what you say is intuitive and I understand what you are telling me. It makes sense for someone to repay a favor or to follow the lead of another or to heed a legitimate authority. But at the end of the day, don't some people just refuse to talk?"

"In my experience? No. Every man has a weak spot. The challenge is in figuring out what that weak spot is. If it is not money, it is women. If it is not women, it is drugs.

If it is not drugs, it is little boys. What the interrogator needs to do is find the other man's weak spot."

"And what about us?" Lars asked. "Are we to become slaves, like you said?"

Chief Wheeler hung his head. "I wish I knew. Reynolds has not said much of anything since first commandeering the ship. So I am trying to plan for the worst. In any case, we will know for sure in about ten days' time."

"Ten days?"

"That is about how long it will take us to reach Venusian airspace. Ten days."

CHAPTER FORTY-FOUR

The sun was uncomfortably large in the window now. They were maybe seventy hours out from the port of Hercules on the planet Venus, and Captain Reynolds had given the order to stow the sail. It had been just under two weeks now since the hijacking.

Once the solar sail was furled, they would use their remaining inertia to coast into Venusian orbit. Then would come their moment of reckoning. Captain Reynolds had announced it over the intercom two hours ago. The ship would be impounded upon arrival. They would all be pressed into military service whether they liked it or not. The women, travel companions mainly, would be dispatched to the Farm, where they were to service Uday's upper echelon.

Reynolds wasn't lying. When the ship docked at Venus Station, armed guards came onboard. There might have been a confrontation then and there.

But the crew had had plenty of time beforehand to discuss what they should do if the *Ticonderoga* was boarded. It was agreed. They were outgunned. A firefight onboard the ship while it was still in orbit would likely wreck the ship, killing them all. They reckoned they had a better chance to survive if they avoided a confrontation.

The decision to surrender peaceably did not go down well with everyone, certainly not with Viscount Henry. He had two very strong reasons to object, both female, his daughter and his consort. He was not about to commit them both to a lifetime of prostitution. This was an outcome he could not stomach.

Uday's goons goose-stepped their way up the catwalk. They had breathers cupped over their faces and force guns slung under their arms.

"You are all under arrest," the Staff Sergeant in charge barked. "Cuff the younger ones. Put the women in a separate room."

Kaleena was in tears. Montera was stone-faced. Two other travel companions and one crewmember's wife huddled together in one corner.

"Get your hands off those women," Viscount Henry yelled.

"Shut the fuck up and mind your own business!" the Staff Sergeant barked. He had taken off his breather and was laboring under the earth-normal atmosphere inside the ship.

"This is my business!" Viscount Henry shot back. "Hands off the women."

"I am telling you for the last time. Step back and let us do our business."

Viscount Henry drew an unseen weapon from his belt, took aim with it on the closest goon.

"Don't do it, Henry!" Chief Wheeler yelled as he began to move in that direction.

But it was already too late. One of the Sergeant's men leveled his force gun at the center of Henry's chest, finger on the contact. He discharged the weapon, and an instant later a moist pink mist painted the wall behind where Viscount Henry once stood. The air was filled with an acrid putrid smell.

Kaleena fell to the floor, began to crawl in the direction of her father's remains. She was crying uncontrollably.

Lars was about to bolt out of line, charge the goon who had murdered the Viscount. But Chief Wheeler grabbed his arm with such ferocity, he was locked in place. "Don't," he whispered. "They will kill you too."

"Get her up," one of the guards said. "Put her with the others. Put them all in the lounge."

"Are you folks ready to cooperate?" the Sergeant asked in broken Terrish. "No one else has to die here today."

Lars looked at the Chief, tried to follow his lead. So did Soldata and the others now in custody.

"Remember what I told you, Lars?" Chief Wheeler said to the boy.

"About us becoming slaves?"

"Yes. Either slaves or soldiers."

"Which do you think it is, Chief? Slave or soldier?"

"This looks to me like old-style conscription. Shove a gun into a man's hands, march him to the front, tell him that if he wants to stay alive, he has to kill the enemy, as many as he can, as fast as he can."

"Just like that?" Lars was appalled. "No uniform, no training, little strategy, few tactics?"

"Do as they say, Lars. Do not argue. Do not put up a fight. Cooperate. Stay alive."

"Stop talking in the line this very instant," one of the goons shouted. "Be quiet or you die. Now, march this way. Onto the Space Elevator."

Captain Reynolds stood dispassionately by as the male crew and passengers were escorted out. Then came the order.

"You too, Captain. Get in line with the others."

"Why me? I did as I was told."

"I have my orders. Come quietly or you will be decommissioned right here, right now."

Lars found some small satisfaction that Captain Reynolds had been double-crossed by the very people who built him.

"What do you think, Chief? Will he put up a fight? Or will he simply comply like a good robot?"

"Unless they made the mistake of programming him with pride, Reynolds will comply. A robot is a tool, Lars. Does a hammer argue about who is gripping the handle when there is a nail to be pounded? I think not."

"There was a song once — *If I had a hammer . . .*"

"Quiet in the ranks! Final warning!"

•

•

The trip to the surface was scary as hell. The Venusian atmosphere was a dense pink sewer, pungent fumes, hot sulphuric-acid clouds, dense layers of carbon-dioxide gas, hurricane-strength winds at the cloud tops.

It would still take years, but the quality of the atmosphere was improving by the month, becoming cooler, less pungent, less poisonous. The surface air pressure, which at one time was nearly ninety times that of Earth, was now only twice as heavy. Each trans-comet that arrived from the distant reaches of the solar system brought the planet millions of liters of fresh water. It also brought the planet sonic booms, extreme lightning, and torrential downpours.

Lars felt sicker by the minute as the elevator descended towards the surface. The air in the cabin, even after having been run through a microbial air filter, tasted putrid, like rotten eggs or diarrhea. He promptly barfed on his shoes. No one laughed. Others felt like throwing up as well. Some did.

Then, as they approached the planet's surface, the sky outside darkened. It was colored green then yellow then brown. The air was thick and heavy.

The male passengers and crew were shackled. It made walking extremely difficult.

The first steps onto the surface were strange. The ground beneath their feet was spongy, like walking on a water bed. It squished with each halting step.

Lars found it hard to breath. Heavy heat. Heavy humidity. Supernormal air pressure. Burning eyes. Tropical undergrowth. Bugs. Bacteria. Fungi. Permanent thermal inversion.

Lars stared skyward, up the cable they had just descended. His visibility was maybe twenty meters. The cable disappeared into the acrid clouds.

The guard outside the elevator docking bay spoke. "This is real simple, fellows. We have a war on. We are losing and we need fresh soldiers on the line. You fight or you go to prison. You may die in battle. But you will surely die in the Gulag. Make no mistake. Our Gulag is no luxury hotel. The food is poor, the air is not filtered, there is no medicine. On the other hand, the prison has no walls. You can walk out of it a free man anytime you choose. There are no guards walking the grounds and there is no electric fence. So feel free to leave whenever the spirit moves you. It is a thousand kloms of dense, dangerous jungle in every direction. No one dares escape. It is a death sentence if you do. So make up your mind right now. Those that wish to be escorted to the Gulag, stand over here. Those that wish to take up arms and help defend our domain, stand on the other side. You have two minutes to decide."

Lars looked to Chief Wheeler for leadership. The Chief moved into the line that would be sent to the battlefield. Lars followed him, as did a dozen or more other men. Soldata got in line along with them. Captain Reynolds, now also a prisoner, stepped into line with the other group, the group headed for the Gulag.

The guard turned and addressed himself to Lars's group. "Follow this road. Follow it for about two kloms. Follow it until you hear the sounds of battle. You will be joining General Petra's group. You can forget about going AWOL. Stay on the road. The jungle will kill you faster than we can. It is filled with dragons and mammoths and other nasties. The pickets will unshackle you at the front, hand you a gun, place you in the line of battle. Now get a move on."

Soldata Fifteen stepped bravely out in front and off they all trudged. Forty minutes later the line of prisoners from the *Ticonderoga* came upon an aid station. Lars and the Chief were near the front of the line. They were still shackled.

Wounded men were everywhere, on the ground, propped up against trees, slumped over beds with no mattresses. Blood and bandages and pained moans. It was a horrible scene. Putrid smells. Warm blood. Flowing pus. The sound of flies.

Soldata walked up to the aid station. "I need water for my men."

The orderly, tired and covered with blood, nodded his head towards the next tent. "See the Quartermaster."

Soldata signaled the others to follow him, and they trudged the fifty meters to the nearest tent. He repeated his request. "I need water for my men."

The Quartermaster was brusque. "Then piss in a cup and boil it yourself."

Now Soldata became unexpectedly fierce. He grabbed the man at the neck and prepared to squeeze. "I will not ask again. I need water for my men."

"But you are a robot," the Quartermaster said. "You are programmed not to hurt me."

"My programming says I am not to harm a human being. You do not presently qualify as such. My men need water now."

"Okay already. Let me go and you can have your water. There are full canteens in that footlocker." He pointed.

Soldata released his grip and went to the footlocker. "Here. Everybody grab a canteen." The men from the *Ticonderoga* rushed over.

"Don't drink too fast," Chief Wheeler warned. "Do not waste a drop. This may be it for a while."

"Geez, Chief. What have we got ourselves into?" Lars asked.

"I don't know, kid. I do not scare easily. But I have to admit. Right now, I am scared. I am not even sure on which side we are fighting."

"Have you ever seen a robot act like that before?"

"Like Soldata just did? No. The sulphuric acid in the air may be futzing with his programming."

"You think?"

"It could be corrosion or something like that."

"Stow those canteens this very instant," a new voice ordered. The man was in uniform, had corporal stripes on one arm, lieutenant bars on his shoulder. "We have little clean water to waste on the likes of you rooks."

The corporal-lieutenant continued. "I heard one of you asking which side you were fighting on. Let us be clear. You are fighting to protect the territory and power of Uday bin Hassan. The Allied Forces under the command of General Bagdonavich are your enemy. Now step aside and let the medic through."

The medic was a young man, red-faced and tired. He had just laid the broken body of a dead soldier on a pile of equally broken bodies. He brushed past them, then reached into the same footlocker, took a fresh canteen of water for himself. He noticed how the men were staring at the stack of dead soldiers.

He said, "If you are wondering, flesh-eating bacteria of the Venusian variety will digest their remains in short order. Come back tomorrow, if you are still alive. This stack of bodies will be nothing but a pile of de-fleshed bones."

Lars turned away. He could not bear to look. When he turned back around, he tugged at Chief Wheeler's arm. "Did you hear what the man said?"

"About the pile of bones?"

"No, the first guy. We are fighting on the wrong side. I thought Uday was our enemy?"

"Not today he isn't."

"Shut up down there and fall in." This was another new voice. The order came from a big man atop an even bigger animal, a bio-stallion. The steed was one of a breed of genetically enhanced horses that prospered in the weird climate of Venus.

“What the hell have we gotten ourselves into?” Lars pleaded to know.

“War is a terrible thing, Lars. Back on Earth, we have mostly forgotten this fact. We have become accustomed to wars prosecuted at a distance, wars prosecuted by anonymous drones directed via satellites parked overhead in geosync orbit. Here on Venus, everything is different. Communications are hash. War has to be prosecuted up close, by real soldiers, firing real weapons, spilling real blood, perhaps our blood. I fear this thing we have got sucked into is medieval. Like the devastating trench warfare of twentieth-century Europe.”

“I am not a soldier,” Lars said. “Not a real one anyway.”

“No, but he is.” Chief Wheeler tilted his head in the direction of the man in the saddle atop the bio-stallion.

“Who is that big guy anyway? The big guy on the horse?”

“If I am not mistaken, that is Ahmed bin Hassan. Uday’s oldest son. He is probably the reason why his father is losing this war. Ahmed is an idiot, plain and simple. Of course, never make the mistake of telling him so. He will have you executed on the spot. Do what the man says. But the only one around here who really knows what he is doing is Ahmed’s XO. I have read that man’s dossier. He is a field commander and a brilliant tactician. Now there is a man who knows the lay of the land.”

“What is the man’s name? This Executive Officer?”

“Petra. General Mustaffa Petra.”

“How will I know him when I see him?”

“Cannot miss him. Big guy. Always has a cigar in his mouth. Built like the motorized all-terrain vehicle he designed. Talks incessantly. Swears constantly.”

Lars chuckled. “You paint quite the picture.”

“Show the man respect. Petra has earned it. One of General Petra’s greatest accomplishments has been development of the Platypus.”

“The extinct animal?”

"Not hardly. An all-terrain amphibious troop transport. Perfectly suited for use on Venus. The planet is like a giant Everglades swamp. There are islands of Amazon-like jungle at every bend. The Platypus has wheels. It has caterpillar-style treads. It has hydrofoil wings and it has pontoon floats like an updated DUK of World War Two fame."

"How do you know so much about this Platypus thing? And what in blazes is a DUK?"

"Oh, some people say DUCK. But this was not its original name. The DUK was a water-capable military transport. The U stood for utility body, I think. The K designation meant front-wheel drive. I'm pretty sure the original had six-wheel dual-driving axles. I know about the Platypus because I am an engineer. I have seen pictures, read the specs. It is quite the machine. The wheels and treads are motorized. There is a pair of twin screws at the rear of the craft for water propulsion. At the front is a dozer blade for knocking down trees and other obstructions. The sides are screened to keep out the bugs and lizards. The roof and floor are double-hulled to help keep the occupants dry. The Platypus can convert in minutes to a submersible and can run underwater at depths up to thirty meters. A standard Venusian infantry brigade counts a dozen or more of these craft as the tip of the spear when they attack."

Suddenly, Chief Wheeler's explanation was interrupted by the voice of the commander atop the bio-stallion, Ahmed bin Hassan.

"Fall in men. Ranks of two. Step off smartly and move forward."

CHAPTER FORTY-FIVE

The battle began at dawn.

Lars Cabot and Chief Lexus Wheeler were next to one another in the second row of soldiers. Soldata Fifteen stood in the next row back a few meters away. They were waiting for the signal to attack.

All night long, it had been the same, bravado up and down the line. Scared men talking big to convince themselves that they were not scared. But of course, every last man was scared.

What young man wants to die? Hell, what old man wants to die?

The battle these men found themselves in was an all-out affair. It was being fought at close quarters, like the First American Civil War, and equally crude. Both sides were ill-equipped. Most of the arms were vintage weapons from Earth, no blasters or force guns. Older weapons jammed in the heavy humidity. Misfirings were common. People regularly blew off a finger or thumb, sometimes worse.

The rain began even before the first shot of the day was fired. The rain would continue without let-up for two days straight. The downpour was part of the sequence of events that marked the arrival of the most recent trans-comet flushed out of the Kuiper Belt and intentionally crashed into the Venusian atmosphere. It was what this war was all about. The soldiers in line had heard the sonic booms the night before, around midnight, a rolling thunder of sonic booms, one right after another after another for hours. Now, as the dirty ice-ball melted in the hot, toxic upper atmosphere, the rain fell in sheets. It was blinding.

Their regiment, such that it was, was second in line of battle. Lars was totally horrified by what he saw happen to the regiment ahead of them. The men, laced tight with piss and vinegar, had paraded up the road and into the arms of the enemy. But they were thrown back in pieces with intense fury.

An artillery shell, lobbed out of nowhere, struck one of the first men in line. The shell carried the man's head off his shoulders. It flew past Lars, a trail of gray matter in its wake. Nothing remained of the decapitated head other than a chin with a bit of hair.

It dawned on Lars that being a soldier was not all it was cracked up to be. The realization was painful. *How had his grandfather done it? How had his grandfather managed to survive a war?* Suddenly Lars was in the middle of one, a real one, one with blood and guts and death and suffering.

It was like Chief Wheeler said. Sometimes even the virtuous have to fight dirty. Sometimes even the good guys are forced by circumstance to do terrible things to destroy great evil. Only thing was, today, here and now, they were being forced to fight on the side of evil.

The devastation was everywhere. It was the same no matter which way he turned. A captain entered a tent and quickly emerged with a sickened look on his face. He had seen a victim of another artillery shell. The dead man's head leaned against his own hand. The lower part of his torso had been blown away. Carnivorous worms were already swirling about the corpse.

Another officer's bio-stallion was heard panting and then fell dead to the ground. These beasts were tough. They had thick, leathery skins. They could run at high speed for untold kloms. But they were also flesh and blood. A cannon ball had passed through the side of this animal — clean through it. The impact blew out its insides.

Lars stayed low, near the base of a giant tree-like plant. It was still raining, and the ground was wet and muddy.

The battle intensified. Men were dropping like flies. Just as quickly, they were being consumed by those same flies. The soldier on the other side of him, a man Lars did not know, had three or four ribs blown out by a heat-seeking artillery shell. The man's still-throbbing heart lay exposed before him. Lars tasted bile in his mouth. The man died before Lars could offer help. The corpse was found three days later. His face had been defleshed and was covered with maggots.

Lars had not realized until now the full extent of the biological hazards they faced. A simple flesh wound could turn septic in no time. This was Venus. Any break in the skin would rapidly become fatally infected. Ahmed bin Hassan would die that way after a simple fall.

Everything on Venus grew at an astonishing rate — plants, bacteria, viruses, mold. Soldiers did not die from gunshot wounds half as fast as they died from infection. Without a constant and aggressive regimen of antivirals and antifungals, any injured man was a goner. Almost no amount of medical care could be delivered fast enough to keep out the microbes.

Chief Wheeler saw Lars's reaction and bumped him on the shoulder with a good balled up fist, as men are wont to do when they want to buck up the other fellow's spirits. But the killing was not over. Nor was the rain.

Another man, this one on horseback, raised himself up in his saddle to get a better view. A bullet struck him behind the left ear, exited the left eye. His hands went to his face, then he crashed to the ground dead.

There were bodies everywhere. Lars looked at one at out of morbid curiosity. The lower torso was laid open like a display case. He was astonished to see a man's insides. The essential parts were all neatly organized, many in their own little membranes, like plastic-wrapped leftovers in a well-maintained refrigerator. This surprised him. He had always assumed that the coils of intestines, the stomach, liver and spleen would all be jumbled together. The tidy reality was strangely satisfying to his organized brain, if horribly terrifying.

With bullets flying, General Ahmed bin Hassan, limping badly from an earlier fall, met with General Petra and a few of the other top field commanders. Suddenly, in the middle of their strategy session, a barrage of smoke and fire tore out of the swamp like a defiant finger. The cannonball sliced through the air along an arching trajectory defined by gravity. An instant later, the ball decapitated the General's aide standing next to him. The General was splattered with brain. Yet another close call for the tyrant's son.

On and on it went. Casualties mounted steadily on both sides. The fighting was fierce. The troops rallied, then fell back, then rallied again. All of a sudden, some of what Lars had learned back in training at Anaconda began to come in handy. He fixed a bayonet to the front of his force gun and charged forward into the blinding smoke like a madman.

Each charge brought more men with more bayonets and more death. All day long, despite appalling casualties on both sides, not a meter of marshy ground exchanged hands. Then, in early afternoon, it happened. The enemy general, Bagdonavich was shot. After that, everything changed.

Bagdonavich was a brave man, probably one of the braver men on the field of battle. Rather than remain safely behind enemy lines while the battle was raging, like Ahmed bin Hassan did, Bagdonavich liked to stay out in front, where the action was. This is what got him shot.

Even from where Lars hunkered down in the short grass, he could hear the Allied general arguing with his aides.

"You need to get back," an aide shouted at him through the rain.

To which the general replied, "You do your duty and I will do mine. Now get out of my way!"

The aide continued to argue. "It is my duty to die, not yours."

Bagdonavich harrumphed, stopped to light his pipe, then turned his steed around and rejoined the battle. Pipe smoke billowed up around the general's head. It made him an easy target.

Lars refused to fire on the man. He would have rathered fight alongside Bagdonavich than fight against him. But others near him were not so picky. A fusillade of bullets rang out.

The general staggered in his saddle. His uniform was torn by bullets in several places. The heel of one boot was cut away. He seemed unsteady atop the big horse.

"Are you hit?" an aide asked, reaching for the general still in the saddle.

Bagdonavich shook his head no. But there was clearly blood at his shoulder. His hand loosened on the reins.

The truth of the matter was that Bagdonavich had been mortally wounded and did not yet know it. A bullet had entered his right leg behind the knee, severing a major artery. Although he was quickly bleeding to death, the wound was masked by his high-top riding boot, which was now filling with blood.

Lars could see blood dripping dark and red from the heel of the general's boot. The aide saw it too. He asked Bagdonavich again, "Are you certain you have not been wounded? I see blood."

Again Bagdonavich shook his head. Then he began to swirl as if he were about to drop from his saddle.

The aide caught him on the way down and lowered him gently to the soaking wet ground. He frantically ripped open the general's shirt searching for a wound. He quickly found the shoulder wound. But that was not what was killing the general; the unseen leg wound was.

A simple tourniquet might have saved the general's life. But by the time anyone recognized the profuse bleeding in his boot for what it was, he had lost too much blood. The dark crimson pool flowed in a long stream from Bagdonavich's body. His eyes were open but his face had turned a deathly pale.

Men allied to Uday bin Hassan cheered his death. But Lars did not. He cried for the loss of such a man. Hours of battle still lay ahead.

With Bagdonavich dead, Petra's forces had the psychological upper hand. They slowly advanced, Lars and the others from the *Ticonderoga* with them. They soon had the enemy on the run. After eight and a half hours of devastating stalemate, the tide was turning in bin Hassan's favor.

Even though victory that day was in sight, the advance was grotesque. They walked through wet fields of dead and dying men, men from both sides in countless number. The corpses, some still alive and barely hanging on, were already being slowly devoured by cannibalistic Venusian moss.

Never before had Lars seen human death, not like this anyway. There had been Sergeant Major Grovosky, of course. But he had died suddenly in space, almost in an antiseptic way, no stench. There had been the bodies in the Space Elevator the day of the rescue. But there had been no blood, no putrid vapors rising from the corpses. There had been the man whose throat was slashed before him that night in Perdition's Cup. But Lars could hardly remember those events anymore.

No, this field of death was entirely different. Each body wore a strange greyness on its skin. The stiffening heaviness of the bodies. Corpses horribly mutilated. Many had missing limbs.

The smell of death hung heavily in the thick air. Bodies were everywhere, in the meadow, in the jungles and glens, in the swamp, near the Kevlar tents that housed the soldiers.

Lars bent over to look at one of the bodies. He could not account for his curiosity. He counted eleven entry wounds, no exit wounds. Then he looked up at Chief Wheeler, who stood nearby.

"Snowstorm effect," Chief Wheeler said.

Lars looked at him with questioning eyes.

"The incoming bullets tumble in flight after they pass through our defensive force field. That is why there is such marked destruction of the body. The number of broken bones is huge. High-velocity bullets fragment and scatter throughout the body upon impact. Medicos call it the snowstorm effect. On an x-ray, the shattered bullet fragments show up like snowflakes in a snowstorm. The frags are so small no doctor can possibly retrieve them all."

"Ain't technology great?"

"I guess it depends on who is holding the gun," Chief Wheeler said. "There is an important difference between cause of death and manner of death. What links the two is the mechanism of death."

"Seriously, Chief. This man was shot in a most horrible way. Need we say more?"

Chief Wheeler acted as if he hadn't heard the younger man speak. "Cause of death is the disease or injury that opens a pathway to a physiological change in the body whereby the disease or injury can exert its lethality."

"Yeah, I got it, Chief. Bullet enters brain. Bullet interferes with brain function. Knife enters chest cavity. Knife pierces aorta. Ruptured aorta disrupts blood flow to the rest of the body. Person dies."

"Sarcasm? That is how you answer me?" The Chief's hair was matted wet with rainwater and sweat.

Lars was still bent over the body. "Why the fuck are you telling me this?"

"Because I am scared. Talking helps me to not be scared."

"If you are scared, how do you think I feel?"

"I know, son. You are scared too."

"Okay, Chief. Keep talking. I am listening."

"Manner of death. We classify it in one of several ways. Natural death. Accidental death. Homicide. Suicide. Things like that."

Lars nodded his head sadly and got to his feet. The two of them moved uneasily across the field of death. The sun was already reddening in the sky when Lars came upon another body. The face seemed familiar. It bore a remarkable likeness to an old friend of his from back home, Granite Irston.

The dead man lay near a small body of water. His thin face was gazing up at the sky. The mouth was open, giving the corpse a vacant, pathetic air. A short, broad sword had opened a frightful gash in his side. Coagulated blood was everywhere. Maggots were already crawling over the body.

Lars began to cry. This was too much to take. His body shook with anger. His tears were the kind a man cries when he loses a son or daughter. *This could have been Granite*, he thought. *His best friend in the world*.

Lars staggered backwards, in the direction of a nearby medic tent. Chief Wheeler followed him in. The tent was filled with wounded, bloody and dying. Doctors and surgeons were in short supply. Medicines and anesthetics were few and far between. What the doctors did, what they had to do, was gross and hideous.

Lars's eyes were drawn to a grisly sight at the back of the tent. A large wooden crate filled with body parts. Hands and feet and arms. All amputated in desperation before gangrene could overwhelm the rest of the body. Every man that left the tent would leave a cripple. The crate was so full, two horrible and bloody feet protruded out over the top.

Wheeler spoke. "Bravery is a good thing, Lars."

"This isn't bravery, Chief. This is slaughter. We have to get out of this thing."

Chief Wheeler nodded. The war — this skirmish — had gone well beyond vicious. In this tent, a tent where men came to be saved, they were dismembered. Arms, legs, hands and feet, just amputated, lay everywhere. In the QM, there was only two days' rations for the men; no forage for the animals. The number of dead, on both sides, was staggering. In a war of attrition, Uday's forces would likely be defeated.

But today's battle was over. After the Allied General Bagdonavich was killed, the opposing army withdrew. Now it was time to suture their wounds and regroup for the next confrontation.

Even tyrants bury their dead; they have to. And the grisly job falls to whomever carries the day. Lars threw up twice before they even began.

The bodies were swollen. Gases inside trying to escape. There were so many bodies and they smelled so bad. He continued to gag through most of the job. Eyes watered, nose ran. Wheeler, scared and nervous, began talking again, spouting all kinds of technical jargon, most of which Lars tried to tune out.

"There is a specific pattern to the decomposition of a dead body . . ."

"We really have to do this now? Now, while they are handing out shovels so we can bury these men?"

"I told you that it helps if I talk. Listen to what I have to say. You might even learn something. There is a distinct pattern, I tell you. Insects come to feed on the body shortly after death, as do these carnivorous worms. The common blowfly is almost always first on the scene. This place is crawling with them. They have a nose for carrion and blood. The flies lay thousands of eggs in the wounds and other body cavities. Once the larvae hatch, they begin to eat the flesh, what we call maggots. They are voracious. If the weather is wet and warm, like it is here, the maggots can reduce a corpse to skeleton within days."

Lars looked at Chief Wheeler and heaved again. "Chief, just the thought of it. Leave it alone, will you?"

"Come on, kid. Take a shovel. Dig."

Soldata joined the other two with a shovel. All three dug. Others joined them in the effort.

Soldata said, "You understand, don't you, that humans have no soul, not one that needs to be buried anyway."

"You are a robot," Lars snarled. "What do you know?"

"This is biology, not philosophy," Soldata said. "Left dead and unattended in a warm environment like this, it will not take long before you cannot tell one body from another."

Lars was insistent. "This is about ritual, Soldata. This is about respect, not souls. You want to live in human society? This is what humans do. Now dig."

Chief Wheeler agreed. "Our job is to dig the holes, lay the corpses side by side in the ground. No coffins. We fire a one-gun salute over the graves, then cover the cold dead bodies with mounds of damp, Venusian clay."

The stench from rotting bodies and hundreds of dead horses proved almost too much to bear. And the effort to bury them was mostly wasted. In the days ahead, virtually all the graves would be uprooted by wild bushpigs and Venusian dragons. Skulls, leg bones, and vertebrae would shortly be scattered across the landscape.

But for now they dug, mostly in silence. Then Lars spoke up.

"Chief, we need to get out of this somehow."

Chief Wheeler leaned back on his shovel. "I agree."

"No, I mean it, Chief. I say we walk away this very minute."

"I would rather not be shot for desertion," Chief Wheeler said.

"I say we take our shovels in hand, move to another part of the battlefield, one closer to the edge of the jungle. Then we start digging again, wait for our moment."

"We would be committing suicide."

"I do not think so," Lars said. "There is no one here to stop us. Everyone else is busy. Plus, we are not armed. We pose no threat to anyone. The other side, the Allied side, is retreating. We slip into the bog and retreat right along with them."

"We will be shot on sight, as soon as any of the Allied Forces see us."

"It is a calculated risk, I agree," Lars said. "But we walk out of here, raise our arms in surrender. We walk into the enemy camp, stay in plain sight, move slowly."

"And we hope like hell that they think first and shoot later."

"Yes, something like that."

Soldata drew closer. For a second, Lars thought he might turn them both in for desertion. But he said, "I may be a robot and I may not understand your ways. But please do not leave me behind when you go to the other side. Promise me."

"You have my word," Chief Wheeler said.

"Mine too," Lars said. "Now what will it be, Chief? Do we break out of here and find our way to the other line? Or do we chicken out? Don't forget. We still need to find Kaleena and the other women. We need to save them before it is too late."

Chief Wheeler stopped digging. He judged the distance to the nearest tree line and the bog beyond.

"Okay," he said. "No sudden moves. Walk slowly and deliberately in that direction. Stop every so often to dig and bury another body. Let's move out."

CHAPTER FORTY-SIX

Montera Cantina and Kaleena Henry huddled next to one another in the belly of the Platypus. They found comfort in each other's arms, the connection they shared in Kaleena's father.

"Why did they have to kill him?" Kaleena asked, her voice cracking.

"He was a brave man, your father. I loved him very much. I know he loved you."

"Love? You want to speak to me about love at a time like this? You are nothing but a common whore."

"There is nothing common about me, I assure you. And in case you are confused little girl, you will shortly be spreading your legs for a gang of unwashed, unshaved heathens. Total strangers. They won't give a flying fig whether they hurt you or whether you suffer badly at their hands. If I were you, I would promptly climb down from that high horse of yours and understand the fix we presently find ourselves in. We may not get out of this thing alive."

"I am sorry," Kaleena cried. "Very sorry."

Just then, the pilot of the Platypus, a big overgrown beast of a man, spooled up the motor and the amphibious craft began to move forward. It could move easily through the swamps and low-lying waterways of Venus.

"Where are you taking us?" one of the other travel companions wanted to know.

"You are going to the Farm."

"We do not know what that is," Montera said. "We need to know where we are being taken."

"The Farm is just that, a farm," the big man said as he guided the machine into the creek. "Pigs, sheep, genetically altered goats."

"Why must we be taken there?"

"Uday considers women to be chattel."

"Like pigs and goats?"

"Yeah, like pigs and goats, but not as likeable."

The Platypus gained speed and then seemed to gain altitude as the hydrofoil wings brought the hull up and out of the water. For a few moments, the craft skimmed the tops of the short vines and bushes at low elevation.

Then, suddenly, the motor whined, the wings retracted, and the Platypus dove straight down into the water. The women screamed at the sudden change in trajectory.

But straight down it went, into the ebony water, under the surface, swimming deeper and deeper into the sinister blackness.

The water outside the craft was cloudy and dark. It was also very hot. The cabin of the Platypus became noticeably warmer the longer they were under.

The submersible's lights came on. But the passengers could not see a thing. The water was murky. The pilot turned on his nav aids. First thermal, then sonar, then e-ping mapping.

The craft slowed its approach. Ahead could now be seen a twin set of large blast doors, tall as a three-story building and nearly as wide. The Platypus exchanged security protocols with the controllers behind the doors. Then the doors began to roll slowly open. They weighed countless klogs and the hydraulics were twitchy.

Beyond the blast doors was a landing bay the size of a football field. Once the Platypus was secured, the doors would be closed and the murky water flushed from the cavernous chamber.

Then, before the hatch could be opened, the outside of the boat had to be pressure washed and cleaned.

The chamber too. The walls. The floor. The ceiling. The entire chamber flushed clean and sprayed down with disinfectant.

They were at the Farm.

•
•

"Our motion detectors are picking up movement at the perimeter. Two, maybe three soldiers."

"Ours or theirs?" the ranking officer asked his subordinate, still at his surveill machine.

"No way to say for certain," the low-level sentry answered. "Not without first apprehending them. But I have to tell you, Lieutenant. Allied soldiers have been straggling in for hours. Most of these boys got separated from their units during the battle. They are filtering back to base camp in small groups of two or three, just like these guys."

"So you think they are okay?" the Lieutenant asked, clearly nervous.

"Our protocol all daylong has been to apprehend and interview. It is time-consuming but highly effective. So far every refugee questioned has been one of ours."

"Okay, Corporal. Then let these three through. Take them into custody. If they resist, kill them."

"Aye, aye, Sir." The Corporal picked up his two-way and spoke to the man at the other end. "Dispatch a roving unit. Have one squad get in behind these three so they cannot bolt. The three unknowns are presently at grid marker 2-B. Have the other squad get in front of them, stop them at the line. Frisk these guys, disarm them, bring them to Interrogation One."

"Rules of engagement?"

"If they resist or try to run, the Lieutenant has issued orders to kill."

•
•

"Stop where you are. Hands up," the squad leader ordered.

Lars, Wheeler, and Soldata froze in place, raised their arms. "We mean you no harm," Chief Wheeler said.

"Shut up and drop your weapons to the ground."

"We are not armed."

"What kind of soldier runs around these woods without a gun in his hand?"

"The kind of soldier that is a conscript."

The squad leader took that information and called it in to the sentry post on his two-way. "Yeah, two soldiers, one synthetic."

"Have your robot take three paces forward," the squad leader said.

Wheeler nodded his okay to Soldata, who advanced the prescribed distance.

The front-most soldier, a private, held out an electronic device and ran a full-body scan of Soldata.

"This one is clean. No explosives, no weapons."

"Robot. Identify yourself," the squad leader ordered.

"Soldata Fifteen. Formerly of the S.S. *Ticonderoga*. Incept date 2304.12.4. Serial number 45GTY682."

"Check the manifest. See if we can verify."

The private typed a series of numbers into his device. "The bot's serial number checks. A robot by that designation was onboard the ship Hassan hijacked."

"Robot. Take five paces forward. Allow my men to place a restraining leash on you."

Soldata obeyed without argument and the squad's second-in-command attached the magnetized device to Soldata's neck.

"Okay. Next man. Three paces forward. Identify yourself."

Chief Wheeler did as he was told. They cuffed him then repeated the process with Lars.

"Okay," the squad leader said. "Take these three before Captain Lewis. You will find him in Interrogation One. The Captain will make the final decision as to the disposition of these men."

"Aye, aye," the private said as he and two other men led them away.

•
•

Captain Lewis was a no-nonsense security officer of the highest order. Everything was by the book.

"Okay you three. I am a busy man. I know you are not Allied soldiers. So you only have a few minutes of mortal life remaining unless I get the answers I want in very short order. Are we clear?"

All three prisoners nodded in the affirmative.

"Good. Now let's start with your names."

"Chief Engineer Lexus Wheeler of the *Ticonderoga*, formerly of the Space Station."

Captain Lewis sized up the other man. Chief Wheeler was a big man, fit and muscular, certainly not a man to be trifled with.

"Chief, you realize this is easy enough for me to check," Captain Lewis said. "We have been in touch with Space Command. We have the ship's manifest. It includes a complete inventory of pictures, retinal scans and genetic markers of every crewmember and passenger onboard."

"I am not lying."

"For your sake, I hope not. Spool up the ship's data, Corporal."

"Aye, aye, Sir."

"Okay, Chief. Look in here." The man held up a portable scanner to Chief Wheeler's face, positioned it close-in at eye-level. "Hold still. We need to do a retinal scan." The machine hummed for a few seconds and then the red light on its back panel turned green.

Captain Lewis said, “Bring up the Chief’s data on my screen. Overlay the scan you just performed. Let me compare the two.”

“Aye, aye, Sir,” the Corporal said. He stood at the Captain’s side as the scans were displayed.

“What do you think, soldier?” the Captain asked, though he had already made up his mind.

“You’re asking me, Cap?”

Lewis nodded.

“My best guess is that these two scans are a match.”

“I would agree. Good work, soldier.” Then Captain Lewis turned to address Wheeler. “Chief, you are clear. Very impressive background, by the way. Now please identify your robot. Remember, we have on file the default code for every Soldata in service. My Corporal here can easily prove or disprove any false claim of identity.”

“You boys really are paranoid, aren’t you?”

“What is your robot’s name? I will not ask you again.”

“Soldata Fifteen,” Chief Wheeler answered in a tired voice. “I haven’t a clue what his default code is. So if you have to shoot me, shoot me. The boy’s name is Lars Cabot. You probably don’t have much of a file on him. He only recently signed on. Now, are you going to clear the three of us or not?”

Captain Lewis hesitated a moment then decided. “Okay, Chief. You three are clear. As for the paranoia, mistakes have been made. There have been some mishaps. We have had instances of people crossing the frontier, saying they want to defect to our side, then committing acts of treason against us. Which brings me to you three. What the hell are you doing here?”

“Well, the first thing you can do is to remove that restraining bolt from my robot.”

Captain Lewis nodded to his Corporal, who removed the magnetized device from around Soldata’s neck.

“Thank you,” Chief Wheeler said. “What are we doing here, you ask? We were conscripted after the bastards commandeered the ship.”

"What bastards are we talking about here?"

"A humaniform robot who we only knew as Captain Nathanial Reynolds. Is he on your manifest?"

"Humaniform?" Captain Lewis asked, as the Corporal studied the ship's complement of passengers and crew.

"Yes. An exceptional likeness. Fooled every single one of us. We only caught on after it was too late. Captain Reynolds proved to be a robot. We only established that fact when we tried to re-take the bridge. We denied the flight deck food and water and we quit recycling fresh air."

"So that crazy megalomaniac finally managed to do it." Captain Lewis appeared stunned.

"Which crazy megalomaniac?"

"Our intelligence sources have told us that Uday has a man inside the Neurological Institute who has been working on this for years. They want to use these things against us, both here and on Mars, maybe Earth as well. We knew it would be only a matter of time."

The Corporal cleared his throat to speak. "Sir."

"What is it, Corporal?"

"I do find this Captain Reynolds on the manifest. He was an eleventh-hour addition to the crew. But I have to tell you. His creds appear to be in order, including a retinal scan. This machine must be very life-like."

"Like I said. — It fooled us."

"And what happened to this Captain Reynolds when the rest of you were conscripted?" Lewis asked.

"We all came down to the surface together. But then Reynolds placed himself in a separate line from the rest of us. That group was being dispatched to some sort of prison, a place our captors called the Gulag."

"He is much too valuable a piece of property to be destroyed. So his ultimate destination must have been somewhere else still."

"I can only tell you what I heard," Chief Wheeler said.

"Okay," Captain Lewis said. "I will send this all up to Command. They will decide how they want to use you. That decision is above my pay grade."

"Sir, if I may," Lars interrupted. "We had women onboard. We think they have been taken to someplace called the Farm. It is imperative we get our women back."

Captain Lewis' voice was flat and without emotion. "Son, if your women have been taken to the Farm, they are already dead. If they are not dead, they will have been tortured. You don't want them back."

"Spare the boy's feelings," Chief Wheeler said. "He has to believe his woman is alive and that she is being treated well. We all have to believe that. The three of us have a duty to try and save them."

"Ah, such a dreamy thought. And uttered by such a sensible man too."

"We have to try." Chief Wheeler was resolute.

Captain Lewis could read the other man's determination. "I can give you an approximate location, Chief. But that is about the size of it. We have never found a reason to target the Farm with our guns. So we haven't collected much intell on the place."

"Fair enough, Captain. But my men and I need weapons and equipment. We also need three additional men."

"No can do. I have absolutely no equipment or weapons to spare. And certainly no soldiers. Not to waste trying to save a bunch of women who are probably dead anyway."

"Don't say that, you bastard!" Lars screamed. "Kaleena is pregnant. I do not want to see her die."

"Captain, try to see it our way. You had a mother once, right? Maybe a wife? Perhaps a daughter? We have to try . . . These women mean a lot to us . . . All I am asking from you is three men. Also, a boat, some firepower, and a few days' provisions."

Captain Lewis sighed. "I will help you. But I have no boat to spare. You will have to steal one from Hassan's men. I know where one is docked not far from here. We can manufacture a diversion to help you hijack a Platypus. You will need to grab a rubber boat as well."

"That is a perfectly fair offer. Thank you."

"Not so fast, Chief. I will want something in return if you succeed."

"I am listening."

"You get your women back from the Farm. Then you help me take out the facility where they are manufacturing these newfangled humaniform robots. Deal?"

"Deal."

CHAPTER FORTY-SEVEN

The Platypus idled quietly in the acrid darkness. The six men and one robot had hijacked the craft from an enemy squad two hours earlier after a short firefight and a series of small diversionary explosions.

The incursion team was led by Chief Wheeler. His second was a man Captain Lewis assigned to him, a man named Fisher, Staff Sergeant Fisher. Captain Lewis considered Staff Sergeant Fisher to be one of his best trackers. Rounding out the team were three more men, all volunteers, Privates Roby and Hall, plus Tech Sergeant Ramirez. And, of course, Lars Cabot and Soldata Fifteen.

Their present target was a large island crawling with bin Hassan's men. Their mission was to try and locate the Farm where the women were being held, scout it for possible weaknesses, figure out how it might be taken or its defenses breached. They were to take the rubber boat from the cargo hold of the Platypus, launch it quietly into the water, and make their way to shore.

Lars got into the rubber boat, now, while Roby and Hall held the mooring ropes firm against the side of the Platypus. Chief Wheeler went in second, followed by Soldata, Fisher, Roby then Hall. They were all dressed in their black jungle caps and dark-blue jungle fatigues.

Tech Sergeant Ramirez was last to board. He had programmed the Platypus' autopilot so that after they shoved off the boat would anchor itself in deep water at a location where he hoped it would not be discovered.

Their training had been brief but severe. Crude skullcaps strapped to their heads for twenty-four hours. Land nav, comm skills, memcon, the finer points of scouting, jungle survival skills — all downloaded into their heads at breakneck speed. You would think in a world of robots and spaceships and satellites and high-tech comm gear that many of these crude skills would not be necessary. But none of that newer stuff worked on Venus, not satellites, not high-tech comm gear, not electronic computers. Even Soldata was a little twitchy. Infiltration had to be done the hard way, the old-fashioned way.

These were not exceptionally brave men. But they were determined. And they did have a single, unambiguous goal. That made them lethal.

They were all in the rubber boat now, paddling for shore. Their backpacks and essential weapons and gear were alongside them on the floor. It was shortly before midnight and the wind was beginning to pick up. The sea was becoming rough, making it difficult to paddle. But Wheeler had no intention of turning back. They would probably get only one chance at this.

They were nearing shore, when Lars quietly spoke up. "Do you see that?" He pointed across the black water to a growing circle of illumination three hundred meters north of their intended landing spot.

"I see it," Wheeler said softly, following the direction of Lars's finger into the night. There, on the distant shore, two or three of the enemy were building a campfire for the night.

"Ignore them," Staff Sergeant Fisher said. "Keep on paddling." He instinctively adjusted his soft jungle cap.

Twenty minutes passed. They drew ever closer to shore. Then the team was on the beach. Roby and Hall deflated the boat, while the others took their weapons and established a perimeter in case they had been seen. Ramirez helped the two hide the boat behind a rock outcropping. Then everyone shouldered their gear.

Soldata took point. He led the team inland through thick kunai grass to the coastal trail. Chief Wheeler took up position at the rear of the team, always watching their backside. Captain Lewis had given them approximate longitude and latitude grid-markings for where they thought the Farm might be located.

The recon team had barely traveled a hundred meters inland before they encountered trouble. Soldata raised his fist in the air. The six team members came to a sudden halt, fists rising in rapid succession down the line. There was dead silence. Soldata came equipped with nightvision. He had spotted an enemy soldier sleeping along the trail. The soldier had to be dealt with.

Lars watched Soldata closely. He could only imagine how the robot was parsing the Three Laws at this moment.

Had the robot done the math? Had he learned to distinguish between friend and foe? Between ally and enemy? Had he come to learn that some human lives he ought value more highly than others?

Soldata drew his knife with one hand, removed his soft jungle cap with the other. He quietly inched his way towards his intended victim. Then, in one swift movement, he placed his cap over the man's face and thrust the knife downward into his chest with crushing force. The whole thing took under a second. There was barely a sound.

Lars said nothing. But he ran his own calculus through his head. He had just witnessed a robot harm a human being in contravention of its programming, and he didn't quite understand how.

Hall and Roby dragged the body off the trail. Then the team resumed its earlier course inland.

The trail turned north and two hundred meters further along they encountered two more soldiers. These were the men they had seen earlier building a fire while the team was still in open water. They could not get in close enough to the two men to use their knives without first being seen. So Fisher and Hall opened fire with their jungle carbines, quickly eliminating the threat.

But then, as Hall and Roby dragged the two bodies into the swamp, they heard movement behind them. *An enemy patrol had moved in behind their position.*

The situation was grim. The team was now boxed in between two pockets of enemy soldiers.

Since they were certain to be killed if they remained on the trail, where they were exposed, Wheeler ordered them with hand signals to do the only sensible thing — *Off the trail. Into the jungle.*

In almost total silence, the six moved about ten meters off the trail and into the jungle.

For the next five minutes they barely breathed. They sat silently with guns poised and watched as a squad of enemy soldiers passed slowly by.

Then they moved even further off the trail. Soldata had downloaded a topo map of the area into his memory core during their day of training. He used it, now, to guide their movements cross-country.

Soldata led the team through heavy swamp and into the closest river. The water was thick with disease and leeches and other ghastly unknowns. But the team had no choice. They would have to cross that murky river from west to east.

On the planet Venus, going into water of any kind was always dangerous. Bacteria was the chief culprit, though by no means the only one. As a precaution, the men took an antibiotic or antifungal every hour or so while in the field.

They waded across the river one man at a time, jungle carbine held over their head to keep it dry. As soon as one man reached the far bank, the next man entered. It took half an hour for the entire team to reach the other side.

"We still do not know the location of the Farm," Lars said. "Isn't that what we risked our lives coming out here for?"

"We still have two hours before the sun comes up," Wheeler said. "We hit the next patrol that comes through, frisk the dead for memory sticks and such, keep one or two of them alive so we can interrogate them, find this Farm."

The men hunkered down beside the trail. They strung trip wires across the path. No one was going to come through without first setting off the alarms.

Lars sat beneath what looked like a large pine tree. But the comparison went only so far. Venusian pine trees were not conifers, not in the conventional sense. They had much thicker bark and strangely shaped leaves.

Lars understood the reasons for the thick bark. Green plant life had it much tougher here than on Earth. Predators were strong and out in greater numbers.

Venusian plants could be attacked by other, more aggressive plants. They could be attacked by insects. By viruses. By bacteria. Fungi. Molds of every stripe. All of these predators had vicious methods. Acidic appendages. Vise-like suckers. Adhesives strong as steel.

To combat this phalanx of predators, trees evolved methods of protection. This included layers of immensely thick bark. It was composed of extraordinarily hard organic matter.

The leaves, too, were quite sophisticated. If one looked closely, the leaves could be seen to actually be chlorophyll factories hidden behind glass. The "glass" was a translucent, organic wax of some kind, tough and durable. A typical leaf ran the entire length of the branch and was curled, like a tube, but open on top. They acted as funnels or collecting pipes for rainwater. After a rain, the water would run down the length of the waxy tube and directly into the trunk, where doors of a sort opened on cue. They would close again afterward, when the tree had had its fill.

Lars marveled at the details. *Life always found a way*, he thought. Then he focused again on the matter at hand. Three of the team members trudged noisily forward through the underbrush. The idea was to flush out the enemy. Very dangerous work.

This is one of those instances where one has to consider the meaning of courage. It is a misused word in today's world. A celebrity reveals that he has a drinking problem. He is described in the press as being courageous. Nothing could be further from the truth. There is no more courage involved in the disclosure of a drinking problem than there is in admitting that one is overweight or going bald. Actual courage is something else. Courage is about risk and choice. Courage is about the decision a man makes when he has the option of caving in. Pappy Boyington. Lech Walesa. Winston Churchill. Liam Kato. Jeremiah Denton. These are men who stood their ground against enormous odds and refused to back down. They earned the right to use that word. Lars felt the members of his team were about to earn that right as well.

They did not have long to wait. Fresh soldiers were moving forward on the trail toward the line of battle. Meanwhile, tired and wounded soldiers were returning home to base along the very same trail.

Now suddenly, Soldata's fist went up. He had been standing point. That closed fist was an unambiguous signal. *Hold.*

The first man on the trail looked in their direction. *Had the enemy soldier seen them?* Lars wondered.

Soldata did not wait to learn the answer. He raised his carbine and fired. The man's head snapped back violently. That is when all hell broke loose.

Within seconds, a second man appeared on the trail. Then a third. Then a fourth. The whole team opened fire. They killed all three then retracted just as quickly back into the jungle. By now, adrenaline was pumping hard through their veins.

An enemy soldier followed them into the thickets. Chief Wheeler turned, knife extended. He struck the man once, straight in the heart like Soldata had done earlier to that first sleeping soldier. The man's blood pumped right up the Chief's arm, bright and red. Carnivorous insects swarmed in almost immediately.

The second guy that followed them into the jungle was not so easy to put down. He caught Roby off guard. Roby had no time to draw his weapon. Private Hall began to pummel the enemy soldier with his fists. Then Private Roby did as well.

But this beating, no matter how severe, was not enough to kill him. Lars was galvanized to action. He ran the man through with his bayonet. Finally, the man stopped struggling.

Following the skirmish with the two men — and before any further soldiers could happen by — the team rapidly frisked the bodies for maps or other documents, anything that might reveal the true location of the Farm.

Then they moved off in the opposite direction. As always, Soldata was in the lead. He did not scare as easily as the others. But then, all of a sudden, he was stopped cold by the sound of a voice.

"Freeze!" Chief Wheeler ordered.

Soldata stopped, foot in midair. Then he turned around angrily, or at least as angrily as a robot could seem to be. He saw Chief Wheeler motioning to him furiously, signaling him to step back, which he did. Robots followed orders, especially emphatic ones.

"Have you lost your mind?" Soldata said brusquely. "We are on silent duty, Chief. You know better than to speak outloud."

Wheeler shone his light just ahead of where Soldata had been standing. The light illuminated a tripwire strung between two trees and rigged to a satchel charge.

"I know the rules well enough, you rusted bucket of bolts. But I need you functional, not blasted into a thousand pieces."

Soldata was flustered. "How did I not see that wire?"

"A polite thank you will do."

Soldata nodded. "Thank you."

The thought crossed Lars's mind. *Was Soldata losing his touch?* Were his senses being corroded by the Venusian atmosphere?

Soldata stepped over the tripwire, being careful not to disturb it or make it vibrate. The others did the same.

Chief Wheeler pulled his men aside. "Let's have those documents you pulled off the dead soldiers. Maybe we can yet discern the location of the Farm. Shine your light over here."

They handed Chief Wheeler all the jungle documents they had collected. He held them in his hand and examined them one by one. Then he handed them off in order to Soldata, who collated the data.

"Here, I think I found it," Chief Wheeler said. He pointed to a grid map, the site of a building and surrounding grounds.

Chief Wheeler was trained in the finer points of land navigation. He knew better than most how to read a map — map symbols, terrain features, grid coordinates. He knew how to read contour lines; how to recognize valleys, mountains, and ridges; how to differentiate between a draw and a spur; how to identify streams and rivers; how to tell the difference between a hilltop and a depression.

There were times, of course, when a man might not have a map. Or he might be trapped in a location that had not yet been mapped. Sometimes even a good map could be rendered useless. On Venus, the dense, ever-changing jungles sometimes made it difficult to spot key terrain features. Roads were few. Mountain ranges were uncharted. Swollen rivers might jump their banks or change course.

Getting a firm fix on one's location was problematic. Venus had no earthlike gps system. It had no visible stars to guide by. All it really possessed in the way of natural guideposts was a fixed magnetic pole. All the rocky planets — Earth, Mars, and Venus — had a magnetic pole. This is where an old-fashioned oil-filled magnetic compass came in handy. Even if a man did not know exactly where he was, with a magnetic compass he could always learn in which direction he was headed. Directional information of that sort might help him find a key river or important coastline that would help fix his location on a map.

Chief Wheeler turned to Soldata. "Upload and fix these grid coordinates into your mapping function. We now have what we came for."

Tech Sergeant Ramirez spoke up. "Chief, I say we mark this spot with a beryllium copper rod. Permit me to drive it into the ground. I carry a ramwrench. Captain Lewis has already outfitted the rod with a locator. He said to place it if we were successful. The placement of the rod improves our odds later. When we come back, we will have a fixed certain point to measure from."

"Your Captain Lewis is full of surprises, isn't he?"

"But, Chief, he is not wrong," Ramirez said.

"Okay, do it. Then I want the whole team back to the boat, back to the Platypus. We have been out here long enough."

Ramirez pulled his ramwrench from his pack and drove the beryllium copper rod he had been carrying into the ground at that spot. He touched a dial on his e-pad and energized the locator. "Okay, we are good to go."

"You have a solid signal?"

"Solid."

"Okay, move out."

Soldata took point and led them back through the jungle to the trail. As they approached the shore an hour later, they realized they faced a new problem. A good-sized storm was brewing just offshore in the bay. Storms were a daily occurrence on Venus, and big ones too. It made rubber boat travel hazardous.

"What should we do, Chief? Try and wait it out?"

"We are running short on meds. We wait this out and we may die waiting. I say we go. Roby, take Hall and find that rubber boat. Ramirez, go with them. Those two are going to need your help re-inflating the boat. Foot pumps and pressurized gas cartridges. Get cracking. The rest of us will provide cover if we get any visitors."

Twenty minutes later, they were in the water. The waves were large. Twice they nearly capsized the rubber boat. But they pressed on.

"Spool up the autopilot, Tech Sergeant. Get the Platypus to raise its anchor and come out of hiding to meet us."

"Working on it, Chief."

"Work faster."

They paddled harder. Tonight's tactical goal had been achieved. Now they had a handle on the precise location of the Farm.

CHAPTER FORTY-EIGHT

When Kaleena woke up from a fitful sleep, she was in a modest room. But she was not alone. With her in the room were seven other women, two from the ship along with five others she did not know. Aside from two oversized chairs, the room was sparse. A bathtub, a lavatory, a small kitchen, and four sets of bunk beds. The ceiling was high, the lights low. Montera was there, as well as Riuanna, both travel companions from the *Ticonderoga*.

"Ah, sleeping beauty awakes," quipped one of the five girls Kaleena did not know.

"Is that a good thing or a bad thing?" Kaleena asked. The other women laughed.

"No, seriously." Kaleena was insistent. "Is that a good thing or a bad thing?"

"Girl, in this hellhole every day begins well enough. And then you wake up. First you get raped, then you get beaten. So most days do not end as well as they began."

"Who are you?" Kaleena asked.

"Name is Rox. Short for Roxanne. And who be you?"

"Kaleena. Kaleena Henry."

"Oh, yeah. I heard about you," Rox said. "Your pappy was a wheel. Got himself killed trying to save some bitches."

"Those bitches he was trying to save was us two." Kaleena motioned to where Montera was seated. "Me and her."

"Why you even out here, girl?" Rox asked.

"There was this boy . . ."

"Isn't there always?" Rox teased.

"He got me pregnant."

"Isn't that all they are good for?"

"It is more complicated than that."

"It always is."

"You got an answer for everything, don't you Rox?"

"Okay, princess. We will all put our lives on hold whilst you regale us with your sob story. We all got one, you know."

"I came back from Mars. We were descending to Earth on the Space Elevator. The Elevator was attacked by terrorists. This boy helped save me and my family. I thanked him one night — the old fashioned way."

"Spread your legs, did you?"

"We were supposed to be married." Kaleena was thinking this was all a real bad dream and that she would soon wake up fresh and relaxed in her warm bed back home.

"You vouch for this sprig?" Roxanne asked Montera.

"I do indeed."

"Me too," Riuanna said.

Another woman, bruised and battered, spoke up. "Rox, you so full of shit. Around here, no day is a good day. I hope they kill me soon."

"Is it really that bad?" Kaleena asked. "What have they done to you? What have they done to all of you?"

"Child, these men are animals. My name, by the way, is Cuzy. And let me tell you, sister. Before long, you wish you be dead too."

"Can I do anything to help you?" Kaleena asked.

"Get me a knife, anything sharp, so I can put myself down," Cuzy said.

"Quit bitching or I will put you down myself," Rox said. "You be depressing our new friends with your pitiful sob story."

"She oughts to know the truth," Cuzy said.

"What truth?" Kaleena asked.

"These men they force us to be with are animals," Cuzy said.

"I do not understand," Kaleena said.

"Well then listen up, sweet cheeks," Cuzy said. "They come in here. They smell of vomit and sulphur and gunpowder. They haven't showered in days. They shove it in your mouth, expect you to blow them. And when they have shot their load, they expect you to swallow it. Then they put it back in their pants and hit you with their fists. I would rather be dead than go through one more day of this crap."

"Is there no way out of here?" Montera asked soberly, looking around.

"Who knows?" Rox said. "I have heard stories, even talked to people. They tell me it is a thousand kloms of swamp and jungle in every direction. But who can say for sure? I am no Leatherstocking."

"I do not know what that means."

"Back in the day, I had an education." Rox chuckled at the memory. "Leatherstocking. Pathfinder. Hawkeye. Long Rifle. Deerslayer. Various nicknames for the same character in a bunch of tales from pre-colonial America. The hero of those stories knew how to survive in the wild, how to live off the land. Like I said — I am no Leatherstocking. A thousand kloms of swamp and jungle would kill me first day out. That is all I am trying to say."

"No one has ever escaped?" Montera asked.

Cuzy answered. "I heard tell once of a village of runaways. Long ways from here. Men who have escaped from the Gulag. Men who have walked off the line, gone AWOL from the war. Women who have escaped from the Farm or from the clutches of one of those dirty men."

"How do they live and eat?" Kaleena asked.

"Who?"

"The people who have escaped; the people who have walked away. Someone had to teach your Pathfinder character how to survive, an indigenous person no doubt. How the hell are we supposed to learn?"

"Don't know, child," Cuzy said. "Hit and miss, I suppose. Anyways, it is only stories. We all gonna die here."

"No, it's true," Rox said. "I heard the same stories. That village exists. It is located due east of here, about two hundred days' walk."

"Two hundred days?" Kaleena exclaimed. "No one could last that long on the trail, not without outside help. That is for sure."

"Hah," Cuzy harrumphed. "A pure blood like you? You would not last ten minutes out there. Place is crawling with beasties of every sort, vipers and dragons and poisonous snakes and lizards. You will die for sure out there without a man to protect you."

"I thought all men were animals? Anyway, I have no man to protect me," Kaleena said sadly. "Not any longer anyway."

"What about Elevator Boy, the boy you were supposed to marry?" Roxanne asked.

"Lars? I hardly think that boy is going to risk his neck, lay it all on the line to come and rescue me anytime soon. How could he even find this place? Besides, I treated him poorly. I seriously doubt whether he cares what happens to me."

"Doll, some boys will up and surprise you," Rox said. "Don't give up hope just yet."

CHAPTER FORTY-NINE

To reach the Farm on foot or by boat meant being in the field and away from regular medical care for days on end without break. It meant crossing kloms of wild, dangerous territory, territory filled with enemy soldiers, treacherous terrain, and fearsome creatures.

Venus was a shithole. This was true in every sense of the word. Which meant they had to place a premium on preparing properly for the planet's many hazards. Every imaginable disease was rampant on the planet, along with untold varieties of fungus, mold, and bacteria. Once Allied Command had given the go-ahead for this mission, Captain Lewis brought in his senior medical officer to speak with them in the hours before they left the compound to head out.

Major Niles Underwood was a big man, broad in the shoulders, burdened by duty. He explained what they already knew to be true from their first battle.

"More men die here from infection and disease than from gunshot wound. As Senior Medical Officer, let me tell you. The watchword here is prevention. You men have to protect your skin. That thin layer of dermis is all that stands between you and a most hideous death."

Chief Wheeler interrupted. "What about an ample supply of meds for my team, Major? On our first mission, when we were scouting for maps and other intell, Captain Lewis issued us antivirals and the like to take along."

"I hate those pills," Tech Sergeant Ramirez said. "They make me sick, give me the runs."

"Nobody has had a solid bowel movement since they touched down on the surface," Captain Lewis said. "You cannot necessarily blame it on the meds."

"Your Tech Sergeant may be right," Major Underwood said. "These are powerful drugs we are giving our men. Diarrhea is definitely a side effect. Soldier, my advice to you is simple. Stay hydrated. Drink plenty of fluids. But refusing to take your meds is not an option. There are three separate regimens — antivirals, antibiotics, and antifungals. Take every last one of them as ordered."

Major Underwood continued. "As I was saying, even a small break in the skin can go septic and lead to a raging infection within hours. Avoid insect bites. At night, always sleep under your mosquito bar. The netting is much like what any Boy Scout earthside is accustomed to when camping in the woods. Keep on your jungle shirt at all times. Each shirt is outfitted on the sleeve with a spray gun filled with repellant."

"And when the repellant runs out?" Lars asked.

"You have a two-day supply. But since exposed skin is the likeliest entry point for infection, proper clothing has to be worn day and night, even when showering."

"Hot and cold running water at this resort we are going to, Major?" one of the noncoms asked.

"The running water in this place comes in two temperatures, soldier. Hot and very hot," Major Underwood replied. "Keep your shirt sleeves rolled down at all times. Keep them velcroed at the wrist at all times. Trousers should be tucked in your high boots or fixed beneath your leggings. Clothes have to be boiled, preferably on a daily basis. In the field, standard uniform for every mission is dark-blue jungle fatigues, shirt and pants, baseball-style soft cap, high-top black boots with leggings. Mud or grease on face and hands. Keeps out the bugs, camouflages exposed skin."

Then Major Underwood issued each man a jungle medical kit and had his aide drill them on its proper use.

"A jungle medical kit is much more complete than an ordinary kit back home." The aide opened the kit and spilled the contents out on a table. "Gather round, gentlemen. First item of note. The kit is stored in a waterproof bag. The reasons ought to be obvious. Authenticate the contents before you leave. Here is a checklist. Morphine. Sulfa drugs. Syringes. Gauze bandages. Laser scalpel. Water purification tabs. Acceleron. Assorted ointments and suppositories."

"Yeah, like any of us are going to bend over and let one of the other fellows insert a suppository."

"A man does what he has to, to survive," the aide said. Then he continued. "You all need skullcap instruction for the rest of it. Run med modules 15 and 16. Those modules will teach you how to do everything from field-dress a wound to how to treat Venusian malaria. Should take you about an hour to run both mods."

Now Captain Lewis took back control of the meeting. "The next man who will speak to you is a specialist on jungle survival. He will teach you which beetles are safe to eat and which are not, which grubs, which snakes, which plants, which leeches, dragons, and rodents. Safe drinking water is an even higher priority. Where can you find it? How can you extract it? There are sources — certain vines, green fruits, rain that has collected on large leaves, gravel runs, blackwater sumps."

It went on for hours like this. Beyond the rigorous medical indoctrination and jungle survival techniques, the next most important skill they had to acquire was rubber boat training. They were rank amateurs when it came to handling a boat, and very little of this knowledge could be accomplished via skullcap, no matter how sophisticated the learning modules. They had to learn some of it hands-on, with direct instruction.

"These tough, soft-hulled boats are your only means of getting into and out of enemy territory."

"We have had some practice already."

"You need more. Patrol boats cannot get in close enough to shore. The Platypus, while unsurpassed in maneuverability, is noisy and impossible to hide. But no form of transportation is more effective in these swamps than a rubber boat. There are islands, narrow channels, ponds, lakes, creeks, every type of water body you can think off, plus at least one large ocean."

The trainer showed them how to inflate and deflate the boat, how to secure it to a large rock or small tree, how to paddle it, how to steer it. Then he moved on to weapons.

The men were armed with knives, of course, and jungle carbines. The carbines were smaller and lighter than a regular-issue military rifle, with a folding stock and waterproof barrel. The jungle carbines rarely jammed. Plus, they were resistant to the planet's high humidity and easy to transport in rubber boats and through dense jungle.

No slot on their canvas pistol belt remained empty. Bullets. Meds. Jungle kit. Two types of grenades, white phosphorous and fragmentation. Also, megaflare incendiary globes. They were a form of grenade that burned at several thousand degrees and were capable of melting steel. What it did to human flesh was downright gruesome.

•
•

Now it was time to go. Allied Command had given them a patrol boat, a pilot, a rubber boat, three days' worth of supplies and four men. Chief Wheeler had made the case to a doubting General that even if there was no strategic value to locating the Farm and freeing its prisoners, those prisoners might have gathered valuable intell from the high-ranking clients they serviced. That intell might help shorten the war. Command had agreed, and now they were in the patrol boat pulling away from shore. Captain Lewis was at the wheel.

The patrol boat got them as close into shore as possible. But the timing was awful. There was a high, rolling surf. They unloaded their rubber boat in the way they had been taught and climbed in, all seven of them.

Almost immediately, the rolling surf grabbed hold of their boat and slapped them against a rocky cliff. The impact blew out the side of the rubber boat and tossed them in the water.

But no one drowned, and no one broke a limb. Somehow they managed to cling to the slippery rocks and climb to the top of the ridge. Exhausted by the effort, this is where they spent their first night.

Besides Chief Wheeler, Soldata Fifteen, and Lars Cabot, there were four other men on their team, all topnotch — Tech Sergeant Ramirez, who they already knew, Sergeant "Red" Roberts, Private Paul Grossberg, and Private First Class Jogn, all fit, all practical, all experienced.

The incursion team was up before dawn. Machine-gun fire startled them awake. Its source was not far away, a disturbing development. This end of the island was supposed to have been deserted. Those reports were clearly wrong.

Soldata hunkered under a downed tree and radioed their coordinates to Command. Within minutes, Allied drones roared overhead. They pelted the enemy positions with .50 calibre gunfire plus hundreds of small incendiary bombs. The sky was suddenly daylight-bright from the fireballs.

When the drone attack began and the bombs started to go off, the team dug deeper for cover. They narrowly missed being struck by friendly fire, they were that close. Bombs exploded all around them. Bullets ripped into the ground nearby.

They waited motionless for the raid to end. When it finally did end, they came out of their holes and discovered three machine-gun nests, along with two hundred meters of camouflaged trenches.

But not every one of the enemy had been killed. In the distance they heard wounded men screaming and crying, as they staggered away from the attack site. Those wounded men would soon die in the jungle, meat perhaps for some passing dragon.

Ramirez pinged the metal rod he had planted in the ground just two days before. The locator pinged back and Ramirez collected positional bearings. Then he uploaded the data to Soldata.

"Take point and lead the way."

As the team moved further inland along those headings, they began to come across telltale signs of the enemy. Broken limbs. Bits of trash. Campfire pits.

They were making good time when all of a sudden, Soldata raised his fist and stopped dead in his tracks. He stood motionless as, one by one, fifteen of bin Hassan's men passed less than ten meters in front of him. The enemy was so close, he could smell the dirty sweat on them. Some of the soldiers were carrying weapons. A few were carrying shovels. Central Command's intell had been very, very wrong. The enemy was unquestionably here, and in great numbers. They appeared to be digging in for an upcoming battle.

There was one other new and unexpected development. Some of these soldiers were not your ordinary, run-of-the-mill grunts. These men were larger than normal. They appeared to be in excellent physical shape and were dressed in neat, well-tailored khaki uniforms.

"Mercmarines?" Lars asked after they passed. The term was short for mercenary marines, a class of hired soldier.

"I don't think so," Soldata answered.

"What then?" Lars asked. "Those were some awfully large men."

"I am thinking humaniform robot soldiers."

"You mean like Captain Reynolds?" Chief Wheeler had caught up with the conversation.

"That is what I am thinking," Soldata replied.

"I say we get some rest," Wheeler said. "We have a long hike ahead of us yet, if we are to reach the Farm before morning and rescue those women. Up into the trees for the rest of the night."

CHAPTER FIFTY

Venus had more dangerous animals per square meter than any planet in the solar system, perhaps the galaxy. The team was bedding down for the night in a tree when they first met up with one of the nastiest.

To avoid the enemy, they would often sit still for long periods of time observing. Sometimes they were on the ground, sometimes in a tree or other high point like a hill or cliff. Lars happened to be up a tree with the other team members when he first observed a Venusian dragon.

The name was somewhat misleading. This animal was not an actual dragon, not the fire-breathing dragon of earth-legend anyway. But to those settlers who first encountered the beast years ago, it did in many ways resemble a Komodo dragon. So the name stuck. The thing had four legs, a long tail, wicked claws, a huge pointy head like a crocodile, and a yellow, two-foot-long, forked tongue. It was mean, and it was fast.

Lars was in a tree, about fifteen meters up, when he first noticed a deer pick its way through the underbrush beneath him. Again, the name was misleading. This plant-eating animal was not an actual deer, not of the earth variety anyway, but something similar, an indifferent herbivore with two tails, six legs, and a leathery outer skin. They made good eating, were completely harmless, and grazed on grasses like their namesake back home.

The deer, colored green like the foliage, was foraging for food. Regrettably, he was about to encounter a Venusian dragon. Even on Venus, nature was still quite red in tooth and claw. Seeing how ferocious the thing was, Lars was reminded of the grizzly bears he and his father used to hunt back in the world, when he was a kid.

Lars had a clear view of the dragon from his perch in the jungle tree. The creature sat motionless, camouflaged by the brush. It was about two-and-one-half meters long and weighed in at about forty-five klogs. Captain Lewis had told them that dragons could get up to twice that size and could run at speeds up to twenty kloms an hour. Its hunting strategy was based on stealth and power. This particular dragon had probably spent hours sitting in this spot, waiting for a Venusian deer or goat to come by — anything sizable and nutritious to eat.

The deer had now wandered to within three meters of the dragon. But surprisingly, the dragon had not yet seen it. Their vision was good — they could see objects as far away as three hundred meters. But there was a downside. Their eyes were more adept at picking up movement than they were at discerning stationary objects. Dragons had poor vision in dim light. Tonight, the tall grass obscured the dragon's view of the deer.

Sight is not the only sense, of course. But their hearing was poor as well. To track prey successfully, a dragon depended primarily on its sense of smell.

That long, forked yellow tongue was in fact a highly sensitive measuring device. Its sensitivity surpassed anything mankind had ever invented. The tongue sampled the air every few seconds, after which the tips retreated to the roof of its mouth. Inside the mouth, the tongue tips made contact with specialized receptor cells, the so-called smell cells. These chemical analyzers "smelled" the deer by recognizing certain airborne molecules and comparing them to its biological database of smells. It was a genuine sixth sense. An adult dragon could sense the existence and direction of odoriferous carrion up to four thousand meters away, when the wind was right. Now it told the dragon to strike.

The dragon turned its head to the left, now, where the deer was standing. The concentration of chemicals present on the left tongue tip was higher than that sampled from the right. This disparity told the dragon that a deer was approaching from that side. Every waking moment of the day, a dragon would swing that monstrous head of its from side to side, the tongue constantly flicking in and out of his mouth, sampling the air. This one now had the scent.

The dragon made its presence known when it was about one meter from its intended victim. The quick movement of its padded feet sounded like a muffled machine gun. Lars was stunned by the bold bloody resolute nature of its assault. When one of these monsters decides to attack, there is no stopping them. Lars quickly flipped on his nightvision goggles so he wouldn't miss the show.

The dragon attacked the deer's feet first. The impact knocked the animal off balance. Then, for a moment, Lars lost sight of them both in the dense vegetation. The leaves were shaking as if there were a hidden struggle.

The dragon's basic strategy was simple. It meant to smash its quarry to the ground and tear it to pieces. Strong muscles drove powerful claws. Those claws did most of the damage.

But the dragon's teeth were its most astonishing and dangerous weapon. Those teeth were large, curved, and serrated. They could tear flesh with the efficiency of a steel plow parting rich black soil.

A dragon's teeth were deadly in yet another way. Hidden within those serrations were bits of flesh marinating from the dragon's last meal, bits of carrion or live prey. This protein-rich residue was like a petri dish in a mad scientist's laboratory. The marinating residue supported huge numbers of bacteria, something Venus was legend for anyway. Most strains were highly septic.

Lars lost sight of the deer in the underbrush. But of one thing he was certain. If the deer somehow managed to escape immediate destruction, chances were high that its victory would be short-lived. Given the super-humid jungle environment, an animal that escaped a devastating attack from a dragon with just a flesh wound was living on borrowed time. An infection would quickly take root in the bite track and kill the animal within days. Then this or some other dragon would come along, find the body, and devour the carcass.

But the more likely outcome was that this deer would fail to escape the present attack, and the dragon would continue to rip it apart with its claws. Once the animal was incapacitated, the dragon would likely break off its attack for a brief rest. By then, its victim would be badly injured and in shock.

Lars stared hard into the darkness. For about thirty seconds, everything was quiet. He craned his neck for a better view. Then, suddenly, the dragon delivered its coup de grâce, a belly attack. Lars saw it clearly from his treetop hideaway. The deer quickly bled to death and the dragon began to feed voraciously.

The muscles of a dragon's throat and jaws allowed it to swallow huge chunks of meat with astonishing rapidity, something like thirty klogs in ten to twelve minutes. The dragon had several movable joints in its mouth, including an intra-mandibular hinge that allowed it to open its lower jaw unusually wide. The stomach expanded easily. The expansion enabled the beast to consume more than half its body weight in a single feast of nonstop engorgement.

Lars had been to the zoo. He had seen vids. But he had never seen anything like this. No large mammalian carnivore fed like this. A lion in the wild would leave as much as one-third of a kill unconsumed. It declined to eat an animal's hide, its intestines, essentially all of the skeleton, plus the hooves.

Dragons were not nearly so picky. This one tore right through the beast. It ate bones. It ate hooves. It ate nearly the entirety of the animal's hide. It also ate its intestines, but not before swinging them vigorously to scatter its contents. This behavior served to remove the deer's feces from the meal. It also served another purpose, a protective one. Since adult dragons were known to cannibalize younger ones, the younger ones often rolled in fecal matter. In this way, they acquired a scent their larger brethren were programmed to avoid.

Attracted, now, by the scent of the kill, other dragons arrived on the scene, seemingly out of nowhere. They shouldered their way in and joined in on the feast. Lars supposed that like other animals, there were girl and boy dragons. But for the life of him, he could not tell one from the other. The dragons, on the other hand, appeared to have no trouble whatsoever figuring out who was who. With a group of them now assembled like rabid dogs around carrion, the opportunity for courtship had arrived. It was the First Corollary to Darwin's Second Law, dragon-style — *Once an animal has been fed, it wants to mate.*

Bellies now full, the dominant males became embroiled in a round of ritual combat in an effort to stake a claim on breeding-age females. At least that is how Lars had it figured. What he supposed were the males assumed an upright posture. Using their tails for support, they began to wrestle. As the combat continued, the protagonists grabbed one another with their forelegs and attempted to throw their opponent to the ground. In no time at all, blood was drawn and the loser hobbled off into the bush.

The victorious wrestler initiated courtship by flicking his tongue on a female's snout and then over the entire length of her body. The fold between her torso and her rear leg seemed to be his favorite spot.

Though Lars could not possibly make out the details, stimulation was both tactile and chemical. Two dragon bodies rubbing against each other generated copious skin gland secretions. Then, something resembling copulation occurred. The male crawled on the back of his intended and jabbed one of his two penis-like structures into her cloaca.

She let out a mournful grunt upon being entered, then dug her claws into the ground for traction.

Lars shuddered with disgust and promised himself to be more careful where he stepped the next time they were on the ground. *One of these bastards could easily tear off a man's leg and leave him for dead.*

The copulation had barely begun, when the rain began to fall. They had heard the sonic boom two days earlier, the sound signaling the arrival of another trans-comet from out in the Kuiper Belt. The comets were designed to cool down the planet and prepare it for full-scale terraforming yet to come. It took about two days' time before they melted fully, and the water began to show up on the surface in the form of a cooling, if torrential rain.

The team threw on their ponchos but it would not change the outcome. Almost no amount of plastic sheeting would keep them dry. The team had several wet hours ahead of them.

CHAPTER FIFTY-ONE

They slept maybe three hours before climbing down from their sleeping berths in the branches of two trees. They were sore, hungry, and dehydrated.

"I want everybody to take a good, long drink from their canteens," Chief Wheeler said. "I cannot afford to have anyone pass out now from dehydration. And take your meds, too. I need everyone operating at full capacity."

"Should I hand out jerky?" Ramirez asked, digging in his bag.

"That's a good idea," Wheeler said. "The jerky will help pump a little energy into everyone's bloodstream."

"Did you see those dragons going at it last night?" Lars asked as he chewed on the salted meat.

"Yeah," Private Jogn said. "And heard it. Like humping hippos, if you ask me. Only grosser."

"I do not ever want to meet one of those fuckers in the flesh," Private Paul Grossberg said.

"Alright, guys," Chief Wheeler said. "Eat up. Drink up. Then let's saddle up. Soldata, you again take point. Get your bearings and take us on the same heading we have been following since we landed."

Soldata nodded and they shortly moved out. As they worked their way down from the high ground, they discovered multiple signs of enemy atrocities.

"Did those mercmarines do this?" Lars asked, sickened by what he saw.

"Or were these atrocities committed by robots? Soldata said those mercs that passed so close to us were humaniform soldier robots."

"Since when can a robot be programmed to do such terrible things?"

In one clearing, they found three men lying dead. Two were Allied soldiers, one was of unknown origin. The Allied officers had been shot in the head and stomach. The third man had been brutally beaten in the face with a club. Based on the level of decomposition, the deaths had been recent, maybe as recently as last night.

A few meters further on, they found a fourth body, a nude male that had been severely violated. Dragons or some similar animal had eaten parts of the corpse. The man had been castrated while still alive. His left hand had been cut off at the wrist. To see such things up close only heightened Lars's anxiety about how Kaleena was being treated.

"Robots did this? Have the Three Laws been somehow repealed? Is nothing sacrosanct?"

"Lars, we have no time to debate this stuff now," Chief Wheeler said.

"Can we at least bury our dead?" Private Jogn asked.

"No, soldier, we cannot," Wheeler answered. "If we bury these men that is proof positive that we have been through here. The enemy will surely come looking for us. Leave them as they lay. Now move out."

Soldata nodded his understanding and they continued to push westward, slugging their way through tall kunai grass. Soldata was out in front, as usual, with Lars behind.

Even though it was night, the sweat poured down their faces like rain. Venus was like that, always hot. Their faces were blackened with grease paint. They blended easily into the jungle environment like trees.

Suddenly, they came face to face with an enemy patrol. The men, dressed in green camou, carried only two rifles between them and were laughing heartily, as if they did not have a care in the world. A moment later, they did not.

With only fifteen meters between the team and the enemy patrol, Soldata dropped to one knee and coolly opened fire. He killed both men. Lars and Tech Sergeant took out three others. The rest escaped into the jungle.

"If they come back, they will come back with reinforcements," Soldata said.

"That is only the half of it," Wheeler said. "Other soldiers may have heard the shooting. We have to get the hell out of here and fast. This way." Wheeler pointed. "We have to run perpendicular to our original bearing. Run!"

They moved like hell through the jungle, flat-out for thirty minutes. Then, after the grueling sprint through the barbs and undergrowth, they stopped.

"Anybody hurt?" Wheeler asked.

"I am," Private Grossberg said. "Thorn ripped my trousers, cut my skin."

"I've got this, Chief," Ramirez said, pulling out his med kit. "I need antiviral cream and a gauze pad. Stat."

While Ramirez patched Grossberg's wound, the others drank some water and pulled out their high-energy ration, dried figs, peanuts, raisins, jerky.

They sat quietly in the dark and ate. Night brought eerie shadows. Venus did not have a moon or the comforting light that went with it. Nor did it have stars. Just an everpresent cloud layer that was puke green during the day and some kind of evil gray at night. It was so dark now a man could hardly see the man beside him.

"Okay, Soldata. Recalculate our bearing and position. Get us back onto our original heading following the hypotenuse of the triangle."

"Yes, sir."

They set off again. But this time they came across two makeshift huts. Soldata's fist went up.

They approached the huts with great caution, guns raised, knives at the ready.

Soldata peered quickly through one window. An enemy soldier was inside sitting on a straw mattress changing his clothes. Jogn pulled the pin on a fragmentation grenade. At Soldata's signal, he tossed it in through the window.

The grenade exploded with great force. But it did not do the job. Soldata rushed in to find the man unharmed. He delivered a crushing right to the soldier's jaw, dropping him to the floor. Then, as the soldier attempted to get back up, Lars raised his jungle carbine and fired.

The other hut was empty, so again they moved on toward their objective. After five kloms of slogging through knee-deep mud, they discovered a woman, half-dead from exhaustion and dehydration. She was barely dressed, laying on the soft wet ground.

"Oh . . ." she said when she saw them. "Are you . . . ?"

"Do not speak, lady," Grossberg said. "Here, drink some water." He propped up her head and tipped his canteen to her lips.

She drank a small amount then began to speak. "Oh, it is so good . . . so good to see a real man again . . ." Then she drifted off to sleep.

"She must have escaped from the Farm," Grossberg said.

"Then it cannot be far," Jogn reasoned.

"We need to get her on her feet," Ramirez said. "So she can walk and talk. Maybe tell us which way to go."

"She comes with us, we all die," Jogn said. "Have you forgotten how we just narrowly escaped an enemy patrol and only because we could run flat-out for half an hour?"

"You want we should leave her here?" Chief Wheeler asked. "A dragon will tear her to shreds before the day is out."

"Better her than us," Private Jogn said.

"The man is right," Soldata said. "We only fight when we absolutely have to. Otherwise we melt away into the jungle and wait until trouble clears."

"Then I will stay with her," Private Grossberg said. "I am already wounded. I cannot keep up with you fellows anyway. I will get some food and water into her and then we will both move back to the boat best we can."

"The rubber boat is busted, remember?"

"When I get her back to shore, I will radio Captain Lewis for help, get him to bring us out another rubber boat."

"Okay, it is decided then," Chief Wheeler said. "Be safe, soldier. Let's hope we all meet up again. Lars, I want you to take point for the next hour. Soldata, pull up the rear."

Almost immediately after Lars took the lead, things got dicey. They had reached a river's edge but decided not to cross it. A short while later, he spied four enemy soldiers walking up the opposite side of the river coming in their direction. Lars raised his fist and they remained perfectly still.

But then he saw three more enemy soldiers following the first group a few meters behind. The troops passed without incident.

But then trouble began. A soldier they had not previously seen shouted across the river to yet another soldier hidden by the foliage. The first man pointed directly at Lars. Chief Wheeler shot him. Then back into the forest they ran.

They headed back inland, where they discovered fresh water. There always was plenty of fresh water to be had in the days after a new comet arrived. This was a boon. The men filled their canteens, treated the fresh water with purification tabs.

Chief Wheeler gathered his men together. "I do not like this. We are running into more and more of the enemy the closer we get. By my estimation, our odds are getting poorer. Eventually, our luck will run out."

"Not much of a cheerleader, are you, Chief?" Jogn said.

"I think we are getting near the Farm," Chief Wheeler said. "I think that is why we are meeting more and more of the enemy."

"What do you suggest we do?" Tech Sergeant Ramirez asked.

Chief Wheeler explained. "I think we should split up into three smaller units. One squad should swing north two hundred meters. The second squad should swing west equally far. The third squad should remain here until the other two are in position. Then we coordinate our movements and all three squads should approach the center of our imaginary circle from the three different directions. Hopefully, the Farm is at the approximate center of that circle and one of the three squads will be successful at finding its way in. The other two squads then move in behind them and cover their flank."

"Sounds like you mean to get us all killed," Jogn said.

"No, just the ones with a smart-aleck mouth," Chief Wheeler said. "Anyone got a better strategy? No? Then let's split up into three squads of two. Ramirez, you are with me. Lars, go with Soldata."

"You sticking me with Private LugNut Jogn?" Sergeant Roberts complained.

"Yeah, I am. Now let's move out. Ramirez and I will swing north. You and Jogn swing west. Lars and Soldata, you are to remain here. I will give two clicks on my squelch when we are in position. Roberts, you do the same."

In the murky darkness that was a Venus night, no one could see a thing. Every step was fraught with danger. Unseen logs and holes, blind shadows, camouflaged obstacles, dangerous animals.

The trail was muddy and dark. But still the three small teams snaked their way to their intended positions. Soldata and Lars. Chief Wheeler and Tech Ramirez. Sergeant Roberts and Private Jogn.

At 0200 hours, everyone was in place. Chief Wheeler had checked in with two squeezes of the squelch on his two-way, followed by Jogn doing the same on his. If the Farm was anyway near the center of the imaginary circle circumscribed by their positions, they would likely stumble upon it soon.

Now each squad slid slowly forward into the murky darkness. Almost immediately, Lars and Soldata came upon another one of those small huts like before. Soldata ran a thermal scan. It came up with five likely inhabitants, probably all asleep.

"There is no way we get this done quietly," Lars whispered to Soldata.

"Cannot be helped. Empty your entire clip, if you have to. But we have to take these guys out if we are to move past them."

Lars nodded, and they both moved forward, guns at the ready. Soldata stuck the business end of his carbine in the front door, while Lars simultaneously did the same through the window. They both blasted away for about fifteen seconds then stopped.

When all they heard from inside were pained groans, Soldata threw on his lumina and charged the door. He fired twice more then quickly withdrew.

"All that noise is definitely going to attract attention," Lars said. "Let's scoot before we have visitors."

Even as the two withdrew, they heard shots being fired ahead of them, both to the right and to the left. The other two squads had probably encountered outposts as well.

We must be drawing close to something important, Lars thought.

A few minutes later, he had his answer. It came in the form of a row of huts. Between them they may have held upwards of twenty enemy soldiers.

"I think we just walked deep into enemy territory," Lars said.

"Only two choices," Soldata whispered. "Push forward and we probably die. Retreat and we have no chance to save the women you came here to save. Robot or not, I do not want to die. But I will leave this decision up to you."

Lars thought a moment then decided. "We push forward. Try to flank the row of huts. Try not to engage the enemy."

"You are the human," Soldata said.

Then suddenly their two-way squelched. No one was to break radio silence unless severely compromised.

"They are in trouble."

"We all are in trouble."

The sound of the squelch woke one of the sleeping mercmarines. He exited his hut not entirely sure what was up. Soldata was on him within half a second, knife extended in front of him.

But, when Soldata struck the soldier expecting a warm explosion of human blood, all he struck was soft metal and electronic works.

"Sparks!" he exclaimed. "This thing is a robot."

So, it's true, Lars thought. *These bastards are machines.* The exclamation "Sparks" was as close to a swear as a robot could muster.

But what happened next sickened his heart.

The mercmarine grabbed the knife from Soldata's hand and jammed it into Soldata's chassis.

The attack was not enough to destroy Soldata.

But he staggered backwards anyway. The mercmarine was much stronger than Soldata and immediately went on the offensive. He was about to tear Soldata's arm from his body when Chief Wheeler appeared out of nowhere and blew the head off the humaniform merc with his blaster.

"Ramirez is dead," Wheeler said. "Run for it and do not stop running. That is an order." Then he led them off to the south at high speed, the way they had come.

Lars was on his tail with Soldata dragging behind. The damage to his chassis had slowed down his reflexes appreciably.

They ran for about ten minutes due south. Then Chief Wheeler slowed and stopped. He bent forward at the waist and tried to catch his wind. The air quality was poor and he could go no further. Lars caught up with him a moment later.

"I cannot go any further," Chief Wheeler said through halting breaths.

"You are dehydrated, Chief." Lars handed him his canteen.

Chief Wheeler nodded and took a sip from the offered canteen. His breathing slowed and the color in his face improved.

They heard noises in the bushes behind them and Soldata staggered in.

"You two should go ahead. I will stay here, protect your rear. It is the only sensible thing for me to do."

Again Chief Wheeler nodded his agreement. "Thank you, Soldata. You are the bravest man I have ever had the privilege to serve with."

"You are welcome, Chief. Now you and the boy go."

Chief Wheeler turned and set off at a more manageable pace. They were aimed straight for the shore, where, hopefully, Grossberg and a fresh rubber boat was bivouacked, maybe that girl as well.

But the fun was not over. Though they did not know it yet, in the rugged mountainous terrain overlooking the beach, bin Hassan's mercmarines had constructed an intricate cave and tunnel system capable of withstanding a lengthy Allied siege. They had stockpiled food, medical supplies, and light weapons. They had also installed several retractable railgun cannons capable of hitting boats far out in the bay.

They became aware of the trouble when, suddenly, there was the boom of the railgun launching a projectile out towards the open water. For all Lars and Chief Wheeler knew, the target might be Captain Lewis and the Platypus. They heard a large explosion and saw a brilliant flash of light. The cannon had struck home on some target in the water.

"Fuck," Chief Wheeler said. "I didn't know they had any big guns out here."

"That is trouble for us, isn't it Chief? Big guns will be defended by lots of heavily armed support troops. We may already be surrounded."

Chief Wheeler did not answer. But the silence said everything. Lars was right.

Inside the cave complex, the enemy had constructed an extensive network of track-mounted artillery. The guns were camouflaged by retractable doors, maybe metal, maybe plastic, which opened and closed using an elaborate pulley system. The doors had been made to look like part of the mountainside. Between the everpresent fog and camouflage coloring they were practically invisible to all but the closest inspection. That is why Allied intell had not been able to warn the team of their presence.

When the guns acquired a target and had a firing solution, the big doors swung open and the guns rolled out on the tracks and boomed away. After being fired, the guns were pulled back into the caves so they could not be targeted. Until Allied Command could take out this emplacement all operations in this area were at risk.

"We have to warn our people," Chief Wheeler said, pulling out his two-way.

"If you break radio silence to warn Captain Lewis, our position will be triangulated. We will be captured for certain," Lars said.

"Cannot be helped, son. We are only two men. The entire Allied front is at risk."

BOOM . . . the guns fired.

"Take an azimuth reading on those guns, Lars. Quick. Remember your land-nav training. Focus on the gun flash. Quick now. Before they fire again."

BOOM . . . BOOM . . . BOOM . . . the guns fired again.

"Did you get it?"

"Very rough numbers, Chief. We need to move in closer for me to be more precise."

"Okay, let me see those prelim numbers." Chief Wheeler opened the contact on his two-way. "Chief Wheeler here. ID number 35XC67. Enemy guns at 21.345 by 87.953. I repeat. Chief Wheeler here. ID number 35XC67. Enemy guns at 21.345 by 87.953. Out."

They moved forward, toward the guns, ever so slowly. The closer they were, the better grid numbers they could obtain.

They were deep in enemy territory now. It was dark. The air was foul. They were on their bellies crawling along the ridge nose-to-heel, head-to-boot, like a long, giant snake.

Twenty minutes later, the big doors rolled open again, and the big guns stuck their noses into the night sky.

"Okay," Chief Wheeler said. "This might be our only chance. Aim your machine at the tip of the closest railgun and shoot me an azimuth and range. I will call the grid numbers right in."

Lars focused his instrument, pressed the contact, and two seconds later the grid-marker numbers appeared on the tiny screen.

Chief Wheeler picked up his two-way and began to speak into it. "This is Chief Wheeler of Allied Command. ID number 35XC67. Updated position on enemy gun battery. Target gridpoint 21.8255 by 88.103. I repeat . . ."

Then the big guns boomed once more and the rest of the transmission was lost. When Wheeler reached to pick up his two-way to try again, an enemy rifle was pressed into his back.

"Give it up buddy. You two may now consider yourselves prisoners of war."

All Lars could think of was:

Shit. Are they going to send us back to the front to fight? Or are they going to kill us right here and now?

They would find out the truth soon enough. Their future home was to be the Gulag, Slave Camp #5.

PART III

CHAPTER FIFTY-TWO

My, how time flies when you are having fun.

That cheery thought flashed briefly through Lars's head. Only, he was not having much fun. The year was 2453. He was a prisoner of war, an enslave, assigned to Slave Camp #5, Domtar Province, planet Venus. He was being readied for his second rejuvenation since being captured nearly one hundred and twenty years ago. The first rejuv had been in 2395, sixty years ago. He was eighty at the time. He was pushing eighty again. Each time a man underwent a rejuv, his biological clock was reset to approximately age twenty.

Thus far, during his confinement as an enslave, Lars had been married to a slave-wife, had two children, been married again, had two more. Near as he could tell, every last one of them was dead.

Since his last rejuv sixty years ago, he had escaped from the slave camp three times and had been recaptured three times.

But now he was too old for even the guards to care what happened to him. Oh, as a slave-laborer in the lithium mines his life was worth something to his captors. But as a man, as a human being, he was just another number, the number tattooed to his arm and again to his leg. Epsilon 1512, the last time he looked. The simple truth was, the guards would not try and stop him now even if he tried to escape for a fourth time. As far as the guards were concerned, he was just too darn old to make it out there in the jungle on his own.

But then again, there was nothing left to hold him back. All his friends were dead. Kaleena was dead. Chief Wheeler was dead. Captain Lewis, dead. Private Grossberg. Soldata. Jogn. All dead. Lars was the only one of the original batch to survive bin Hassan's labor camp into old age.

Lars could never figure out why. *Why had he lived while the others died?* He supposed it might be because of his earlier experiences, his rustic upbringing, his Boy Scout training, those days hunting with his father, that Yeager-syndrome thing his grandfather once talked to him about. Lars was a survivor. He knew how to survive. Hell, he had outlived both his slave-wives and all four of his children.

But now the bastards were going to rejuvenate him for a second time. Then, when he was young again, they were going to make him work for yet another lifetime.

So, Lars had come to a decision. He was not going to let them do this to him again, not this time, no way. This time, when they made him young again, he was going to escape, walk away for good. He had heard of a place, first from Kaleena who had heard it from Roxanne and Cuzy. Others had told him of this place as well, including prisoners who had escaped and been recaptured. The place was a thousand or more kloms away, a place they called Industry. It was populated by escaped POWs, soldiers awol from the war, pirates and profiteers. That is where he was going after this second rejuv, to that brave new colony in the middle of nowhere. After that, who knew? Maybe he could someday make his way back to Earth.

Lars thought of his good friend Chief Wheeler. Lars could never bring himself to call the man Lex or Lexus. To Lars, he would always be Chief Wheeler or just Chief. Theirs was a friendship like no other. In their many days together — on the Station, onboard the *Ticonderoga*, on the battlefield, in the slave-camp — he and Chief Wheeler had touched at one time or another on practically every subject. Lars revered the man. Chief Wheeler had taught him a lot. Lars cried when he died.

- The gods always fight on the side with the heaviest artillery.
- Ninety percent of everything is crap. But the other ten percent is worth dying for.

Those were two of Chief Wheeler's favorite sayings. But there were others.

- If you cannot afford your habits, change jobs.
- If a man's word is no good, of what value is his signed contract?
- If something is unsustainable, have patience. It will stop. This applies in equal measure to a bull market as it does to a runaway train.

And then there were Chief Wheeler's questions. He had many. All of a philosophical nature. He would ask Lars:

If you read a book on how to ride a bicycle, do you know how to ride a bicycle? *No, you do not.* You can strap on a skullcap, you can read everything about bicycling that you can get your hands on. The history of cycling. Who won the great races. What sort of bicycle they rode. How a bicycle works. You can study the physics, you can watch a bike race on the vid, even squirt oil on a chain in your driveway. But still you know next to nothing about bicycling. To learn how to ride, you have to take a bicycle in hand. You have to go out on the driveway, sit on the seat, put your feet on the pedals and take off down the street. You must physically learn to do it, and why? — *Because the part of the brain that learns how to ride a bicycle is different from the part of the brain that sits on a couch and reads about it.* When the wind blows through your hair on that sprint down a hill, when the adrenaline courses through your body when you realize you are about to fall, this is the animal brain, the get-your-fingers-dirty part of the brain, not the book-learning Ph.D. part of the brain. All of life is that way, Lars. Do not let anyone tell you different. How can a politician make a rule for a businessman if he has never run a business? How can a university professor teach a student how to write or draw or speak or sell if he himself has never been rejected by a publisher or refused by a gallery or booed by an audience or snubbed by a customer? He cannot. Theory is Crap. Experience is Everything.

Then, on the Chief Wheeler's final day, just before they wheeled him away for good, he looked hard at Lars and cried. With questioning eyes, he said to Lars:

Have we finally reached an Orwellian age? An age where entitlement has replaced responsibility? Where those who wield power have redefined coercion as compassion? Where compulsory redistribution has come to be called sharing? Where quotas substitute for diversity? Where suicide is prescribed as death with dignity? Where eternal life is a death sentence?

Then they wheeled Chief Wheeler away. The rules of the Gulag were simple. Wheeler understood. An older man, in good health, with no heart disease, with no cancer, no stomach problems, no problem peeing or getting it up — such a man would be rejuvenated to enjoy another fifty or sixty years in the slave labor camp.

But an older man like Chief Wheeler, who had smoked and drank as a youth and who was not presently in the best of health, would be put down like a dog. It was simple economics, if you can put those two words in the same sentence. You have heard of an oxymoron, haven't you? Legal profession. Army intelligence. Sensible woman. Simple economics.

That was nearly ninety years ago. Now it was Lars's turn, his second turn actually. Lars's fate would be much worse than Chief Wheeler's. They were going to let Lars live. Hell, they were going to *make* him live.

The nurse approached him now. She was wheeling a rolling bed that Lars was supposed to lie down on. She checked the bar code on his arm and the matching code on his leg against the alphanumeric on her clipboard. Satisfied that she had the right patient, she strapped a facemask over his nose and mouth.

"Relax," she said.

Lars noticed that she was attractive. He had been through this before.

"Relax and close your eyes, Epsilon 1512. Good. Now take a deep breath."

Lars did as he was told. Then everything went black.

•
•

Lars could feel them inside him now, the spiders, moving this way and that, fixing all the parts that were broken or injured or damaged. Hundreds of spiders, maybe thousands, all tiny, each under a thousandth of a millimeter in size, weaving their way through his body, his blood vessels, his lymph ducts, his nerve channels, stopping at each layer of tissue, rearranging what was out of place, setting straight what was wrong.

Age had done most of the damage, age and liquor and exposure to radiation and forbidden drugs. Tiny mistakes cumulated through time.

But nowhere within the double-helix chemistry of deoxyribonucleic acid was there an organized apparatus — a biological subroutine — for repairing each and every broken copy. Selfish genes replicated in casual abandonment. The same mechanism that allowed evolution allowed death. The chemistry of life lacked a Darwinian imperative to keep its host alive indefinitely. Everyone was born into this world with the seeds of cancer — and heart disease and dementia and arthritis. Only the manmade spiders, injected into one's body before it was too late, could fix them.

Lars did not want to die. No one really does. But out here in the slave camps of Domtar Province, death was no longer an option, not if a man had skills, not if a man was healthy.

Lars had skills. He had been a soldier. He had worked on the Space Station. He knew his weapons. He was mentally and physically tough. He could survive in the wilds. He knew about the jungles and he knew about the fearsome creatures that roamed free out there. But he had made the mistake of being captured alive when they tried and failed to liberate the Farm. Now he made his home in Slave Camp #5.

As slaves, the prisoners mined lithium. It was a soft, silver-white metal. It was a reactive metal and one that was dangerous to mine. With the rot and the viruses and the bacteria, slave-laborers did not last long. Like the metal they mined, which corroded in the moist Venusian air, changing color from silver-white to dull gray then to black tarnish, the workers corroded into uselessness as well.

But since it was cheaper to rejuv an existing slave than to purchase a new one on Earth and import it to Venus or build a humaniform robot to replace it, the choice was clear.

Lars felt the pain, now, in his abdomen. A burning sensation just below the sternum. The spiders were gathering, now, in the liver, the last and most complex organ to be rebuilt. That it had gotten this far meant he would live — the rejuv had been successful. It was not a hundred percent, you see. It hadn't worked on the tyrant Uday bin Hassan. After his son died, he wanted to live forever. But he waited too long. He could no longer be fixed.

Imagine the irony! The man who had set this hell in motion had himself escaped it by dying. Hah!

Technology had changed the meaning of dead. It was no longer an absolute. Chemotherapy. Open heart surgery. Organ harvesting. Radiation treatments. Corrective gene therapy.

But all these many things were done at the macro level, an artery here, an organ there. And almost none of it was permanent. The spiders were the first to get at the heart of the matter. The first to fix things at the micro level. Tiny little manmade gizmos not much larger than a virus. Built to attack aging and disease at the cellular level, down in the mitochondria, down where messenger RNA and all her obedient soldiers held sway.

Certain things could not be fixed, of course. Macro things mainly. That rib you broke as a kid, falling out of a tree. That scar on your knee where you hit the pavement, falling off your bicycle. That finger you lost when you blew it off playing with daddy's force gun.

But what could be fixed were the ATP factories inside each cell, the mitochondria. What could be fixed was the depreciating number of telomeres at the end of each chromosome. What could be fixed were the errant cells, the tumors, the cancers that might spin out of control killing the host organism, which is to say, you. What could be fixed was the lung damage from smoking, the liver damage from alcohol, the brain and kidney damage from Deludes.

Suddenly, with all the damage fixed, you inhabited a body with the strength and endurance of a twenty-year-old, a body with yet another prime to live.

But it was no longer a case of youth being wasted on the young. Your new, more agile mind still possessed all its memories. Plus, it was even keener than before. *All that you had once learned you still knew.*

Now, in your second life, you had the body of a twenty-year-old and the accumulated knowledge and experience of an eighty-year-old — or in Lars's case, a one-hundred-and-forty-year-old — a potent combination of assets for a man contemplating escape.

He had decided.

CHAPTER FIFTY-THREE

It takes a hardheaded man to casually stroll out of Slave Camp #5 and walk twelve hundred kloms northeast across central Domtar Province, transecting all the wild jungles and many dangers that lie between bin Hassan's kingdom and the vast Venusian Sea.

It takes a harder head still to conceive of doing it alone and on foot. This was a vast, unknown terrain. To attempt such a crossing in a single, sustained, expeditionary trudge was beyond irrational.

Domtar Province was a dangerous place, like central Africa back on Earth, only worse. Hot, humid, acrid air. Overgrown plant-life. Hazardous animals.

Plus, there were physical obstacles. Rivers to be bridged or forded. Swamps to be waded. Ravines to be crossed. Vast thickets to be carved by machete. Active warfare to be avoided. Thorny vines. Biting flies. Stinging ants. Giant ticks. Sharp-toothed vipers. Flesh-eating termites. Poisonous vosquitoes. Foot worms. Leeches. Dragons. A few nervous mammoths. The occasional armed mercmarine. And just to keep things interesting: a dark, spooky jungle about midway along the route that was believed to harbor an Ebola-like virus. The virus, whatever it was, had caused lethal epidemics up and down the province.

The human costs of such a journey were many. Fatigue. Hunger. Extreme loneliness. Tedium. Diseases less mysterious than Ebola. Headache. Diarrhea.

Callouses. Blisters. Infected feet. It takes a great measure of obdurate self-confidence to begin such a journey, let alone complete it. *But why make it at all?* Because Lars had heard from other prisoners that out here somewhere lay a colony, a colony of freedom-loving refugees. On such a basis a new civilization might be founded.

Whether he could survive such an undertaking was yet to be seen. In the queer mass of human history, the determining factor has always been luck. But Lars had some things that improved his odds.

Lars had the advantage of a recent rejuvenation. He was a young man in body, mind and spirit. Hard, virile, horny. Once again he had the fearless intrepidness of a twenty-year-old. But now he was armed with the experience and commonsense of someone much, much older.

Under conditions of high metabolism, in the steamy jungles of the planet, survival of the fittest took on new meaning. Here, the ceaseless fight of life proceeded with special intensity. Bacteria. Viruses. Gelatinous fungi. Pathogenic microbes of every stripe. They were all virulent. And let us not forget the flesh-eating fungi. A man will think twice the next time he orders a grilled Portobello sandwich or asks for mushrooms on his pizza.

In the beginning, when the first spacejockeys set foot on the surface, not a single product of Earth's medical labs worked to protect them from this hellhole. Not vaccines, not immunizations, not antibiotics, not antivirals, not gene busters. The analogous but different diseases of Venus had to be combatted with a new set of pharmacological tools. Some people, by chance, had a natural immunity. They were naturally resistant. They could move with relative ease and little danger on the ground.

But for others, it was a nightmare. Imagine the worst of the fungoid-type skin diseases you ever heard of. Imagine a common fungal infection like athlete's foot magnified a thousand times over. Imagine something so wicked, it grew quickly, before your very eyes. Add to that horrifying picture what you may have experienced of mold, of mildew, of damp rot, of toadstools in the forest feeding on decay. Then imagine those messy things speeded up in their processes a hundredfold, speeded up by the oppressive heat, visibly crawling across the landscape in real time as you watched.

Can you see them now? — attacking your eyeballs, your armpits, the soft wet tissues inside your mouth or your nostrils or your penis. If you are a woman, imagine them taking root inside your vagina, sending their slithery tentacles higher, up into your womb, along the pathways of your fallopian tubes. Picture them working their way down into your lungs from your mouth. Or up into your kidneys from your penis.

This is what it meant to sit in the wrong spot on Venus. Or cross the wrong stream. Or eat the wrong food. Or sleep in the wrong tree. The worst manmade torture ever devised by the sickest bastard on the planet could not be as horrible.

The first Venus expedition was lost entirely. The second had a surgeon along, one with enough sense to sever gangrenous limbs and bathe the infected tissues in ultraviolet radiation. What was left of that team soon turned tail and sped back home. Only three of them made it back alive.

It took seven more expeditions and nearly one hundred years of trying to establish a self-sustaining colony. Even robotic creatures found it difficult to survive in the harsh conditions.

Permanent colonization depends on adaptation to an environment, not insulation against it. The moon colonies were a case in point. Luna City was many things. But it was not a self-sustaining colony. Luna was an outpost. It would never be more. No matter how much water and other volatiles would be found on the Moon, people could not live there freely. No one would ever be able to walk outside without wearing a protective enviro suit. It would forever after be a mining station, an observatory, a dumping ground for hazardous wastes, a refueling stop for outbound vessels.

Venus, on the other hand, was a true colony like Mars. There was a settlement, several settlements. The colonists breathed the air of Venus. They ate its food, drank its water, exposed their skin to its climate. They slopped barefoot on the marshy soil in true ecological balance, daily battled its natural hazards. Only the cold, polar regions were tenable by terrestrials. Even those regions were roughly comparable weather-wise to an Amazonian jungle on a hot day during the worst of the rainy season.

Lars was headed for just a spot, on foot and alone, the Botany Bay of Venus, a place some called Industry.

•
•

Lars had made the decision to go. *But what to take along with him?* He would need shoes of course; several pairs. But what else besides shoes does a man take along with him if he is going to try and slug his way across twelve hundred kilometers of jungle, desert, and swamp?

On a trip that long, it is not possible for a man to carry along all his food. A man needs to know how to forage enroute for food. The same goes for water and shelter and clothing. Plus, he must have a way to start a fire. Fire-starting is the most basic survival skill of all. Without fire, a man cannot cook. He cannot get dry when he is wet or cold. He cannot lift his loneliness through the long, dark night. And he cannot chase away predators.

Lars had with him practically none of the elements of a basic survival kit. He had no hat, no sunblock, no sweater, no wool shirt. What he did have were things he could scrounge on the grounds of the slave camp. He wore sandals and a light-weight cotton shirt.

Lars had no sleeping bag or tent. He did have a large leaf bag made from durable materials. He also had fifty meters of strong cord, a knife, a machete, a wire saw, and the makings of a sturdy hammock.

He had no signaling devices or lights. But he did have any number of body maintenance items. Aspirin. Safety pins. Hook and line. Antiseptic ointment. Needle and thread. Gauze. Surgical tape. Acceleron tablets. Magnetic compass. A length of steel wire. His grandfather's wristwatch.

Most importantly, he had with him in a waterproof bag a quantity of materials with which to start a fire. Waterproof matches. Butane lighter. Spare flints. Wax candles. Chemical heat tabs. Trioxane packs. Dryer lint.

All of these fire-starting materials Lars could find in great quantity inside the prison camp. Trioxane packs were to be found everywhere, leftover from the war. Each pack was a small, lightweight heat source used by the military in the field. Candles were equally easy to obtain in quantity. Prisoners rendered animal fat to obtain stearin and tallow. Dryer lint was lightweight and highly flammable. Volunteer for a couple weeks in the camp laundry and a man could have as much dryer lint as he could carry.

But building a fire and lighting a fire were not the same thing. To have a fire large enough to cook on required fuel. Logs and downed wood were obviously preferable. But in a survival situation, many things could serve as a source of fuel for a fire — scrub brush, a fallen tree, spare tire, shredded bark, cattail fuzz, floor mats, animal droppings, anything that burned. A man had to use his head and improvise.

To build a sustainable fire required that one use proper architecture. That, plus adequate tinder and a proper firestarter. The ignition system could be a reliable lighter or a strike-anywhere match or, as last resort, ordinary friction.

In pre-modern times, friction was the only workable method. Early man used the hand drill or the bow drill or the flint and steel method. Hot sparks were struck from a piece of steel or iron onto suitable tinder and fanned into flames. Any hard stone like flint or quartz would produce sparks when struck by another that contained iron.

The dryer lint or other material used to hold the spark would be held above the flint or quartz, tight against the stone. The steel or iron striker was then brought against the stone in a quick, straight downward motion. The hard stone tore steel flakes off the striker in the form of hot, molten sparks. When the hot sparks made contact with the tinder, they smoldered just this side of fire.

Suitable tinder could come from many sources. Lars departed camp with a couple weeks' supply in the form of cotton balls he had soaked in lighter fluid then stored for portage in a waterproof ammo canister. He also had with him a small duffel full of candles and trioxane packs. When these ran out, he would have to get more creative.

The saturated cotton balls would stay soaked for many, many months, perhaps as long as a year, when properly sealed for transport. Once ignited, a saturated cotton ball would burn long enough, several minutes at least, when placed at the bottom of a stack of more substantial tinder.

Lars preferred wax candles. They were easy to make, easy to carry, lightweight. But all sorts of substances made excellent tinder. Fuel soaked fiber. Candle stubs. Wax-impregnated wood strips. Any jellied-petroleum product. Fuel pellets.

To build a proper fire, a man needed three stacks of wood. Tinder to start the fire and to get the kindling burning. Kindling and small branches to get the fire hot enough to consume larger fuel. Fuel in the form of large branches and logs.

Even in the wet jungles of Venus, dry tinder could be found if a man knew where to look. Lars had learned these lessons as a boy when he and his father camped in the High Country of Montana.

Dead branches — even dead branches that were wet on the outside — would be dry inside once the bark was peeled back. To find dead branches, Lars looked under trees, sometimes under larger logs or beneath boulders. He would push over standing deadwood. Once down, the deadwood would usually break easily. Dry wood could be found in the center.

With enough kindling and fuel, and tinder on hand, Lars would begin his firebuilding ritual. One spin of the butane lighter and he could ignite a small amount of tinder.

The rules of firebuilding were simple. As soon as the tinder burst into flame, he needed to add more tinder to increase the flames. Patience was important. It could not be done too quickly or in too great a quantity or he risked smothering the fire.

But as the fire grew and more tinder caught flame, he needed to add small pieces of kindling. Then, keep adding kindling until the fire was big enough to consume larger fuel.

As the fire grew stronger, he needed to continue to add fuel. But it had to be done a certain way, stacking the fuel standing up in the shape of a teepee. This is where the architecture of firebuilding kicked in. To keep the fire from going out, he had to be sure it wasn't starved for air. Every fire must have oxygen. If necessary, he could blow on the base of the flame to increase its heat.

Finally, after the fire was safely ablaze, it was time to add larger pieces of fuel. Again, architecture was crucial. The key to success was to arrange the larger pieces of fuel like spokes on a wheel, with the fire at the hub. As the wood burned, it was customary to use another stick to push fresh fuel into the center. The end result of all that effort would be a controlled fire suitable for warmth and for cooking.

Building a proper fire took time and planning. Lars knew that if he did get into trouble on the trail and needed heat or light or comfort, time was of the essence. His father had taught him this. *The longer a man waits to build a fire the more likely he will die of exposure.* That is what his father said. The colder a man became — or the wetter or the more scared — the tougher it would be to gather the materials and build a fire. He told Lars: *Always stack the odds in your favor. Make the first effort good. Do it right. Avoid shortcuts. Gather and arrange your tinder, kindling and fuel. Then fire up.*

Lars did not forget his lessons.

CHAPTER FIFTY-FOUR

Lars was hungry. It had been two days since he left camp, two days since he last ate. He had been moving fast. His idea was simple. Put as much distance as possible between him and the camp as quickly as possible. Do not stop for anything. Do not eat, do not sleep, keep on moving.

But now he was hungry and tired. He pulled out his heavy-duty garbage bag, crawled into it and fell fast asleep. When he woke six hours later, his head was pounding and his stomach hurt.

Dehydrated. The thought moved groggily through his head. *Need water.*

He pulled out his canteen and took a slow drink. *Don't drink too fast or you will surely barf.* His Boy Scout training was coming back to him.

He carefully wrapped up his garbage bag bed and began to forage for food and materials to build a fire. Lars knew that his choices of wild food to eat were limited. It was not like this place was a delicatessen.

But he was not desperate or in a rush to choose. He had with him a two-week supply of wild-bushpig jerky. This is what the prisoners made for themselves from the food thrown away in the slave-camp.

He pulled out a short piece of bushpig jerky and began to chew. It was heavy with salt and garlic to mask its otherwise putrid taste.

The rules for gathering food in the wilderness were pretty straight forward. No mushrooms or other fungi. While some of these sprouts were known to be quite delicious, they offered little in the way of nutrition. Most were downright dangerous.

No beans or peas or similar plants. The legume family was not to be trusted, not on Earth nor on Venus. Many were poisonous. When they grew in the same spot year after year — as they did in the wild — they absorbed and concentrated heavy metals from the soil. Each generation became more toxic.

Avoid plant bulbs. Though there were a few that were edible, most were poisonous. The only exception was those bulbs that looked, smelled, and tasted like onion or garlic. These were edible, though not in large quantities. Lars had foraged for these before. It was what the slave-prisoners added to their wild-bushpig jerky to make it palatable.

Avoid weird looking plants. Ugly plants were not to be trusted. Hairy leaves or stems. Thorns. Spines. Shiny leaves. These were all danger signs. They shouted keep away.

Avoid plants with milky saps. Every known variety was poisonous.

Avoid plants with berries of any sort, especially bright colored berries. The toxicology risk was fifty-fifty. More than half of all red-berried plants were poisonous. The only known exceptions were aggregate berries, those with individual juice cells. Essentially all of those were edible.

But knowing what not to eat solves only half the problem. A man also had to know which parts of the plant were safest and how those parts could best be prepared for eating. Some plants needed to be boiled in water long enough to soften the skin. Others could be eaten as is. Some needed to be baked. Others needed to be ground into a fine powder and mixed into a drink.

The upshot was that safely foraging for wild food on the trail was the product of trial and error. At each step, a man had to choose the path where the odds of a bad result were kept to a minimum. Lars had it boiled down to a bit of a science. He called it his PET Project. That was short for Plant Edibility Test.

Step One: Select a plant that is both plentiful and easy to recognize. *Why risk testing a food source that is too rare to provide a useful number of calories or one that is too easily confused with some other plant?* Plus, the test had to be run all the way through on a given plant before moving on to a second one.

Step Two: Select the part of the plant that appears most palatable, while avoiding the obvious dangers like berries and the like. Crush some of what you have selected against a rock and carefully examine the juice or sap. Again, no milky saps. But if the sap is clear, touch a drop of it to your tongue. Be alert to the danger signs. A bitter taste or a numbing sensation on your tongue or lips or mouth is a clear cut signal to stay away. Watch especially for a sick feeling or for nausea. Under no circumstances are you to swallow what you touched to your tongue. Spit it out. Rinse your mouth with cool, clear water and spit that out too.

Step Three: If the tongue-tip test produced no lasting ill effects, you are ready to get braver. Place a teaspoon-sized chunk of that same part of the plant in your mouth and chew it without swallowing. Do this for five minutes. Be alert for the same warning signs as in the previous step, bitter taste or numbing sensation. If there are still no ill effects at the end of five minutes, swallow the sample you have thoroughly chewed and wait eight hours. Eat nothing further until the eight hours are up.

Step Four: Get braver still. If you still feel all right at the end of those eight hours, try a larger portion of the same part of the same plant, about half a cup. The quantity is not crucial, the process is. Again, wait eight hours. If you do not get sick or suffer numbness or burning or itching or have an allergic reaction, consider that part of the particular plant edible. But whatever you do, do not gorge yourself. Always go easy and always stick to the same portion of the plant you have successfully tested.

Lars knew his PET Project was both tedious and time-consuming. But he had always possessed a scientific mind, and this was the only way he could figure out how to survive in this hostile, unknown environment.

The tedium arose, in part, because he had to repeat the test for each part of each plant he sought to use as a food source. And he had to repeat the test for each different method of preparation. This was a rule he could not bend, no matter how hungry he became. If he first tested the plant-part raw, then he had to eat it raw every time. If he boiled that part first, he had to boil it before eating each and every time.

To do it any other way meant gambling with his life. Plant poisons reacted differently to various methods of cooking. While heat would kill most toxins, it was also known to turn some benign chemicals toxic.

By the same reasoning, if at any point his test revealed that digesting a certain part of a given plant might cause him grief, he had three choices. Give up and try another plant. Switch to a different part of the same plant. Or try preparing that particular part of the plant some other way.

He could perhaps soak it in water first. Water had long been known as a universal solvent. Among its many valuable properties was how it could often neutralize or render dangerous substances less toxic. Boiling hot water was known to neutralize even more toxins.

Which reinforced, once again, the importance of fire. Reducing toxicity was where food tasting intersected with firebuilding. Boiling a plant in water was one of the most effective ways early man knew for eliminating the undesirable effects of plant poisons. In Lars's case, if his test of a very common plant netted him nothing more than a sore mouth or a mild bellyache, he could improve his odds of finding a suitable food source by trying to neutralize the offending chemical with boiling hot water. This worked more than half the time.

But of course, man is not a herbivore. Man is an omnivore. And probably for good reason. In the survival game, catching critters was a heck of a lot easier than running a taste test on every frigging plant in the forest. Plus, critters offered more in the way of calories, and almost all of them were safe to eat.

In the absence of some special equipment, like a shotgun, a man in Lars's position had no choice but to zero in on little critters and let the big ones go. All mammals were edible, and the easiest way to catch one was with a snare. The idea was for him to take a length of steel wire from his survival kit and twist a small eye into one end. Strong cord would work just as well. Then he needed to push the free end through the eye to form a loop. The loop had to be just large enough to admit the head of his intended quarry. Finally, he had to secure the opposite end to a tree or log or rock and suspend the open loop above the ground at the height at which his quarry normally carried its head.

Lars knew from his experiences hunting with his father that it did little good to place animal snares at random. To be effective, observation was required. The snares had to be set in heavy traffic areas. Thus, they were most useful with "trail" animals, like rabbits or squirrels.

Venus had its own crop of little critters, though hardly any of them could be comfortably described as a squirrel or rabbit. But he did know that he could increase his odds of catching something by "funneling" any trail animal toward the snare. He put out bait. Then, to force the animal into the snare, he placed a brush barrier both to the left and right of the trail. Finally, he did not depend on just one snare; he set loads of them all along the animal trails nearby his campsite.

Another very simple device for catching small animals or birds was the box trap. Lars used to build them all the time as a kid back in Minnesota and caught all manner of critters in his traps, from the neighbor's cat to hapless sparrows. Here in the wilds he would have to improvise, of course, and make his own box. But it was not hard to do. He simply tied sticks together, log-cabin style, and fashioned a top made from rows of parallel sticks. Many things could serve as string. Thread from his clothes, thin strips of bark, hardy blades of grass. They would all work for tying.

To set a box trap, he simply had to place the box, open side down on the ground, and prop up one end with a stick. The stick had to be just long enough to admit his prey. Then he had to place the appropriate bait on the ground, well inside the confines of the box, and tie a string to the stick.

That part was easy. What was to come was much more difficult. Lars had to step back out of sight, string in hand, and wait. And wait. And wait. If he was lucky and supper stepped under the lid of the box to have a taste of the bait he had set out for him, Lars would yank the string, pull out the prop, and hopefully trap the bugger long enough for him to secure the box.

An equally appropriate alternative to the box trap was to use a log or heavy flat rock to create a manually triggered deadfall. This saved him the trouble of having to secure the beast long enough to kill it.

Finding the appropriate bait was the hard part. Lars knew precious little about the local wildlife and even less what they fancied as food. So he had to experiment, sometimes with leeches, sometimes with little frog-like things, sometimes the occasional worm or snake or lizard, stuff that he would ordinarily not eat himself.

With so many lakes and ponds and rivers dotting the landscape, one of his first thoughts was to fish for food. He had line, and he had a safety pin which could double as a hook. Once again, bait was an issue. However, with a certain amount of experimentation, he came up with several sources of suitable bait to fish with, little bits of lizard and the like.

Lars's problem was different. Everything he caught on the line was so large and so strong, he could not possibly reel it in. The animals — whatever they were — would break the line and sometimes swim away with his hook still stuck in its craw. Lars quickly gave up on the whole idea.

After a few very careful taste tests and one terrible bout of barfing and diarrhea, Lars found that — except for the heads, which very often contained hidden poison sacks — almost all the snakes, lizards, frogs, and turtle-like things were edible. Most were quite tasty, especially if skinned and cooked. And most were easy to catch. They did not move fast. He could often just simply whack them on the head with a strong stick. He began to carry with him a club for just this purpose.

The turtle-like things were the easiest to cook because they came with their own pot. He simply needed to lay them on their backs in the coals. A few of the shells he kept with him afterwards then put them to use as soup bowls.

People have a natural aversion to insects. But they were probably one of the easier sources of survival nutrition. This was especially true on Venus because the insects were generally larger than their Earth cousins. All a man needs is plenty of drinking water to wash them down. Insects were protein-rich. Nearly all of them were clean, no dirty intestines to dispose of, few poison sacks or sharp teeth to avoid. Most were quite tasty.

What passed for ants and bees and grubs were all highly nutritious and available in great quantity. Lars could find them nearly everywhere. He would turn over rocks, pry open rotting wood, or dig directly into anthills. It was best done early in the morning, when the soil was still relatively cool, and the little beasties were more sluggish.

He found that most insects tasted best when roasted or fried, though they were generally safe to eat right out of the box, so to speak. To roast a larger insect, he would lay it near a hot coal in the fire and wait a minute or two until it became crispy.

Diarrhea was more than an occasional hazard, prevalent under survival conditions. Nervous tension. Eating unfamiliar foods. Intestinal infection from contaminated water. It was not always possible to identify the source.

But one thing was for sure. He had only one change of underwear. Diarrhea was uncomfortable at best and debilitating at worst. The worst side effect was dehydration, which could only be remedied by drinking an abundance of water.

The diarrhea itself was relatively easy to control, even without access to a pharmacy. All Lars need do was eat fresh (but cool) natural charcoal from his campfire. It did not take much and the taste was not unpleasant. With essentially all of the pitch and cellulose burned away, what remained was natural charcoal. A couple tablespoonfuls was all he need ingest to get things back under control.

And then it was back on the trail headed north.

CHAPTER FIFTY-FIVE

Sweltering heat. Impenetrable thickets. Shrubs that oozed burning sap. Four-inch-long wasps. Lethal snakes. Killer bees. Giant ticks. Stinging ants everywhere he sat. Sprays of red orchids. Downed logs covered with orange mushrooms. Swarms of glistening blue butterflies that bit a man when he moved. These were the jungles of Domtar Province, all twelve hundred kloms of it.

Yes, he was in the jungle now. Thick dripping jungle. Club moss fuzzing on bent branches. Seed pods, hard and green, dangling from every tree. A canopy of forest overhead. Lush sweeps of green. Green of every shade, from blue-green to yellow-green to purple-green. It was jungle. Growth and decay and the stench of chlorophyll. Jungle sounds and jungle depth. Soft, humming jungle noises. Buzzing. Singing. The sounds of wings. Insect wings. Bird wings. The wings of unknown animals. Greenery deep in greenery. Itching jungle. Biting jungle. Dark, lost jungle. A botanist's nightmare.

And where was he standing? — Right smack in the middle of it.

But he was less standing than staggering. He didn't know how much more of this he could take.

When he could, Lars would follow animal trails, deer or mammoth or dragon. When he could not, he made his own trail using a machete or wire saw, always pushing north. Twelve hundred kloms, 453 days. That is not much progress, not even three kilometers a day, barely two miles.

There was weight in the air. It was always there. Heavy, wet, pungent air. Smells came together from every direction. They mixed in the wet, damp air and the final smell was always of rot. It kindled images from his days as a soldier in bin Hassan's army, those dead rotting bodies.

But how long ago was that now? Lars could no longer say. Memories were beginning to blur, beginning to run together like colors in a stream. It might have been the heat, which was intense. Or the lack of water. Or hunger. Or some crazy psychedelic chemical that inhabited the meat of whatever crappy salamander he had last eaten the day before.

Each day, in the early afternoon, when the heat became unbearable, he would find a place to stop. A shallow creek ran roughly parallel to the animal trail he was presently following. He would stop there, dip his hands in the water, splash some on his face. Then he would drink, refill his canteen, remove his sandals, lay back with his feet in the stream. No giant leeches here. Soon he would be asleep.

The dreams would come hard and fast. He would think how nice it would be to have a cold glass of ale. Or a tray of ice from the freezer. Or a fresh orange from Florida. *Could he even remember how they tasted?* And what about a woman? How did a woman smell? Oh, how he missed a woman's soft, wonderful touch.

Then suddenly the dream was over and the nightmare resumed. Lars would sit up quickly, check his feet for blisters, rinse out his dirty socks. *Did it matter?* His callouses were so thick. *Did he even need to wear shoes?*

Then he would bound to his feet. The terror inside him was rising. He had to move quickly, before the carnivorous lichen could get his scent and start moving in on his inert body. *Just one more klom*, he would say. *Just one more*. Then he would move on.

At night he would sleep on a hammock strung between two giant trees. High off the ground, away from the tree trunks. It seemed the carnivorous lichen could not “smell” him unless he was in close contact with it. Hanging in midair like that, the lichen would leave him alone.

But if only that were true about the insects! They would just not leave him alone when he slept. Especially the vosquitoes. They would drain him of blood before morning. And the leeches. God, they were everywhere! He would be covered with them when he awoke. Even on his mouth and lips. They would crawl in during the night, while he was sleeping. He would not feel them. They secreted some sort of paralyzing toxin. It numbed his skin. Then they would begin feeding.

About the only spot on his body where the leeches did not attach themselves were his one arm and leg, where the prison camp bar codes had been tattooed into his skin. A series of thin black bars on a fading field of white, with a number and a letter underneath — his identifier — Epsilon 1512. Lars guessed the little buggers did not like the ink. Lars was not particularly nuts about it either. He would have removed the tattoo himself if he could. Nothing was more degrading to his manhood than to be branded.

In the morning, he would start off again. He would remove the leeches, drop them into a pot of searing hot water, wait until they stopped wriggling. Then he would fish them out and grind them into a thick paste. At night he would spread the paste onto a harmless leaf and eat the combo like a sandwich. It seemed a fitting revenge for such a horrible animal.

But in the morning he would start off again. Remove the leeches, eat a light breakfast, take down his camp and shove off, always pressing north. It was hard work. The jungle was thick and seemed to be getting thicker. He would plod through groves of banyan and neem trees, then forests of palm-like trees, then acres of shag bark trees, then stands of trees he could not name, plus vines and deep brush and insects of every sort. He found that the bark of the neem tree had a resin he could spread on his skin to ward off insects.

The jungle was thick. He would trudge along slowly, painfully, stopping often to work with the machete, try to clear a path. Hacking. Sometimes crawling. Chopping. Hacking some more.

Then, all of a sudden, the animal trail would give out entirely. It would simply end. He would be standing in impenetrable jungle, surrounded by trees on all sides.

What should he do now? Hack his way through a wall of trees with nothing more than a machete and his bare hands?

Exhausted, he would chop through blunt jungle for an hour. First one hand, then the other. His fingers would bleed. Blisters would form, break, bleed, form again.

It was hard, awkward work. The machete handle would turn slick from sweat, from blood, from blisters, later callouses. There was no room to swing the blade, no leverage. Tangled thickets. Air full of heat. Heat he had never known before. He measured his breathing. Inhaling. Holding it for two counts. Swinging the machete and exhaling at the same time. Pausing. Inhaling. Holding his breath. Swinging.

After twenty rounds of it, he would drop to the ground exhausted. Sweat poured off his body as if from a fire hose. He would forage in the nearby branches for food to replenish his calories. Drink from his canteen. Dip into his dwindling supplies of bushpig jerky.

Then he would get to his feet and start again. Swing. Breath. Hold. Swing. The earth was damp now, springy with crushed ferns. Poisonous mushrooms. Ancient smells. A dank hush. Like before a summer storm. He would hear a noise and get spooked. *Geez, Lord, let it not be a dragon.*

The heat came in layers. It was a sucking heat, the sort that drew moisture out of living things. He was a living thing. *Or was he?*

He kept pushing. Near dusk on that day the narrow trail widened. The trees thinned out. The trail slipped down into a gully, soon a wide, dark river. Lars had no map. Trees grew to the river's edge. Their roots snaked down the muddy bank and into the slow, murky river. His compass said he had to cross the river, get to the other side.

The water was very still, almost too still. The river was like a pond without current. It flowed but very slowly. Dusk gave the water a murky brown color. Lars was scared.

Rivers were dangerous. So were swamps. So were lakes and ponds. Fuck, everything on this planet was dangerous. Lars knew the dangers of water from his days as a soldier in the field with Chief Wheeler. Crocs and leeches and bacteria of every sort.

But this time he was lucky. He floated across on a downed log. Most times he had to wade across or worse. Then spend half an hour pulling leeches and god knows what else off his skin.

Each day was the same. 453 days. He would roll out of his hammock at daybreak, pull off the leeches that had attached themselves to his skin overnight, then slug his way through thick jungle until midafternoon, when the heat clicked on like a furnace.

Then he would rest, spinning out the hottest hours in sleep or petty conversation. He would talk to himself, argue actually — about politics, about women, about money.

Sometimes he would tell himself stories, stories about summer camp, about hunting grizzly bear with his father, about Kaleena and the few happy hours they spent together. Those few hours may have been the last time he was truly happy.

Then the late afternoon shadows would appear. His delirium would pass. The air would cool ever so slightly. He would resume his march north until dusk.

Each day the decision would be the same. Each day he would have the same argument with himself, with Chief Wheeler, with whomever he was walking the trail with. Sometimes his grandfather, sometimes his mother, sometimes Sergeant Major Grovosky.

Okay, decision time, he would say. *Do I keep on with this shit? Or do I call it quits? Do I keep on walking? Or do I sit down and die? Tell me, you asshole, what the hell should I do?*

He would scream it at the top of his lungs. Sometimes the trees would answer. Sometimes they would just stand there, unmoving, and laugh at him.

But each day, his friends, his family, would answer him the same way. If he went back, if he returned to Slave Camp #5, all he faced was a firing squad.

Plus, there was no way back anyway. The jungle grew back in to obscure his trail almost as fast as he cut it. And if he sat down, if he refused to take another step, he was a dead man. The jungle would get him within a day or two. If not the dragons, then the carnivorous lichen. If not the lichen, then the leeches. Or the vosquitoes. Or the wild bushpigs. Something would come along and kill him dead.

No, he had no choice. He had to press forward. He had to find the colony. He had to make a new life for himself.

•
•

453 fucking days. Lars kept count on his walking stick. Little notches in groups of five. All up one side and down the other, in neat little rows. The stick came in handy when he had to push aside a plant sporting thorns to avoid breaking his skin or to cross a shallow lake or river, as he often did.

The simple truth was that Venus was wet and getting wetter all the time. It was all courtesy of the parade of comets coming in from the Kuiper Belt. Rivers, streams, lakes, swamps, mud, guck, everywhere. Almost daily he had to ford some body of water. Usually, it was a blackwater sump, a zone of intermittently flooded forest. The water's sleek black surface would be dark as buffed ebony. Its depths would be punctuated here and there by large trees. Their roots and buttresses remained submerged beneath the surface.

But how deep was the water? That was always the question. *And how far to the other side?*

Imagine a flooded thicket. A tangle of dense, scrubby vegetation. Low branches and prop roots interlaced in a thick latticework like mangroves. It was impossible to see past them or to imagine anyway to pass through them. Lars would wade into the water, hoping the sump was not too deep. That was where his walking stick came in handy, to probe the bottom, to check the depth one step ahead of his feet.

So he would advance into the thick water. In no time at all, he would be waist deep. Then chest deep. Then armpit deep. Now his walking stick no longer touched solid bottom. Soft mud in every direction. He probed ahead with his feet, fearful of a sudden drop.

Each step forward was tentative. When the water seemed too deep, he would back out a step or two, always seeking the shallowest route. He would try to probe the dark water ahead of him with his long stick. He would try not to get his feet and sandals caught in the sucking mud. With every step he could feel more leeches attaching themselves to his legs and chest. It was frightening. They were sucking the living blood right out of him.

Leeches in moderation were no big deal. Lars would pick up ten just rinsing off in a stream after a hot day. They did not hurt and as a general rule did not cause infection or harbor disease.

But in one pond he crossed, they numbered in the tens of thousands. They swam up to him in schools. They were aggressive, like hungry piranha. They hooked their thirsty little maws onto his ankles and calves, a half-dozen here, another half-dozen there. When he tried to pull them off, they resisted slimily. He had leeches under his sandal straps, leeches between his toes, leeches racing to every open sore and blister. *Good grief, what had they lived on before he arrived?*

A day or two later, Lars had his answer. Mammoths. At least that is what he called them. This massive elephant-like creature with six legs spent half its time in the water, where it grazed. Lars could only guess at its role in the planet's food chain.

He thought of them as the sauropod of the jungle. Thank God, they were herbivores. They considered him more of a nuisance than a food source. The thing was enormous, with tree-trunk-like legs and an anteater-style snout. These giant animals dined on the hard, green seed pods that were ubiquitous in the jungle. The pods dangled from every other tree in the canopy.

The mammoth's favorite tree was a towering hulk with shaggy bark. It had a gracefully tilted trunk and a wide, multi-footed buttress. Lars called it the "shag." The shags grew to magisterial size — two meters in diameter, fifty or more meters tall, with straight, clean trunks. The shag tree would have made his father eminently happy. It was lovely wood, grist for a sawmill should one ever be built.

The big green fruits that the mammoths considered a delicacy were globular and heavy. Each was filled with a sweet-smelling, pumpkiny orange pulp. A little chalky for Lars's palate. But the mammoths traveled a considerable distance to scarf them down. And it was a good thing too. When these big, six-legged monsters moved, they carved out wonderful trails, trails that were easy for Lars to follow. The mammoth trails saved a lot of wear and tear on his machete arm. Plus, the fresh mammoth dung they left behind made for a first-rate insect repellent, when spread smoothly over his exposed skin.

One other nice thing about the mammoths and the trails they left behind were the bushpigs. They followed the trails just as Lars did. This symbiotic relationship manufactured the perfect conditions for Lars to snare a few pigs and cook them up for dinner. The bushpigs had a fair amount of blubber, like a raccoon, and made for excellent eating and even better jerky. They waddled along like flightless ducks at a speed that made them easy prey. From this point forward on his trek, Lars almost never went hungry and actually gained back all the weight he had lost and then some.

For a short while, life was heaven.

CHAPTER FIFTY-SIX

His father was there when Lars woke up. Hogan was going on and on about Pamola, the Storm God.

Lars tried to settle his father down. But the man would not stop rambling. He claimed his Night Spirit had crept away from his body during the night. It had gotten into a fight with another man and the two of them had battled to within inches of their lives. Now his back hurt and every muscle was sore.

Lars's father was always that way. All worldly things had a metaphysical explanation. It wasn't that the ground he slept on was hard; it was that his Night Spirit had been thrashed by an enemy while he slept. It wasn't that a pebble had gotten into his boot, causing a blister; it was that he had been irreverent when walking on sacred ground. It wasn't that he had a runny nose because he was allergic to some offending pollen; it was that he had mistakenly sniffed the flower of a sacred tree. Science did not exist for Hogan Cabot, only spirits, medicine men and superstition.

Now his father started going on and on about how, as hunters, he and Lars had to respect their prey before they hunted it down and killed it. Grizzly bears represented power and manhood. *Heed Pamola,* he shouted at the top of his lungs.

Lars thought he was asleep, that he was having some sort of terrible dream. Was he on Venus now or back at home with his father? It all seemed so real. Had he eaten something weird for dinner last night? Was he now hallucinating from some strange chemical he had ingested? Or had he smoked a joint and was again time-traveling? What the hell was going on?

Heed Pamola, his father shouted again.

But now it was coming back to him. Last night the two of them, Lars and his father, put up a tent. They built a fire, laid out their sleeping bags inside, cooked dinner. They ate foil burgers and baked potatoes. Lars had never tasted anything so good. Then, when it got dark, a river of stars began to flow overhead.

Lars's father, Hogan Cabot, began drinking whiskey. He lit up a cannabis joint. Father and son started talking. Hogan was getting drunk. Time and again, he handed his son the joint and encouraged the boy to smoke. Lars was already flying.

Lars looked at his wristwatch. It was late, nearly midnight. But hadn't he lost his watch? Back before his first rejuvenation? That did not make sense. Was he on Earth now? Or was he still on Venus? What sort of mind-altering drug had he taken?

"Put away that silly watch," Hogan ordered. He lived in a world inhabited by supernatural forces. No place in that world for timepieces. No place in that world for technology.

"But Grandpa gave me this watch. He said it was valuable, that I should take good care of it."

"That crazy old man. It isn't even a real watch. How can it possibly be valuable?"

"He said it can help a man find his way," Lars argued.

"Yes, yes, yes. Something about the hour hand and the direction of the sun."

"You see, Father? That is precisely what makes an old-style wristwatch so valuable. Grandpa Flix was right. You cannot use a digital watch to find due north."

"But, son. We are on Venus not Earth. Your timepiece will not help us much here. You know that, right?"

"So am I having a dream?" Lars asked his father. "Or are you actually here with me now?"

Hogan laughed, tossed his son another burger off the coals. Lars was hungry and happy for the second helping. But his father was stoned. Not everything that came out of his mouth made sense in this state.

Hogan laughed again. "My two favorite things in the world. Hiking and fucking. They are the same, you know. Walking is like sex. Basic. Simple. Repetitive. And yet, both are capable of great sophistication."

"I would not know about that."

"Ah, but you must learn, Lars. You must learn. Hiking and fucking. One is as likely as the other to be banal, almost boring. Both can be completely meaningless, without emotion. It all depends on the woman — and the trail. Each is capable of great passion, of endless adventure. A good walk is like a good woman. One is as likely as the other to lead a man into strange and unknown territory. There is no map in this land. If she is quiet like the trail, if she lets you have your way, you will come away satisfied."

"Talk about a land with no maps. This must be a dream. Do you not know where we are, Father? This is the planet Venus. I am walking across Domtar Province on my own and by myself. Do you think this is fun?"

"What have you been smoking, son? Some illegal hash laced with lysergic acid?"

"Father, I have been on the trail for more than three months already, maybe five. I have lost count. I have been hungry. I have been thirsty. I am constantly horny. I have been attacked by leeches, by insects, by flesh-eating lichen, by unimaginable things. I am scared shitless every damn day out on the trail. I can tell you for certain. Hiking is no fun at all."

"So now what are you going to do? Give up? Sit down and die? After you have come all this way?"

"You do not know what I have been through. I left for a reason. I was tired of being a slave, of no longer being a free man. I was tired of being property, of being rejuvenated against my will, of being made to live the same ugly life over and over again."

"Ah, but don't all men yearn for eternal life?"

"Not like this they do not. I walked away from that prison camp. I have been on the trail for months. Alone. Afraid. Hungry. Thirsty. This has not been fun, not fun at all."

"And you think losing an eye was?"

"The accident at the mill? I could never understand why the gods would permit such a thing to happen to you."

"Ruddy gods." Hogan sighed as he looked up at the night sky with his new eye.

Lars followed his father's stare skyward. The aurora borealis shimmered overhead, as it often did this time of year. Ribbons of light danced across the northern sky. Flashes of white, yellow, and indigo violet.

"That is not right," Lars said.

"What is not right?"

"Venus cannot possibly have Northern Lights. The atmosphere is all wrong. I must be back on Earth again."

"You are where you want to be, Lars," his father answered.

"What kind of philosophy is that?"

"I am not a religious man, Lars. If it is moral lessons you seek, talk to your mother. If you want parables, get yourself down to church. If you want to study philosophy, find someone with a Ph.D."

"But I have read the *Book of Lore* from front to back. I still cannot figure it out. Is there just one god? Or are there many?" Lars asked.

"Why the hell are you asking me? Your mother would be the first to tell you how I am nothing but a drunken fool."

"I am asking you because I want to know what you think."

Hogan turned pensive. "What does it matter how many gods a man believes in? Religion. Magic. Physics. They are all the same. If there is a difference between them, I cannot see it. The god you love, the god of science and mathematics — He can destroy religion just as readily by totally ignoring it as He can by trying to disprove it. As far as I know, Lars, no one has ever demonstrated the nonexistence of Thor or of Zeus. Yet, in this day and age neither one of them has much of a following."

"I am confused. Are we talking about god or are we talking about religion?"

"Maybe we are talking about neither. Maybe we are talking about alien beings."

"Now you have really gone and lost me."

"Lars, most of us would describe God as being omniscient and omnipotent. We ourselves are neither. So how can we puny humans distinguish without fail between a God who actually and truly possesses these traits and an extraterrestrial who possesses these traits in sufficient quantity to seem so?

The answer is we cannot. In fact, if God were only relatively more knowing and powerful than we are, then by definition such a deity might be considered to be an extraterrestrial."

"I see what you mean. You are talking about Clarke's Law."

"Who the fuck is Clarke?"

"You might not have heard of him. Arthur C. Clarke. One of my idols. He was likely one of the farthest-seeing visionaries of the last thousand years."

"Do tell."

"Arthur C. Clarke said that any sufficiently advanced technology would be indistinguishable from magic. He set out the following thought-experiment. Consider a tribe of alien creatures only one thousand years ahead of us in technological terms, a mere pittance of time. These alien creatures are about as far ahead of us as we ourselves are ahead of, say, the Middle Ages. Now suppose you traveled back in time to medieval Europe with a modern vid unit in hand. Leave aside for the moment the issue of having no place to plug them in for power."

"I don't follow."

"What I mean is that electricity had not yet been invented."

"Yes, I see."

"No, you don't," Lars said. "The point is this. If a technology is sufficiently advanced, an ordinary person might perceive it as being magic. Take a famous scientist from our past, Aristotle or Isaac Newton, bright men both. Show either of them an ordinary video device, and he would run screaming from the room. Show him a skullcap or a microwave oven or a space elevator and he would faint. When he came to, he would claim it was all witchcraft, that you were possessed. He would not understand the devices at all and you could not adequately explain them to him either, not in five years of trying. He lacks the intellectual background. He knows not from electromagnetism or light wave propagation or particle physics. To him, these ordinary mundane appliances are possessed of magic, as if from an advanced alien being."

Hogan Cabot nodded his head. "You make some very good points. Maybe religion is magic. I myself am a bit of a fatalist. There is a plan, you see. A plan for each and every one of us."

"I do not accept that. Men have free will."

"Do they? . . . Or have they just deceived themselves into believing they do in order to avoid confronting their reality?"

"I am scared of the future."

"That does not make you special, Lars. Every man is afraid of the future, even the big strong ones, even the boastful ones, even the ones who are full of themselves."

"Even you?"

Hogan looked at his son then spoke the words that had stuck in Lars's head, now, for some two hundred years.

"Son, I want to be able to die at a time and in a place of my own choosing."

"But you take such awful risks on the job. The things you do. Aren't you afraid of being hurt? Aren't you afraid of being killed?"

"I am not afraid to die, Lars. But I want it on my own terms."

Lars scoffed at the idea. He was scornful of his father's statement. "Me, I do not want to die at all. I want to live forever . . ."

That is what he told his father that day, that he wanted to live forever. And in truth he practically had. Two involuntary rejuvs had seen to that. Lars was currently hip deep into his third lifetime. Now all he wanted was to die of old age, the natural way.

Suddenly Chief Wheeler spoke up, pushed Hogan aside. "But you have so much to live for, Lars. Why would you possibly want to die? Have you even thought about that girl you spent such a wonderful night with? Her father sacrificed his life that she might live. Or have you forgotten?"

"What are you doing here, Chief? I thought you were dead and gone long ago? I must be having a very vivid dream."

"The mind is a funny thing, lad. People can live on in your memory long after they have passed from this world."

"So that's what this is then? Scotched up memories of people long dead? You are not real. My father is not real. None of this is real. Have I finally descended into madness?"

"Not madness," Robota said. "Put on your skullcap. You possess one of the finer skullcaps money can buy. Put it on and think. What makes the most sense? That this is a fantasy? Or that this is actually happening?"

“Ah, grow a pair, you worthless rook,” Sergeant Major Buster Grovosky said. “Buck it up and keep walking. Don’t let these lugnuts confuse you. Your father is right. This is no time to fold up and die. Move along!”

“Forget the damn skullcap,” Chief Wheeler said. “Use your head, Lars. Use your skills. You were born into this world with a boatload of commonsense. Use it, for god’s sake.”

“You got my daughter pregnant,” Viscount Henry boomed. “What the hell do you intend to do about it?”

“The right thing, of course,” Lars said sheepishly.

“But you never did.”

“How was I to know the ship would be hijacked on the way to Mars and that we would all end up as prisoners of war on Venus?”

“This is an excuse? Rubbish! What did you do to try and protect my daughter?”

“I went looking for her, honest I did. I tried to find her. I tried to rescue her. They had taken the women to someplace called the Farm. We all died or were captured trying to free those women.”

“I did not know that.”

“How could you? By then you were already dead and buried yourself.”

“And did you?”

“Did I what?”

“Did you find my daughter? Did you free her from that evil place?”

“No, sir. I failed.”

“You are pretty good at that, aren’t you?”

“Pretty good at what?”

“Failing.”

“That is unfair.”

“Well then. Quit babbling. Wake up from this drug-induced nightmare and start walking again in the morning. Time is a wasting.”

CHAPTER FIFTY-SEVEN

453 days. 1200 kloms.

The jungle turned into savanna and then desert, something Lars did not believe possible on Venus. In the space of a few kloms the landscape morphed from lush green to scraggy brush and prairie grass to stark brown sand. Lars put it down as an unintended consequence of the trans-comets being brought in from the outer reaches of the solar system. Somehow the addition of all that cold water must have disturbed the air-circulation pattern over the center of the continent and altered the climate. *Would wonders never cease?*

As Lars pushed farther north, now, and as conditions began to change, so too did his survival strategy. Desert was different from jungle. Exposure was much more of a problem now than before. After months and months of never having to worry about water, it was now suddenly his only worry.

Lars knew the basic protocol for desert survival. Walk slowly to conserve energy. Stay in the shade. Rest often, at least ten minutes each hour. Avoid talking. Do not smoke. Drink no alcohol. When you do have water, never ration it, always drink it. People have died in the desert with water still in their canteens. Breathe through your nose, not your mouth. Avoid eating if you are short on water. Digestion consumes water. Do not strip off your clothing. Clothing helps ration sweat by slowing evaporation. Wear a hat. Keep on your shirt. Wear sunglasses. Travel in the evening or at night or early in the morning. Avoid the midday heat.

Of course, half that information was useless gibberish in his situation. Lars did not smoke. Except for an occasional sip of prison-camp hooch, Lars had not consumed alcohol in over a hundred years. *Talk?* Who the hell was he going to talk to anyway? Lars was traveling alone. He did not have a hat or sunglasses and not even much of a shirt. The best he could do was to travel at night or early in the morning, when the air was cooler.

The deciding issue in desert survival is water, or rather the utter lack of it. A man can forget all the other rules of desert survival so long as he has enough clean water to drink. It is a question of biology. Water is by far the largest component of the human body. Yet, a man has little to spare. In the hottest desert humans can sweat out water at a prodigious rate — up to seven or eight liters a day while resting in the shade, as much as fifteen liters a day while walking.

Even when a man is dehydrated, he continues to lose water at nearly a constant rate. Thus, the only way to stretch one's life is to reduce his water needs. He has to stay put, stay out of the sun, and, by all means, keep his clothes on.

Stay put? What a laughable idea! *Why would anyone in his right mind stay put in the middle of an unforgivable desert?* Was some friendly barmaid going to drive by with a beverage cart? *Not very damn likely.*

Staying put would not help him get any closer to his destination. Staying put was a form of suicide. *No, if he wanted to live, he had to keep moving.* Which meant he had to find water — and soon.

Thirst is first felt when the body has lost just one-half of one percent of its weight to dehydration. For an average-sized man like Lars, this amounts to little more than one pint.

With a two percent loss — say, two quarts — the stomach is no longer large enough to hold as much water as the body now requires. People at this stage of dehydration, even if they are given ample fluids, will stop drinking well before they have replenished their deficit.

At a five percent loss, you are in the danger zone. The symptoms are many. Fatigue. Loss of appetite. Flush skin. Irritability. Increased pulse rate. Mild fever. A man in this condition will feel just plain miserable. Waves of nausea will destroy any desire he may have to drink. If he does vomit, he will lose even more precious fluids. Then things will start to go downhill in a hurry. Beyond this point lies serious trouble. Dizziness. Headache. Labored breathing. Absence of salivation. Blue skin. Slurred speech.

At a ten percent loss, a person can no longer walk. The point of no return is around twelve percent. The tongue swells. The mouth loses all sensation. Swallowing becomes impossible. A person this dehydrated has lost in excess of eleven liters of fluid and cannot recover without medical assistance. The scary part is that it may take as little as half a day to get to this advanced stage.

A man in this condition is a horror to behold. The skin begins to shrink against the bones. It will soon crack like dry kindling. Both eyes sink into their sockets. Vision and hearing become dim. Urination is painful, if at all. Delirium sets in. The blood thickens. The end comes with an explosive rise in body temperature. Convulsions follow. Then blissful death.

Not a pretty end, Lars thought, as he stumbled forward across the harsh sand. There was water to be found, he knew, if he looked in the right places. But he had to be smart about it,

He figured that the best place to start looking was where water had recently run. At the base of a rock cliff, perhaps. Or in the gravel wash off a mountain valley. Along the outside edge of a sharp bend in a dry streambed. All possible places. Look for wet sand. Dig down one or two meters to find seep water. Or look for green vegetation. Or along an animal path. Or near a flock of birds. Or near a cluster of trees or shrubs. Or follow an animal trail to their watering hole, maybe a pond or stream.

Lars surveyed the landscape. The land was flat, bone-dry, and lifeless. No dry streambeds here. No animal trails. No animals, period. No vegetation. Nothing green whatsoever.

I am so screwed. He thought to himself. *First, more water than I know what to do with. Now this?*

Lars stumbled forward. The arrow on his compass pointed him in the direction he was to go. Behind him, through the clouds, the sun was growing with intensity. Its yellow heat silhouetted his lanky frame against the burning sand. Unlike the jungle, with its oppressive humidity, the clouds that hung overhead here were thin and far apart. Before long the temperature would become unbearable.

How was he going to survive out in the open like this?

There were no trees in this stretch of landscape to find shade under. No trees to hang a hammock between. No trees meant no firewood. No trees meant no furry little animals to catch, no water to drink, no protection from the elements.

I am so screwed.

All around him was noise. Not animal noise, not like in the jungle. But weird dangerous noise nevertheless. This surprised Lars. He had always thought of a desert as silent and dead.

But then again, he was out of his element here. He had heard stories, however. Chief Wheeler had told him about those concrete arrows in the desert, about growing up in a clapboard house on the high desert mesa of New Mexico. Lars had learned about the dust storms on Mars, how deserts were legend on the Red Planet, how dust permeated everything.

In all cases, the story was the same. Whether Earth or Mars or Venus, the story was the same. Nomads traveling across the desert have reported hearing mysterious sounds. In most cases these travelers were put off as delirious from the heat. But they all reported the same phenomena. They thought the sounds were made by ghosts or demons or lost souls.

The stories go back countless centuries, back into the dim reaches of early human history. Marco Polo reported that evil spirits filled the desert air with the sounds of musical instruments, sometimes drums, sometimes the clash of arms. Other listeners, in more recent times, likened the sounds to bells or trumpets or foghorns. Some even compared them to cannon fire. Thunder. Low-flying aircraft.

Different dunes were known to produce different sounds. Moaning. Like a woman in heat. Ringing. Like a church bell. Whining. Like a string instrument. Droning. Like the low cadence produced by the aboriginal instrument, the didgeridoo.

But the really frightening sounds were the booming sounds, the ones that produced explosively loud cannon-fire-sounds, sounds that could be heard up to ten kloms away. These occurred almost exclusively deep in the desert among large, isolated sand dunes. It was one of those sounds that held his attention now, the thundering sonic boom of a distant dune-avalanche.

Lars walked in the direction of the sound. He instinctively knew that there were no evil spirits lurking out here. The sounds he heard had something to do with the laws of acoustics. Blow across the lip of a bottle and you get a certain range of sounds. Surely the dunes must twist the wind, much like the bends in the tubing of a brass instrument. *How else to explain the deep, trombone-like sounds?*

Lars walked in the direction of the sound. The physics of dune formation were legend. Strong steady winds lifted sand particles into the air. Later, those same winds deposited the sand particles in colossal linear dunes. Mixed with a little rainwater and made sticky by sea salts, the sand formed a type of cement. That made the dunes hard, more like rock than loose sand. So each dune had to be climbed. In the valleys between dune peaks, the heat was intense.

Lars continued to follow the sounds. Before long he stumbled upon a patch of green, a short plant that vaguely resembled a cactus. It had tiny flowers and what resembled a fruit on one branchlike spur.

Lars was not only thirsty, but thirsty with a strong adjective in front of it. He split open the base of the cactus stalk and chewed on the pith. This was risky behavior, no doubt about it. The plant could be poisonous, for all he knew.

But Lars was not stupid. He knew better than to swallow the pith outright. He chewed on it awhile. Somehow, the chewing did help alleviate his thirst. He rested awhile beside the plant, then moved on.

The sun climbed higher above the horizon, now, and with it the temperature. There was bright sun here, not clouds, not like back in the jungle. The jungle had shade. The jungle had running water. The jungle had nourishment.

But not here in the desert. The trick, now, was to move quickly enough to avoid dehydration, but not so swiftly as to become winded. He knew it was not smart to walk during the day. But there was no shade anywhere. He could not see how it would help for him to just sit down and fry in the heat.

He wiped at his forehead with the back of his handkerchief. He was dripping wet. He had to get out of the sun. *But there was no place to hide.*

A stream of perspiration poured off his face and onto his hands. The day's heat was rising in full force now, making it impossible for him to even hold onto his walking stick.

He stopped, wiped his sweaty fingers against his tattered shirt to dry them, gripped his stick with renewed determination.

He wanted to take a deep breath to calm his frayed nerves. But for some strange reason his mouth would not open. His throat was constricted and he could feel it coming on, the panic. He grunted out a staccato obscenity.

How fucking stupid can you be? He swore at himself.

Those who knew Lars, knew him to be a hardheaded man. He was not known as one who gave in easily.

But now he was beaten. He had backed himself into a corner with no possible way out. An unknown distance of impenetrable desert still lay between him and his goal. He had no water, no food, no transportation.

How dumb can you be, Lars? You are going to die out here, you know that don't you? Hell, you aren't even certain this place Industry exists. Just stories around the campfire. Have you seen even one sign that people have crossed this desert before you? No, you fool! You are the first! You will be the last! What a fool you are! Such a fool . . .

Anxious fear began to grasp at his bowels and for one long instant he thought he would be ill. Then reason took hold. *He had to avoid being ill at all costs.*

Swallowing hard, now, he struggled to flush the cobwebs from his throat. They were lodged there in his parched airway like so many logs caught in a snag. His head was pounding. His back was starting to ache. It was straining under the weight of his bedroll on his shoulder. He knew that sundown would bring relief. *But would he last that long?*

Every once in a while, now, feelings of resentment would bubble to the surface. Nasty primal feelings. Anger at Chief Wheeler, at Viscount Henry, at Kaleena, at his mother. Where these feelings came from, Lars had no idea. But they were ripping at his soul. Anger.

Resentment. Prejudice. Lars tried to suppress them. But the heat was beginning to exact a toll.

Why the fuck did I have to walk away from the slave-camp? Why could I not have just died like the others? What the fuck am I trying to accomplish out here anyway?

Lars was angry. But the anger helped. He reached up inside himself for renewed strength, found it, and continued to trudge on, one halting step after another.

He was really thirsty now.

He tried to spirit away the feeling of emptiness in the pit of his stomach. But like an unwanted guest it would not leave.

Each step he took seemed shorter than the one before. His legs were tired. His kneecaps felt like they were about to explode.

He was totally drenched in sweat. His breathing was shallow. He licked at cracked lips with a tongue swollen to twice its normal size. Then he stumbled and fell to the ground. He could not go on, not like this.

The sun beat against his upturned face. Lars was not a man given easily to defeat. But it would be easy, oh so easy, to just lay back on the hot sand and let it happen. Just fall asleep and kiss his worldly cares goodbye.

Lars tried once or twice to get back up but found he could not. He closed his eyes and cursed his stupidity and bad luck.

Like before, the sand began to speak to him. Booms and whistles and cannons firing. Then the sounds changed. Now it was moaning like a woman in heat. He knew this sound. It was Kaleena. They were in bed together. She told him he was a fool. He never should have left her side. They never should have listened to her father. They never should have boarded the *Ticonderoga*. He never should have left her arms. He never should . . .

CHAPTER FIFTY-EIGHT

This time, when Lars awoke, he was cold. It was dark, and he thought he was dead. The only clue he had that he was still alive was that he was alone. He figured hell had to be crowded. So he must be still alive.

Cold was a killer. He knew that. But it was also a life-saver. If he could now find water, he might just live to see another day.

A desert cools off rapidly as soon as the sun sets. The risk is hypothermia. In a survival situation that can be a killer, and a sneaky one at that. When your body starts to shiver, it is trying to tell you that it is losing core body heat faster than it can be replaced. The shivering reflex exercises a whole bunch of muscles and increases heat production by burning more fuel, which is to say food. Taking in more calories in the form of food heats your body. Breathing, perspiration, and radiation cool it.

Shivering alone is not likely to rewarm someone. Active prevention is the key. If a man has dry clothes, he should put them on. He can run in place or do calisthenics, anything to force his muscles to burn more fuel and generate heat. The downside for a hungry man like Lars is that he will be consuming fuel he cannot easily replace. The desert was not like the jungle, with food at every turn. He had not eaten, now, in two days.

To prevent hypothermia, he had to act fast. That meant reducing his heat loss as much as possible with shelter, fire, and additional clothing.

He had no additional clothing to put on. But he did have his bedroll. Lars wrapped his hammock around his shoulders like a shawl and kept pressing forward. If he had had any wood to burn, he would have stopped to build a fire. But the landscape was barren, not a bush or tree in sight. Lars knew he was now living on borrowed time. If something did not change for the better, and soon, he would go downhill fast. It would go something like this:

You are shivering. The circulation to your hands and feet is being choked off. This is one of those automatic reflexes designed by evolution to keep your vital organs warm. By reducing the flow of blood to your extremities, your body is reducing its loss of heat.

But it is doing so at a cost. In no time at all, you will begin to experience fatigue. That, plus muscle tensing and poor coordination. Your hands are about to become cold and stiff, even though the last thing you need in a tight situation is clumsy hands. Those hands are going to have to build a fire, put up a shelter, perhaps button a coat. Fingers stiff with cold fumble the job when they try to strike a match or blow air carefully into a fledgling fire.

Next comes a surprise. As your core body temperature continues to drop, you stop shivering. This is not good news. This is a sure danger sign, one you are not likely to recognize. The biggest danger from hypothermia is that it robs you of the necessary will to help yourself. About the time you quit shivering, you also quit worrying. You are dying and you could not care less.

At this point, your body has lost its ability to rewarm itself. Even if you have unlimited clothing or a thick sleeping bag to crawl into, you will continue to cool off until you fall asleep and die. Your only hope, now, is to add external heat. A warming fire. A hot drink. Another human body pressed close.

But Lars was lucky. He did not get down that far. Not thirty minutes later he stumbled across the half-frozen carcass of a dead bushpig. This unlikely piece of meat saved his life. It was fresh, or at least fresh enough to eat. Out here in the desert, things were dry. Dead things did not rot, or at least not as quickly as they did in the jungle. There were no gelatinous fungi to avoid, no carnivorous lichen, no flesh-eating bacteria. Things did not rot, they baked.

That dead bushpig meant one other thing. He was nearing the end of the desert. This part of his trek was nearly over.

•
•

Digesting protein consumes water, much more than digesting carbohydrates. Luckily, Lars found a water hole about an hour after he found the dead bushpig. The desert was coming to an end. In its place was a low range of mountains. He had made a smart move and cut off some of the bushpig's hide to fashion into a coarse coat. For the moment he lacked the skills or inclination to clean or tan it properly, so it was kind of gamey. But the extra layer kept him warm as he began to ascend the angled foothills.

Much like the desert, hypothermia is also the leading cause of death in the mountains. Humans are basically warm-weather animals. Cold is hard for us to cope with. Not that Lars was particularly afraid. He knew that staying calm in the face of adversity greatly increased his chances for survival. Fear could kill a man as fast as any other hazard he faced in the wild.

Nights were cold. Not Colorado Rocky Mountain cold, but cold enough to freeze standing water into a mushy slush. With his newly acquired hide and the chance to eat more regularly, his odds improved sharply. Over the course of the next several weeks, as he crossed the low range of mountains, he added to his collection of furs.

While Lars would have preferred some actual wool clothing Earth-style, he learned to make do. He had grown up with natural wool. His father wore it all the time. It was the classic fabric of the outdoorsman. Between the layers of fiber was an insulating "dead air" space. Wool retained much of its insulating value even when wet. Plus, because of its lanolin content, wool tended to shed water, keeping its wearer dry. Not true in equal measure of the local fur.

At night, Lars would have to find shelter. He had been pressing north since he escaped from the slave camp many months ago. Now the nights were getting progressively colder. His idea was to find rather than build shelter. Why exhaust himself unnecessarily? Why drag around heavy logs to build a shelter when there was a simpler way? The only thing all that heavy lifting accomplished was to make him sweat and thus get colder.

So, whenever possible, Lars would use the natural shelter around him before trying to construct something from scratch. Lars would find a natural depression in the ground and cover it with branches or leaves for insulation. At night, he would stay out of the valleys. Cold air falls. That means that the floor of a valley can be the coldest spot on a mountain. Plus, sunlight gets there last in morning. He would stick to wooded areas, where game was plentiful, and build himself a roaring fire.

His compass would not work properly in the mountains. Lars could not understand why until he decided the local rocks must be lodestones and thus magnetized. As a boy, he used to find such magnetized rocks all over the Mesabi Range near where he grew up. He knew their properties.

But now, to stay on course, he had to resort to an older technology. This is where his grandfather's ancient wristwatch would come in handy. The wristband had long ago disintegrated. But the watch still worked. It was an old-fashioned watch with face and hands. Definitely a collector's piece. Probably worth something too. Grandpa Flix was into all that antediluvian stuff. Now Lars understood why.

Just as an old-style manual lighter had its advantages over one of the newer electronic ones, so too did a conventional wristwatch have certain advantages over the newer digital ones. For starters, with a little sunlight it could be converted into a passable compass. All a man had to do was hold the watch parallel to the ground and point the hour hand in the direction of the sun. An imaginary line drawn precisely halfway between the hour hand and the twelve o'clock position would point due south. An about-face and he was back on track north. Just one of the many survival tricks his grandfather had taught him when he was a kid.

It was on such a day that with wristwatch in hand Lars found his first footprint in over fifteen months.

At first he thought it was his own, that he had gone in circles, that his makeshift compass was useless on a planet where the sun seemed to be everywhere at once.

But then Lars compared the tread to his own. The two sets of tracks most certainly did not match. *The shoeprints did not belong to him.*

He followed the trail of footprints with his eyes. It went down the mountain, across a small river and off into the distance. In that same distance he saw buildings. Buildings and streets. Streets and people.

He had made it.

CHAPTER FIFTY-NINE

"Now that wasn't so bad, was it?"

Lars stared unknowingly at the she-person speaking to him.

"Who . . . where am I?" Lars felt strange. The room he was in had a vaguely antiseptic smell to it.

"Come on, boy. Snap out of it," she said as she very slowly removed the skullcap from atop his head. There was a slight pop as the neurofeeds detached from the e-nodes imbedded in his shaven head.

"Where am I?" Lars repeated. "And who are you?"

"The where is the Feldman Neurological Institute. As for who I am, I am Robota. We have met. You know me. I am Doctor Feldman's personal assistant. He assigned me to work with you until you were fully synched. I realize that you have not asked, but I will answer your question anyway."

"What question?"

"The question you were about to ask."

"Can you read minds?"

"No. But I am a fully sentient being. I am fully capable of anticipating a man's questions. This is your second day, Lars. We were performing a Level One Synch. You passed out on our first try."

"My second day? Maybe you stood too close to a lightning rod in a thunderstorm. Sentient being or not, a wire has been crossed in that silicon brain of yours. In case you missed it somehow, I have lived two lifetimes, been to space, crossed Venus on foot."

"I am indeed sorry to disappoint you, Lars. But no, you have never left this chair, not for one second. You have not been to space. You have not been to Venus. You have been here the entire time, all of five minutes. We have been doing a Level One Synch. You have been downloading data at a very high speed. Very high."

"Are you suggesting that everything that has happened to me over a lifetime of living is somehow fake, that it is not real at all?" Lars was still seated in the chair he had been sitting in when he came to. Now he was getting restless, eager to get up and move about.

"Oh, it is real enough, Lars. You and I have talked about this before. Whatever your brain believes to be real is real."

Lars could not take this on faith. "You mean to tell me that my entire life has been imaginary, something I cooked up in my brain? Everything I have experienced for the past two hundred years — all the pain and suffering, all the love and joy — they are all just part of some vivid, five-minute-long fantasy? I feel like I am going to explode."

"You are overwhelmed. I can see that. But, Lars, you are still very much a boy. Indeed, I promised your parents I would return you to their custody within 30 days."

"They are still alive? My parents?"

"Of course."

"And I am still a boy?" Lars looked down at his scrawny young frame in disbelief. "But I was a man, an old man."

Robota spoke into her recording device. "Extreme patient disorientation. Not a good sign." Then she turned to Lars. "Next time we hook you up to the skullcap we will slow the rate of dataflow but lengthen the contact time. Many people are like you. They have to work up in stages to regular full-time connection."

Lars got to his feet. He was unsteady. He looked at his arm and again at his legs. No barcode. That was solid evidence to support the notion that his entire lifetime had been a dream.

"Skulltechs call it the pruning effect," Robota said. "The idea is that . . ."

"Yes, yes, yes. You explained it to me once before. Even gave me examples. Pruning a tree. Cutting back on staff in an office building. Lopping off a dead tree branch. Pruning."

"And do you recall what it means in this context?"

Lars sighed in a heavy voice and replied. "With each life experience, the brain changes shape at the cellular level. Synaptic connections that prove useful are strengthened. Those that stay idle or remain unused for long periods are sloughed off. This pruning process adjusts and modifies the brain to survive in the particular environment it finds itself."

Robota nodded with approval. "And each new session with the skullcap improves the odds of a successful synch."

"So how does it end?"

"How does what end, Lars?"

"My life."

"Your life? It is impossible for me to know. You are but a boy. Your life has barely begun. The future is not yet written. You cannot tweak a few knobs on some machine and fast forward it to its logical conclusion, no matter how sophisticated the machine."

Lars shook his head. "Hook me back up, Robota. I want to know how it ends."

"I can only reconnect you if Doctor Feldman gives his okay. But even if he does give his okay, I must warn you. A skullcap is no time machine. It cannot predict the future. Nor can I."

"I want to finish the story."

"I am not authorized to hook you back up. Not without prior clearance."

"First Law, Robota. First Law. *A robot may not injure a human being or, through inaction, allow a human being to come to harm.* I state categorically that I will be harmed if you do not do as I instruct and hook me back up to my skullcap this very instant."

Robota twitched and briefly cocked her head to one side. There was an inherent conflict in its programming. *Which was the stronger command?* Doctor Feldman's order to seek his permission? Or Lars's order to reattach the skullcap in order that he not suffer harm?

"First Law, Robota. Your programming leaves you no wiggle room. You must do as I say or harm will befall me. This takes precedence over any orders to the contrary that Doctor Feldman may have given you. I must finish the story."

By now Robota had sorted out any discrepancy in her programming and come to a decision.

"Okay then," she said. "Sit back down and we shall begin."

EPILOGUE

CHAPTER SIXTY

I am an old man now.

Kaleena is dead, and I am alone.

The prison barcodes, which were once stark on my arm and leg, have now faded into nothingness.

I am in pain. My bowels do not function properly. My skin is thin and blotchy. My eyesight is weak. My hearing is poor. Two of my teeth are loose. Three are broken. My breath is short. I am angry and confused. In all my railing against rejuvenation, it never occurred to me that getting old would hurt so much.

We had a good life together, Kaleena and I. We met again in Industry. She and the other girls had escaped from the Farm after the fall of bin Hassan's empire. She too had been rejuvenated and was again young, though not quite as young as I.

When I arrived in Industry after my long trek cross-country, the locals did not greet me with open arms. But I was not placed in shackles either. Every citizen in the colony was a fugitive of some sort or other. Newcomers were few and far between. All were viewed with suspicion.

I was a sight when I arrived. Long hair. Ratty clothes. Gaunt face. No shoes. People came out of their homes to stare at me. Once in a while, I would stop and stare back.

The settlement was built on the temperate slopes of the mountain range I had just crossed on foot. Not too hot, not too cold, just right. The site was a natural. Plenty of clean, running water. Abundant quantities of wild game. Forests of tall trees. Pastures for grazing. Soil suitable for raising crops.

Word of my arrival spread through the town fast. Before the first day was out, Kaleena had learned of my presence. She vouched for me to the others and gave me safe haven that first night.

Relations between us were strained. She was angry, and after all this time, we were complete strangers. Her experiences at the Farm nearly broke her. She blamed me for not rescuing her. I explained that we had tried but that we had been taken prisoners ourselves. Eventually, Kaleena and I found a way back into each other's arms.

Kaleena and I married. We had children, eventually returned to Earth. We found good jobs and lived comfortably. Our children had children of their own. We traveled extensively — Africa, Asia, South America — lived in a nice home, enjoyed all that life had to offer.

Our comfort was due in large part to a substantial inheritance. That, plus the power of compound interest. Viscount Morgan Henry died a wealthy man. He left behind but two heirs. One of them, Kaleena, though a prisoner, was known to still be alive. Her share was held in trust for more than a century before she came to claim it.

Plus, my grandfather had left me a little something as well, the house in Maine, a collection of old guns, some property in England. I never found his final resting place, though; which was a shame, for I owed him so much. Probably a military cemetery somewhere. The man was a hero. He deserved to be buried among other heroes.

I took Kaleena back to the place where I grew up. Ironwood, Minnesota. The area had once been called the boundary waters. But that particular border between two countries no longer had meaning. The Great War had seen to that. Widespread devastation up and down the line.

I found the home where I grew up, now forgotten beneath a paper mill. I found where my mother was buried. The gravestone said she lived a long life. A holographic image of her lovely face still hovered over the marker, a technology I never felt at home with. A tiny solar battery kept the holo lit.

I wondered if my mother ever thought of me. Probably. Mothers always think of their sons, even the bad ones. They cannot help themselves.

But this holographic image seemed somehow morbid. I solemnly kissed her gravestone, removed the battery and said my goodbyes.

I found no gravesite for my father. That did not surprise me. He probably died elsewhere. Perhaps chose to be cremated. That would fit somehow with his philosophy.

The dreams of my childhood?

No, they have not all been realized. I remember as a ten-year-old boy wanting to be a pilot. The closest I ever came was flying my grandfather's airchop east across the United States. Do not get me wrong, that was great. But there have been regrets. Soldiers I fought with, women I slept with, friends I outlived.

For those of us who are old, there is something infinitely pathetic about this matter of regrets and growing old. Every gray-haired man has had his share of disappointments. Frustration and disillusionment are part of what makes us who we are. I am what I am, at least in part, because of the pain I have suffered.

The quality of the dreams I have not attained is a matter for self-reflection, perhaps remorse. But let no person judge either the dream or the man who has dreamt it. These are the words of Samuel Clemens. The value a dreamer places on his unattained dream is the only fair standard by which to measure its worth. What makes another man's lost dream worthy of our respect, what makes that loss large and great and fine is how much grief that man sheds for his loss. We cannot measure it ourselves. Only he, the dreamer, knows how much his failure has cost him.

Put yourself in the dreamer's place. Respect what he seeks. Do not ever laugh at the dreams your friends cherish and reveal to you. Do not laugh. Do not even smile. These dreams are precious cargo to the mind that carries them. Should your friend fail to attain his dream, he will be left scarred by his failure. Do not pity your friend. We all need our pain, every bitter ounce of it. Remorse is what turns heads that were once brown when they were young, white or gray as our years near their end. Listen to what these old men have to say, for they truly know.

So comes the penultimate question of every mortal man. It usually arrives on his lips near the end, when he is alone.

Name one good thing about getting old. Just one!

Stiff joints. Poor eyesight. Droopy tits. Erections that will not stand tall on their own. Incontinence. Forgetfulness. Constipation. Wrinkles. Hardening of the arteries. Cancer. *Good God, is there no way out of this?* No way to put a stop to this? No way to turn back the hands of time, to stay young forever? Is there no way to meld technology to flesh? No way to help keep us fit and in our prime forever?

What in blazes? *Did you hear what I just said?* Am I crazy? Can I really have forgotten so quickly? How could I forget so soon about the spiders, about the forced rejuvenations, about what the bastards did to me, how they messed up my life?

My stars, I have been confined to a slave camp. I have walked across a continent, alone and near starving. I have journeyed between planets. I have seen death. I have taken pleasure from life. Three lifetimes actually. Each one littered with successes, with failures, with dreams, defeats, love and loneliness.

No, by God. I have not forgotten. Getting old is not just about failed erections. It is also about Patience. About Determination. Perseverance. Wisdom. Confidence. Charity. Foresight.

By the gods, I have done it all. I was not old, I was seasoned. I was not worn-out, I was broken-in. I was not soft, I was hard, tough as nails. Experience had made me that way. I was, by all accounts, now the oldest man in the solar system.

So now ask yourself and dig deep for the answer. Should Man live forever? Should he be rejuvenated over and over again in a never-ending cycle of young and old, adolescent and adult, greenhorn and veteran, constantly living but never quite dying? Is this really what you want for yourself? For humanity?

If we could manage it in some distant future, should we allow people to live for a thousand years, perhaps even demand that they do so? Would natural life, shortened life, then become a sin, much as abortion or suicide already is?

And if we could manage it, would it not rip apart our society? Think of the changes. Sons who can never escape the shadows of their fathers. Fathers who are themselves still trapped in the shadows of their own fathers. Heirlooms that are never passed down by dying parents to their children. Family feuds that are never settled. Marriage vows that crack under the accumulated weight of uncountable years. Directionless people who always have time to take the road less traveled, who feel no pressure to complete what they started. *Why rush to finish any project when one has infinite life?* There is always tomorrow, if not the next day.

And what will become of God? Infinite life means no deathbed declarations, no final words of forgiveness. The death of God himself. What meaning is there to an afterlife when the one you are living has no end? No longer will there be Valhalla. Forget about Heaven. No fear of Hell. Only Purgatory.

Infinite life may bring our kind infinite wisdom. But it may also bring us infinite pain. What of the brutal dictator who can go on brutalizing for however long he pleases? What of the serial killer who can now contemplate an endless string of victims, committing an infinite number of murders? What of the terrorist who can continue terrorizing without end?

Can you imagine such a world? I cannot. Finite life has its virtues. It means the end of a lot of good people, yes. Loving fathers have heart attacks and die. Brilliant scientists contract cancer and wither away. Patriotic leaders. Talented musicians. Amazing athletes. Captains of industry. Military heroes. All dead.

But finite life also means the end of ruthless dictators. The demise of murderous psychopaths. The death of cruel child molesters.

What do I want from life, you ask? The same thing my father wanted, to die at a time and in a place of my own choosing . . . And, I will.

ABOUT THE AUTHOR

Steven Burgauer is a former stockbroker and investment advisor. He is the author of several science fiction books, an investment guide, a history of World War II, and a fictionalized, but well-researched story of Neanderthal's first encounter with man. Steven currently resides in Lady Lake, Florida.

Printed in the United States
By Bookmasters